happily ever after

cinder & ella

KELLY ORAM

BLUEFIELDS

For Karie, since this book really is all your fault.

1

MY EYES DROOPED AS I LAY STRETCHED OUT ON THE PLUSH couch, head propped up on the armrest, staring at the computer on my lap. It was getting late, and the words on the screen were all starting to blur together. I must have been closer to sleep than I thought, because I jumped when my instant messenger dinged at me.

Cinder458: I miss you.

I snorted. He was such a goofball. Shaking my head, I couldn't help typing a response.

EllaTheRealHero: Ha! You're such a dork.
Cinder458: I'm serious.
EllaTheRealHero: That makes you even more of a dork.
Cinder458: No, it makes me *romantic*. You're such a brat.
EllaTheRealHero: And you're *annoying*. Leave me alone. I'm busy.
Cinder458: But I miss you. I need you. Right now.

When a hand began to lightly tickle my sock-covered foot, I glanced over my laptop and huffed in exasperation at the man typing on his phone at the other end of the couch. "Seriously, Brian," I groaned. "I take the GED *tomorrow*. You told me that if I came over, you'd let me study. So far, I haven't done much studying."

"You've already passed two practice exams. How much more studying do you need?"

Brian, having had enough of my ignoring him, stole the computer off my lap and set it on the coffee table. My heart spiked as he crawled across the couch toward me, being mindful of my scarred and damaged legs. He had that look in his eyes again, the one that made women around the world fantasize about having his babies.

I still couldn't believe that of all the women in the world, he chose to give that look to me. We'd been an official couple for a week now, and the novelty of dating one of the country's hottest movie stars still hit me on a regular basis. Especially at times like this, when he was trying to melt me with his smoldering bedroom eyes.

He came to a stop inches from my face. His tall, muscular, perfect body hovered above mine, waiting for my permission to fall against me. Just waiting. Building tension without even touching me.

Shivering, I sucked in a sharp breath. My head swam as he filled my senses. His body heat warmed me. His cologne—a subtle spicy musk—hit me as I breathed in, triggering my hormones as if it had been designed to do so. It was probably called *Eau de Bottled Lust*. "Brian, come on. Seriously."

"Ellamara," he whispered softly. Dangerously. "Forget about your test already, and kiss me."

That did it. The man knew my weakness. With a groan, I lifted my arms around his neck and pulled his mouth to mine. He was more than ready for the kiss. We connected with passion, and he kissed me deeply. It was as if he'd been waiting his whole life to kiss me, and not just the last couple of hours.

"It's really not fair when you use your audiobook voice on me," I breathed as soon as he released my lips.

He smirked against my mouth. "I know." His head moved to the side of my face, his lips finding something new to torture: the soft spot of sensitive skin just behind my ear. "Why do you think I used it?"

My eyes rolled back in my head, and I buried my fingers in his soft, dark hair. Brian took that as the okay to turn our kiss into a full-on make-out session. He lowered his body on top of mine, angling himself slightly to the side so as not to squish my small, frail body under all of his weight. I nearly gasped, both from pleasure and fear.

Having his hard muscles pressed against me from head to toe and his hands wandering over the top of my clothes was a new experience for me. We'd only been dating for a week now, but even for a week, I'd been pretty shy about getting physical. I'd never been serious with anyone before my accident, and after... well...I'd been downright scared of dating. Terrified, even.

I pushed away my nerves for a few minutes, letting my desire rule my actions. Brian felt so good, and as anxious as I was, I craved him as much as he wanted me. As he readjusted our bodies, making us comfortable on the couch that suddenly felt way too small, my hands found his chest.

I'd touched his amazing, award-worthy chest once or twice before. I'd rested my hands there while he held me and kissed me, but I'd never been in a position to *explore* it before. Fueled by lust and not thinking clearly, I dragged my fingers down his abs, feeling each individual muscle, hard and defined.

I shuddered again. He was *perfection*.

Brian seemed to like me touching him, because he paused for a moment, as if surprised. And then something inside him just snapped. He found my mouth again, devouring me in a heated kiss.

My heart pounded, and it became hard to breathe, but in the best possible way. My hands found the hem of his shirt and slid beneath the material. When I felt his blazing hot skin, I came back to myself. I squeaked in surprise and stilled my fingers. Brian growled in response. "*Yes*, Ella. Do it. Put your hands on me. I want you to touch me."

I wanted to. I wanted to more than anything, but I hesitated, surprised and a little embarrassed by what he said. His words had been a desperate request more than a command, but they had been so direct. Brian had a lot more experience in the dating department. There were only three years' difference between us in age, but sometimes it felt like twenty. Every time things got physical between us, I felt like an innocent little schoolgirl dating a full-fledged grown-up man.

When I didn't act, Brian ripped his shirt over his head. He covered my trembling hand with his large strong one and guided my fingers to his body, splaying them across his stomach. This time, we both shuddered.

His skin, so soft and hard at the same time, burned beneath my touch. It felt as if he were on fire, and it made me nearly combust as well. I quit being shy. I let my hands roam, exploring every inch of his stomach, chest, and shoulders.

My lips found his neck and drifted to his bare shoulder as my hands met his back. His whole body tensed, and, with a low groan, he squeezed me to him, being a lot less gentle with me than he ever had been before.

His hands slipped under my shirt, doing some exploring of their own, but when his fingers slid over my scars, they doused my desire as if I'd fallen into an icy lake. Gasping, I scrambled to sit up, and Brian immediately sat back, giving me space. His eyes bore into mine, filled with concern. "Did I hurt you?"

My face heated with embarrassment. "No."

"Then what…" His voice trailed off as he solved the mystery. His expression turned pained. "Your scars?"

I took a deep breath and chewed on my lip.

Brian took my damaged hand in his and rubbed his thumb over the back of it. "Your scars are part of you, and I love *all* of you." His thumb stilled, and he met my eyes with a searching gaze. "You believe that, don't you?"

"Of course I do. I just…" My throat closed up, and my eyes started to burn. I hated that this bothered me. It shouldn't have. I knew he didn't care about the scars. I *knew* that. But *I* cared. His body was flawless and beautiful. Mine was…not.

"Ella," Brian rasped. His voice was too full of emotion to take on that low, rumbly quality that makes me melt, but this new, strained voice was just as overwhelming. He squeezed my hand. "I love you so much."

He'd said those words often this week, and they nearly burst my heart every time. Now, with the emotions flying high between us, they nearly brought me to tears. I'd spent the last year thinking I would never be loved again. Brian had proved my insecurities unfounded a thousand times over. "I love you, too," I whispered, swallowing back the raw feelings that were choking me.

Brian tucked a loose strand of my hair behind my ear, caressing my skin as he did so. "You are the most beautiful woman I've ever known. Stay with me tonight, and I will spend every minute until I take you home in the morning proving to you just how beautiful you are. Every. Single. Minute. Ella. You have my word."

He was doing the smoldering gaze thing again. The desire in his eyes would have melted most women, but it spiked fear in me. "I'm sorry." I shook my head, trying to keep the movements slow so that he wouldn't guess just how panicked I was. "I'm not ready for that."

Seeing through my flimsy facade of calm, Brian sat back and let the lust fade from his eyes. "Okay."

He didn't question me. He simply accepted that I'd put on the brakes. He was the most perfect man in the world. My heart swelled with love, and yet guilt wracked me, too. So much so that I felt the need to try and explain. "It's not just because of the scars."

Brian surprised me by chuckling. "Yes, I can see that."

His playfulness evaporated my guilt, but it tripled my

embarrassment. I covered my flaming face with my hands and lay back on the couch, groaning. Brian had no sympathy. His chuckle turned into real laughter.

I glared at him through my fingers. "Are you seriously laughing at me right now? Thank you so much, you jerk."

He pulled my hands away from my face, and I swatted his arm. He caught my hand in his, grinning down at me, his eyes sparkling with delight. "What? I think it's adorable."

Now that was just hard to believe. I sat up again and gave him my most challenging stare—the one I saved for when we argued about books and movies. "I'm not ready to sleep with you, and you find that *adorable?*"

Brian rolled his eyes but kept grinning. "Ella, I *know* you. I know you've never dated anyone seriously. I know your grandparents were very strict Catholics, and that your mom was *way* paranoid about you getting involved with boys too young."

"Yeah, and now I know why," I grumbled. Considering I was an accidental, unwanted surprise that caused my parents eight years of strife, my mother's paranoia made perfect sense. Unfortunately, it had turned me into an inexperienced prude and maybe even made me a little afraid of sex.

"Whatever the reason," Brian said, his smile turning from playful to serious, "I know this is all new for you. Yeah, I hoped you'd agree to stay tonight—had to give it a shot—but I'm not the least bit surprised you turned me down."

"And you're really okay with that?" I bit my lip again, uncertainty creeping into my thoughts. "I know that's not what you're used to."

Brian shook his head, giving me a rueful smile. "You are nothing like what I'm used to. That's exactly what I love about you, and you *know* that."

"Yeah, but—"

"But nothing. Stop feeling self-conscious. I consider myself the luckiest man in the world to have found a woman who loves *me* instead of the movie star. I'm not going to screw something this special up by pressuring you into things you aren't ready for. I promise."

His words were so romantic. He was being so amazing, and understanding, and supportive. Still, I had to go and ruin the moment with an obnoxious snort of laughter. "That sounded a little too perfect. I really hope it wasn't a line from one of your movies."

One thing I'd learned about myself this week—for all that I loved sappy romance in books and movies, I couldn't handle it in real life when it was directed at me. I loved it; I just had a hard time believing I deserved it. I was no silver screen princess. I wasn't a heroine from a novel. I was just a normal girl with a million flaws, too much emotional baggage, and a broken body.

Brian sighed. "One of these days, Ella, you're going to learn how to take a compliment."

He rose to his feet with a yawn and a stretch. He still had no shirt on, and watching his muscles expand and contract beneath his golden skin, I regretted killing the mood. My eyes snapped back to his face when he cleared his throat. He flashed me a cocky smirk, which I answered with a sheepish grin. "Sorry. Just taking advantage of the free show. Most girls have to buy a ticket to get this view."

Brian cocked a brow at me. "Who said this show was free?" He'd been kidding, but his voice quickly turned heavy, and his smile disappeared. "Being my girlfriend comes at a very steep price."

He wasn't joking. The past week had been insane. The world was obsessed with Cinder and Ella. The only peace we'd found was inside the privacy of our homes. And considering my house came with an awkward family who gawked a lot—and usually a bunch of my stepsisters' friends all hoping to meet Brian—we'd spent most of our time together holed up in his house.

"You're worth it," I promised, sliding my arms around his waist. He squeezed me tightly against him, and I reveled in the feel of his bare chest against my cheek.

"I hope you still think that after the newness wears off."

The worry and insecurity in his voice broke my heart. "I'll always think it," I assured him. Then, wanting to lighten the mood again, I brushed my fingers over his stomach and said, "Especially when you have abs like these."

Brian's eyes flashed with desire. He released a growly purr of approval as he lowered his mouth to mine. "So it's my body you love me for, is it? Not my brains? Or my sense of humor? Or my charming personality?"

"Mmm. Nope. Just your body." I ran my hands up his stomach and twined them around his neck. "And maybe your kissing abilities."

"Maybe?"

He sounded genuinely hurt, but then, he was an actor, so he *should* sound sincere. I knew he was only trying to work me over, though, so I shrugged. "Eh. It could be your money, I guess. It's hard to tell exactly what does it for me."

Brian snorted but didn't bother with a witty comeback. Our time for the night was coming to an end, and he apparently would rather spend it kissing me than bantering. I indulged him until the alarm went off on my phone. We both sighed. "Time for this Cinderella to get home."

Brian slipped his shirt back on—a travesty, though necessary, I supposed, if he was going to drive me home. After handing me my cane, he collected his wallet and keys. "You know," he said as we headed out to his garage, "I'm pretty sure Prince Charming got to keep Cinderella at the end of the movie."

I laughed as he helped me into his car. Once he was seated behind the wheel, I said, "I'm pretty sure Cinderella didn't have an overprotective father she was trying to reconcile with."

Brian cracked his neck and tightened his grip on the steering wheel. "Your father doesn't deserve the respect you give him."

I resisted the urge to sigh as he opened his gate and pulled out onto the winding, narrow canyon road he lived off of. There was a lot of tension between Brian and my father. The day after the premiere, my dad had a background check done on Brian. Never mind the gross invasion of privacy; all he cared about was that there had been a strong theme in the results—women.

Needless to say, my dad wasn't too thrilled with the idea of such a notorious playboy dating his daughter. Brian, on the other hand, didn't think my father had any right to an opinion where I was concerned. Balancing the two dominant men was proving difficult.

"This is almost the last time you have to worry about it," I said, patting Brian's hand. "After Christmas, you'll help me move out. Then I'll only have to respect Vivian's dads' rules." I giggled at the thought of them issuing me a curfew. "Given the way both Steffan and Glen adore you, I doubt they'll care what time you bring me home."

Brian turned onto Mulholland and zipped along the top of the ridge to the neighboring canyon that my father and Jennifer called home. It was a little mind-blowing to think that all these months I'd lived less than three miles from Brian and never known it.

"What if I *didn't* bring you home?" Brian asked.

"What do you mean?"

He shot me a quick glance before turning his gaze back to the dark, twisty road. His brows were pulled low over his eyes, and his leg bounced nervously. "I mean, what if, when I help you move out, I bring your stuff to my place instead of Vivian's?"

2

Did he just suggest I move in with him? I laughed, but it quickly died. When it became obvious he wasn't joking, my jaw fell open. "Are you *serious?*"

He pulled into my Dad's small lane and parked in front of the gate to my house, but he didn't open his window to punch in the security code. Instead, he turned in his seat to face me. "Hear me out."

"*Hear you out?* Brian, you just asked me to *move in* with you. We've been together for a *week*."

"I've been in love with you for three *years*, Ella. We're more than a one-week-old couple."

I opened my mouth to argue but couldn't find any words. I had to settle for frowning. "No. I can't. That's crazy."

Brian shook his head. "It's more than just that I want you there. If you're really going to move out of your dad's house, then you should at least consider coming to live at my place. If you aren't ready for it to be a live-together situation, it could be a roommate thing instead. You could have your own room, your own bathroom. You could even label your own food if you wanted, and I'd only steal it when you annoyed me."

I laughed despite myself, but wariness quickly crept in. He was being awfully insistent. "Why?" When he hesitated, I knew my suspicions were founded. "What aren't you telling me?"

He sighed. "I'm worried about you living at Vivian's."

I laughed. "What on earth for?" The notion was ridiculous. "Vivian and her dads love me. They're excited to have me come. I'll be much better off there than I am at my dad's house."

Brian cut me a serious look. "It's not Vivian's family I'm worried about. It's the security at her apartment."

Vivian lived in a typical LA-style apartment complex in West Hollywood. It was built back in the sixties and modeled after a two-story motel. There were only eight units in the complex—four downstairs and four up. Each of them had front doors that opened to the outside. The complex didn't even have parking, much less a gate.

I frowned. "Her apartment building doesn't have any security. Unless you count the dead bolt on her front door."

Brian's grim face seemed to say, *That's exactly my point.*

I smiled when I realized what he was worried about. "It's not a bad neighborhood. Maybe it's not the Hollywood Hills, but Glen and Steffan assured my dad it's completely safe. They've never had a problem. Vivian said it's a great neighborhood, and she loves her neighbors."

Brian sighed. "I'm sure it's a great place for Vivian and her dads, Ella, but you're different now."

"What do you mean?"

Brian rubbed his hand over his face and then reached to take mine. He brought it to his lips, forcing a pained smile at me. "I told you dating me comes at a cost. It won't take long for the media to realize you've moved, and it'll take even less time for them to figure out where you've moved to. You'll have no privacy at Vivian's. You'll be stalked all the time by everyone from paparazzi, to fans, to tourists."

"Oh come on, the novelty of us will wear off soon. It won't be that bad."

Brian laced our fingers together and let our hands fall to his lap, but he didn't return my smile. "You don't understand. Celebrity hype like mine doesn't wear off. I've had trouble this past year with obsessed fans. A lot of trouble. I've had to get a few restraining orders. I've had a number of people try to break into my home. That's why I moved to the place I'm at now. The security is state-of-the-art."

"Whoa. You seriously had people break in?"

Brian's face was grave. "My level of fame is intense, Ella. Fans don't see celebrities as real people. They won't respect your privacy or your personal boundaries. I don't want you to have to deal with that on your own."

I began to think twice about staying at Vivian's. Sinking back in my seat, I stared out the windshield at the gate to my father's house. I'd always considered gated homes pretentious, a way for rich people to feel self-important. I never considered some of them might need the security. Or privacy.

But move in with Brian? That was a *huge* commitment. Yeah, he said we could live like roommates, but could we really? I wasn't so sure. And I just wasn't ready for a live-in relationship. Not even close.

"I see what you're saying, and it's really thoughtful of you. Thank you for being so concerned about me, but I don't think moving in with you is necessary."

When Brian frowned, I kept talking so that he couldn't argue with me. "Things are just crazy right now because we created huge drama with the whole Cinderella thing. I'm sure it'll die down soon. We'll be old news by New Year's."

Brian searched my face. I detected disappointment in his gaze and tried not to let that sway me. I couldn't accept his offer. Not if my current amount of anxiety was anything to go by. I tried to hide how panicked I was. I loved him, but the thought of moving in with him terrified me. It was also insanely appealing. And maybe *that* was what was so scary. It was too much, too fast.

Giving up for the moment, Brian finally rolled down his

window to punch in the security code to my gate. As he pressed the buttons, a bright flash went off, and a dark figure jumped out from behind the trees.

Brian, of course, said nothing to the guy. He'd always encouraged me to do the same, but I wasn't very good at it. "Seriously?" I asked, leaning around Brian to scowl at the man. He continued to click away, blinding me with his flash. "You don't have anything better to do than stalk my house at one in the morning, hoping to get a picture of us?"

"Ella, don't bother." Brian sounded tired, and I knew it wasn't because of the late hour.

I couldn't see the man outside, but I could picture his smarmy smile as he laughed and said, "Are you kidding? Brian Oliver having to get his girlfriend home before *curfew*? That's front-page news. You're gonna earn me some serious cash tonight, sweetheart."

The guy's condescension irritated me so much I was tempted to jump out of the car and smash his camera. "It's a *self-imposed* curfew, thank you very much."

"Ella…"

"My father worries about me, so while I'm still living under his roof, I make sure to be home at a reasonable hour."

"Ella…"

"I'm not a *child*."

Okay, so maybe the guy's comment stung because it hit a little too close to home. I may have been granted all of my legal rights as an adult now, but I hated that I'd lost them for a year. And I hated even more that the world knew it.

The first night Brian brought me home after the premiere of *The Druid Prince*, a couple of extra-crafty paparazzi managed to follow us back to my house, and my identity had been discovered. It had only taken hours after that for the papers to report all about my accident, my disabilities, the loss of my mother, and my unstable mental health. The custody thing with my father because of my attempted suicide had come out, too.

Brian rolled up his window and pulled through the gate, watching his rearview to make sure the paparazzi stayed off the property. Once his window was shut, I slammed my head back against my headrest and groaned. "That guy was being a jerk on purpose, trying to get a rise out of us. I hate that it worked."

Brian squeezed my hand. "Learning to ignore them takes practice."

"I know. It's just embarrassing. I mean, the guy's right. I'm coming home by *curfew*."

"True. But you were right, too. You're doing it out of respect for your father, which I think is beyond admirable."

"Yeah, well, I doubt that bit of information is going to make it into his headline."

"Who cares about his headline? You know the truth. I know the truth. Your dad knows the truth."

I huffed in frustration, trying to let my anger go. Nothing was injured but my pride, and that only hurt if I let it. "You're right. Sorry. I'll get used to it."

Brian gave me an apologetic smile. "Have I told you how grateful I am that you're willing to deal with this for me?"

I gave him a wry smile. "Like you gave me much of a choice? Do you know what would have happened if Brian Oliver's personal Cinderella *didn't* show up to claim the glass slipper, or in our case a pair of gloves and an autographed book?"

"It was definitely an underhanded move." He chuckled. "I don't feel bad. Living without you was unacceptable, so I had to guarantee myself victory."

I snorted, and after checking to make sure the gate was all the way closed behind us, opened my car door. Brian jumped out of the car and rounded it to help me stand. I waved him away. "It's okay. I got it."

"Ella—"

"Call me vain, but my ego is already bruised enough for the night. Let me at least stand up on my own."

He backed up, not offended that I was grumbling at his offer of assistance. He knew me too well. He smiled at me and shook his head as I slowly pulled myself from the car. "Stubborn woman."

"It's a good thing, too, otherwise you'd be helping me into my wheelchair right now."

"I know." Brian shut the car for me like a gentleman and walked me to the front door. "I love that you push yourself to get stronger. But it also hurts my male ego when you won't let me rescue my damsel in distress."

He was teasing, but my heart still melted a little. "You've already rescued me plenty," I said as we reached the front porch. "You're my knight in shining armor. Literally, *Prince Cinder*."

Brian's grin turned goofy, and he stepped back to give me a courtly bow. I had no doubt it was authentic—something he'd learned in preparation for his role as the cherished Druid Prince. "M'lady," he mumbled as he bent at the waist and dropped his lips to my hand. "Fair Priestess, I bid thee good night."

I couldn't help the giggle that escaped me. I loved it when his inner fantasy geek came to the surface. It was so utterly dorky, but he was *my* dork. I curtseyed as best as my body would allow. "And to you as well, Your Highness."

Brian let go of my hand and snaked his arm around my waist, pulling me tight against him. "Screw the Old World manners. If you refuse to come live with me, then I need a real kiss to get me through the separation."

Laughing, I wrapped my arms around his neck. "Who am I to deny a prince?"

"As the powerful mystic priestess, you're the only one allowed to deny me anything, but I wouldn't recommend it. I tend to get cranky when I don't get what I want."

"Mmm. That's because you're a celebrity. You're a very spoiled lot, you know."

Brian chuckled, pulling me just a little bit tighter to him. His hands started to glide up and down my back, as if he were attempting to memorize the feel of me before he had to let go. "Yes," he agreed shamelessly. "Very spoiled, indeed. And self-centered. And needy. I'm afraid I'm going to be an extremely high-maintenance boyfriend. Are you sure you're up for the task?"

I pretended to think about it. "It'll be difficult, but you do drive a Ferrari, so…"

"Ah. So it's the car you really love me for."

Grinning, I glanced behind us at the fine Italian automobile Brian referred to as his *Precious*. It was ostentatious, but I couldn't deny it was fun to ride in. "It's definitely the car."

"And the truth finally comes out." Brian shook his head, and then his gaze landed on mine with a new look that was hard to label. "Say it again for me."

I understood the look now. It was love. Pure and simple. The man standing in front of me, holding me in his arms, was head over heels in love with me. *How in the world did I ever get so lucky?*

I tried to suppress a smile as I rolled my eyes, but I was only half successful, and I couldn't deny his request. "Car," I said, throwing a little extra *H* into the word, exaggerating my Boston accent.

Brian's face lit up with delight. "You are *so* cute."

I was in the middle of rolling my eyes again when Brian finally captured my mouth with his. I forgot about everything the moment we connected. My only thoughts became of him. I would never get tired of the feel of his lips, the minty taste of his mouth, or the way he made me tingle all over from head to toe and left me lightheaded because he took my breath away. He could light a fire inside me with a single touch and make me weak in the knees with just one look. Kissing him was magical.

I must have had some of the same effect on him, because when he finally released me, he was panting, and his eyes looked feverish.

"Think that'll get you through the night?" I teased.

Brian sucked in a long breath and licked his lips before answering. He looked as if he was considering dragging me back to his car and keeping me forever. If he'd tried it, I'm not sure I'd have stopped him. But he remained a gentleman and took a small step back. "Don't be surprised if I show up at sunrise."

"Don't you dare. This Cinderella needs lots of beauty sleep."

"Fine. After your test." Brian sighed and leaned in for one more kiss. This one was soft and quick. A chaste good-bye kiss. The perfect farewell. "Goodnight, Ella. I love you."

I quietly opened the front door and turned back to Brian with a smile. "I love you, too. I'll call you tomorrow."

Brian hopped down off my front porch and slowly started walking backward to his car. "I miss you already."

"Good-bye, you dork."

3

BRIAN

ELLA'S PARTING KISS HAD BEEN INCREDIBLE, BUT IT HADN'T HELPED me walk away from her last night. And it definitely hadn't helped me sleep. I lay awake forever, and when I finally did pass out, I dreamed. I dreamed vivid, sexy dreams all night. They were so hot and so detailed that when I woke the next morning to the smell of fresh coffee being waved in my face, I thought maybe the dreams were real and that taking Ella home had been the dream. I rolled toward the waiting cup with a low moan of pleasure. "You made me coffee? You are seriously the perfect woman."

"I didn't make it, and I'm actually quite far from being perfect or a woman, but I'll still take the compliment."

Fantasy dead, I pulled my eyes open and groaned. *"Scotty?"*

My personal assistant leaned over my bed, flashing me a bright smile as he held out a warm paper cup from my favorite coffee house. "Morning, boss."

Accepting my defeat—because though I didn't have a clue why Scott was here, I knew he would not be letting me stay in bed—I sat up and rubbed the sleep off my face before accepting my coffee. "What time is it?"

"Not early enough to warrant a lecture from you."

"Meaning…?"

"Almost nine."

I groaned again, eliciting a chuckle from Scott. "Rough night?" he asked.

I sipped my coffee, unsure how to answer as I remembered all of my sexy dreams. They'd left me frustrated, but they hadn't exactly been unpleasant. "Depends on how you look at it."

Scott quirked a curious brow. The twenty-six-year-old Christian virgin was so innocent he probably didn't want the details, but I couldn't resist at least giving him the right idea. He was too fun to tease. "Let's just say being together with Ella and having to take her home every night is causing some seriously hard, painful, and *blue* complications that have been affecting my sleep and making me extra uncomfortable first thing in the mornings."

"Oh." Scott's cheeks turned pink, and his eyes popped open so wide I forgave him for waking me up. He tried to cover his shock and act like he was used to this kind of conversation by clearing his throat and shrugging. "So…you and Ella haven't… gone there yet?"

Damn, he was fun. I rose to my feet with a laugh and clapped him on the shoulder. "I wish, buddy. Ella's as pure as you."

Scott chuckled good-naturedly. I ribbed him a lot about his goody-goody moral ways, but he knew I was teasing. I actually really respected him. Not only must his way of living be extremely hard to uphold, but he was also just such a good guy—trustworthy, hardworking, loyal. The best personal assistant I'd ever had.

"We need to find you a woman, Scotty. A good one like mine, who has a thing for Boy Scouts."

"No, what you need to do is get dressed quickly. I've got family coming into town today. I have to go to the airport in an hour, so I can't stay long."

I glanced down at my bare chest and pajama pants with a smirk. "So no showering first this time?"

"You're not sweating out two days' worth of booze this time, so that won't be necessary." Scott laughed as he headed out of my room. "Hurry up, boss. Time's a wastin'."

As he wandered down the hall, I called out after him. "You are way too cheerful in the mornings, Scotty!"

It wasn't until I threw on a T-shirt and followed Scott to the kitchen table that I thought to question his presence. I asked the million-dollar question as I popped a couple slices of seven-grain wheat bread into the toaster. "So what are you doing here? I swear I don't have any meetings scheduled today that I'm forgetting about."

Scott glanced at me from behind the laptop he already had open on my kitchen table. "No, you *don't* have any meetings scheduled yet. That's the problem."

His reason for being here finally clicked, and my good mood vanished. "Forget it."

"Brian." Scott leaned back in his chair and rubbed a hand over his face. "Your entire team is hounding me day and night."

"So don't answer their calls. That's what I'm doing."

A very rare look of annoyance flashed across Scott's face. "I *know* you're ignoring them. That's why they're calling *me*. I would like to enjoy my holiday, boss, so I'm not leaving until I have something to tell them. Preferably a scheduled meeting time."

I returned his look of irritation and reached for my toast. After tossing the hot bread onto a plate, I went for the bottle of raspberry jam in the fridge. Scott continued to pester me as I covered my toast with the jam. "You can't avoid this. Hiding out like you've been doing all week isn't going to make it go away."

Damn the man for having a point. This past week hiding out with Ella as if the world didn't exist had been amazing. I'd known it would come to an end; I just wished it didn't have to be so soon. Scott was right, though. The media frenzy wouldn't go away until we addressed it.

I leaned against the counter, eating my toast, frowning at Scott while he held a no-nonsense stare and waited for me to break. It didn't take long. *"Fine."* He was very good at that I-mean-business stare. "Schedule a meeting."

"They'd like you to come in today, if possible."

I snorted. "Of course they would."

Ignoring my sarcasm, Scott opened up both of our calendars on his laptop and scanned our days. "How about right after lunch? One o'clock work for you? I'll be back from picking up my relatives by then and can get away for a while."

"Fine, whatever. The sooner we get it over with, the sooner we both get to enjoy our holiday."

Scott glanced up from his laptop, all hints of annoyance replaced with a sarcastic grin. "Very astute observation, boss."

I tried to mimic his I'm-serious-and-you-will-do-what-I-say stare but lost my composure and cracked a smile. I'd never admit this to Scott, but his sass is one of the reasons he got the job. I can only handle so much ass-kissing. I'm well aware I can be difficult at times. What makes Scott so good is that he always seems to know when to give me what I want, when to push back, and when it's okay to give me shit.

With the tension broken, I rolled my eyes and threw the crust of my toast at him. "Shut up."

He dodged the flying food, chuckling, which made me laugh. "Fine. One o'clock."

"Great. And you'll bring Ella with you, or should I send a car for her?"

I froze, with my second piece of toast halfway to my mouth. Why had this caught me off guard? It shouldn't have. My team was hounding me about Ella, after all. Of course they'd want me to bring her in so they could talk to her.

Abandoning my toast and coffee, I sat down across the table from Scott and folded my arms. Now it was easy to hold a serious stare. Scott sat up straight, matching my attitude. "Brian, you know this would be easier if you would just bring her with you."

"No."

"Why not? This is about her as much as you."

"Because they're a bunch of pushy bastards. They will railroad her into agreeing to things she doesn't want to do. All they'll have to do is tell her it's best for me, and she'll sign on no matter what it will mean for her."

Scott closed his laptop, which was a sign that he was *really* serious now. "Like it or not, Brian, she is *in* this. Up to her eyeballs in it, in fact. She won't be able to avoid it forever, and when it catches up to her, she's going to have some real choices to make. If you don't bring her in with you, then your management team— along with everyone else in town—will bypass you and go straight to her. Do you really want her to meet with people and make decisions *without* you?"

My jaw clenched. Hollywood people could be nice enough, but they were all sharks in sheep's clothing. Ella was a strong, smart woman, but she wasn't used to playing their game. No way did I want her having to navigate this business on her own.

"You're absolutely right that your team will try to use her as much as possible," Scott said. "That's why you should be there when they do. At least if you're together, you can tell her when they're trying to work her over."

Damn him again. Why did he always have to be right? Letting out a breath of defeat, I scrubbed my hands over my face and then raked them through my hair. "All right, all right, fine. Let's schedule a meeting with Ella. But not yet. After the holidays. After New Year's."

Scott's posture eased up a little, and he gave me an apologetic smile. "I don't think they want to wait that long. You guys are in the headlines *now*. You're the biggest story of the year. With the movie releasing in two days, they want to take advantage of all this free publicity."

I huffed in exasperation. "*The Druid Prince* is the biggest release of the holiday. The studio has put millions of dollars into advertising. How much more publicity does it need?"

"Not the film, Brian; *you*."

"I don't care about the publicity. I don't want the attention."

I shot to my feet with a groan and headed for my coffee again. It wasn't as hot now, so I chugged it as if it held the answers to all my problems.

"You *do* want it this time," Scott insisted. "And so does Ella."

I was still frowning, but I leaned against the counter again and gave him my full attention. He jumped on the window of opportunity but spoke cautiously, as if he was afraid I might explode if I didn't like what he said. "How you and Ella deal with this attention will affect your future, and you know it. The world loves you guys right now. You're a real-life fairy tale. People are dying to see the two of you live out the happily-ever-after you promised them."

"Forget the world. *I* want that. But if the freaking media doesn't leave us alone, no one will get that happily-ever-after, because Ella will dump my famous ass."

Scott's snort of disbelief was only mildly reassuring.

"She's not like everyone else, Scott. She doesn't care about the money, and my fame is a *problem* in her eyes, not a fun perk. She's fragile. If this gets too crazy, she'll throw in the towel. She'll have to. And I'll have to let her."

"If you would just make a couple of appearances together, do an interview or two and a photo shoot, that would satiate the public, and things would die down."

"Tell that to Kim and Kanye."

Again, Scott spoke right over my cynical mutterings. "It would help you both in other ways, too. Ella is *exactly* what you need for your career. This relationship will completely erase your last year or so of debauchery."

I cocked an eyebrow at Scott, trying my hardest not to smile. It wasn't easy. *"Debauchery?"*

His cheeks turned a little pink, but he stood his ground. "Do you have a better word for all the partying and womanizing?"

I held his gaze a moment longer but then cracked. "Fine.

Debauchery."

"Right. And after a few appearances with Ella, as in love as you guys are, not even Kyle Hamilton will remember your previous reputation as an arrogant, immature playboy."

My eyebrow went up again, and this time it was Scott who relented. "Okay, *Kyle* might. But no one else will; I guarantee it. You'll be the mature down-to-earth A-list actor who chose to be with a physically-disabled woman when he could have *anyone*. You'll be admired by all of Hollywood. And a man like that might just win himself an Oscar, whether he earned it on-screen or not—that's simple Academy politics. Not that you haven't earned it, but no one in the Academy would hesitate to vote for you. And no director will hesitate to consider you for a role in the future. Play your cards correctly right now, and you'll be earning thirty million a picture for the Cinder Chronicles sequels and turning down roles you'd beg for right now."

A year ago, that would have been a persuasive argument. "It's not me I'm worried about. I'll earn my A-list status eventually; I don't need to use Ella to get there."

"She might want to use this opportunity, though. You should at least explain to her what is going on and what it means for her. From what you've told me, she's an extremely independent woman and isn't going to want to live off of her father's money forever, or yours. This could be a very lucrative time for her. It could help her with her future and even give her something to focus on. It could give her positive reasons for living with the fame and maybe help her make sense of how much her life has just changed."

I shot Scott a glare, hating that last accusation, and got his Super-Assistant-Stare-Down again. "Like it or not, Brian, the moment you gave that Cinderella interview on *The Kenneth Long Show*, you changed her life. There's no going back for her, so help her move forward. Help her make the best of a hard situation. Ease this transition for her by being straight with her. You know no one else will."

I rubbed my head. All this thinking about the future first

thing in the morning was giving me a headache.

"Sorry, boss, I know it's not what you want to do, but it is what you *need* to do. I'd let you keep ignoring them and turn off my phone over the holiday if it wasn't."

My hands dropped to my sides as all the fight left me, and I met Scott's gaze again, frowning. "Do you ever get tired of being right?"

The corners of Scott's mouth twitched. "Not really, no." I snorted. "So, will you bring her with you this afternoon?"

I relaxed a little. I still had some time. "Can't. She's taking her GED today."

"Oh." He blinked a couple times and stopped to think. Mr. Always Had An Argument Ready had no defense for that one. "Good for her. Okay...then...how about..." He looked at his laptop again.

"Not until next week."

"Brian—"

"No. I've waited three years to be with this woman; the press can wait another week. Ella and I have only had a week to get to know each other in person, and it's still a little strange. I want to keep her to myself a few more days before I have to share her with the whole damn world. It's a holiday. I intend to enjoy it. I'll talk to Ella about everything after Christmas, and we can schedule a meeting then. That should be enough of a promise to get the team off our backs for a few days, and if not, stop answering your phone."

Scott appraised me through narrow eyes and eventually nodded, accepting the compromise. "Fair enough." He leaned back in his chair, and after stretching, looked at his watch. "I've got about forty minutes still. Do you want to go over everything you need to discuss with Ella? It might help her feel less overwhelmed if you've got a plan to take care of it all when you drop it on her."

That was a good idea. I couldn't imagine how it was going to feel to Ella when she realized she was now a bona fide celebrity. "Yeah. Let's."

"Okay. And while we're at it, there's something I wanted to run by you, too, an idea I had for Ella."

I frowned. His words didn't match his sudden tension. "Why did you make that sound ominous? Is this going to require more than a piece of toast?"

Scott sighed. "Because you're not going to love it, but it's a good idea that I think Ella will be excited about."

I gave him my best frown, but he stared back with determination. Curse the man and whatever brilliant-yet-inconvenient idea was running through his head. "Right. Omelets it is. You want one?"

Scott shook his head and began pulling up e-mails or files or whatever he does on that laptop of his. "I had breakfast a couple hours ago, boss. Thanks, though. You knock yourself out. I can type up a list while you eat."

"Deal."

Half an hour into our planning session, I was full. I'd had a second cup of coffee, and I was feeling a lot more confident about having to explain to Ella she was Hollywood's new It Girl. I'd even forgiven Scott for his brilliant plan that I both loved and hated. Life wasn't so bad.

Then, with one ring, my phone destroyed all the progress I'd made with my good mood. Okay, it wasn't the phone so much as it was the person calling me. I thought about sending him to voice mail, but my father was a lot like Scott in that if I ignored him too much, he'd show up and lecture me in person.

With a sigh that Scott found curious, I picked up the phone. "Hey, Dad."

"Well, what do you know, Christmas *is* the time for miracles. The prodigal son answered his phone."

"Like you said, it's Christmas. I was feeling generous."

Dad laughed, despite my dry tone. Probably because he couldn't see my eye roll.

"What's up, Dad?"

"I've just been informed that you and Ella haven't RSVP'd for my party yet. I've got a lot of people asking if the reclusive Cinder and Ella will be there."

I smirked. Ella said she wouldn't mind going, but I was more than happy to cancel on him. I did *not* want to have to attend Dad's annual Christmas Eve party, where he would use Ella's and my current hype to boost his own popularity. He'd find a way to take credit for us somehow and would probably spend the evening insulting me and sexually harassing my girlfriend.

"Sorry. We agreed to dinner at home with her family for Christmas Eve."

"What? Seriously? I throw my party every Christmas Eve. You know that."

"And *you* know that we decided to cancel any and all crazy plans this year. That includes huge parties where there will be lots of people wanting to get in our faces and ask us a ton of questions. I told you that. Ella even canceled on her extended family that was planning to come down for Christmas to meet her. And I canceled my trip out to Mom's. We just need some time to lie low and adjust to all the changes."

"Come on. Canceling your trip to Wisconsin I get, but my party? It's just one night. You're seriously going to leave me hanging?"

"Yes."

While I waited out my father's dramatic sigh, Scott glanced at his watch and signaled that it was time for him to go. I nodded, and he began to pack up his laptop.

"Fine," Dad said. "Christmas Day, then. Come see the movie with me in the afternoon."

"The point is to keep things low-key this year, Dad. Ella's been through a lot recently, and she's overwhelmed with the fame thing."

"Really?" He sounded genuinely surprised. "I'd never guess."

"You haven't seen her away from the cameras."

"Exactly my point, Brian. I met her for a few minutes at the premiere, and that's it. Come to the movie Christmas Day. It'll be low-key; I promise. I've rented out a whole theater, and I'm keeping the guest list small."

My father's definition of *small* and Ella's would be much different. "Dad, we already promised Ella's family we'd go see it with them Christmas Day. Ella wants to see it with her stepsister."

"So bring her. Bring the whole family." His voice cheered up at the thought of having more people to impress. "I'm sure watching it with all of us in a private viewing will earn Ella some cool points with them, right?"

You'd think so. But considering how much her father was against her dating a celebrity, I wasn't sure that would be the case. There was something terrifying about having to introduce my dad to Ella's family, but I knew her family was planning to see the film Christmas Day anyway, and having our own private viewing *would* be nice. "All right, I'll ask them. But no promises. I'm not sure they'll go for it."

"Oh, please. Of course they'll say yes. I'll put you guys down for it. Don't bail on me. And after the movie, you and Ella should sneak away and do Christmas dinner with me. Just the three of us. I'll have it catered."

I sighed. "Dad, I think her family—"

"You're already giving them Christmas Eve. They can spare the two of you for a couple of hours Christmas evening."

"But—"

"Come on, Brian. It's *Christmas*. Our first movie together is releasing, and it's going to be a huge hit. I want to celebrate with you, and I want to spend some time with this woman who is apparently more important to you than your own parents. Yes, your mother called and chewed me out when you canceled your trip to Wisconsin. As if that was *my* fault. Like I conspired with you to ruin her Christmas or something."

I winced. Mom was the other person whose calls I'd been avoiding the last few days. I'd planned to spend Christmas with her this year, but after Ella showed up at the premiere, I canceled my trip because I couldn't leave Ella home to have to deal with all the media attention on her own. Mom had begged me to bring Ella to Wisconsin, but I just couldn't do it. I'd only just finally got her the way I wanted her. I couldn't bring myself to share her yet. Mom said she understood, but I'd heard her disappointment. If she'd called my father, then she must have been *really* upset.

"Son, can't you at least pretend you'd like to spend some time with your old man, for once?"

And here came the guilt trip. Typical of him. But it worked, because he had a legitimate complaint. I was his only child, and I really didn't spend much time with him. That was because he was a bit of an asshole, but still, he loved me. Or...I was his favorite trophy, anyway, and he liked showing me off. But I think that amounted to love in his eyes. "All right, look, I will commit to the movie in the afternoon, and I will *talk* to Ella about Christmas dinner. Fair enough?"

Dad sighed. "I suppose if that's all I'm going to get, it'll have to be."

I ignored the jab and forced cheer into my voice. "Great. Text me the details about the movie, and we'll see you Christmas Day."

As soon as I hung up, I leaned forward and banged my head against the kitchen table with a long, tortured groan. Scott—all packed up and on his feet—chuckled. "I feel your pain, boss. I'm the youngest, and the *only* boy in my family. I have *six* older sisters, who are all in town for the week. All of them are happily married, with housefuls of children, and I haven't had a steady girlfriend in two years. As if that's not bad enough, I'm about to go pick up my grandfather, who believes I've let the family down because I'm twenty-six and have yet to produce an heir to carry on the family name, and a grandmother, who will doubtlessly have a dossier of suitable marriage candidates in her hand when she gets off the plane. It's going to be a *long* week."

Six older sisters? That explained so much about Scott. His story also made me feel better about my own problems. Laughing, I climbed to my feet and walked him to the door. "Good luck with that, man. Anytime you need a break, shoot me a text.

I'll be happy to play the role of the spoiled, demanding, celebrity employer. It just so happens I might need someone to bring me a six-pack and watch the football games with me."

Scott opened the front door, flashing me his signature Boy Scout grin. "Oh, I'm counting on it, boss. Have a Merry Christmas."

"You too. Enjoy your gift."

"What gift? You already gave me a Christmas bonus."

Glancing over his shoulder at the crappy beat-up Toyota parked in my driveway that was at least a decade old, I grinned. "You'll see."

4

I ACED MY GED, BUT I COULDN'T THINK OF A SINGLE ACCEPTABLE Christmas gift for Brian. Now, it was the day before Christmas Eve, and I was at the mall. This was supposed to be a fun, relaxing day with my girlfriends, but between the noise, the chaos of frantic people desperate to finish their last-minute shopping, and the fact that Ana and her new boyfriend Jason had crashed the party and come with us, I was quickly getting stressed. And sore. We'd been here for hours now. This was the most physically demanding activity I'd done since my accident. When we passed an empty bench, I stopped the group. "Sorry, guys. I have to rest for a while."

I slowly sat down on the bench, sighing in relief when the weight was taken off my feet. Ana shrugged and turned her attention to Jason, but Juliette and Vivian both frowned in concern. "You okay?" Vivian asked.

"Yeah. I just need to sit for a few minutes. Why don't you guys go help Juliette find a gift for Dad and then come back?"

"You sure?" Juliette asked.

"Yeah, I'm sure. You guys go ahead. I already got him a gift, and I really do need to sit for a while, or I'm going to have to go home early."

"I'll stay with you," Vivian offered, sitting down beside me. "I'm done with my shopping, and I have no idea how to help Juliette with your dad."

Juliette shot me a hopeful expression, as if I might suddenly have the answer to her problem. She'd been having trouble this morning deciding on a gift. I shrugged. "I got him a briefcase."

Juliette's frown deepened. "He's going to love that." She glanced at Ana. "What'd you get him?"

Ana gave her sister an evil grin. The two of them had a competition every year to see who could get their parents the better gifts. Ana had been very secretive about Dad's present, but since Christmas was only two days away now, she finally spilled. "I got him a copy of the new Janice Bishop novel. The one that doesn't come out until *March*."

"*WHAT?*" Juliette screeched. "He's not even going to care what I get him now! How did you manage that?"

Ana shrugged a shoulder and smirked in my direction. "Ella. Publishers give her whatever books she wants."

"That's cheating!" Juliette's eyes bulged, and she shot me a wounded look. "You helped *Ana* with Dad's gift?"

"I didn't." I shook my head, confused. "I didn't even know Dad likes to read."

Juliette rolled her eyes. "Why do you think he was so excited when he found out you were a book blogger? It was something you guys had in common."

This news settled in my heart, creating both warmth and sadness. "He never said anything."

Juliette shrugged. "He probably just felt awkward. He was so scared of you when you first got here."

I felt bad about that but not too much, because I think I was as equally terrified of him. "I've never seen him read. What kind of books does he like?"

Ana snorted. "The ones where the good guys always catch the bad guys."

That made me smile. Dad hated nothing more than losing a

case. From what I'd heard, it didn't happen to him often, but it was devastating for him when it did. I could easily picture him reading about the underdog detective catching the notorious criminal against all the odds. "I've never even seen him pick up a book."

"He doesn't have a lot of time for it, " Ana said, "but it's his favorite hobby."

She shot Juliette another smug smile, and Juliette sighed, defeated. "There's one author whose books he always makes time for—Janice Bishop. He's going to *flip* when he sees the early copy." She scowled at Ana. "You totally win this year."

"I know." Ana smirked at me. "Thanks for the hookup, Ella."

I shook my head emphatically when Juliette shot me another wounded look. "I swear I didn't."

"But you always leave your e-mail open on your laptop," Ana pointed out, "and your e-mail address goes a long way with publishers."

My jaw fell slack. "You used my e-mail? You pretended to be me?"

"Ana!" Juliette gasped. I wasn't sure if she was more horrified that Ana had done it or just mad that she hadn't thought of it first.

"What? Sorry. That was before I thought Ella would help me if I asked her to. It was just one e-mail. And I was totally professional about it. They were excited to hear you're interested in testing out a new genre. They said if you like it, they have a lot more books where that one came from. Oh, but I think you have to post a review about it now."

Juliette punched her sister, while I slapped a hand over my face. But, really, no harm was done. I would have helped her if she'd asked for it, and now I was curious to check out these books my father liked so much. I was desperate to find things we had in common. There didn't seem to be much.

"Fine. Whatever. Just…please ask in the future, okay?"

Ana rolled her eyes. "Fine."

"I can't believe this." Juliette groaned. "I've been stressing over Dad's gift all day, and you knew all along I didn't stand a chance!"

Ana's eyes lit up. "On the bright side, now you can get him that bottle of cologne he's been not-subtly hinting about for weeks."

Juliette rolled her eyes but still nodded. "I guess. I've got nothing better, and I'm ready for lunch. We can hit up Sephora and then go eat."

The thought of going into a shop with all of those smells which would make my head pound worse than it already was made my stomach roll. "Or...you guys can go get the cologne and then come back and get me to go to lunch."

Both twins nodded, no questions asked, and headed down the crowded mall. Once they were out of earshot, Vivian nudged me with her elbow. "Did you really need the rest that badly, or did you just need a break from Ana and Jason?"

"Both."

Ana and I, though we were making an effort to be civil, were still not friendly by any stretch. And Jason was the guy who'd accidentally torn my skin graft near my elbow back before Halloween. Needless to say, hanging out with either of them was never high on my list of priorities. But Jason was Ana's boyfriend now, and both he and Ana were making an effort to smooth things over with me. It was awkward, but I was trying to play nice, too, because I wanted the rift between Juliette and Anastasia resolved. It wasn't technically my fault that they weren't close the way they used to be, but it felt that way.

"She actually hasn't been that horrible today," Vivian mused. "I think Jason mellows her out."

"That, and Mom and Dad have been sending her to weekly appointments with my therapist."

Vivian snorted. "Good. If you ask me, that girl had plenty of issues long before you ever showed up. Anyway, enough about her. How are *you*? I've hardly heard from you this week. Things must be going well, huh?"

She waggled her eyebrows suggestively, and though I knew she was only playing, I still blushed. "It's been good." My face flamed even brighter, causing Vivian's eyes to nearly bug out of her head. "Not *that* good," I amended. "We've just been hiding out. Things have been crazy. We both needed the peace and quiet and some time to get to know each other face-to-face."

Vivian burst into laughter. "Yeah, face-to-face. And *body-to-body*."

"Shut up! We haven't done anything more than kiss."

I pushed her in the side so hard she nearly fell off the bench. She laughed even harder. "Hey, I'm not judging. I'm living vicariously. Are you seriously still only kissing?"

I shrugged. "Not that he wouldn't love taking it further. He asked me to move in with him last night."

Vivian gasped. *"No way!"*

"*Way.* We were talking about moving day, and he asked if he could bring my stuff to his place instead of yours."

My spunky redheaded friend sat beside me, wide-eyed and utterly speechless. I understood her incredulity. I was still reeling from the shock of his request. "I said no."

Vivian shook herself from her frozen state and chewed her lip a moment before saying, "Are you sure that's what you want? I'd understand if you want to ditch me."

She was completely sincere, and as much as I would have considered her feelings in the matter, I didn't need to. "No." I shook my head. "I can't move in with him. I'm not ready for that."

Vivian let out a puff of air, as if she'd been holding her breath. "Good." Her face exploded with exhilaration, and she grabbed my hands. "I love Brian. I really do. But I am *so* excited for you to come be my roomie."

Her enthusiasm was contagious. "Me too. I'm going to need my girl time even more now. Brian's so intense. I don't want to get completely wrapped up in our relationship and forget about everything else. Brian might be ready for that, but I'm just getting to a point where I can finally start living my life again. I don't want Brian to be the only thing in it."

"Oh, don't worry. I'm not about to let you ditch me, even if you have left me alone at school and snagged the most amazing boyfriend in the world. Now that Brian has transitioned to boyfriend status, that makes me your new best friend. You need me even more now."

I laughed. She was joking, but in a way, she was also right. "Yes, I do. And after lunch, I really, *really* need you to help me figure out my gift dilemma."

"We'll figure something out."

"You guys ready to walk again?" Juliette asked, returning with a small Sephora bag added to her pile of booty. "'Cause I'm starving."

"Me too." I hadn't eaten much for breakfast this morning, and I'd definitely burned through those calories by now. "Not the food court, though. Let's go somewhere dark and quiet, where we can hear each other talk and no one will stare at me or ask for an autograph while I eat."

I'd been recognized a number of times today. It was so weird every time some stranger stopped me. I think it was starting to get on all of our nerves.

"Good idea," Juliette agreed. "I know just the place."

The restaurant we wanted was downstairs, and since the elevator was out of service, I was forced to use the escalator. Escalators weren't my best friends. I could use them, but I had to be really careful getting on and off of them. It was a slow, mildly-embarrassing task, but even as difficult as escalators could be, they were still better than a long flight of stairs.

As I finally placed my weight onto the moving step, I was shoved aside and nearly lost my balance. Vivian had to grab me to keep me from falling and severely hurting myself.

"You know what you need?" Juliette asked, glaring at the jerk who'd muscled his way past me onto the escalator.

"Magical force fields?" I grumbled, rubbing my throbbing hip. "A personal shopper?"

Seriously, I use a *cane*. I *limp*. You'd think people might give me a wider berth but no. Those four feet Mr. Pushy got ahead of me on the crowded escalator must have been *really* important to him.

"A Taser gun," Juliette answered, pretending to shoot the man in the back with her finger. "So you can fry jerks like him."

I laughed, but I wasn't sure she was kidding.

"Hey, buddy!" a strange voice called out from behind me, grabbing the attention of the guy who'd pushed me out of his way. I glanced over my shoulder, just in time to see a hottie holding a bulging Macy's bag glare at the jerk in front of me. "Do you treat all women so disrespectfully, or is it just the beautiful ones with disabilities?"

Mr. Pushy's face paled when he glanced at me again and noticed my cane. "Sorry," he muttered. "I thought you were just talking to your girlfriends and not paying attention."

"Nope. Just slow because I'm handicapped."

"Sorry." The man grimaced again, and as soon as he reached the end of the escalator, he took off as if his pants were on fire.

Both Juliette and Vivian snickered. "Serves the jerk right," Juliette said.

Vivian high-fived my defender. "Right on, dude."

After I carefully stepped onto solid floor, I turned to the guy behind me. He looked college age, had tousled honey-blond hair, and was wearing a rumpled T-shirt and basketball shorts. He'd definitely just rolled out of bed and found something semi-clean off his bedroom floor before coming to the mall, but somehow it was still endearing. Might have been the striking green eyes or the boyish smile that saved him.

Behind him, Juliette was pulling swoony faces and fanning herself. I'm pretty sure she mouthed the words *I want*.

Swallowing a laugh, I smiled at my rescuer. "Thanks. You didn't have to do that, but thank you."

He glared in the direction Mr. Jerk had run off. "Yeah, I really did. I can't stand people like that. Sorry. I hope I didn't offend you by mentioning your disability, but that guy needed to realize what he'd done."

"It's okay. I think you taught him a pretty good lesson."

Vivian laughed. "Yeah. Did you see his face when he saw you leaning on Candy Cane? Classic."

"*I* missed it," Juliette said. "I was too busy noticing Ella's hero." She grinned at the stranger. "So, Mr. Knight in Wrinkled T-Shirt, do you have a name to go with all of your nobility? Or do you prefer to remain anonymous while defending women from inconsiderate shoppers?"

The guy glanced between the three of us, as if we were overwhelming him, but then he laughed and stuck his hand out to Juliette. "I'm Erik."

After brief introductions, Erik took in Juliette's and Vivian's bags and eyed my empty hands with a grin. "Either you're all done with your Christmas shopping, or you're the worst procrastinator I've ever met."

I sighed. "I only have one left, but I'm having trouble figuring out what to buy."

Erik nodded sympathetically. "Shopping for your parents can be tricky."

I swallowed hard, but it had been long enough now that I was past breaking down into tears when my mother was mentioned. He was wrong, though. My mom had always been the easiest person in the world to shop for. Not like Brian. I shook my head. "Wrong guess."

"Sister?" he asked hopefully. "Brother? Best friend?"

"Boyfriend," I admitted.

He winced. "Damn. Strike one." He looked to Juliette and Vivian with a flirty pout. "Don't tell me you're both here shopping for your boyfriends, too?"

I smiled despite myself. He was adorable. And he had both of my best friends gazing at him wistfully. "We're both single," Juliette said. "So the real question for you is, do you prefer blondes or redheads?"

It always amazed me how forward she could be. But I guess when you looked like Beverly Hills Barbie, you had a reason to be confident. I used to resent girls like her, but after getting to know Juliette, it was more fun to sit back and watch her work her magic. She'd have a date with the guy by the end of lunch.

Erik's eyes bounced between the two of them, and his grin grew. "Can I keep my options open for a little while? At least through lunch? My treat?"

"That's fair," Juliette replied. "We were just headed to the Piazza Lounge."

5

I DIDN'T MIND THE EXTRA COMPANY WE'D ACQUIRED. ERIK DID A good job of keeping both Juliette and Vivian entertained, which gave me an opportunity to text Brian.

Hey, stranger. Surviving another day without me?

No. I'm lonely and miserable, woman. I can't believe you ditched me two days in a row.

I laughed. No doubt he was annoyed. He only ever called me *woman* when I was driving him crazy. But there was something adorable about his grumpy text. I could just picture him checking his phone every ten minutes for the last few hours, getting crankier every time he had no waiting message. He'd been that way since I first started e-mailing him. If I waited too long to respond, he'd message again, yelling at me for ignoring him.

Back when we first started talking to each other, I figured he was just some lonely guy who didn't have many friends or much of a life. But I quickly realized it was the opposite. He had a million friends and a crazy life. He got everything he wanted when he wanted it. He wasn't lonely and friendless; he was spoiled and had no patience. Once I figured that out, I'd keep him waiting every now and then just to drive him nuts.

Oh, and I forgot to tell you this yesterday, but my father called me. We have to hang out with him for a while on Christmas Day.

Why do you make it sound so awful?

Because it is. Trust me. But at least he's rented a theater for a private viewing of the movie so we won't have to deal with the public. He's invited your whole family to go, if you think they'll be up for it.

That's generous of him. I'm sure they'll be okay with that. They were planning to go, anyway. They'll probably think it's cool.

All right. He mentioned doing Christmas dinner afterward, just the three of us, too. I tried to get out of it, but he seemed pretty desperate. He doesn't really have anyone else of real meaning. I think he feels it during the holidays. I couldn't say no, so I'm sorry in advance, but you're going to have to add dinner with my dad to the to-do list this week.

He made it sound like the end of the world, but I was less afraid of meeting his family than I'd ever been of meeting mine. His dad seemed like a bit of a sleaze, but I could tell that beneath the animosity Brian held for him, he still cared for the man. At heart, Brian was still just a kid who wanted to make his father proud. I also got the impression he was a total momma's boy, which I found *beyond* adorable.

You're a good son. And it's okay. I'm sure it'll be fine.

Okay. Thanks. So, how's your day going? Still shopping?

I groaned internally. I didn't need to see his face to know he was smirking right now. He knew I was having trouble with his gift, and he was being such a pain about it. The man enjoyed torturing me way too much.

You *know* I am. You are IMPOSSIBLE to shop for. Can't I at least have a hint?

I told you I don't need a gift. You are my gift. Now that I have you, there's nothing else in the world that I want.

UGH! You're driving me crazy right now. Did you get me

a gift?

Of course I did. You're going to love it.

BRIAN!!! You suck!!! Just tell me what you want for Christmas!!!

I told you. All I want for Christmas is you.

I gave up. No doubt he was singing the popular Christmas carol right now. At the very least, he was humming it in his mind. He'd been singing the song to me all week every time I asked him what he'd like for Christmas.

AGH!!!! FINE!!!! I have to go. I'll call you after I get home.

Looking forward to it. Good luck with the shopping. ;)

I groaned again and shoved my phone into my back pocket. Vivian laughed as she slid into one side of the booth we'd been ushered to. "I take it Brian's still not being helpful?"

When Erik slid in next to her, I sat across from them. "Helpful? Please. He's being a downright pain in the rear. I don't know why he loves to torture me so much."

I scooted all the way in so that Juliette could sit next to me, but she squeezed in on Erik's other side. When I cocked an eyebrow at her, she gave me a sheepish grin and nodded toward Erik.

Ana studied the seating arrangements and only hesitated a second before sliding into the booth next to me, letting Jason take the end. Before things could get awkward, Erik smiled across the table at me and asked, "So Brian would be the boyfriend you can't figure out a gift for?"

I sighed. "Yes."

"Maybe I can help. I am a guy, after all."

"Ooh. Good idea," Juliette said.

"Okay, fine." I really did need the help. "As a guy, what would you want for Christmas from your girlfriend?"

"That depends," Erik said. "How long have we been going out?"

"A week," I said, while both Vivian and Juliette answered, "Three years."

Erik's eyebrows rose high up his forehead, and rightly so. He waited for an explanation. I was going to change the subject, but I was so confused about my current relationship that the idea of a guy's perspective was totally appealing. "It's complicated. We've known each other online for three years, but we only got together in person a week ago."

"Hmm." Erik fell into thought as if he was really taking this task seriously. I found myself holding my breath for his answer. "Were you together as an online couple before you met?"

I shook my head. "Just friends, but we fell in love."

"And it's definitely a relationship now…?"

"Yes. Exclusive."

"You've told each other that you love each other?"

"Yeah."

He frowned. "So…why are you having trouble finding him a gift? Don't you know him really well by now?"

I groaned at the question and fell forward, banging my forehead on the table in front of me. "I know everything about him," I whined, leaving my forehead against the cool tabletop. "The problem is, he's really rich and already has everything he could possibly ever want or need. Whenever I ask him to give me a hint, he says he doesn't need a gift. He just sings me that stupid song: 'All I Want for Christmas is You.'"

Ana snorted. "You're making this way harder than it has to be. I know exactly what you should do." All of us looked at her, waiting for this miraculous answer to my dilemma. She slid me a sly look and shrugged her shoulders. "Give him your virginity."

Erik choked on the ice water he was sipping, and Jason burst into obnoxious laughter. Both Juliette and Vivian yelled at Ana, but she'd only been teasing, so their scoldings came with laughter. I wasn't angry, but they had no idea how sensitive a topic that was for me. Since I didn't want them to know just how deep my insecurities went, I forced myself to laugh along with them. "Shut up, Ana. That's not happening."

"Actually, that's really not a bad idea," Juliette said.

"Juliette!" I gasped at the betrayal and threw my napkin at

her. "I'm not going there with him after only a week."

She rolled her eyes. "You guys aren't a week-old couple, and you know it. Maybe you guys don't have to go all the way, but a nice, romantic evening together taking the relationship to the next level—whatever that is to you—might be the best gift you can give him."

My blush deepened. I scrubbed my hands over my face, but it did nothing to remove the redness from my cheeks. "Oh my gosh, you guys, can we, like, *not* have this particular conversation in front of Jason and some guy we met five minutes ago?" I glanced at Erik with a grimace. "No offense."

He laughed. "None taken. But if I could just weigh in here a little, I think your friends are right."

I laughed once. "Of course you do. You're a guy."

He shook his head. "No, seriously. If he really does have everything already, then maybe he's not teasing when he says all he wants is you. Maybe he's giving you the hint you've been asking for."

We all sat there for a moment, contemplating Erik's suggestion. It made a lot of sense. Maybe that's what Brian really did want. He'd asked me to *move in* with him, for heaven's sake. Maybe he was desperate for a deeper connection.

"That was very insightful," Juliette crooned, grinning at her prey. "You must be a pretty sensitive guy."

He shrugged, a light blush dusting his cheeks. Yeah, Jules definitely had this one in the bag.

I looked to Vivian, and she surprised me with an apologetic shrug. "I think he's right, too, Ella. You know how much Brian loves you. And you know he worries about you getting tired of…" She glanced at Erik and censored her words. "…his crazy life now that you're together in person. This week has been intense for you guys. He's probably pretty stressed about it. And you know a guy like him can't be used to feeling vulnerable. Maybe this is his way of reaching out to you. Maybe he needs a more solid commitment from you, and he's just afraid of asking for it because you two are so new."

"Maybe," I agreed.

Ana shrugged. "So, what's the problem? It's not like you've really only known each other for a week. You guys have been in love for years. You know everything about each other. What would it hurt to make things a little more serious?"

My stomach twisted into knots. Everyone seemed to agree with Ana on this one, but anxiety had my hands trembling beneath the table. "It's not that easy, you guys. You're right: we've loved each other for years. But that's what's so scary about our relationship. It's intense because we're ahead of ourselves emotionally. On one level, Brian and I are brand-new to each other. But in other ways, we're like a couple that's been together for years. A couple like *that* would be ready for things like sex and living together, but I'm not. I feel like I'm in both relationships—the old and the new—and I don't know how to merge the two."

"Something tells me Brian will have no problem combining them," Juliette muttered.

I nodded. "Exactly. And if I give him the kind of gift you guys are talking about, then I'm going to find myself in over my head. He's three years older than me. He lives on his own and has a stable career. He's been with like a *billion* women. I'm basically a naive little girl dating a grown-up man. He might be ready to jump right in, but it's going to take me some time to get used to us being an us."

Juliette sighed, and Vivian slumped back in the booth. "So, we're back to square one. How about a personalized license plate that says *Precious?*"

I laughed, grateful that the conversation had gone back to trivial and away from my love life. I didn't have the heart to tell her that was already what his license plate said.

"Forget *Precious,*" Vivian said. "It needs to say *Sorry, ladies, I'm taken.*"

Erik laughed. "I don't think you can fit that on a license plate."

"We'll get it tattooed on his forehead, then." Vivian said, winking at me. "Trust me. The man needs it."

I rolled my eyes.

"Enough about Brian and Ella," Juliette interrupted. "Let's move on to finding *me* a boyfriend. Now that Ana and Ella are both in steady relationships, I've got to get a move on it. I can't be the only single sister of the bunch. That's not cool." She leaned around Erik to grin at Vivian. "Would you mind horribly if I call dibs and ask Erik to take me out sometime next week?"

Erik's eyes bulged so wide all of us girls cracked up. "He's all yours," Vivian teased. "No way am I going to get mixed up in a Coleman sister competition."

6

JULIETTE CONVINCED ERIK TO STAY WITH US AFTER LUNCH TO finish his shopping, but it turned out everyone was done except me. The group decided an intervention was necessary and began dragging me into store after store. I didn't put up any fight. I was getting desperate, and six brains were better than one.

"Oh!" Ana came to a halt so fast Vivian crashed into her from behind. "Yes. This."

I groaned when I saw all of the underwear in the windows. "I seriously doubt Brian wants a pair of matching lacy black bra and panties for Christmas."

Ana looped her arm through mine, grinning. "For once, I completely agree with you. With your skin tone, we can go much brighter. I'm thinking vixen red."

So shocked by her friendly playfulness, it took me a minute to realize she was leading me into the store. I put on the brakes really fast and pulled my arm from hers. "Ana, we are not going in there. There are *guys* with us."

She turned to Jason and Erik with a frown. "Do either of you have any objections to going in there and helping Ella pick out something sexy to wear for her hot-as-hell boyfriend?"

My face flamed when Erik smirked and shook his head. "It would be my pleasure."

"Do I get to help pick something out for my sexy-as-hell girlfriend, too?" Jason asked.

Ana shot him a slow wink, and he smiled from ear to ear. "Sweet. I'm in."

"Ana, come on. I'm not getting Brian lingerie for Christmas."

She started dragging me into the store again. "Stop being such a prude, Ella. When else are you going to have the opportunity to have two different guys' opinions while you pick out something sexy?"

"It doesn't matter. I already told you, I'm not going there with Brian."

"You might, if you owned something as sexy as that." She marched over to a wall of very fancy lace bra and panty sets and picked up a ruby-red bra. "Trust me, Brian will *love* this."

"I love *this*," Jason said, grinning as he picked up a pair of skimpy panties—he went with traditional black.

I snatched the bra from Ana, glaring at Jason. He didn't seem to care. He smiled at me again and held up his find against Ana's body. "I know what I want for Christmas, babe."

Erik cleared his throat, and when I whirled around to face him, he smirked. "Your sister's on to something. I don't think you can go wrong with that." He pointed to the bright-red bra still dangling from my fingertips, then reached for a pale-pink cropped bustier and shortie panty set. "Or this would look great, too. I've always been a fan of pink."

I narrowed my eyes. "Seriously? I don't even know you, and you're trying to pick out underwear for me?"

His grin doubled, taking his cuteness factor up a notch in the most infuriating way. "I'm just trying to be helpful."

Juliette placed a hand on his arm. She smiled for him and them flashed that grin at me. She must have recognized the fire in my eyes, because she laughed and said, "Hang on there, *Señorita Snark*. Let's keep the temper in check. This isn't his fault."

"No, it's *Ana's*."

I shot Ana a glare. Yeah, I was trying to play nicer with her now, but this was *embarrassing*, and I was really annoyed with her. My attitude only fueled hers. She flashed me a saccharine smile. "I take full responsibility. Someday, you will thank me for it. And here. You *have* to try this on." She held up a bright-blue lacy teddy with a matching thong and garter. "This was made for you. It matches your eyes."

I started to argue, but before I could, Vivian took the teddy from her and held it up to me. "Oh, Ella," she crooned. "You know I hate to agree with Ana on anything, but she's right. This would look stunning on you. You *have* to get it."

"No way. I'm not buying that."

"But Ella, it's perfect," Juliette said. "It's beautiful *and* tasteful. It's so you."

I gritted my teeth. They were right. It was very pretty and much more tasteful than the things Erik and Jason had picked up. Unable to help myself, I took the garment from Vivian, imagining what Brian might think if I were to wear this for him.

Brian would *love* this gift, but could I wrap it up and hand it over? It wasn't just a joke. A gift like this came with a promise. Was Ana right? Would I be ready to make that promise if I felt beautiful enough? Because that was really what was holding me back with him. I loved him, and if this week together had taught me anything, it was that I wanted him. But I was scared. Afraid he wouldn't find me beautiful.

I rubbed the silky material between my fingers. It was amazingly soft. I could almost envision myself wearing it, but then I caught a glimpse of my scarred hand, and the moment was ruined.

I glanced around the store at all of the playful underwear. Before my accident, I used to love this store. I'd never been brave enough to venture to the naughtier side we were in now, but what girl doesn't appreciate cute underwear? Now, though, the shelves and bins full of pretty things meant to make you feel sexy and the walls plastered with pictures of beautiful, flawless bodies seemed to laugh at me. "I can't wear something like this," I muttered, setting the beautiful teddy down.

"Why not?" Ana asked.

I glared at her again. Why did she always have to push? "Why do you *think?*" I gestured to my body. My clothes were covering my scars, but she'd seen them before. She knew what I was hiding. "How about the obvious reason?"

"Um…" Erik interrupted hesitantly, as if sensing how real this conversation suddenly was. "Sorry. What's the *obvious* reason? If I can be a little forward here, you're absolutely beautiful. Your boyfriend is one lucky guy, and I'm sure he would *love* to see you in that."

My anger faded into a deep depression. Erik was trying to be nice. I even believed he was sincere with his compliment. I only wished *I* believed it. With a sigh, I held up my bad hand and pushed my sleeve up my arm. Erik's eyes widened slightly, but he otherwise didn't react to my scars except to curiously take in the sight. "I was in an accident—trapped in a burning car. These scars cover over 70 percent of my body. God was merciful enough to leave me my face, but…" I glanced down at my body and gulped. "Over 70 percent. Think about it."

Juliette was suddenly there, wrapping me in a warm hug. "Ella, you know Brian doesn't care about that."

"He says that," I muttered, soaking in my sister's support before facing the small group of people I'd suddenly made feel very awkward. "Even if he doesn't mind my scars, I'm dating a guy who is physical *perfection*. Before me, he dated girls as beautiful as he is—models and actresses. Those women probably wore stuff like this for him all the time." I picked up the teddy again, trying to picture it covering my scarred body. I couldn't imagine it.

I waved a hand at the pictures all over the store. "Take a look around you. There's not one picture of a woman in this store with a single flaw on her. Not even a freckle. Those models are all perfect. You think that's coincidence?" Holding up the teddy, I started shaking it angrily. "Wearing something like this isn't going to make me look sexy. All it's going to do is make it seem like I'm trying too hard to be something I'm not."

I sucked in a breath and let it out slowly, forcing back the threat of tears. I'd lost a grip on my emotions with that last admission, but I couldn't help it. They may not have meant to, but they were forcing me to face one of my greatest insecurities. "I'm going to go get some air. There are some benches right outside. I'll wait for you guys there."

I only got one step before Vivian stopped me. Her eyes were glossy, and her voice shook when she spoke. "Ella...true beauty comes from within. You *know* that. You are the most beautiful person I've ever met. Why else do you think you managed to snag a guy like Brian? And you didn't just snag him, girl, you have that man so wrapped up in you he can't even *see* other women anymore. They don't *exist* for him anymore. You are that man's everything, and you know he'll think you are beautiful no matter what is under your clothes."

"Maybe. But I don't feel beautiful."

"That," Ana said, stepping into the conversation with a confidence that broke the tension, "is because you refuse to wear things that make you feel sexy." She added the pink bustier and panties to the teddy in my hands. "Dress for success, Ella. Even if you're not ready to show yourself off to your man, you've got to start dressing sexy to feel sexy. Do you know what I'm wearing right now?"

Both Jason's and Erik's heads snapped in her direction, their eyes doing elevator moves up and down her body. Jason snaked his arms around her and began kissing her neck. "What are you wearing, babe?"

She swatted him away with a smirk. "That's my sexy secret. But look at how much confidence I have."

I seriously doubted her confidence came from her underwear, but it was pointless to argue.

"I can't believe I'm going to say this a second time," Vivian said, "but I agree with Ana. If you can't start feeling sexy, you'll never be ready to go there with Brian. You should start treating yourself like you deserve to wear this kind of stuff. Because you *do*."

"She's right," Juliette said. Her mouth curved up into a crooked smile, and she plucked the black lace panties from Jason's hands, adding them to my pile. "It's time for you to start feeling as sexy as you are, so woman up and buy yourself a new thong."

Everyone laughed, and while I was completely mortified that Jason and Erik had witnessed this conversation, I also loved my friends more than anything in the world. Even Ana, in her overbearing too-aggressive way, was trying to make me feel better. I think. Or she was trying to embarrass me in front of these two guys because she knew I was a prude and liked to razz me about it? Either way, she was successful. I did feel a little better. Not enough to buy myself a thong or a teddy, but better.

"Fine. Maybe you guys have a point, and I promise I will start making more of an effort to be proud of myself. But let's start with some cute short-sleeve tops or a skirt, okay? I'm not ready for *this*." I lifted the pile of lingerie in my hands for emphasis, and then set it down, flicking the tacky black thong at Jason. "Besides, how is anyone supposed to feel sexy with a string tucked up their crack?"

Everyone laughed again, but as we started to leave the store, Juliette grabbed the teddy. "Fine. If you won't, I will." She shot me a smirk and headed for the cashier. "Merry Christmas, Ella."

"Good idea," Ana said, grabbing the pink set Erik had picked out. "I wasn't actually going to get you a gift, but I'm feeling generous now."

I rolled my eyes, but then I saw Erik's grin, and I blushed. "I really do like the pink one," he said. "If you ever get tired of your boyfriend, give me a call."

Vivian snorted. "Yeah, I don't think that's going to happen. You're going to have to stick with Juliette."

Erik's eyes drifted toward the sales counter where the twins were making their purchases. Juliette's gorgeous locks were falling down her back in big ringlets, and her mile-long legs were on display thanks to the short skirt she had on. "Not a bad deal," he said.

He was still checking her out as she approached us. He slid his arm around her shoulder and tucked her to his side. "So, beautiful, I've got to get going, but before I leave, do you have plans for New Year's Eve yet? I've got an invite to a killer party, and I still need a date."

Juliette shrugged nonchalantly. "I have plans, but maybe I could be convinced to ditch them for a better offer."

"Well then, I'll just have to convince you that mine is the better option. Give me your number, and I'll text you later."

He handed her his phone, and as she programmed her number in for him, she shot me a sly wink. I shook my head with a laugh. I never would have guessed I could be so close with a girl like Juliette, but I really did love my new stepsister.

I CAME HOME FROM THE MALL EMPTY-HANDED, BUT AT LEAST SOME good came from our hours of shopping—Juliette was glowing as we came into the house that evening. She'd played it cool with Erik, but the second he was gone, she went nuts with excitement, claiming he was the nicest, funniest, hottest guy she'd ever met. I was happy for her. Jules needed a good guy, and even though Erik had picked out a sexy bra and panty set for me, I could admit he was cool and that it would be okay if Juliette started dating him.

Dad and Jennifer were down in the family room watching *Love, Actually*, but Jennifer paused the movie when she heard us come in, and they came upstairs to greet us. "How did it go?" She plucked a bag from Ana's hands. "Can I see the goods?"

"Mom!" Ana shrieked, yanking the bag away from her. "Your present is in there. Stop trying to peek. You're as bad as Dad."

Juliette laughed. "Yeah right. No one is as bad as Dad." She shot me a sardonic look, clutching her own shopping bags as if her life depended on it. "There's a reason we wait until the last possible minute to shop for our parents."

She glared at Dad, who was inching closer to her as she spoke. "What?" he asked, with an expression so innocent I burst into laughter.

"Did either of you peek at the gifts *I* got you?" I asked.

One look at Dad's face, and I knew. "Dad!" I whacked his arm.

"What? You left the bag on the kitchen counter. I thought it was groceries."

Sure he did. "I left it on the kitchen counter for five minutes, because I couldn't carry everything at once, and I warned you not to look."

"Come on, Ella. You can't leave a surprise for me on the counter, tell me not to look, and then *leave the room*. What did you expect?"

It was odd to see such a formidable attorney who was used to cross-examining ruthless criminals sputtering without any defense. It humanized him a little, and even though I was busting him, I still cracked a smile. "Ugh. You're as bad as Brian. I should take it back and get you something else."

"Don't do that. I've needed a new briefcase for a while, and I love the one you picked. I was tempted to ask if I could have it two weeks ago." Dad grinned at whatever exasperated look I gave him. "I really do love it. Thank you in advance."

"Whatever. I need to go rest for a while."

Dad's face fell. "Did you overdo it at the mall today?"

"A little bit." I shifted my weight off my bad leg with a sigh. Both of my feet ached, and I was throbbing all the way from my toes to my hip. "Daniel will probably say the exercise was good for me, but I'm going to have to soak in a hot bath for a long time tonight if I want to be able to move tomorrow."

"Use some Epsom salt, if you're swelling," Jennifer said. "And don't forget the lavender oil. If you're really sore, try mixing some bergamot and eucalyptus in there, too."

Jennifer was big on essential oils. I used to think she was just a California fruitcake, but I can't deny her tricks have been heaven for my body. "I will, thanks."

It took me a while to get in the tub. I was sore enough that I was moving like a ninety-year-old woman. I really had overdone it physically. Walking is something I can barely do, and it wears me out. We'd been at the mall *all* day. I'd often had to sit down and wait for the girls while they browsed. But even resting periodically, I'd done a lot more walking than normal.

This was the first time since my accident that I'd been on my feet most of the day, and my body was voicing its protests. Still, it had been worth it. Wandering the mall with my two best friends, shopping, gossiping, and picking up boys made me feel like a normal teenager again. Well, minus the handful of times I was recognized. The fame thing was not normal no matter how you looked at it. I wondered if it would ever feel less strange.

So exhausted from my day, I accidentally dosed off after my bath. After getting dressed, I'd lain down on my bed just to rest for a minute, with my hair still twisted up in a towel, and didn't wake up until the next morning.

7

I WOKE TO THE SOUND OF MY PHONE RECEIVING AN INCOMING text. It took me a minute to comprehend where I was, and that I'd fallen asleep after my bath. Yawning, I untangled the towel from my head. My hair was dry and crusty from not being brushed after my bath. I'd have to wet it down again if I wanted it to be the least bit manageable. Filing that thought away for later, I stretched and blinked several times when I realized it was morning.

My phone dinged again—another text—and then it dinged again. And then it rang. As odd as that was, I ignored it. I was still too groggy, and it was probably just Brian wanting to whine at me for not calling him last night. He could wait long enough for me to brush my teeth. Or maybe he could wait another half an hour...

I rolled over and snuggled under the covers, but that only lasted about two minutes before Juliette barged into my room. "Ella! Get up! You have to see this!"

"Go away," I groaned. "I'm sleeping."

"No, seriously."

She grabbed my laptop and climbed onto my bed. I yawned again as she booted the thing up. "What is it?"

"Don't you check your phone?"

"Not this early in the morning. Brian can wait until I'm out of bed."

"You might want to call him back."

What the heck was so urgent? I grabbed my phone while Juliette pulled up the Internet on my laptop.

My texts were from Vivian and Rob. Both seemed urgent and told me to check out this website called *Get Real Hollywood* right now. There were multiple exclamation points used. Even *Rob's* text used one, so I knew something big had happened.

As I rubbed the sleep out of my face and slowly sat up—I was beyond stiff after having rested on my sore muscles—Juliette shrieked. "No way! No freaking way!"

"What is it?" I asked.

She was too focused on the laptop to explain, but I could tell her shock was not from any kind of good news. She looked a scary combination of horrified and pissed.

I moved my legs over the side of the bed with a groan. Daniel was going to kill me in my next PT session for overworking my body so much. Probably right after he told me it was good for me and recommended I do it more often.

My phone started to ring, but I ignored it. Whoever was calling was only going to tell me to look at the website Juliette was gawking at. "What's going on?"

"That sneaky rotten *bastard!*"

"Juliette!" I snapped. It was the only way to break her concentration.

Juliette's face was stark white except for the angry red splotches on her cheeks and the back of her neck. When she met my confused and curious gaze, her eyes misted over. "Ella, I'm so sorry."

She moved my laptop onto my lap. I looked at the screen in front of me, but it took me a moment to understand what I was seeing. "Hey, that's me. Is that lunch at the restaurant yesterday? What…? Where…? How…?"

"Erik," Juliette whispered. "He's some big-time celebrity gossiper."

"What do you mean?"

She clicked out of the video and went back to the home page for *Get Real Hollywood*. It was a celebrity news website. Erik's picture was in the upper left corner with a short bio. The lead story was front and center, and huge: *Cinder's Ella Gets Real About Her Physical Relationship with Brian and Her Own Insecurities.* The video of me at the lunch table in the mall yesterday was right beneath it.

"We were totally duped," Juliette said. "He must have known who you were from the start. That's probably why he stuck up for you. He'd probably been following us for a while, looking for some kind of opportunity to talk to us. We fell right into his trap."

I wasn't ready to believe this yet—still in the denial stage of my shock. "How was he recording this?"

Juliette shrugged, staring once again at the video playing on the laptop. "I don't know. He must have had some kind of hidden camera on him."

"Is there audio?"

Juliette's grimace answered the question for her. She clicked on the video, and my voice rang out loud and clear. "…whenever I ask him to give me a hint, he says he doesn't need a gift. He just sings me that stupid song: 'All I Want for Christmas is You.'"

My stomach rolled. Bile clawed up my throat, and I had to swallow it back down as I realized exactly what Erik had captured on video and posted for the entire world to see. "How much did he get?" My question came out shaky.

Juliette scrolled forward through the video and swallowed. "It looks like the whole conversation at lunch…and everything in the lingerie store."

I cringed. "Everything?"

Juliette nodded.

I fell back against the bed, so shocked that I didn't even notice the physical pain the movement caused. That conversation at lunch had started with Ana telling me I should give Brian my virginity for Christmas and only got more personal from there. I felt ill. The room started to spin, and my eyes began to sting. "Jules..." My voice started to shake.

"I know," she whispered, equally distressed. "And all of us only made it worse. Ella..."

My phone rang again, and when I saw Brian's name on the caller ID, tears pooled in my eyes. Unable to answer the phone, I threw it across the room and slapped my hands over my face. The phone went to voice mail and immediately started ringing again. Juliette retrieved it and held it out to me. "Talk to him, Ella."

I shook my head. "I can't. If he's calling me, he's already seen this. He heard that whole conversation at lunch about him being a grown-up and me being his silly little prude of a girlfriend. He saw me refuse to buy sexy underwear and confess that I wasn't ready to sleep with him because I'm insecure about my body. He *heard* that. The whole *world* is currently hearing it."

Juliette wiped a tear from her cheek. "Ella, I'm so sorry."

"It's not your fault."

"Still, I feel—" She cut herself off when the phone started ringing a third time. "You need to talk to him."

"I *can't*. Not yet. I need a minute to freak out."

Across the house, there was an earth-shattering shriek, and then seconds later my bedroom door burst open. "Did you see it?" Ana cried.

One look at me answered her question. She began pacing. "That asshole! I'm going to kill him!" She glared at me. "Did you know who he was? Did you let me make a complete ass of myself on purpose, knowing he was filming all that?"

Was she kidding?

"Shut up, Ana," Juliette snapped. "Not everything is about you."

My tears vanished, and, for once, I probably managed a scarier glare than her. "Oh no, this is *totally* about you, Ana," I argued, taking the easy target to vent some of my anger. "I *totally* called

Erik up and invited him to come secretly film us making fools of ourselves at the mall. And I *totally* confessed to him that I'm not ready to sleep with Brian because he's perfect and my body is a horrific mess because I *wanted* the whole world to know that. And I *totally* asked you to bring up my sex life and drag me into a lingerie store. You got me. That was all my big, evil plan to make *you* feel stupid."

Ana glared again, but she wasn't pissed off at me. Her angry look turned to one of frustration as she plopped down into my desk chair with an angry huff. "This is a nightmare."

"On the bright side," Juliette said, glaring at the laptop so severely I feared for its safety, "Dad is going to *destroy* him in court. That jerk messed with the wrong family."

"NO!" Ana and I shouted together.

Juliette flinched, startled to be so heartily opposed.

"Dad will *kill* me if he sees that video," Ana said.

Yeah, I might have looked stupid and insecure, but Ana came across as pretty skanky. She'd never be allowed to date again if Dad saw this video. "And he'll want to have some kind of awkward father-daughter talk with me," I added. "If he doesn't just launch into another lecture about his disapproval of me dating Brian."

Juliette scoffed. "I hate to break it to you both, but Dad is going to see this anyway. It's going to be everywhere. If he jumps on it now, maybe he can get a cease and desist order before it makes it into Kenneth Long's monologue."

A loud knock made me groan again just as Dad's nervous voice rang out. "Girls? Are you all decent? I found the website on Ana's computer. Can I come in…?"

Juliette frowned at Ana. "You woke the whole house screaming and then left your laptop open when you came running down here? Good job. Way to keep Dad from finding out about it."

"Girls?"

"Go away, Dad!" Juliette yelled.

Apparently *go away* means *come on in* in Dad speak, because he opened the door and poked his head in. When he saw that we were all at least covered, he stepped fully in the room. "Dad, please," I begged. "I don't want to talk about this."

Whatever expression I wore on my face was enough to make my dad pause. His face fell, and he sighed. "Sweetheart, you've chosen to date a celebrity. As long as you're seeing Brian Oliver, things like this are going to happen."

I didn't want to fight, but the man knew exactly how to push my buttons. "This wasn't Brian's fault."

He rolled his eyes. "I'll beg to differ on that, but it's a moot point. What I'm saying is, you can't let these things control your life. It's already happened. There's no use hiding from it."

Ha! *I'd* beg to differ on that.

While we were locked in a stare down, the doorbell rang. I didn't need three guesses to know who was here. I didn't even need one. Sure enough, once Jennifer answered the door, Brian's voice rang out loud and clear and full of concern. "Ella?"

When he appeared at the threshold of my room, I lay back down and pulled my covers over my head. "UGH. Ella's not here right now. GO AWAY, PLEASE."

"Ellamara," Brian cooed. "Relax. It's going to be okay."

For once, his voice did nothing to soothe me. "No, it's NOT!" I was so worked up my voice cracked on the last word. "How could I be so *stupid?* I said stuff, Brian. We got caught up in our conversation, and I wasn't thinking. I said some really personal, embarrassing stuff. I'm sure you've seen it all. We joked around in a *lingerie* store. Juliette and Ana bought me Christmas presents when I wouldn't buy anything for myself. The whole *world* is going to see that."

I sucked in a breath as a sob hit me. I swallowed it. I didn't want to cry. But no matter how hard I tried, I still sniffled. I'd been tricked. I felt violated.

When the weight shifted on my bed, I knew Brian had traded places with my father. He plucked my blankets off my head and gently pulled me into a sitting position. When he wrapped his strong arms around me, I broke. I collapsed against his chest, letting my tears flow. "How could he do that to us?"

Brian squeezed me tighter and quietly said, "May we have a minute alone, please?"

I didn't look to see if they listened. I knew they would. When Brian used his serious voice like that, he tended to get his way. Oh, I'm sure my father shot him a nasty look, and I didn't hear the door click shut because he, no doubt, refused to shut it all the way with Brian in the room. But when Brian pulled my face out of his chest and tucked my hair behind my ears, I knew we were alone.

I took one look at his pain-filled eyes and broke down as if I were at a confessional. "I'm *so* sorry. We had no idea who he was. He—"

He shook his head and spoke over me, unwilling to let me keep apologizing. "You have nothing to be sorry for. It wasn't your fault. The guy's name is Erik Clarke. He's notorious around town for stunts just like this. He doesn't get the celebrities as often because we all know to look out for him, but he tracks down the families and friends of the celebrities and gets them talking. He gets all kinds of dirt on people."

Great. "Some luck. What were the odds I'd end up next to him on the escalator the *one time* this week I went out in public without you?"

Brian's face fell, and he shook his head again. "It wasn't luck. You were spotted at the mall. He knew you were there without me, and that you most likely wouldn't know who he was. He took advantage of you."

Brian growled that last little bit and had to stop speaking to take a breath and calm down. I knew the feeling. I was just as pissed. "And I completely fell for it, because I am a stupid, naive little girl who only thinks she can handle adulthood."

"Don't do that. Don't belittle yourself. That was not adulthood. That was fame. Being new to it doesn't make you stupid." He huffed in frustration. "I'm sorry, Ella. I was really hoping you'd have time to adjust to everything before something like this happened."

"How do you *live* like this? I mean, *geez*. As if I didn't feel stupid enough before? Everyone knows about the suicide attempt and the legal custody my dad had. I have a freaking *curfew*. Which they also put on the front page this week. Now I'm the naive little virgin girl scared to have sex with my boyfriend. The nation thinks I'm a joke. UGHHHH. I *am* a joke." I gave my hair a good yank.

"Ella, *stop*. Look at me." When I didn't, he repeated himself, throwing some force into the command. *"Look at me."*

I met his gaze.

"Tabloids are always going to twist the facts to create the best headlines. That doesn't make what they say true. Anyone can be made to look their worst if you can pick and choose only a few key facts from their life. What those people don't know, but I do, is that you are a strong, smart, kind, and compassionate woman. You are *not* a joke." Brian brought his hand to my face and softened his voice. "You are the best thing that's ever happened to me. Do you understand me? No matter what anyone says or prints, I love you. I will *always* love you."

Brian's declaration, though I'd heard it before, was exactly what I needed in that moment. I couldn't find words to express the amount of gratitude in my heart, so I leaned forward and pressed my lips to his. The kiss was frenzied. I kissed him as if his lips on mine would make all of my problems disappear.

Brian returned my frantic kiss with calm strength. His gentle touches and the way he held me were confident and loving. They filled me with a sense of security, easing away the torrent of emotion I'd been racked with. After I calmed down, Brian broke the kiss and gave me a soft, teasing smile. "Feel better yet?"

I did. I felt a million times better. Better enough that I could match the playful glint in his eyes and tease him back. "Nope. I don't think so. I'm going to need a lot more of that before I'm better."

When I wrapped my arms around his neck and kissed him again, he laughed but indulged me for a minute longer. Only, now that I wasn't on the brink of an emotional breakdown, Brian's response was much more heated. The kiss became less about soothing me and more about his own set of needs and desires. He was the one to break it again, but this time he had to rip himself away and suck in a deep breath. "That's enough of *that*," he said, trying to cool his lust. "At least while your family is out there waiting for us to come out."

I sighed. Time to get back to reality. "All right. Let's go get this over with. They've all seen that stupid video this morning, so it should be nice and awkward, and my dad, no doubt, has an awesome lecture all thought up."

I started to move, but Brian stopped me. "Ella..." Wariness crept into his tone and expression. "About what you said in that video..."

And just like that, all of my anxiety was back. "No." I shook my head frantically. "Don't. Please."

"But—"

"Please? I am embarrassed enough right now. I really don't want to have this conversation."

He frowned. "We *need* to have this conversation. Actually, this particular conversation is one you should have had with me in the first place instead of with your girlfriends."

My face flamed, and I dropped my head, unable to meet his probing gaze. "Girls will always need their girl talk."

"I know, but I can't stand the thought of you worrying that I won't find you attractive. I promise you, that is *not* the case. Far, far, far from it. And if you're feeling scared, or confused, or overwhelmed with our relationship, or you don't know what I'm feeling, the best way to fix that is to talk to *me* about it."

Ugh. See? And this was exactly one of those things that set us apart. "Said the mature grown-up man to his clueless baby of a girlfriend," I grumbled.

"Ella."

"I know. Sorry. I'm wallowing in self-pity." He quirked an eyebrow at me, and I caved. "Fine. We can talk about it. But not right now, okay? Just give me some time to get over the shock and stop feeling so stupid."

Brian raked his eyes over me, trying to figure out if I was serious about being too overwhelmed or simply trying to get out of the conversation. I must have passed his test, because he let out a breath and nodded. "Okay. Not now. But you promise? After you're feeling better, you'll talk to me about this? About *us?*"

I hesitated simply because I felt like being defiant. But I *did* want to figure things out between us so I could stop feeling so stressed out and so…so…I don't know…immature, I guess. Talking was inevitable. "I promise."

"Good." He pressed a quick kiss to my lips and pulled me back into a hug, seemingly in no real hurry to get up. I happily snuggled against his chest. "Then I just need to say one last thing," he said. "About everyone's favorite sound bite…"

My heart missed a beat or two when it dropped into my stomach. I pulled out of his embrace to gape at him in horror. "What sound bite? There's already a favorite sound bite?"

Brian laughed, a real, gut-bursting laugh, and squeezed me close again. "My girlfriend accused me of being with a *billion* women. That's not disappearing from the front pages anytime soon."

Okay, I was glad he'd pulled me back to his chest, because he couldn't see the way my face set on fire.

"I'd just like to set the record straight that while I may not know the exact number, I assure you it's not a *billion.*"

He was being obnoxious, but his tactic worked, and he successfully cheered me up. "Whatever." I cracked a smile and let a soft laugh escape. "Fifty…a billion…if you've lost count, it's all the same."

We laughed together, which felt amazing, but the moment ended quickly. Sighing, I stole one last kiss. "Thank you for coming."

8

When Brian and I finally emerged from my room, everyone was in the kitchen. Jennifer was starting a pot of coffee, fretting as she glanced back and forth between the three of us girls. Anastasia was sitting at the dining table, texting on her phone with a scowl on her face. Dad was leaning stiffly against the counter, his arm elbow-deep in a box of Lucky Charms. Guess he was done pretending he didn't sneak contraband into the house. Apparently, he needed the comfort food to settle him down.

Juliette was going to need more than some marshmallow cereal to bring her down from her rage. She was pacing back and forth, muttering to herself under her breath. At once, she stopped mid stride, whirling on Dad. "Why aren't you making any calls right now?" she demanded. "That stupid entertainment creep should be on his way to jail already. Nobody messes with the Coleman family and gets away with it!"

I looked over just in time to see Dad cringe. The expression made my heart skip a beat. "What?" Juliette asked. She knew there was bad news coming, too.

Dad glanced back and forth between us and sighed. "Erik Clarke did nothing wrong."

"WHAT?" Juliette roared.

My heart sank into my stomach.

"Morally," Dad said, talking over Juliette's shouts of protest, "what he did was despicable. Legally…" His shoulders drooped. "He's done nothing outside of the law."

I blinked in disbelief. Could that really be true?

"He filmed us without our knowledge!" Juliette ranted. "How is that *not* illegal?"

Dad shot her his calm-down-now-or-you'll-be-sent-to-your-room look. "Everything you girls did and said yesterday was in public."

"But it wasn't meant for the whole public to see."

Dad shook his head. "It doesn't matter. Public is public. Clarke's first amendments rights protect him on this matter. This is his *business*, ladies. I'm sure he knows exactly what the laws are and was very careful not to break them. You're not his first angry victims by any means. He's long since figured out the system. I *did* make a call. Clarke's got his own team of lawyers, and my friend says they're some of the best. He gets sued often but usually settles out of court, and he's never been slapped with any criminal charges."

Juliette plopped down at the table beside Ana—arms folded tightly, face pulled into a petulant frown.

"So much for seeing that pretty face behind bars," Ana said.

"Lucky for him," Juliette muttered. "He'd make a lot of the inmates happy, for sure."

I cracked a smile at that. "Definitely too bad we can't get him thrown in jail, then."

Anastasia laughed, and Juliette huffed. "Fine. We'll just have to settle for suing him."

"My lawyers are already looking into that," Brian offered. "I called them on my way over."

He was trying to be helpful, but Dad's eyes narrowed again.

Anger rose up in me—Dad really didn't have a reason to hate Brian so much—but I choked it down. Things were bad enough.

I didn't need to get into a fight with my dad on top of it. "I'm sorry to change the subject," I said, "but I really need to take some painkillers and sit down for a while."

My request set everyone into motion. Brian pulled out a chair from the kitchen table for me, while Jennifer grabbed a bottle of Tylenol from the cupboard. "Not those," I said. "I'm going to need the heavy-duty stuff today."

She put the Tylenol back and reached for a bottle of prescription painkillers that I only ever used when I really needed it. After yesterday's all-day mall excursion, I needed it. Dad grabbed me a V-8 from the fridge and brought me the medicine. "You're still sore from yesterday?"

"Yeah. I'm going to have to take it extra easy for a few days."

Dad's brow creased. "Should I call Daniel?"

Daniel was my gorgeous and cool, but ruthless, physical therapist. I liked the guy, and I had to admit I'd come a long way since working with him, but still, I didn't want to have to see him more than was necessary. "No *way*. Do you know how painful it would be if he made me do my exercises right now? He promised me a torture-free holiday. I'll be fine until next week."

I swallowed the pill my dad gave me and smiled. Once Dad wandered into the kitchen to dump a bunch of sugar into his coffee, Brian pulled out the chair next to mine and sat with me. He threw an arm casually around the back of my chair, and the simple gesture went a long way in helping me relax. "So..." he said, "have this morning's events convinced you to reconsider my offer at all?"

Juliette plopped down across from us with a curious expression. "What offer?"

"Nothing," I said, while Brian answered her loud and clear.

"I asked Ella to move in with me instead of Vivian. I'm hoping I can convince her before moving day."

Juliette choked on surprise, and, as I knew would happen, my father heard this and completely overreacted. *"WHAT?"* he roared, slamming his coffee mug down on the counter so hard he nearly shattered it. As it was, he spilled coffee all over the counter and his shirt, and Jennifer was forced to clean up the mess while my father fumed.

There was a reason I hadn't mentioned Brian's offer to anyone. I knew it would make my dad flip. Brian knew it, too. I couldn't believe he'd brought the subject up in front of him. After shooting Brian an annoyed glance, I turned around to face my dad. I tried to look and sound completely calm, hoping I might rub off on him. Doubtful, considering the dark red shade of his face. "Relax, Dad. I didn't say yes."

"Yet," Brian interjected stubbornly.

I glared at him again. Surprisingly, he returned the annoyed look before locking his eyes on my father. Ditto for my dad with him. He looked ready to murder Brian. "How *dare* you suggest such a thing to her? You've only been a couple for a *week*. She's barely nineteen!"

Brian was completely unruffled by the outburst, save some eye twitching and teeth grinding that suggested he wanted to tear into my dad. He resisted the urge, though, and sat up straight in his chair to give the scary prosecuting attorney a confident, challenging stare. "I know you don't understand my relationship with your daughter," he said calmly, "but Ella and I have been best friends for years. The way we know each other—*love* each other— is not new, and it's not casual. I'm not going anywhere, Richard, no matter how much you disapprove of me, and if Ella wants to move in with me, that is her choice, not yours. She's an adult."

I was stunned. Maybe even more stunned than my father. Brian had called him by his first name on purpose. He'd spoken to him man-to-man. He'd let him know that while I might be someone Dad could push around and treat like a child, *he* was not going to accept that. And he'd completely pulled it off, is the thing. Ana's boyfriend Jason would have peed himself if my father had thrown that kind of hostility at him. But not Brian. He might only be twenty-two, but he'd been thrown into an adult world at a young age and forced to grow up. He was a man now, in his own right—a mature, confident one, who was used to having people answer to him, not the other way around.

Dad was *not* happy to be put in his place. "You smug son of a—"

"And, not that it's any of your business," Brian continued, talking over my father and his would-be insult, "but my offer to Ella was about more than just our relationship. If she's going to move, her privacy and safety have to be taken into consideration."

"What do you mean?" Jennifer asked before Dad could yell some more.

Brian barely spared her a glance before meeting my father's eyes again. "Like it or not, Ella is a celebrity now. Vivian and her fathers are wonderful people, but their apartment isn't equipped to handle Ella's fame."

My father swallowed whatever argument he was about to spew and frowned at me. In turn, I shot Brian a nasty glare. I wanted to kill him for bringing this up with my family after I'd already turned down his offer. He ignored my anger as easily as he'd ignored my father's outburst. "I'm serious about this, Ella. I know you think things will die down, but you have to trust me. I've been dealing with this my entire life. I know what it's like. And with the stunt Erik Clarke just pulled, it's only going to get worse."

"Oh," Jennifer said, grabbing Dad's arm with a worried frown. "He's right, Rich. We never thought about that."

Dad, still glaring and clenching his jaw, nodded slowly and turned his furious gaze from Brian to me. "If your safety is at risk, I don't want you going to Vivian's."

Great. Now he was going to try and stop me from moving out. I'd do it anyway, but he'd be pissed at me for it. *Thanks a lot, Brian.* "He's being paranoid, Dad."

The argument sounded weak, even to my ears. I was starting to see Brian's point. Erik Clarke had shaken me up. I'd been completely blindsided, and I'd never once suspected him. If someone was willing to ambush me with hidden cameras like that, I could only imagine what the paparazzi would do when they realized I'd moved to Vivian's apartment. I don't know that my safety would be in jeopardy, but I'd definitely never have a moment's peace.

I sighed, not willing to accept defeat but not in the mood to argue anymore, either. "Look, now is not the time for this discussion. I haven't agreed to anything, and it's Christmas. Can we please drop it before we get into a huge fight and ruin the holiday? We're all worked up because of the Erik Clarke thing. Let's wait until we can discuss this rationally. It's breakfast time, anyway. Maybe if we eat, we'll all be less grouchy. How about I whip up some spinach quiche?"

There was a tense moment of silence before everyone gave in and accepted the obvious subject change. Jennifer was the first to move. "Ella, sweetheart, you're not feeling great this morning. You take it easy, and let me handle breakfast. I may not be able to recreate your amazing quiche, but I can handle egg-white omelets." She glanced around for approval, and when everyone nodded, got to work.

Dad was still glaring, so Jennifer shoved an apron at him. "Would you mind helping me? I need some onions and some bell peppers chopped. *Richard.*"

Dad sucked in a breath, sent Brian one last death look, and threw the apron over his head, muttering under his breath.

I glared at Brian and didn't hold back my irritation when I snapped, "May I speak to you *privately?*"

Brian turned his unrelenting gaze on me. "Yes. Let's."

I dragged him back into my bedroom and rounded on him the minute the door was closed. "Are you *kidding* me? You had to go and bring that up in front of my father, when not just me, but the *twins*, are all over the media right now?"

Brian's eyes flashed for a brief instant, letting me know that he was just as upset as I was, even if he hid it better. "That's exactly why I brought it up. You blew me off too easily. You aren't taking this seriously. I'm worried about your safety."

"Fine. Maybe I don't really grasp the whole fame thing well enough yet. But still, you can't just spring something as huge as living together on me all of a sudden when I'm about to get out of the car, and then blurt it out to my family before we got the chance to really discuss it, just because you were mad that you didn't get your way."

He rolled his eyes. "That's not why I mentioned it."

"Bull."

He spun around and half leaned against, half sat on my desk, folding his arms tightly over his chest. I gave him a challenging look, and he huffed, throwing his hands in the air. "Fine. I was mad! Sue me."

I scoffed. "Jerk."

"You didn't even *think* about it, Ella. I asked you to *live* with me—something I've never even come close to doing with anyone before—and you blew me off without blinking. Worse. You shot down the idea like it was a freaking warplane coming to drop nukes on you."

I felt like crap when I realized he was upset because he felt *rejected*. "Brian…" My shoulders slumped, and my anger deflated. What could I say? I wasn't ready for what he wanted.

"It's not like I'd try to take advantage of you," he muttered, pinning me with the full force of his Oscar-Award-worthy expressive eyes. "Don't you trust me?"

I had to look away from him. I couldn't handle the hurt and confusion in his gaze. I sat down on the edge of my bed and wrapped my arms around myself, feeling strangely vulnerable. When I had a good grip on the whirlwind of emotions swirling inside me, I looked back up. "Of course I trust you. It's not that I think you'll pressure me for anything; it's just that you're so intense. Everything about you is intense. So is this relationship. And the fame is downright *crazy*. It's overwhelming. Trying to add living together on top of everything…" I blew out a breath, beset by the very idea of it. "It's too much all at once."

Brian pushed himself away from my desk and raked his hands through his hair. "I'm sorry," he said, with a frustrated shake of his head. "I was raised with this. My father was well-known in the industry long before I was born. I've been famous my entire life, even before I started acting. I can't imagine how hard getting thrown straight into all of this must be for you."

"No. You can't. *I* can't even grasp it. That's why I need a little time and space. Just some breathing room where I can escape it, if I need to. Just until I get used to it. That's all I'm asking for."

With another long breath, Brian sat beside me on the bed. "I'm sorry this is overwhelming you, but Ella, my life *is* intense. There's no escaping that. I'll do my best to buffer you from it when I can, but there are going to be things about this relationship that will force you out of your comfort zone. I can't help that."

"Yeah, but—"

"I know what you're hoping for, but moving to Vivian's would not be an escape. The insanity would follow you there, and it would only be worse because you wouldn't be prepared for it. Plus, you'd bring it down on Vivian and her fathers, too. You would pull them into this bullshit, whether you wanted to or not."

I closed my eyes and sucked in a breath. That was something I hadn't thought about. If the paparazzi was going to start hounding me at Vivian's the way they did here, then they would doubtlessly hound Vivian and her dads, too. They didn't need that.

"Why do you think I never told you who I was?" Brian asked softly. "I knew this would happen, and I didn't want this life for you. But I'm selfish, and now you're stuck with it. You don't have to do that to Vivian. Moving in with me might not be something you're completely ready for, but you may just have to learn how to swim straight from the deep end. I *want* you to live with me, but I *need* you to be safe, and if that means asking you to do something you're not fully comfortable with, then so be it. Sacrifices are going to have to be made if we're going to work."

I wanted to be mad, but he was being so *reasonable*. It was super annoying because I couldn't argue with him when he was thinking smartly, being rational, and, most importantly, being straight with me. He might try to protect me from his world, but he never sugarcoated things. I was glad he seemed to be of the *ignorance-is-not-protection* opinion.

Things weren't always going to be pretty or easy for us. Brian knew that. He didn't like it, but he always warned me ahead of time. I was grateful for that. I'd read a million books where the hero kept the heroine in the dark in an attempt to shield her from bad things. Those heroes were idiots. Their lies always ended up hurting the heroine.

Brian didn't try to hide the bad things. He wanted me to be prepared so that we could face them together. He trusted that I could handle it. For that alone, I owed him the courtesy of trying my best to make good on that trust. For him, I would find a way to handle the things that came at us.

"All right," I said, quietly letting out another breath. "We don't have a solution to this yet, but I acknowledge that it is important, and in the future, I will take your suggestions much more seriously. I promise, no more blowing off anything you say just because it makes me uncomfortable."

Brian frowned. "That's not a promise to move in with me."

"No, it's not," I agreed with a wry smile. "But it's an *I'm-willing-to-sit-down-and-discuss-the-issue-to-try-to-find-a-reasonable-compromise.*"

Brian didn't respond right away. He studied me with a searching gaze that I decided was him trying to figure out why I was so hesitant to live with him. I figured he needed some reassurance even if he'd never admit to feeling insecure, so I stood up, pulling him with me, and slipped my arms around his waist. "I love you, Brian Oliver."

As if my words were magical keys that unlocked the tension in his body, he sucked in a breath and wrapped his arms around me, melding his body to mine. "I love you, too, Ellamara Rodriguez."

"Good," I said, snuggling into his embrace as much as possible. "Then, could you do me a favor and *not* try to use my family against me to get your way in the future?"

Brian sighed, but he chuckled, too. "I was unhappy that I didn't get my way—I'm definitely not used to being told no—but

I swear I didn't mean to do that."

"Liar."

"Fine. I didn't *only* mean to do that. It was for your father's benefit as much as yours."

"Nice."

He groaned and hugged me tighter. "I'm sorry. Your dad just gets to me."

"I know." I sighed in full understanding and placed a small kiss to his neck. "I'm sorry he's been a jerk to you. I think he's overwhelmed, too, and nervous about what this could do to our family, but that's not an excuse to treat you so horribly. He doesn't deserve your patience, but would you try to play nice as much as possible? He's frustrating, but he's the only parent I have left. Please? For me?"

Brian pulled back and lifted my chin so that he could see my face. I managed my best puppy-dog pout, and he cracked instantly. "Wicked woman," he said as he lowered his mouth to mine. "You are not allowed to give me that look ever again." He moved his lips to my neck. "It's not fair."

"You use your audiobook voice on me *constantly*." He kissed me beneath my ear, and I shivered. "Talk about unfair."

The dangerous, low chuckle that escaped him set my insides on fire. "Oh no. We are not doing this right now," I said, though I made no attempt to escape his attention. "Not while my whole family is out there and knows we're back here fighting."

"We *were* fighting," Brian murmured, as he continued to rain kisses on my neck. "Now we're making up."

His mouth finally reconnected with mine in a tender kiss that left me unable to do anything except melt in his arms.

"I'm sorry, Ella," he whispered between kisses.

"Me too," I gasped.

Truth be told, I couldn't remember what we were fighting about.

We gave it a minute or two longer, but then forced ourselves to rejoin my family. Dad and Jennifer were still cooking, and both

Juliette and Anastasia were at the table, with omelets in front of them. Both girls smirked the second they saw us. "All finished with your lovers' spat?" Ana teased.

I didn't think I was particularly flushed or anything, but Juliette scanned my face and snorted. "Looks like they worked it out just fine."

I was dying, but Brian seemed to enjoy the attention, and being the stupid actor that he was, he hammed it up for his audience. He walked between the two of them, resting an arm on the backs of each of their chairs, and ducked his head down near theirs. "We worked things out, all right," he murmured, low enough that my dad and Jennifer couldn't hear him. "You remember the make-up scene in my movie *Senior Trip?* It was like that but hotter." With a slow, provocative wink, he added, "It's okay to be jealous."

Ana nearly snorted juice out of her nose while Juliette inhaled her omelet and started hacking up a storm. Their reactions were justified. How that movie got a PG-13 rating with that scene in it was beyond me. "Oh my gosh. *Brian!*" I hissed, slapping a hand over my face. "Shut up! We did *not!*"

All three of them laughed at my mortification. "Yeah, you wish," Ana told Brian. "You're dating *Ella.* I'm sure it was closer to something out of your movie *V is for Virgin.*"

Brian frowned, but the corners of his lips twitched. "Burn," he admitted with a grudging nod. "Well played."

Juliette, finally done choking on her breakfast, dissolved into a fit of giggles and held up a hand to Ana for a high five. "Nice one, sis."

"You're all idiots."

I rolled my eyes and headed into the kitchen, needing some juice and to escape the three stooges.

Brian wrapped his arms around me from behind just as I reached the kitchen counter and placed a small, soft kiss to side of my neck. As far as apologies went, it was pretty nice. I suppressed a shudder and leaned back against his chest. "Smells good," I said.

Jennifer and my dad looked up from their places near the stove, and Dad said, "Well, you kids sit down, if you're hungry. How do you like your omelets, Brian?"

Brian and I were both surprised by the invitation. Either my father had been lectured by Jennifer while we were gone—Jennifer, as most women did, had a major soft spot for Brian—or Dad actually felt bad for losing his temper at my boyfriend. It was probably the former, but either way, I'd take it.

Brian glanced at me and then shook his head. "That's okay. I didn't mean to intrude on your family time. I only came to make sure the girls were okay after I saw that video."

Judging by Jennifer's smile and Dad's soft grunt, Brian earned a few brownie points by including the twins in his concern. I'm not sure it was genuine in Ana's case—he wasn't her biggest fan—but I was sure he felt bad for Jules, and that was enough for the worry to come across as sincere.

"Well, you're here," Dad said gruffly. "May as well eat."

Brian looked down at himself and then shook his head again. "Thank you, but I suppose if the fire's out, I should run home and shower and put some real clothes on or something."

I realized for the first time that he was in pajamas and slippers and had bed hair, having sped straight over here when I refused to answer my phone this morning.

"What?" he asked, noticing the grin on my face.

"Nothing. Just...thanks for coming over this morning."

He matched my smile and kissed my cheek. "Thanks for not picking up your phone so I had an excuse to come over."

"Gag," Juliette said, as she walked past us to put her empty plate in the sink. "I'm going to get out of here and go shower before the lovebirds make me puke."

Laughing, I smoothed down the side of Brian's hair that was sticking up. "Come on, I'll walk you out."

As we reached Brian's car, he slid his arms around my waist and pulled me against him. "You could come with me," he murmured, ducking his head to my ear. "My shower's plenty big enough for two."

He was teasing, and he wasn't. He knew I would say no, but at the same time, the offer was real. With his mouth so close to my skin like that, his invitation was a lot more tempting than he knew. Suppressing a shiver, I swatted him on the chest. Unfortunately, my hand clung to his shirt when I hit him, which didn't help much in convincing him I wasn't interested. "That's not happening."

His mouth moved down my neck, raising goose bumps on my skin. "Forget the shower, then. How about a nice, long drive up the coast? Maybe we can find a deserted overlook to relax and...*talk*."

I laughed, but it quickly morphed into a groan. "You have no idea how good that sounds. Go home now, before you convince me and I ditch my family all day, making my father disapprove of our relationship even more."

Brian's mood flipped like someone had thrown a switch. "Who cares what he thinks about it? As soon as you move, it'll be none of his business anyway."

His frown turned to a dark glare, so I wrapped my arms around his neck and forced his lips down to mine. The kiss put a smile back on his face. "Just hurry back," I said.

Laughing, Brian found my lips again. "Are you sure I should? With all the Erik Clarke drama, I don't know if I could keep from fighting with your father if I spent the whole day here."

"I don't care. With all the Erik Clarke drama, *you're* the one I want to spend the day with. Not him. You're the one who makes me feel better. *Please* come back soon."

I used that face he warned me not to use again, and he sighed. "As you wish."

Yes, he was totally quoting *The Princess Bride*.

As he opened the car door and climbed behind the wheel, he shot me a grin and said, "You won't even have time to miss me."

I tried to keep quiet. I tried to swallow the words wanting to tumble out of my mouth. I really, *really* tried. But I couldn't do it. After he closed his door, I gestured for him to roll down his window, and then said, "I miss you already."

His chest shook with laughter as he turned on the car. "Now who's the dork?" he called over the roar of the engine. "Love you, woman. I'll be back soon."

9

BRIAN KEPT HIS WORD AND WAS BACK WITHIN AN HOUR. THANK-fully, no more arguments arose. We spent the day playing board games. Unbelievably, Brian had never done that before. He'd been an only child, and with no siblings to play with, had never had the opportunity. He'd also been auditioning for parts on TV by the time he was ten, and essentially missed out on a normal childhood of any kind, so things like Sorry! and Monopoly were a new experience. It was surreal watching him turn almost childlike every time he took his turn.

My personal favorite was watching him play The Game of Life. It's like the stupidest game ever, but he was thrilled with every turn. He joked about finally having the time to go to college and kept landing on the baby spaces. He ended up needing two of those little cars to carry all his people around. The dork actually named them all and gave them each positions on the family football team.

Not even my dad could resist the charm of Brian Oliver getting to be a kid for the first time in his life, and the two of them teamed up together against us girls for a few rounds of Battle of the Sexes. Then they played a few hands of poker with each other while Jennifer and I cooked Christmas Eve dinner.

It was a perfect day. Well, it was—until we turned on the TV after dinner. Jennifer and Dad shooed us kids all off while they did the dishes. We migrated back to the family room and turned on the TV. Ana plopped down into Dad's armchair, and Juliette sat on the end of the couch nearest her, while Brian and I claimed the other end. We'd just snuggled up together when Ana turned on *Celebrity Gossip*. I used to love the show, but it was quickly losing its appeal. The show was more of a tabloid rag than a respectable entertainment news show. Brian wasn't a fan, but he didn't protest, and Ana didn't offer to change the channel.

As soon as the opening credits were over, my picture filled the screen. "Cinder and Ella are making headlines again tonight, and we've got the full scoop," the show's bubbly blonde host announced. "Erik Clarke of the website *Get Real Hollywood* is here with us to dish the dirt on the reclusive couple."

Brian's grip on me tightened, and my stomach rolled. "We'll change it," Juliette said quickly.

Unfortunately, Ana was the one holding the remote, and she had a different idea. "No way. I want to see what the jerk has to say."

"Ana," Juliette hissed, glancing in my direction.

I was with Juliette. I had no desire to see what was coming, but Brian said, "No, it's better to hear it so we know what we're going to have to deal with." His jaw clenched, and he muttered, "And so I know how much to kick his ass the next time our paths cross."

We all sat quietly, mentally cursing Erik Clarke—Okay, Ana and Brian cursed him out loud—while the commercials played. When the show returned and Erik was sitting on a couch with the blonde host, my whole body tensed up. "I'm right here," Brian whispered in my ear as he rubbed my arms. "It'll be okay."

I wanted to believe him, but it was pretty hard to do with Erik's smug smile staring at me from the TV, as if he had a giant secret he was about to share.

"Erik!" The host was so excited she could hardly contain her excitement. "Welcome to *Celebrity Gossip!* Thanks for coming in today. You managed to get the scoop of the century, and we're all dying to know how you did it. Brian Oliver's not known for being very friendly with the media, and so far, his new girlfriend, Ella, has proven to be even more elusive. Not a single press statement or interview has come from the couple since their relationship was made public. How on earth did you manage to get this interview with Ella, and how did you get her to open up like that?"

Erik shot the woman a sly grin. "I have my ways."

Juliette, Ana, and I all scoffed while Brian muttered more words best not repeated.

"All right. Keep your secrets," the host teased. "But tell us... how was she in person? That interview was so heartbreaking and real. Was she like that off camera, too? What are your thoughts after having met her?"

I scoffed again. "Of course it was real. I didn't know I was being filmed. How can that lady possibly believe that footage was an actual interview?"

"She knows it wasn't," Brian grumbled.

"But it's too good a story to ignore, and it'd be too tacky to admit the truth on camera, so she's playing dumb," Juliette said.

Judging from the way Brian's teeth ground inside his head, I guessed he'd been thinking along the same lines.

Erik leaned forward, the wide smile that had won over my friends and me plastered on his face. "You know...? I can't say this often about the celebrities I meet, but I was really impressed by Ella. She's a very cool woman. She's fun, witty, friendly, down-to-earth, and an all-around stand-up person."

Brian let out a quiet breath of relief that I wouldn't have heard if I weren't snuggled up next to him. I was relieved to hear a positive review as well, but having Erik tell the world he thought I was cool didn't make me feel any better about what he did.

"She's...raw," Erik continued, "genuine. There's no pretense with her. That's what I like. Real. That's why I run my website the way I do. Hollywood is so fake. I like to see the people behind the image, and most of the time, it's not a pretty picture. It's nice to see someone like Ella, for a change."

Oh, please. First of all, I wasn't really a part of Hollywood. Well, I guess *now* I was, but I hadn't been part of it long enough to be changed by it. And second of all, like he could talk about being fake? He's the biggest phony in the city.

"At least he's not trashing you," Juliette offered with a grimace.

I rolled my eyes. "Yeah, he liked me so much he felt the need to exploit me."

"Oh, I'm sure he liked you. He just likes money more," Juliette said, ever so helpfully. She shot me a wink and added, "I like you, too, but I have to admit, I might sell you out for that kind of scratch."

Ana shook her head in disgust, but a small laugh escaped me, and my mood lightened. I was grateful to Juliette for breaking the tension. Sighing playfully, I grinned at my stepsister. "Sadly, I might sell me out, too. He's probably making enough money off me with this to pay for college."

Brian's chest shook with silent laughter, and he kissed my cheek. Some of the tension bled out of him as if he was relieved that I wasn't falling apart as we watched this interview. He had a lot to do with that. I'd be freaking out a lot more if he weren't sitting here holding me and lending me moral support.

On the screen, Erik was still chatting about me with the blonde host. I started paying attention again just in time to hear her tease him, saying, "Sounds like someone might have a little bit of a celebrity crush."

Erik flashed the woman a crooked smile. "I'd definitely have asked her out if she weren't so obviously head over heels for Brian. He's a lucky guy. And interestingly enough, meeting Ella gave me some newfound respect for him."

"Really?" the woman asked. "How so?"

Erik shrugged. "Well, obviously the guy's got a reputation."

The woman smiled. "You mean, those *billion* women he's

been with?"

Brian snorted at the same time Erik laughed, and I groaned. "I'm never going to live that one down," Brian teased.

I had a feeling I wasn't, either. My face flamed, but Brian didn't seem upset. He was more amused by everyone's favorite sound bite, if anything.

"He was a playboy, for sure," Erik continued, "and moody and standoffish with the press. After all of that publicity crap with Kaylee Summers leading up to the release of *The Druid Prince*, I was sure he was the biggest arrogant douche bag to come out of Hollywood in years, but if he's smart enough to want a woman like Ella, and you consider the way Ella and her friends talked about him, I'm betting there's a lot more to Brian Oliver than he lets the world see."

"No shit, Sherlock," Brian grumbled.

I shook my head. "No, not really," I teased. "Arrogant, moody playboy about sums it up."

"Oh, gee thanks," Brian said.

I flashed him a wide grin, and he poked me in the ribs, making me squeal. "You're a brat."

"I am not. I am an *all-around stand-up woman*. You heard it yourself. And look!" I pointed to the screen. "Erik Clarke respects you now. I'm so awesome that just dating me has improved your reputation."

"And you're so humble about it. It's nice to know your new-found fame isn't going to your head."

"Well, yeah. I've got to puff up my ego as much as possible if we ever want to have some balance in our relationship."

Brian smirked, but the light in his eyes had a giddy quality to it, as if he was thrilled with our banter. I knew the feeling. I was having enough fun that I didn't really care that I was the topic of the interview currently being played. Maybe fame wouldn't be as bad as I feared. Maybe Brian was right, and that if we stuck together through it, everything would be fine.

As if he could read my thoughts, Brian's face softened into a loving and proud expression. His gaze dropped to my mouth, and that was the only warning I got before he pulled me all the way into his lap and kissed me senseless. It was such a heated kiss that I forgot about the world around me until we were smacked in the head with a throw pillow.

"Gross," Ana said.

"Yeah, get a room, hornballs," Juliette added.

My face heated hotter than Brian's kiss, and I tried to pull away, but Brian wasn't ready to let me go. Eyes hooded, he continued to brush his lips over mine while teasing the twins. "What's the matter? You guys pay money to watch me do this on-screen."

"That's different," Juliette argued. "That's Movie Screen Brian—who is *so* not the same—and Movie Screen Brian doesn't make out with my sister."

Brian grinned at me. "He would, if she was willing to get in front of a camera with him."

He looked a little too eager about that idea, so I set him straight immediately. "Never going to happen."

He shrugged and pressed another soft kiss to my lips. "That's okay. This works, too."

I am definitely not a PDA kind of girl, but as Brian captured my mouth in another passionate lip-lock in front of my stepsisters, I found that I didn't care about the audience. "Sorry, Jules," I breathed as I twined my arms around his neck. "I can't seem to stop. I think he's got powers of compulsion or something."

Brian waggled his eyebrows at me. "Guess my secret's out."

He started to kiss me again, but Dad and Jennifer chose that moment to come downstairs. I felt my father's annoyance before I saw him. "What's going on here?"

I wanted to shrivel up and die of embarrassment, but Brian smiled as though he didn't have a care in the world. "We're surviving fame together."

The words warmed my heart so much that I didn't stop him when he gave me one last kiss before turning his attention back to the TV. My dad wanted to say something—probably tell Brian to get his hands off me and get out of his house—but he got distracted by the television. Erik "The Sleaze" Clarke was still on-screen. "She makes an interesting point," he was saying. "Hollywood is very stuck on perfection. It's all about image, and that image has to be flawless. But it shouldn't be that way. Personally, I would *love* to see Ella Rodriguez in some sexy lingerie."

My dad sputtered at his candidness, and my humiliation grew. Brian gave me a reassuring hug and leaned his head against mine. I tried to relax, but it was hard, considering Erik was now talking about seeing me half naked.

"I've got a poll up on my website, so you can go vote for yourself. Blue or pink. I think the blue was winning last time I looked, but I'm still a fan of the pink. I think she should model the winner for the whole world to see."

I gasped at the thought. "Are you kidding me?" I screeched. No way could he be serious! Except he was.

This wasn't so fun anymore. Brian was tense again, too, and glaring at the television.

"Oh! That would be so fun!" the host said, clapping in excitement. "I'd love to see that!"

"Right?" Erik said, leaning forward as he got more excited. "Aside from the fact that she would look gorgeous, scars or no scars, it would just be cool if she did it. She could sort of say, *Screw the world. I may not be perfect, but I'm beautiful the way I am.*"

"Oh!" the host said. "That would be great."

I scoffed. "Oh, yeah. That would be *so* great."

"It's just a shame that she doesn't know how beautiful she is," Erik said. "She seems so confident in every other way." He turned his attention to the camera. "Guys, if you agree with me that Ella is beautiful, and if you'd like to see her model the winning outfit, bearing her scars with pride, hop on my blog, and let us hear it. Vote for your favorite, and then give Ella some encouragement in the comments section. Let's see if we can help Brian out a little and give his girl a boost of confidence, eh?"

I couldn't believe this was happening. I hated Erik Clarke

for doing this to me. "The nerve of that…" I let out a frustrated scream. "He's joking about my insecurities! And now the whole world is going to treat my condition like it's a fun game! It isn't a game! It's my life!"

I got to my feet and turned off the TV because I couldn't hear one more second of this garbage. I was so angry, I started pacing.

"Ella, just ignore it," Brian said. "He's a sleazy paparazzi scumbag."

"*How?*" I roared. "He may be a sleaze, but he's getting attention. You think the world is going to ignore that? They won't. This is going to get thrown in my face over and over again. People are going to be asking me to show off my scars for the rest of my life. I can't *believe* he did that!"

The room fell silent. I was ready to explode, and everyone could see how close I was to losing it. Brian seemed to know I didn't want to hear any comforting words. He stayed silent as he got up and stopped me from my angry pacing. He let his strong embrace speak for him as he pulled me into his arms.

"Screw him, Ella," Juliette said. "We'll figure out a way to extract revenge on him. You have a *huge* following. There's got to be some way we can make him pay for this. Humiliate him publicly, like he did to us."

"Juliette," Dad warned with a tired sigh. "There will be no retaliation. People will have fun with the voting, but then they'll all forget about it. This will blow over. If you try to get back at him, it will only make it worse."

"That's what a guy like him wants, anyway," Brian said, glaring at the dark TV. "If Ella or I speak out about this, then he gets even more publicity. Your dad's right; the best thing to do is completely ignore it."

Juliette and I both huffed, but for different reasons. My vindictive stepsister was mad that she couldn't make the jerk suffer. I just didn't believe this was going to *blow over* as easily as they seemed to think it would. But I was completely biased on the issue, so hopefully I was wrong. Only time would tell. The situation was completely out of my control.

My anger dissipated as defeat sunk in, and I suddenly felt drained. "You know what? It's been a long day, and it's getting late. I'm going to go to bed."

Brian looked into my eyes, trying to judge my mental state to figure out what his next move should be. I was tempted to ask him to take me to his house for the night so that I wouldn't have to stew in my own thoughts alone this evening. But then I knew I'd only have to face him, and he'd want to talk about this. He'd also revisit the moving conversation and want to talk about the things I'd said in that video. He'd already made me promise I would discuss it with him. I wasn't ready for that. Especially not now.

I walked him to the front door, and though I didn't ask him to take me home with him, I did make him the opposite offer. "If you want, you could stay, since you're coming back tomorrow morning anyway."

He raised an eyebrow. "Stay…where…exactly?"

My lips twitched. "The guest room. Or the couch. My father would flip if you stayed in my room."

He thought about it but then shook his head. "I'd better not. He seems to abhor me a little less at the moment. Best not push my luck, because if I stayed, I'd for sure find my way into your room before morning."

He opened his mouth to say something else and then thought better of it. Perhaps it was an invitation to come to his place instead that I was half praying for and half dreading. Instead, he gave me a small smile and shook his head again. "It's okay. I'll just come back in the morning sometime."

"You sure?"

He nodded. "You guys don't have to wait on gifts for me, but you do have to save me some of your sopaipillas."

My grin turned sincere. "No promises. If you sleep in forever, I'll eat them all myself."

He chuckled and then dropped a soft, sweet kiss to my lips. "You going to be okay?"

I let out a sigh. "Yeah. I guess. It's not the end of the world."

"That's my girl." His proud smile was tinged with sadness. "I love you, Ella. I'm so sorry you have to go through this with me."

"You're worth it," I promised, leaning forward to instigate another kiss.

CHRISTMAS MORNING, I WAS STARTLED AWAKE WHEN MY BEDROOM door flew open and the most excited chirp came from the grumpiest Coleman. "Get up," Ana said.

I rolled over with a groan, refusing to look at the clock because it was still dark out, so whatever time it was, I didn't want to know. "What?" I moaned. "What's wrong now?"

"Nothing's wrong. It's *Christmas*. Get up, lazy, and come downstairs."

"Seriously?" What was wrong with this girl? "We aren't five anymore. Can't we do this in an hour or two?"

She yanked the covers off me and threw them on the floor. "Get up."

She was gone before I finished rubbing the sleep from my eyes. I wanted to stay in bed, but the wench had deprived me of my covers, which was unacceptable.

Ana's voice hollered from across the house. *"COME ON, ELLA!"*

"I'm coming, you deranged psycho!" I yelled back as I forced myself out of bed.

"Still dark," I muttered to myself as I put on my robe and slippers.

This was so not how it had worked for me in Christmases past. Before my papa and *abuela* passed, Mama and I would go over to their house and stay up late, laughing and celebrating with loud music, dancing, games, and food. We'd party until we dropped on a couch somewhere, and then we'd all sleep in late Christmas Day. When we finally did get up, we'd turn on the Christmas carols and sing along while we made a breakfast feast that could feed an army. After they both died, the only thing that changed was that Mama and I could pass out in our own beds once we were too tired to keep our eyes open any longer.

I was glad to see I wasn't the only zombie in the crowd. Ana was the only one completely bright-eyed and bushy-tailed. Everyone else looked half dead. But they seemed in good spirits, so I smiled along with the rest of them and told myself I'd get to go back to bed soon. "You guys could have warned me about Buddy the freaking Christmas Elf," I said through a yawn as I made my way down into the family room. "I can't remember the last time I was up before eleven o'clock on Christmas morning."

Dad's chuckle was one of understanding—it may have been over a decade ago, but he'd been through plenty of Rodriguez family Christmases. He shot me a small, knowing smile and hugged me before I claimed my spot on the couch. "Merry Christmas, baby girl."

There was a little extra emotion in the greeting, so I knew Dad was also feeling a little sentimental this year. "You too."

"All right, now that Ella's *finally* here…" Ana was in such a good mood that she flashed me a gorgeous smile. A real one. Not one of her evil smirks but a genuine, excited grin. "Dad, open mine first, before we all dig in!"

She ran over to the Christmas tree and began sorting through the mound of packages, looking for a specific one.

I'd never seen so many presents in one place before. The

Coleman family managed to single-handedly boost the economy between Black Friday and Christmas. Not that I thought they were selfish. After all, there were so many presents because they all enjoyed giving gifts and had been generous in their shopping. I'd just been raised in very different circumstances and wasn't very good at handling anything excessive. This family was all about excessive.

Ana found what she was looking for and handed Dad a book-size package with a tiny squeal of excitement, then stood there anxiously waiting for him to open it. Juliette groaned and scowled at both Ana and me. "You both still suck."

"Juliette!" Jennifer scolded with a laugh in her voice.

Juliette's glare turned into a pout as she looked at Dad. "I got you a stupid bottle of cologne. Ana wins. Even Ella's briefcase is better, and she didn't know it was a competition."

Dad and Jennifer both burst into laughter. Clearly, this rivalry was a well-known family tradition.

Dad needed no other prompting to tear the wrapping from the gift. His face lit up with delight at first, but his brow quickly fell in confusion. "I didn't think Janice Bishop had a new book coming out for another few months."

Ana puffed up her chest. Her smile grew to something that could rival one of Brian's. "She doesn't."

Dad examined the book a little more closely, and his eyebrows flew up when he read the small type at the bottom of the book that the publisher had printed on the front cover labeling it as an advanced reader copy. "This is the one that isn't out yet?" he asked, stunned. "How did you…?"

When he looked up, Ana grinned again. "Ella helped me get it."

Juliette scoffed, and I rolled my eyes when Dad turned his surprised eyes on me. "You helped Ana with this for me?"

"In a manor of speaking."

Ana winked at me as if we were coconspirators. It was so strange. "You love it, though, right, Dad?" Ana asked.

He laughed and opened his arms for Ana to fall into. "Of course I love it! This is fantastic. And now, because I have the whole week off, I can actually sit down and read it without falling asleep after five minutes. Thank you, honey." He hugged her again and then turned to me. His face clouded over with emotion. "Thank you, Ella."

"I really can't take credit. It was all Ana," I said, causing Juliette to scoff again and Ana to finally smirk. "I didn't even know you liked to read. You never mentioned it."

Dad shrugged, and a tiny layer of pink rose on his cheeks. "I'm not quite the aficionado that you are, but I enjoy a good book when I have the time. Janice Bishop is excellent." He held up the book so that I could see the cover. "She weaves fascinating mysteries, and her knack for detail is unparalleled. You should try them sometime. I know they aren't your usual read, but they're good. I've got a couple lying around the house somewhere. *Murder in Motown* is even being made into a movie right now. It comes out this March, I think."

I nodded. "I think I've seen the preview. I'll check it out, and maybe I can get us some press passes to see the movie early, if you'd like that."

Dad's face lit up again. "Really? You'd take your old man to one of your special events?"

There was so much pleasure oozing from his voice that I felt bad I hadn't offered to take him to a screening before. I hadn't thought he'd care, but he was almost as giddy as a true fanboy. Ana and Juliette were right about him. And Ana definitely earned her victory in the gift-giving competition this year. "Sure," I said, shrugging off the slight awkwardness between us. "If you want to."

Dad nodded. "I'd like that."

"Okay, okay, okay, awesome," Juliette cut in. "Father-daughter bonding is great and all, but the rest of us want presents now, or I'm going back to bed."

Dad laughed and nodded his head toward the tree, which had a mound of presents stacked beneath it. Juliette and Ana both dashed for the pile of gifts and began tossing them to their respective recipients. Presents I'd had no clue were coming my way began to pile up around me. There were multiple gifts from each of them to me—apparently Ana had been lying when she said she hadn't planned to get me a gift—and there were also a bunch from my extended family.

My grandparents and my uncle's family had shipped a ton of gifts down to us after I'd asked to cancel our meeting this year. I'd felt bad for asking them to wait, but I hadn't known how the sudden fame was going to go, and I didn't want my cousins exposed to it. My youngest cousin, Mason, was only eight. He didn't need to be hounded by paparazzi. Apparently, they hadn't held any resentment for my canceling their Christmas plans, because I had boxes of things from all of them with my name on them. It was more gifts than I'd ever received at one time in my entire life. Maybe more than I'd received *combined* my entire life.

For me, growing up, Christmas had always been about baby Jesus and the food. I usually got two gifts. One from Mama, and one from Papa and *Abuela*. After they both passed, there were two gifts beneath the tree every year. One from me to Mama, and one from her to me. It was small, intimate, and familiar.

Christmas with the Colemans felt like the opposite. No one had lit a candle, said a prayer, read the Christmas story from the Bible, attended a mass, or set out a nativity. I wondered if Ana and Juliette even knew Christmas was about the birth of Christ. I didn't hold it against them—I knew they weren't religious—it just gave the holiday a completely different feel.

Unable to dig into my gifts the way they all were, I sat back watching them and just took in the moment. It wasn't bad. It *wasn't*. I just needed to come to terms with the differences and accept the loss of my former life.

Everyone was laughing, smiling, and fawning over their gifts. There were hugs and kisses, along with teasing and banter. It was moving, and yet, none of it was *me*. It was nothing like any Christmas I'd ever had. These people were a family, but somehow, right then, they didn't feel like *my* family. Logically, I knew that they were, and I'd been getting better at feeling as if I belonged, but at the moment, I felt like an outsider. And I really missed my mom. I missed *Abuela* and Papa. I missed my family and my old life.

"Ella...you aren't opening your gifts," Jennifer said, bringing the room to a halt.

All eyes turned to me and my pile of unopened presents. I couldn't speak around the lump in my throat, so I just shook my head. Dad's head snapped up. "Sweetheart, are you okay?"

My eyes glossed over, and Jennifer jumped up to bring me a tissue. Everyone waited while I composed myself. "I'm sorry," I whispered. I couldn't meet their expectant gazes. "I'm fine."

"Sweetie, you don't look fine," Dad said. "You're pale."

"I'm okay. It's nothing."

"It's not nothing, Ella," Jennifer insisted. "Please tell us what's wrong."

She waited expectantly. As did my father. Juliette looked concerned, and Ana looked at my unopened presents and then at me as if I were nuts.

"I'm sorry. It's nothing. I was just still in and out of consciousness last Christmas, so this is the first one without..." *Without Mama.* I couldn't say it out loud. "Sorry. I didn't expect it to be so hard."

I totally killed the happy mood, but Juliette immediately jumped to the rescue. "Well, it won't be different for long. Don't think I forgot about the sopaipillas you promised to make for me."

I barked out a surprised laugh that bordered on hysterical because of the emotions I was struggling with and threw my arms around Juliette. I was eternally grateful for the kindred spirit I'd found in my stepsister. Somehow, she always understood me and knew exactly what to do or say to make me feel better or break the tension that I constantly created.

At my whispered thanks, she squeezed me tightly back. I sunk into her embrace and let out a breath. I could get through this. I didn't have Mama, but I had Juliette. And I had Brian. Or,

I would in a few hours, when he finally woke up.

After we broke apart, I felt much better. I took a deep breath and got ahold of myself. "Sopaipillas do sound good. Maybe I'll go start those."

"Don't you want to open your presents first?" Juliette asked. "There's one in there I'm dying for you to see."

Her excitement was contagious, and I finally smiled. "Whatever it is, I'm sure it can't top the tickets you got me to FantasyCon for my birthday."

"True. That was pretty epic."

"So is this," Ana said, tossing me a box. "You should open it."

I had a feeling, judging by the size, shape, and weight of the box, that I knew what was inside it. Ana's amused smirk confirmed it.

"Well, there's not much need for me to open it, is there?" I shook it and heard the faint sounds of material sliding around inside. "The whole world already knows what's in here."

"Whatever." Ana took the present back with a roll of her eyes. "It's not really for you, anyway. I should have put Brian's name on it."

"Anastasia!" Dad sputtered.

Juliette laughed as she tossed a similar-size box to her sister. "I *did* put Brian's name on mine."

Dad groaned. "You're both going to put me in an early grave. You do not need to be encouraging that young man."

"Dad, relax," Juliette said. "We're just giving Ella a hard time. And you don't have to worry. Brian's a good guy. Plus, Ella's got him so whipped he'd probably take the Abstinence Challenge for her if she asked him to."

"Which she probably would," Ana added.

I stuck my tongue out at her and nearly fainted when she returned the gesture. Dad was just as surprised by the playful banter as I was. I think that's the only reason he let the subject drop without another lecture on modesty and self-respect like the dozen he'd spouted off since he saw the Erik Clarke video. He simply eyed both gift boxes with a grimace and said, "The Abstinence Challenge is not a bad idea. I think you should all take it. And *please*, Ellamara, do not open those in front of me." He shuddered.

I blushed, but Ana, Juliette, and even Jennifer all broke into fits of giggles. Torturing Dad was one of their favorite pastimes. The poor man was always so outnumbered.

"Hey, I wonder which one he'll like better," Juliette said suddenly. A hopeful look bloomed on her face. "The blue is killing it online. I bet I still have a chance at winning with at least one person."

"No way. Brian was not a competition." Ana argued immediately.

Juliette's grin doubled. "Well, he is now, and I am so going to win."

"That doesn't count. I didn't even pick the pink one. Erik did. I picked out the blue one."

"But you didn't buy the blue one. I did. You're giving him the pink."

Ana scoffed.

"I'm so asking him," Juliette said, whipping out her phone and presumably sending Brian a text about which lingerie outfit he liked better. After she hit send, she gave Ana a smug smile. "You know he's going to say the blue, and when he does, I so win him. And I won Mom, too, which means I win overall."

"You do not. Mom said she liked ours equally, and Ella hasn't even opened hers yet. Don't be a sore loser."

Dad and Jennifer laughed at the twins, and again, I got the feeling that this argument was an annual occurrence. I couldn't believe they were getting so worked up over who was the better gift giver. It was amusing to watch them, though, so I joined Dad and Jennifer with the laughter until something else occurred to me. "Hey, wait. What do you mean *the blue is killing it online?* Did you seriously look up that stupid poll on Erik Clarke's website?"

The twins stopped arguing and both shrugged with chagrin. "We were curious," Ana said defensively.

Juliette cringed and suddenly blurted, "I totally voted for the blue. I'm sorry! I couldn't resist!"

My mouth fell open. "You traitor!" The insult was hardly harsh when I couldn't stop myself from laughing.

"Oh come on, you know you planned to look eventually," Ana said. "And you are going to freak when you see how big of a response it's getting. It's *huge*. Erik Clarke's video has over 34 million views, and people are going crazy over it. You're gonna have to do it."

"What?"

"It's turned into some kind of cause or something," Juliette said. "People love the idea of you taking a stand and saying that you don't have to be perfect to be beautiful."

When my jaw fell slack again, it wasn't out of play this time. "Seriously?"

Jennifer smiled proudly at me, as if I'd had something to do with it. "There are only a handful of people in the world who really fit the media's idea of beautiful, Ella. With over seven *billion* people in the world, that's a lot of imperfect people. Plenty of them would love to see someone stand up for them."

I scoffed. "Yeah, I'm one of them."

Jennifer smiled, as if she understood, but some of the light left her eyes.

In the sudden quiet that fell on the room, Juliette's phone chimed. When she read her incoming text, her eyes bulged, and she slapped a hand over her mouth to cover a laugh. Ana snatched the phone from her hand, read the text, and smirked.

I groaned internally, imagining all the different answers Brian could have given to Juliette's question. The possibilities were endless. Before I could ask, Jennifer snaked the phone from Ana's fingers. Like Juliette, her eyes got really wide. "Well." She slapped a hand over her cheek, as if to cover a blush. "I think it's probably safe to say you girls tie for Brian's gift this year."

The curiosity was killing me, so I took the phone. Juliette had texted, **Quick question. You must answer truthfully. It's life or death. Blue or pink?**

Brian's response was, **I couldn't possibly answer such an important question based on color alone. Nor could such a decision be made quickly. I'll need to see them in action, and I'll need to be able to take my time studying them in a very intimate, hands-on fashion in order to form a true opinion. Convince Ella to model them both for me, and I will give you the truthful life-or-death answer you seek.**

My face-palm prompted my Dad to read the text, too. The phone was in his hand before I realized it was gone, and the growl that escaped him had me half convinced he'd turn into a wolf on the next full moon.

"Oh, relax, Richard," Jennifer said, swiping the phone from his hand before he crushed it, and handing it back to Juliette. "It wasn't that bad. And how would you expect a young man his age to respond?"

"How about with a little respect for my daughter?" Dad snapped. "Ella is too good for that arrogant pervert."

The insult had me seeing red, but surprisingly, Jennifer beat me to Brian's defense. "Oh, please. He may be a little arrogant, which is hardly surprising considering his situation, but you know that man respects Ella every bit as much as you respect me."

Dad scoffed. "I would *never* say something so—"

Jennifer cut him off. "Would you like me to open up my texts and read you the conversation we had a couple weeks ago when you had to work late and cancel our dinner plans?"

"Jennifer," Dad gasped, flushing red.

To my horror, the color was from an embarrassed blush and not anger. GROSS.

Ana and Juliette agreed with me and started squealing and screeching in mutual disgust. "I think it's time to make sopaipillas," I muttered, rising from the couch as quickly as I could.

"Good call," Juliette agreed, escaping the room before I could even make it to the bottom of the stairs.

Ana was right on her tail. "I'll help, too." She shuddered as she ran out of the room. "Ugh."

Unfortunately, I couldn't move as fast, so I had to hear the rest of their argument.

"He is a normal twenty-two-year-old man with a healthy sexual interest in the woman he loves. There's nothing wrong with that. You were that age once. You remember what it was like."

"Yeah, I do!" Dad roared. "I was just as arrogant he is. I thought I was infallible, too! And look what happened! I was irresponsible. I made the biggest mistake of my life because of my *healthy sexual interests*, and I have regretted it for the last twenty years!"

Ouch. It wasn't really surprising anymore whenever my father accidentally reminded me that he considered me a mistake that he regretted, but it never failed to hurt. I continued my slow ascent up the few family room stairs, ignoring his comment because it wasn't worth getting involved. He was caught up in his argument with Jennifer and hadn't even realized he'd hurt my feelings. Pointing it out might make him feel bad, but it wouldn't keep him from accidentally doing it again in the future. That would be kind of hard, considering he genuinely regretted the fact that I existed.

"Richard, I am so tired of this argument, and I'm sure Ella is five times sicker of it. You are being completely irrational when it comes to that young man. Don't punish Brian because *you* regret *your* mistakes. Even if Brian and Ella did end up in your shoes— which considering how levelheaded, responsible, and modest your daughter is, is highly unlikely—it wouldn't be the same. Those kids are not you and Lucinda. They love each other in a way I've never seen before in two people so young."

Dad barked out a disbelieving laugh. "You honestly believe he *loves* Ella? A guy like that? With his looks, and his money, and his fame, you really think he's going to settle down at *twenty-two* and remain faithful to Ella forever? He's not the type. Ella said it herself he's already been with too many women to count."

I reached the top of the stairs and made my way into the kitchen where Ana and Juliette were sitting on barstools, waiting for me. They met my grimace with matching awkward smiles. I couldn't force one in return with my father's voice still wafting through the house.

"She's a shiny new toy to him right now," Dad continued. "She's a wonderful girl who makes him feel special. He may fancy himself in love with her at the moment, but it will never last. Heartache and permanent consequences are all she's going to get from that relationship. I know what it's like to have to live with that, Jennifer. I don't want that for her."

Okay, that pissed me off, and I opened the fridge with too much force, causing all the jars in the door to clank against one another. "That's ironic," I snapped. "Considering he already gave me a life of heartache and permanent consequences."

As I started slamming ingredients on the counter, Ana sighed. "Well, I will say one thing, Ella; I certainly don't blame you. If a guy like Brian Oliver ever *fancied himself in love* with me, you bet your ass I'd risk permanent consequences. Hell, I'd beg for them."

Juliette and I both laughed, but on the inside, I was stunned. Who'd have ever thought *Ana* would be the one to come to my rescue with a good icebreaker?

BRIAN SHOWED UP NOT TOO LONG AFTER DAD AND JENIFER'S argument. I imagined it was just enough time to shower and make himself presentable after receiving Juliette's earlier text—which I assumed woke him up. When he buzzed the gate, I'd just set the dough for the sopaipillas aside to rise for an hour and had gone back to bed with Dad's new book.

The twins had been right about Dad's excitement over the advanced copy. It was by far his favorite Christmas gift. I was still mulling over his reaction. He'd gotten all giddy over it the way I do about my favorite books. It was a new side to my father that I'd never seen before, and it warmed me to him in a way I'd never felt would be possible. To be able to connect with my dad over my biggest passion felt like a godsend for our feeble relationship.

When the doorbell rang, I only had a couple more pages to the end of the chapter and didn't want to get up. Ana must have answered the door, because my dad and Jennifer had disappeared into their room right after their argument—whether to fight some more or make up, I did *not* want to know—and Juliette had gone back to sleep once she realized how long the sopaipillas were going to take.

Brian wandered into my room just as I flipped to the last page in the chapter. He immediately lay down on my bed, snuggling up next to me as if he liked the idea of falling back to sleep. Plucking the book from my hands, he flipped it to the back and scanned the summary. "Serial killers, huh? That's new."

I nodded. "Apparently, Janice Bishop is my dad's favorite."

"Janice Bishop…that name sounds familiar."

I took the book back and reached over Brian to place it on the bedside table. He caught me in his arms when I tried to lie back down and pulled me against his chest. I happily nestled in. "She's pretty big-time in the crime thriller genre," I explained. "Got several books turned into movies. Dad said they're filming another one right now. *Murder in Motown?*"

Brian's eyes lit up with recognition. "Oh yeah, yeah, yeah. My friend Rhett is working on that one. Said it's a good script."

"Your friend Rhett?" Ana asked, appearing in my bedroom doorway. "As in…*Rhett Kessler?*" She covered a yawn and plopped down in my desk chair. "He's hot. If you're not going to hook me up with Logan Lerman, Rhett Kessler would be an acceptable alternative."

Brian laughed, but I was still stuck on the fact that Ana was choosing to hang out with us, and that Juliette wasn't even present. What was going on here? Not that I was complaining, but it was as if she'd finally let go of whatever resentment she'd held for me since the moment she learned I existed. That, or she was just really bored because it was the holiday, and she was stuck at home with the family. It was either hang out with us or watch *A Christmas Story* or James Bond marathons.

"I told you, I don't know Logan," Brian said. "I *could* set you up with Rhett, but your father would probably kill me for it, seeing as how he's twenty-five and you're seventeen."

Ana frowned as she swiveled from side to side in my desk chair. "Well, what good are you, then?"

Brian laughed again. "I'll tell you what. If your parents okay it, you and Jules can come with Ella and me to my agency's New

Year's Eve party. It's usually huge and A-list only. That way, you can ogle hotties all you want, I can keep an eye on you, and your father doesn't murder me."

Ana stiffened and narrowed her gaze on Brian. "Are you serious?"

"Sure. Why not? Ella would probably appreciate the company."

I didn't know how much I'd appreciate *Ana's* company, but if she remained as tolerable as she'd been the last two days, it wouldn't be so bad, and I'd definitely like having Juliette there.

"Seriously, though, your parents would have to agree, and your dad basically hates me, my lifestyle, and pretty much everything I stand for, so he'll probably be a hard sell."

Ana chewed on her bottom lip as she considered this. "Mom will be super easy, though. I'll start with her, and we can work on him together. I'm sure she'll help. You should have seen her rip into Dad on your behalf this morning."

Brian jerked in surprise and looked to me for an answer.

"It was the usual," I said. "Dad was being judgy, stubborn, and unreasonable. He thinks I'm just a shiny new toy to you, and as soon as I lose my appeal, you'll go back to all your women, leaving me with nothing but a long life of *heartache and permanent consequences*."

Brian sighed. "Ella, it doesn't matter. Even if he never gets it, you and I know that's not what this is."

"I know." I snuggled up against him some more. Not that I could get any closer than I already was, but I liked making myself comfortable on his chest over and over again. He was perfect for snuggling against. "I didn't burst into tears this time when he called me a mistake that he's regretted for the last twenty years. I didn't even bother to argue with him or tell him he'd hurt my feelings. There's no point. I think that's why Jennifer lit into him so bad."

Ana laughed. "I think she's sick of his whining. We're all getting tired of it. He's just being stubborn. Dad can never admit it when he's wrong, but he *is* wrong about you."

Brian and I were both stunned speechless at Ana's compliment to him. Then she smirked and said, "I don't know what his problem is. It's obvious to the rest of us that Ella has you completely whipped for life."

After a heartbeat of surprise, Brian laughed. "That is very true," he admitted with a sorry shake of his head. "The woman has completely destroyed the bad-boy player reputation I worked so hard to build for myself." He squeezed me to him and kissed my temple. "Thanks a lot, Ella."

The doorbell on the front gate rang, halting our conversation before I could get out a good snarky reply. Ana and I frowned at one another. "Is Jason coming over?" I asked.

She shook her head. "Vivian and her dads?"

"No. Not that we'd planned."

"Family?" Brian asked curiously.

Ana and I both shook our heads. "Our grandparents and uncle's family all stayed up north. They're not coming down until spring break. We don't have any other family in Southern California."

"Who would show up on Christmas Day without calling?" Ana asked.

Across the empty house, we heard Dad's deep voice answer the intercom. "Hello?"

"I have a delivery for Ellamara Rodriguez."

"On Christmas?" Ana asked, voicing my exact thoughts.

I tried to remember if I had books coming from a publisher or something, but those wouldn't come on Christmas. My stomach fluttered with excitement and anxiety—mostly anxiety—as Brian climbed off my bed and helped me up. He hadn't brought a Christmas gift with him that I'd noticed, and he'd talked about nothing but how much I would love my gift all week. He's not one to think small. If it was something that had to be specially delivered on Christmas Day, the possibilities were endless. "What did you do?"

He seemed genuinely surprised by the accusation. "Me? I didn't do this." He smirked. "If we were at Scott's house, that'd be a different story. But I left *your* present at home because you've been so stressed about exchanging gifts, I figured I'd wait until you were ready."

That was incredibly sweet of him. If I weren't going crazy with curiosity at the moment, I'd kiss him for being so thoughtful and understanding. Instead, I laced my hand through his and headed for the front door. "Well, if you didn't do it, what could it be?"

Juliette and Jennifer were up now, too, and we all followed Dad outside after he opened the gate for the delivery guy, equally as curious about my unexpected arrival.

The truck that pulled into the driveway was a dark SUV with a custom paint job advertising a twenty-four/seven courier service. By the time I reached the vehicle, the delivery guy had unloaded six boxes from his trunk, and it looked like he had at least that many more to go.

The delivery guy was a hefty man probably close to forty years old. When he saw me, his face lit up with recognition, and he gave me a friendly smile. He set the box in his arms down next to the rest of the stack on the driveway and pulled a clipboard from the front seat of his car. "Miss Rodriguez, if I could just get your signature?"

"Yeah, sure." I took the offered pen and scribbled my name on a line at the bottom of a delivery slip. "What *is* all this?"

The man took the clipboard back and tore off a carbon copy of the delivery slip. When he handed it back to me, there was a slight blush in his cheeks. He glanced quickly at Brian and then cleared his throat. "It's, uh, from that lingerie store. The...uh... one from your video."

"It's *what?*" I blanched.

I watched the guy unload another box from the trunk of his car. There had to be over a dozen total. "Why is it here? Who would send this to me?"

The deliveryman set the box down and offered an apologetic shrug. "Sorry. I just got paid to pick it up from the store and bring it here. I don't know the details."

My dad stepped up to my side, glaring down at the boxes as if he could scare them away. "The *store* sent them to her?"

The man nodded as he reached into his trunk for the last box. "Yeah. It wasn't a private third party. At least, I don't think so. The company footed the bill for the delivery. Oh, and they wanted me to give you this, too…" He grabbed a red envelope the size of a Christmas card out of the front seat and handed it over with a grin. "Seems to me it's a Christmas gift. I don't usually work holidays, but the store manager called me last night and offered me triple my normal rate if I'd deliver it today."

I let out a long groan, scrubbing a hand over my flaming face. The lingerie store was sending me Christmas presents now? As if the ones Ana and Juliette got me weren't enough? "This is crazy."

"Crazy *awesome*," Ana said, picking up one of the boxes and giving it a shake. "Do you know how much this stuff costs? They must have given you the whole store. Can we open it? Whatever you don't want, I'm totally claiming right now."

The blood drained from my dad's face, but before he could say anything, Jennifer clapped her hands and added a giddy, "Oh, me too! I hope there's some stuff in there my size."

Brian, who had a box of his own in his hands and looked as if he was considering opening it, whirled on Ana and Jennifer. "Hold on now; no one get too excited yet."

Yeah, I thought. *Because I'm sending everything back.*

Brian and I weren't exactly thinking on the same page. He shot Ana and Jennifer a wicked smile and a wink and said, "I get first dibs on Ella's behalf."

Juliette burst into laughter.

Choking on mortification, my jaw fell open, and I gawked at the excited gleam in my boyfriend's eyes as he pulled his keys from his pocket and used them to break through the tape on the box he was holding. "Brian!" I hissed.

He ignored me. "You ladies can have whatever's left after I go through it."

"Oh my gosh, BRIAN! You are *not* opening that!"

He finally looked in my direction, wearing a mask of innocence. I was not buying it for anything. No way. I thrust a finger at him. "Stop. No one is going through that, because I'm sending it all back."

I turned to the deliveryman, who was still standing there with pink cheeks. "Is there any way you can take this all back? Give the store my warmest regards and tell them thanks but no thanks?"

"I...well, um..." The man rubbed the back of his neck, seeming surprised and unprepared for the question.

Brian stepped over to him before he could answer. "That won't be necessary." He slipped what looked like a freaking hundred-dollar bill into the man's hand. "Thank you for bringing this over. You can take off now. We'll sort the details ourselves. Have a Merry Christmas."

The man blinked at the cash in his hand, gaped at Brian, glanced at me, looked back at Brian, looked back at me...

Brian was crazy if he thought we were going to look through this mound of lingerie together, but he did have a point in that it was Christmas and this guy should be home with his family instead of dealing with my drama. Sighing, I forced a smile to the man. "He's right. We'll take care of this. Thank you. Go home to your family, and have a wonderful Christmas."

He didn't waste any time. "You too! Merry Christmas!"

After the courier was gone, everyone grabbed a box or two and brought them into the living room. It took two trips to get them all inside. I sat down on the couch and just stared at the pile of boxes, still stunned by what had just happened.

Brian sat down beside me and took my hand in his. "I'm sorry, I should have warned you. This sort of thing is common for celebrities."

I slanted him a dry look. "People send you lingerie often?"

His lips twitched. "Okay, lingerie is a new one for me, but

free stuff, yeah. People send their products, hoping I'll wear them or endorse them."

"But underwear?" my dad grumbled. He was still glaring at all the boxes. "Lingerie? How could they possibly think this is appropriate?"

Brian shrugged, as if receiving a roomful of lingerie was the most normal thing in the world. "Intentionally or not, Ella gave their store a lot of free publicity. They're going to make a lot of money from this. Of course they'd want to send her their gratitude. That's all this is."

Dad grunted. He continued to frown, but the rage in his gaze died.

"It's just like when publishers and studios send her books and movies for review," Juliette said.

"Exactly," Brian agreed. "With celebrities, we get a lot of clothing, accessories, skin care products…things you can be seen with."

"Sweet!" Juliette said. "Bring on the freebies."

Ana opened a box and peeked inside. "Nice." Thankfully, she didn't pull out whatever was tucked away, but she did give a low whistle. After closing the lid, she smirked at me. "Next time you get caught on camera, you should say how much you love Louis Vuitton."

Brian chuckled. I rolled my eyes. Hopefully, there wouldn't be another next time like the Erik Clarke debacle.

"Open the card," Juliette demanded.

She looked so curious she was about to tear the envelope from my hands and do it herself. I'd completely forgotten about it. Glancing around the room at all the curious eyes, I supposed I had no reason not to. I took a deep breath and braced myself for whatever explanation it contained.

As if knowing I needed the support, Brian slipped his arm around me. I didn't necessarily want to read this with the whole family watching, but I knew they'd never leave me alone if I didn't. After a quick scan of the contents, my jaw dropped again. "It's from the owner of the company."

"What's he say?" Jennifer asked, sounding as excitedly curious as Juliette had.

I read the note aloud.

Dear Miss Rodriguez,

Season's Greetings from all of us at Lindon's Lingerie Boutique! I was so moved by your interview with Erik Clarke that I wished to send my sincerest compliments and this small token of appreciation. You are a truly beautiful woman who would only enhance the sex appeal of anything Lindon's has to offer. I would be proud to have you representing my products. It would be my honor to have you join the team and model my upcoming spring line. I am prepared to offer you a generous contract. Please consider it.

With Sincerest Regards,

William C. Lindon

Founder and CEO of Lindon's Lingerie Boutique

I was grateful for Brian's arm around me, because I was so stunned I felt light-headed. His touch was the only thing keeping me sane at the moment. There was a collective gasp around the room, and my poor father looked as if he were having an aneurysm.

Ana was the first to break the silence. "Are you freaking kidding me? They want *you* to be a *Lindon's model?*"

The disbelief in her voice would have been completely insulting if I didn't feel the exact same way.

"No. Absolutely not," Dad insisted.

I wasn't the least bit annoyed that he was trying to make decisions for me since I agreed with him 100 percent. No freaking way was I going to do it.

"Hang on, Rich," Jennifer said. She sounded ecstatic. "Don't just dismiss this so easily."

Dad and I both gaped at Jennifer. She shrugged and looked at me with imploring eyes. "Do you know what kind of an opportunity this is for you?"

"I don't care what kind of opportunity it is," Dad roared, all his earlier rage back with a renewed vengeance. "My daughter is not going to parade around in her underwear in front of the entire world!"

"Richard, be reasonable!" I was shocked when Jennifer raised her voice at him again, for the second time today. She was usually so nonconfrontational all the time. But she was also a professional model, and I could imagine this job had major significance in her eyes. "Being a Lindon's model is one of the most coveted gigs anyone could land. I could only *dream* of getting a chance like that. It's a respectable job that would open all kinds of doors for her, and it would pay enough to give her financial stability, despite all of her medical needs."

When Dad's face turned a scary shade of purple, I joined the argument before he could have a heart attack. "It doesn't matter, because I'm not doing it."

Dad let out a breath of relief, but Jennifer shook her head emphatically. "Ella, you should really consider it."

"I'm sure it's a great opportunity, Jennifer, but I wouldn't even feel comfortable wearing any of that stuff privately. There's no way I'm going to *model* it."

"But sweetheart, think about what it could mean. This is something this world desperately needs. You could do so much good for so many people by taking this job."

So Jennifer had jumped on the bandwagon with the online commentators. Not a big surprise, I guess. Being a model, she'd gotten a lot of criticism over the years, and had, at one point, nearly destroyed herself trying to mold herself into the world's idea of perfection.

I agreed that the world could use a few models that were more average looking, but I wasn't average looking. Beneath my clothes, my body was covered with hideous, angry scars. They were raised, blotchy, discolored, and pulled my skin in awkward directions. It wasn't beautiful. I didn't care how many people tried to tell me otherwise.

None of them meant it, anyway. It was just the popular or polite thing to say. It was an idealistic fad at the moment, but it wasn't sincere. And in Lindon's Lingerie Boutique's case, it was worse than that.

"This job offer wasn't sincere," I said, shaking my head. "It's damage control because I badmouthed the store for only using perfect models. They probably already have a handful of feminist groups gearing up to sue them. Offering me this job is the easiest way to smooth that over. Not to mention the publicity they'd gain from it. It's nothing but a gimmick. A gimmick that exploits me and my physical condition."

Jennifer sighed. "Just because it's a good opportunity for them doesn't mean it's not a worthy cause. If the lingerie is uncomfortable for you, there are plenty of other—more modest—ways to accomplish the same thing. Swimsuits, for example. Those aren't suggestive the same way lingerie is."

I wasn't sure how modeling bikinis was much better than lingerie, but I didn't bother to argue.

"I'm sorry, I just can't. I don't want to show the world my body. I *hate* my body. There's no way I could do it."

The light finally left Jennifer's eyes, and she nodded her acceptance. She looked disappointed, but she seemed to understand. I was surprised at how much I hated to let her down. I wished I could be the courageous hero she wanted and stand up to a world of judgmental, shallow people, but there was just no way I could do it. I was nowhere near brave enough or strong enough.

"It's a dumb statement for you to make, anyway," Brian said suddenly, squeezing my hand. "Your looks are too perfect."

Though he wasn't trying to make a joke—I didn't think—I snorted a laugh. Brian grunted and nearly growled his next words like a warning. "Ellamara, I wasn't trying to be funny. I was *complimenting* you."

"Sorry?"

I gave him a sheepish smile, still having a hard time containing my giggles, and he sighed. "You are so unromantic."

"Unromantic?" I teased. "Or just not cheesy?"

Brian scoffed. "I am *not* cheesy."

That opinion was worth a decent argument, but now wasn't the time, and despite the corny compliment, Brian had succeeded in cheering me up, because cheesy or not, he meant it. Knowing there was at least one person who loved me exactly the way I was went a long way to protect my damaged soul. Making me laugh never hurt, either.

"If you say so." Pecking his cheek with a playful kiss and giggling at the irritated frown I got in response, I turned my attention back to my family and the room full of lingerie boxes. "Anyway… let's just…figure out what to do with all of these and forget this happened. We have to leave for the movie in a while."

Brian squeezed me tight. "Just set them aside for now. I can have Scotty help me bring them back to my place tomorrow. I have his and hers closets in my master suite, so we can just put it all in your closet for now, and you can go through it later. Or better yet…" He grinned wolfishly at me. "You and I can go through it together, and you can try out the modeling thing with an audience of one before deciding how to answer Lindon's offer."

I wasn't sure what was more shocking—that Brian was asking for a sexy underwear show in front of my entire family, that he thought I might actually consider Lindon's offer, or that he already considered the extra closet in his bedroom mine.

"Brian! Oh my gosh! *No!* I'm not going to model any of this stuff for you, and there is *nothing* to decide. I'm not taking that job."

When Brian smiled triumphantly, I knew I'd been had. And he'd gotten me good. I'd totally believed he was serious that time. Curse him and his brilliant acting skills. "You jerk!" I swatted his arm, and he burst into laughter. "That's not funny. I thought you were *serious.*"

"And the Oscar goes to…" He laughed.

"And you say *I'm* a brat."

"You are. And you were being a brat first. It was my turn."

The man had a point. And when I realized that, a smile cracked through my scowl. "Okay. Fine. I was. But now we're even."

Brian's face lit up brighter than the sun, and he pulled my lips to his for a quick kiss. "I love you, woman."

Someone in the room—my guess was Jennifer—sighed, and I flushed all the way from the top of my head to the tips of my toes when I remembered we had an audience. Dad was watching Brian with hawk eyes that promised death if Brian ever stepped out of line, but at least he wasn't shouting and kicking him out. "Sorry," I muttered, stealing his attention. "So um, yeah, I'm just gonna go shower and get dressed." I scowled at Brian. "Behave. Which means no opening all this junk and stringing it all over the place. *Please.*"

BRIAN

Ella and I drove to the theater separately from her family because we planned to go to my dad's for dinner after the movie. We ran into my father and a few of his friends in the lounge on the first floor of the entertainment complex. "Brian!"

He was sitting on a couch in the theater's lounge with two other men and two women. Well, one woman and one almost-woman. The fake-redhead bombshell dressed like she was ready to go clubbing looked barely old enough to order alcohol.

Unfortunately, we were a little early, so we'd have to sit and chat for a while. I was tempted to walk right past them into the theater and pretend I hadn't heard my father call my name, but he rose to his feet and shouted at us as he waved us over. "Brian! Ella!"

"Damn."

Ella chuckled at my muttered curse and squeezed my hand. "Could he be any worse than my dad?" she whispered.

"The same. Just a different kind of awful."

Ella gave me the most intriguing smile then. It was wry and

mixed with something that said she thought I was adorable. I wished I knew what she was thinking, because I couldn't imagine what she thought was cute about me disliking my father.

"It's all good," she said. "We can do this. Game faces."

She flashed me a dazzling smile that would convince even the severest skeptic she was thrilled to be here mingling with strangers. I matched it with my own million-dollar smile and teased her. "You could be an actress with those skills."

She snorted. "Yeah. Maybe I'll try it after I get bored with my lingerie-modeling career."

I was grateful for her light attitude. It went a long way in calming me down. There was nothing I loved more than my sexy little *mamacita's* feisty, snarky, sarcastic humor.

Bright smiles perfectly in place, we walked over to greet my father and his friends. Well, I bet the redhead was more like his *special* friend, but I really didn't want the details.

"Aw, you see?" he said to his friends, who all stood to greet us as well. "I told you they would be here."

Keep the smile in place, Brian. He's just a proud father who likes to show off his kid. It's nothing more. "Hey, Dad."

"Hello, Mr. Oliver," Ella added.

After a quick pat on the back, Dad brushed me aside and took Ella's hand. "Please, Ella, call me Max," he crooned as he kissed her cheek.

Never relinquishing her hand, he guided her to the seat next to him on the sofa, barely leaving any room for his date on his other side. The redhead didn't seem to mind all that much, considering she was already making bedroom eyes at me.

Suppressing a groan, I sat down next to Ella and forced a smile at the three strangers on the opposite couch. When they all gave me their attention, Dad immediately made introductions. "This is Lloyd Wright and Michael Hobson. They're both from New Gate Films. Brian, you know Maya Sutherland. Ella, Maya is my brilliant agent." He lifted an arm around his date and somehow managed a dignified smile. "And this lovely little thing is

Noémi Virág."

After polite greetings and handshakes, Noémi giggled like a ditzy schoolgirl and reached across Dad to place her hand on Ella's leg. "I heard your great news this afternoon. Congratulations! I have to admit, I kind of hate you right now. I would kill for the opportunity to be a Lindon's girl. That's as supermodel as it gets."

I stiffened, and Ella's face paled. "You heard about that?" I asked, since Ella didn't look like she could speak at the moment.

"Of course." Noémi waved away the question as if the answer should have been obvious. "Mr. Lindon himself went live on Facebook saying he thinks you're beautiful and that Erik Clarke's idea was a fantastic one. He's the one who announced that he made you the offer. *Everyone's* talking about it."

"Fantastic," Ella grumbled.

Noémi completely missed the sarcasm.

I cringed. I wasn't surprised by the power play, but I should have thought to warn Ella that this might happen. Lindon's *had* to comment on the situation as a way to do damage control. They had to be fairly sure Ella would reject their offer, and if they didn't say anything before she did, making the offer wouldn't have done them any good.

I'd told Scott I'd sit her down for a good business-type talk after her family left, but at this rate, we were going to have to do it sooner. Like tomorrow morning. Hopefully, Scott was serious about me stealing him away from his family for a while. For now, the best I could do was change the subject so that Ella wouldn't mention turning down the offer and have to defend herself to a group of strangers.

I sat forward and took Ella's hand as I looked at the two people sitting across from me. Dad had already said they were from New Gate films, but I could have guessed they were from some studio or another. There are only two types of people in Hollywood: the creatives and the suits. The creatives physically make the films, and the suits control the decision making since they're the money.

There's a reason the execs in the industry are called suits, and it's exactly the one you'd imagine. Most of us embrace casual in both appearance and behavior in the workplace. Suits don't seem to understand the concept. I mean, here we were, seeing a movie on Christmas Day, and these two stuffy pricks were sitting here in their designer sharkskin suits and power ties.

"So… New Gate, huh? Why am I not surprised?"

I let plenty of arrogance seep into my voice while still seeming polite. All part of the game. These men were here with an agenda, whether I wanted to do business or not. I couldn't be rude and burn any bridges, but I couldn't entirely accept their underhanded attempt to get a meeting with Ella, either. Letting people in Hollywood think you're a pushover is one of the worst things you can do.

"I seem to recall that name coming up in a number of phone calls with my agency recently."

"Actually, Brian," Dad interrupted, wearing an innocent smile that wasn't fooling anyone, "they came to see the movie and chat with me about possibly directing a film adaptation of *Drive Hard*."

Ella coughed, and I had to bite the inside of my cheek, because I knew that cough was only to cover up a laugh. "The video game?" she asked primly.

Ella was never prim about anything. The tone was all too polite. She was definitely trying to keep from laughing.

Dad's face lit up with pride. "One of the biggest sellers on the market. It's about time they make the film."

Ella leaned toward my dad and placed her hand lightly on his forearm while flashing him a smile so beautiful I almost got jealous. "Mr. Oliver—Max—I honestly don't think there is any other director in the world more right for that project than you."

Now I was the one coughing to cover a laugh. No one sitting there with us could have ever suspected how much Ella loathed the majority of my father's work. No doubt she believed *Drive Hard* would be the biggest, flashiest, most ridiculous piece of trash to come out of Hollywood this century, and I was sure she wasn't lying when she said she thought Dad would be the perfect director for the film. Only I caught the condescension hidden beneath her compliment, and that was only because I knew her so well.

I couldn't help elbowing her softly. She cut me a glance, and her grin turned wry. I had to rub my hand over my mouth and jaw in an attempt to literally wipe the smile from my face. When she saw me struggling to keep my composure, she gave me a subtle wink and turned her smile on the suits from New Gate. "Seriously. Max Oliver is definitely the man for that job. If you haven't offered him a contract yet, you'd better get on it."

The woman was *incorrigible*. I poked her in the ribs a little harder, tickling her in warning that she'd better cut it out before she made me laugh and got us both busted. She was so going to get it when we finally had a moment to ourselves.

The urge to snicker vanished when Lloyd and Michael smiled back at her like a pair of sharks circling a bleeding fish. "Well, I suppose if Ellamara has departed such *words of wisdom*, then we'd better get that contract written up first thing after the holiday," Lloyd said.

Michael nodded. "And since we're on the subject of contracts and proposals, Miss Rodriguez, it's very fortunate that we've run into you today."

"Yes," I said in a clipped voice. "Fortunate indeed. And purely coincidental, I'm sure." Sarcasm and disdain dripped from my voice. I wasn't happy, and I wanted these jerks to know it. They needed to sweat a little.

Dad sat up a little straighter and lost that casual, easygoing edge he'd had before. "Relax, Brian. This isn't an ambush."

"No. It's *Christmas*. This is hardly the appropriate time to be discussing business, and you promised us low-key if we came today."

Ella patted my leg and whispered, "Brian, it's okay."

It really wasn't. Scott was right that people were finding their own ways to get to Ella since I wasn't returning their calls. That they would bother her on Christmas Day, when they knew she would be with her whole family, was appalling. I'm sure she was the only reason they were here. And I'm sure my father was more than happy to help them corner her when they dangled the *Drive Hard* project in front of him. Jerks.

"What proposal could you possibly want to talk to me about?" Ella asked.

I kicked myself again. I knew what was coming, and it was yet another surprise I hadn't warned her about ahead of time.

"We're interested in acquiring the film rights to your story," Michael said.

"Film rights!" Ella gasped as I grumbled, "You, and everyone else in town."

When Lloyd and Michael both looked at me, I said, "Don't play dumb. You know everyone is trying to get this project. Studios a lot larger than New Gate."

Ella turned her incredulous gaze on me. "They *are?*"

I sighed. "Yeah. They're all asking me because you don't have any contact info set up yet. I was going to tell you about it; I've just been waiting because you were so stressed about your GED test and your family coming. We need to sit down and go over all of this. I just wanted to wait until after the holidays."

I shot a look at Lloyd and Michael as I said that last bit. Neither seemed very sorry. But at least Ella wasn't acting upset that I'd kept this news from her. She looked stunned, but she was calm and pensive as she slowly processed the information. "Yeah, okay. That's probably a good idea. Film rights." She shook her head, blinking at her lap as if she still couldn't believe it. "That's *crazy.*"

She pulled herself together and smiled at me. "Thanks for not dropping that on me last week. You're right. I was stressed enough."

She leaned over, puckering her lips, and I can't tell you how thrilled I was when she gave me a quick, grateful kiss. She's so shy about the physical stuff and gets very embarrassed when the subject of our relationship is brought up. This tiny, chaste acknowledgement of what we were to each other felt like a huge step.

Ella took a deep breath, let it out, and then shook herself from her daze. "All right. Let's definitely sit down and talk about all this Hollywood stuff soon. Maybe after New Year's we can escape to your place, order in some take-out, and have a powwow?"

Despite that idea sounding like heaven, I winced. "Actually, with the Erik Clarke drama and the Lindon's stuff, I'm thinking we shouldn't wait that long."

Maya finally jumped into the conversation. "Oh, I agree," she said. "This is something you should act quickly on."

I glared at the hungry gleam in her eyes. I'd been so focused on Lloyd and Michael that I'd forgotten Maya would have an angle of her own. "Ella," she crooned in a sugary-sweet voice that set my nerves on edge. "You have no idea how hot a topic you and Brian are right now. You need to act quickly if you want to take full advantage of that. I could really make some amazing things happen for you."

Ella frowned. "What do you mean?"

Maya handed her a business card. "I would love to represent you."

I tried not to grind my teeth down to the nerve endings. Ella glanced at me, astonishment once again showing in her expression, and took the card from Maya. "You want to be my agent?" she asked, confused. "For what? I'm not taking Lindon's offer. I'm not going to become a model."

"You aren't?" Noémi gasped. "Why on earth not? Are you *crazy?*"

I feared Ella would get mad and lose that infamous Latina temper of hers, but she just rolled her eyes at me and smiled sweetly at the woman she clearly considered an idiot. "I'm just not interested."

Noémi's jaw dropped, and Maya stole Ella's attention back. "You'll still need representation for a number of other opportunities that will come your way now. Film rights being one of them."

She flashed a big smile at the New Gate guys, who grinned back as if the deal were already set.

"Yes," I said, grinding my teeth so hard my dentist would lecture me the next time I went in. "Ella *is* going to need representation, but again, you aren't the only agent looking to represent her."

Ella sighed. "I guess we have a *lot* to talk about, huh?"

I pulled her tightly to my side. "I'll help you sort it out. It won't be so bad."

"Okay."

Maya bristled. "I may not be the only agent wanting to represent you, Ella, but I'm the best."

I snorted. That was quite arrogant of her, considering she knew who *my* agents were, and they actually *were* the best in town. "Whatever. You've made your offer. She has your card. She'll add it to the pile." I shot a stern look at Lloyd and Michael. "I have your offer and contact information as well."

They both frowned but kept their mouths shut and didn't interrupt when I told all three of them, "I promise Ella will look over everything that's been thrown her way this week, and someone will get back to all of you on Ella's behalf once she's had time to consider her options and knows what she wants to do. In the meantime, she and I are going to head into the theater now. Her family will be here soon, and we'd like a few moments to ourselves before they arrive."

I stood, and Ella smiled to the group as she rose with me. "Thank you for the interest. I promise I'll get back to you after I've learned a little more about what's going on. Have a wonderful Christmas. It was lovely meeting you all."

Dad stood, too, and took Ella's hand. "You're still coming over for dinner after the show, right?" he asked, bouncing his gaze between both of us.

"I don't know," I said, as Ella nodded. "Is it really going to be just the three of us? Or will there be other agents and producers waiting to have an advantageous chat over dinner? Some reporters, maybe? Or photographers?"

I didn't want to be a douche, but I was pissed at my dad. He'd basically exploited his connection with Ella to get in good with the New Gate people. I wasn't surprised. My father is as Hollywood as a person can get. He's always working every angle. But I was still pissed.

"Oh, Brian." Dad sighed playfully and then grinned at his company as if he considered me a silly little boy whose antics he found amusing. "Always so skeptical and reclusive. You really should loosen up a little. You'd get further in this business if you weren't always so rigid."

I gave him my million-dollar fake smile. "It's a cutthroat industry, Dad. We all know that. I just don't appreciate being worked over by my own father, and I'm not about to let Ella get taken advantage of. I also value my privacy. What little I have left."

Dad backed off. For all that he was, he wasn't an idiot, and he knew he was pushing my buttons. "All right, all right. You kids go do your thing." He turned his smarmy smile on Ella and leaned in close to stage whisper in her ear. "You make sure to help him relax a bit during the movie, eh? He's always so cranky."

Good grief. I hoped Ella didn't see that for the sexual suggestion that it was.

Ella kept her smile up like a pro. "Really? That's odd. He's never cranky with me." She shrugged. "Must just be you."

I choked on a laugh. She'd just insulted him to his face but had delivered it with so much innocence he was forced to play along. I'd never been so proud of the woman in all my life.

"Hmm." Dad's smile tightened. "Perhaps you're right. But you know how fathers and sons can be."

"Of course." She shot him a sweet smile and an innocent bat of her eyelashes. "Don't worry. I'll make sure he has a good time today. And we'll be there for dinner. Promise."

Dad's tension eased. "Great." He gripped her hand and held up his phone when she tried to walk away. "How about a picture before you guys disappear? A picture with the mysterious Ella will give me all kinds of street cred with the younger crowd, which I could really use if I'm going to be directing a video game adaptation." He laughed boisterously and winked at her. "Plus, I need proof for Brian's mother that I'm being a good father and paying attention to my son and his new girlfriend."

"Dad."

"It's true." He shot me a pout. "She's sent me a dozen warning texts this week about Christmas being the time for family and that I needed to put in an effort with the two of you."

I groaned. He probably wasn't lying about that. "Fine. If it'll make Mom happy."

Dad handed his phone to Maya, who was—no surprise—more than willing to take the picture that would get her client even more exposure. Then, he squished in close enough to Ella that I almost punched him and slid his arm low enough around her waist that her eyes bulged.

"Dad," I growled.

The douche had the nerve to chuckle as he kissed her cheek and let her go. "Thank you, love. We'll see you guys in there. I look forward to meeting your family, so make sure to introduce them at some point."

When I started dragging Ella away, she seemed more than ready to go. It wasn't until we were sitting in the theater that she leaned over and whispered, "I think your dad grazed my butt on purpose when he put his arm around me."

And that was it. Things went red. I stood, with every intent to go kick my father's sleazy ass, but Ella yanked me back down. "Chill. There's no need to go all Druid Prince on him. Just, next time, *you* get to stand beside him for the pictures."

Whatever combination of curses I grumbled made Ella burst out laughing. I took a deep breath. If she was fine and laughing about it, then I didn't need to go make a spectacle of myself by punching out my father in public. But I wanted to. "I'm sorry. There's really no excuse for him."

"Hey, at least he seems to like me, right?"

She was teasing, but that was *not* funny. She didn't realize my dad would have no problems trying to get my girlfriends into bed if he thought he could manage it. She'd be no exception.

I tipped my head back and groaned as I scrubbed my face with my hands. "Not funny, woman. Do me a favor, and keep your distance from him, if you can. Please? In fact, let's keep him as far away from your family as possible, too. *Especially* your step-sisters. Your dad hates me enough as it is. He'd lose his shit if my father hit on the twins."

Ella sighed but smiled and leaned her head on my shoulder. I lifted the armrest between us, and she snuggled in close, instantly relaxing all of my muscles. I let out another long breath and leaned my head on top of hers.

"What a week we've had, huh?" she asked. Her voice got softer, as if matching the sudden shift in mood.

I squeezed her gently and kissed the top of her head. "I wish I could tell you it won't always be like this, but my life is a three-ring circus, and you've just signed on to star as the main attraction."

"As long as they get someone awesome to play me in the movie," she teased, surprising me with her light response to the situation. "Oh, and your dad is *so* not allowed to direct it. Sorry. Just, no."

"Deal. Thanks to your glowing recommendation, he'll be too busy making *Drive Hard* anyway."

Ella laughed again, and this time I laughed with her.

WATCHING THE MOVIE AFTER HAVING SPENT MOST OF THE LAST week with Brian made it a little hard to see Cinder up on the screen instead of Brian, and it was really weird to watch Juliette swoon over my boyfriend. It was still fun, though.

I was surprisingly not jealous at all that someone in the audience hooted and hollered when Cinder took his shirt off or when I had to watch the kissing scenes between both Cinder and Ellamara and him and Ratana. Though, admittedly, the scenes with him and Kaylee Summers were harder to stomach than the other ones. But that was just because I hated her. Not because of Brian's job.

I was relieved to see that that part of his job wasn't going to bother me. I'd known going in that this was all just acting, but I'd still wondered if it would upset me. It didn't. It was impossible to be jealous when I knew how much Brian loved me. Knowing what he really thought about Kaylee helped, too. But, again, that could have just been my petty side speaking.

Max had been true to his word, and the guest list was small. Though he'd bought out the whole 4:30 showing, only a third of the seats were filled. None of the other cast members were there—thank heavens Max had enough sense not to invite Kaylee—but a couple of the guests were very recognizable from other films. I was surprised to see Susanna Salazar, a very popular teen pop music star, there. I guessed her parents were friends with Max.

After introducing herself to me and saying hi to Brian—whom she was obviously very familiar with already—she was surprisingly interested in talking to Juliette and Ana. When I asked Brian about it, he explained that it was hard for famous teens to meet other people their own age. Susanna was probably starved for attention from girls her own age who wouldn't just fangirl on her. And thanks to Brian's presence over the past week, the twins weren't as affected by celebrities anymore. As soon as Susanna realized Ana and Juliette would be cool, she clung to them as if they were her new best friends.

By some small miracle, Max and my family managed to meet without the world coming to an end. Oh, I was sure my father would have plenty to say about Max's date once they got home, but Max managed not to hit on any of the Coleman women, and my father didn't tell him I was too good for his son, so I considered it a win.

Overall, things were great—until we all left the theater. Word had spread during the movie that Brian and I were here. We didn't think anything of the completely packed complex—Christmas Day was always a big day for the movies, after all. And when the fans lined up in the lobby waiting to get into the next couple of showings started screaming and shouting at us, it seemed normal enough.

Brian and I waved and said hello, smiled for a few pictures, and told them we hoped they enjoyed the movie as we walked past them. That was no big deal. I could handle that. But as we made our way across the lobby, the theater manager stopped our whole party. "Forgive me, Mr. Oliver," the man said to Max, forcing a nervous smile, "but word has gotten out somehow about your party being here. I'm afraid we've had to call in police for crowd control."

"Oh." Max paused, as if surprised, and glanced outside the front doors, where a huge crowd had gathered. After taking in the situation, he smiled again and patted the guy's shoulder. "Thank you for the heads-up. Most of us have parked with the valet. Will they still be able to bring our cars around?"

The manager sagged in relief to see that Max wasn't upset and blaming him for the leak to the press. "Oh, yes, of course," he gushed. "You may have to wait a few minutes longer than normal, but the police will be able to get you safely out."

None of the unrecognizable people had anything to worry about and left after a few quick good-byes. The few other celebrities in the party waited inside with us after handing their valet slips to the manager, but they all seemed rather blasé about the chaos.

"How come they aren't upset?" I whispered to Brian.

Brian certainly looked concerned, but when he glanced at the other famous people, he shrugged. "They probably expected it. With so many of us in one place, people were bound to notice. I'm the idiot for not realizing Dad would have invited other celebs. When he promised me a small, low-key guest list, I naively thought it would just be us and a few of his closest non-famous friends."

Brian shot an annoyed glare at his father, who was laughing with Susanna's parents. And she looked thrilled to have the attention. She was grinning as she greeted fans in the lobby and posed for pictures while she waited for the valet to bring her car around.

Cell phone flashes were going off like crazy in the crowded lobby, and outside the front doors to the theater, it looked like last week's premiere all over again, minus the red carpet. My stomach churned. "Will we be safe?" I asked. I hated to sound worried. I wanted to be strong and prove to Brian that I could handle his world, but memories of being swarmed at FantasyCon and having to be carried to safety by Brian made my body shake with anxiety.

Brian's jaw clenched at my question. His brooding scowl turned impossibly darker. He was *really* not happy.

I felt terrible. I knew Brian was only upset right now for my sake. He was used to this kind of thing. Without me, he'd probably be as blasé as the other celebrities, instead of seconds away from punching someone.

"It's a short walk from here to the valet stand, and the police are here. They'll keep you safe," he promised.

My dad was hovering closely enough to overhear Brian's promise. He looked as angry as Brian, only his anger was not directed at Max. "She had better be safe," he grumbled.

When Brian returned his glare, I gripped Brian's arm to hold him back and keep him calm. Now was not the time for the two of them to butt heads again. "Brian! Dad! Both of you, calm down," I hissed. "Fighting about it is not going to make things any better. Worry about it after we're all home."

The warning seemed to put them both in check, and the tension eased up a little. Brian's phone rang, and he glanced at the display as if he didn't plan to answer it, but when he read the name on the screen, he frowned and put it to his head. "Hey Scotty, what's up?"

He ducked his head and plugged one ear so he could hear whatever his assistant was telling him. While they talked, I turned to my dad. He—along with the rest of my family—was standing there taking in the spectacle around us with a stunned expression. "Dad, I'm sorry. Max promised us low-key. We're not sure how—"

"Brian's dad posted about it on Instagram," Juliette said, holding out her phone. "It's all over the Internet. Ana and I started getting texts from kids at school before the movie started, asking if we were with you guys."

"What?" Brian gasped, whirling toward Juliette with wide eyes.

Juliette frowned at his incredulous expression and held out her phone for us to see. Sure enough, Max had posted the picture he'd taken before the movie with Brian and me on his Instagram feed. It wouldn't have been a problem, except in the caption he mentioned the name of the theater we were at and the showtime of the movie. When Brian read that, he sucked in a sharp breath and started trembling with rage.

"It's okay, Brian."

"No, it's not," he growled. "It was bad enough that he ambushed you before the movie with his agent and those producers, but to pull this shit on us just to get more publicity? *DAD!*"

Max shook the hand of another of his guests and then floated over to us, looking completely serene. Brian held up Juliette's phone to Max and glared so hard his face turned bright red. "Are you kidding me with this?" he hissed.

Max frowned. "What? I told you I was going to post the picture."

"I don't care about the picture. You posted our *location*. You planned this all along." He waved toward the mob outside. "This is the whole reason you even invited us today, isn't it?"

Max rolled his eyes. "Of course not. I invited you because you're my son. And I didn't *plan* this; don't be so dramatic. I just wasn't thinking when I posted the picture. I don't have the same problem with fans that you do."

Brian scoffed.

I didn't believe Max, either.

"It's not that bad," Max said, giving up his attempt at innocence after seeing our disbelief.

I glanced outside at the crowd again. Susanna's car had just pulled up to the valet, and when she and her parents left the theater, the roar of noise outside was so loud Ana and Juliette exchanged nervous glances and moved closer to Dad and Jennifer.

Max winced at the noise and shook his head at Brian and me. "You'll only be outside for a minute, and that's totally worth what this is going to do for ticket sales. You should really stay for a little while and take advantage of this opportunity. You and Ella haven't made a public appearance since the premiere. For the two of you to come surprise the fans on opening day is amazing publicity. The media will love it."

Brian shut his eyes and pinched the bridge of his nose. He let out a breath and shook his head as he tried to calm down. "You're unbelievable, Dad. You know what? Forget dinner tonight. We're not coming. I'm not, anyway. I suppose Ella can, if she wants, but I doubt she does after the way you've just spent the afternoon exploiting her for your own gain."

I shook my head. "Not really. My family wanted us to have dinner with them anyway." I looked to my dad and Jennifer. "You guys don't mind if we join you, right?"

"Of course not," Jennifer said.

"What?" Max looked genuinely offended. "You guys don't have to bail on me. Ella, honey, Brian's just being overly sensitive. I swear I didn't—"

"The New Gate people, Dad?" Brian asked. "Seriously? You're going to tell me you didn't invite them today just because they wanted an in with Ella, and you wanted the *Drive Hard* deal?"

Max groaned. "I didn't mean any harm. I thought she'd be excited by their offer, and what else could I do? They were already in talks with Ridge Davies when I contacted them about the project." He pointed his pout in my direction. "Ella, sweetheart, I'm sorry if that upset you. That wasn't my intention. And I can't thank you enough for that wonderful endorsement. I don't think you realize how much pull you have in the industry now. I really wasn't their first choice for the film. If I get the contract, it'll be because of you."

"Glad I could help," I said drily.

I wasn't as pissed as Brian was. From what Brian had told me about his father, I wasn't all that surprised. But I was upset on Brian's behalf. He was making a big deal out of it for my benefit, but I also knew it was bothering him a lot more than he would admit to anyone. I can't imagine how it would feel to be used for my fame by my own parent.

Ignoring my sarcasm, Max rolled his eyes at Brian again and held his elbow out in an offering for me to take. "Well, there's no use crying over it. What's done is done. You may as well go mingle with your fans while you wait for your ride."

When Brian's whole body tensed again, I gripped his arm tighter and pulled him close to me. "Actually, we'll wait here with my family. They aren't used to this type of thing."

Max frowned, looking at my family as if just realizing they were still there. He immediately flipped into smarmy mode, but before he could say something to my father that would surely piss him off, Dad shook his head and said, "There's no need to wait with us, Ella. Our cars are here, and your public is waiting. You and your boyfriend can go mingle with your fans."

I was so shocked—and hurt—by his disdain that I couldn't hold back a snarky reply. It was a miracle I managed to not shout at him. "My *boyfriend* has a name," I snapped, gritting my teeth. "And he had nothing to do with any of this. Nor did I. We only came to the theater today because *you* all wanted to see the movie, and we thought Brian's father genuinely wanted his son's company on Christmas. We didn't mean to be such an *inconvenience* to you." Glaring daggers at him, I ground my teeth and shook my head. "Maybe we'll skip Christmas dinner with you guys, too. You've clearly had enough of us and our drama for one day."

I tried to give Brian a smirk. "Looks like we should have gone to see your mother in Wisconsin, after all."

His face softened at my joke. "I'm sure she'll call us tomorrow to say *I told you so.*"

The half smile he managed was just enough to make me relax. Sighing softly, I took a breath and spoke in a calm voice. "Dad, I'm really sorry about all of this. You guys all go ahead. You're better off leaving separately anyway. You won't be recognized that way, and no one will bother you."

"Actually," Brian said, "Juliette and Anastasia should probably come with us."

When everyone gaped at Brian, waiting for an explanation, he grimaced. "My assistant called a few minutes ago. He saw the news and said people are talking about them almost as much as Ella." He shrugged. "They were in Erik Clarke's video, too, and I guess people are intrigued by the Cinderella's stepsisters angle."

Juliette's jaw dropped, and Ana's eyes bulged. Dad flinched, as if the news of his daughters' new fame literally shocked him.

Brian ran a hand through his hair. "Scott called a limo service for us so that we can all stay together. He said things are crazy enough out there that it would be best to let a professional driver worry about the crowd since you guys aren't used to it. I'm *really* sorry."

It took my dad way too long to respond to this, and when he did, he couldn't speak. He simply clenched his hands into fists and stomped off toward the bathroom. I'd never seen him so angry.

"Well," I muttered, "there goes my relationship with my father. Wonder how Dr. Parish will try to spin this one."

"Ella, I'm so sorry."

I smiled sweetly at Brian and kissed his cheek. "Not your fault."

When Dad came back, he was still not speaking to anyone—not even Jennifer. Brian and I decided to give him space and went to talk to the fans lined up waiting to see the film. Not that we were in the mood for it, but thanks to Max, who was schmoozing the crowd and kept calling out to us to join him, we really didn't have any other option. Blowing them all off would have made Brian look bad.

It took nearly half an hour for the limo to arrive, and when it showed up for us, two police officers came to escort us out. "Just hurry to the car," Dad growled at the twins. "Don't say anything. Don't even *look* at the cameras."

"Ella and I will go out in front of you," Brian murmured. "That should take the attention off the rest of you."

His valiant effort only earned him another nasty glare from my dad. I wanted to scream at my father. He was being totally unreasonable. None of this was Brian's fault. *None of it.*

"You ready?" Brian asked.

I nodded as I sucked in a deep breath. "At least they have the crowd barricaded off this time so you won't have to carry me."

Brian's shoulders sagged, and he barely choked out my name.

"Ella…"

I shook my head. "It's part of the package." I forced a smile. "I knew what I was signing up for."

He pulled me into a hug and then wrapped his arm around me before nodding to our police escort to open the doors.

The noise that had greeted Susanna had been crazy, but it was nothing compared to the chaos that erupted when Brian and I left the building. The sidewalk from the main entrance to the drive-up loop where the valet waited was only about ten to fifteen yards or so, but when both sides of it were lined with a mob of fans and reporters being pushed back by the good old LAPD, the walk to the waiting limo felt like an eternity. Especially because I was the world's slowest person.

I tried to hurry and almost asked Brian to carry me after all, because this crowd was crazy. The theater people had dragged a bunch of velvet ropes out to line the sidewalk, and the police were making sure the crowd stayed behind it, but I didn't exactly feel safe. This crowd was a lot rowdier than either the group at FantasyCon or *The Druid Prince* premiere had been.

These people had had a good two and a half hours to gather here. Every paparazzi in town was here as well as all the local news teams. There were a lot of random people there, too. They shouted how brave I was and how proud they were of me and how beautiful I was.

That wasn't so bad, but aside from the normal excited shouts, this particular crowd had a much more obnoxious side to it. The first woman to make me realize we were in for some trouble pushed herself against a cop and shouted, "Forget Ella, Brian! If she won't fill your needs as a man, I will!"

"So will I!" someone else shouted.

"Me too!"

"You can have us both!"

Brian ignored them all and kept me securely tucked into his side. He remained 100 percent focused on the car ahead of us.

Then, a group of college guys jeered and threw panties at me as we passed. "I got you a present, too, Ella!"

"Model these for me, sexy!"

"Forget the panties! Show us everything, baby!"

Next to them, someone else shouted, "Forget that ugly, deformed bitch! Give me the sexy stepsisters!"

"Hell yeah!" someone else chanted.

"I got dibs on the slutty one!"

A gasp behind me had me looking over my shoulder. Ana had stumbled to a stop and was gaping at the guy who'd just called out to her. When he caught her attention, he grinned at her and said, "Hey, Ana, why don't you ditch your lame boyfriend and date a real man?"

His friend elbowed him and laughed. "At least show us what you're wearing under your clothes this time, you skanky little tease."

He made a really crude gesture with his fingers and tongue that made Ana gasp again and bury her face in her father's chest. The crowd hooted, laughed, and whistled when Dad wrapped his arms around her. "Go!" I shouted to him. "Hurry and get her in the car!"

My shout pushed my poor stunned family into motion, and they hurried ahead of us. "Damn, Ella," someone shouted as they climbed into the car, "your stepmom's a total MILF. Can I get her number?"

My eyes burned as we kept walking, but I refused to cry. If they saw that they could upset me, things would only get worse. I kept walking with my head held high and a stony expression on my face, but I was sure Brian felt the way my body trembled. We picked up our pace, moving as fast as I was capable.

The worst of it hit us when we neared the limo. A man who was probably pushing fifty had been standing against the red velvet rope nearest the car, and because he was so calm, the police were focused on other people. As we approached him, he smiled at me in a way that made me shiver. His leer alone made me feel dirty. "You want to see how sexy you are, baby?" he called to me.

Before anyone could stop him, he hopped over the little velvet rope and jumped in front of us. He opened his jacket to show me that he already had his pants open and was fully exposed. "Here's your proof. See what you do to me, baby?"

It happened so quickly that I still caught a glimpse of him grabbing himself before I whirled around and hid my face in Brian's chest. I tried to block out the lewd sounds the man made as the police knocked the pervert to the ground, but I couldn't, and that was enough to break through my control. I started to cry as we waited for the police to tell us it was okay to get in the car.

The man was still shouting horribly crass things at me as Brian climbed into the limo behind me and shut the door. I was shaking so hard that Brian had to buckle my seatbelt for me as we pulled away from the theater. He held me in his arms as tightly as our seatbelts would allow and whispered apologies to me over and over again. That he blamed himself for that mess only made me feel worse.

Across the car, Juliette watched me with concern, and both Ana and Jennifer were crying. Dad had them both tucked into his sides and was holding them tightly, comforting them as best he could. The glare he flashed Brian and me over the tops of their heads assured us his calm facade was solely for their sakes. He blamed Brian and me for this.

NONE OF US SPOKE THE ENTIRE DRIVE HOME. IT WASN'T UNTIL
we all piled out of the limo, and Brian told the driver he could
leave since he planned to stay with me for a while, that my father
finally exploded. "Actually," he said to Brian, "you can climb right
back in that fancy car and leave. You're no longer welcome in my
home."

"Dad!" I gasped.

Jennifer, Juliette, and Ana stopped heading for the house and
turned to see what was happening. Brian asked the driver to wait a
few minutes, and the man nodded, then kindly rolled up his window to give us a little privacy. When Brian turned back around to
face my father, he looked surprisingly calm. I knew it was taking
him some serious effort, though.

He stepped away from the car, holding his hand out to me
while never taking his eyes off of my father. My heart melted at the
way he reached for me. Even with my father telling him to leave
and never come back, he wanted me at his side. I happily indulged
him, sidling up next to him and leaning into him when he put his
arm around my waist.

"Mr. Coleman," he said, his low voice filled with apology, "I can't tell you how sorry I am for what happened today. My father was completely out of line, and you have my word that I will never involve your family with him again. He and I will be having a long discussion later."

My father wasn't moved in the least by Brian's apology. "Well, that's good for you," he spat. "But I still don't want you anywhere near my family ever again. It was not your father's fault that my girls were exposed to that horror today."

"Yes, it was, Dad. Max posted our location online. He—"

"Stop making excuses for him, Ellamara!" Dad glared at me so hard that Brian stiffened, and his grip on me tightened. "It wasn't Max Oliver that made Erik Clarke come after you girls at the mall the other day. It wasn't Brian's *father* that has destroyed your life and stolen all of your privacy. You girls were bombarded today because of *him*." He thrust his finger at Brian. "All of this has been *his* fault, and it ends *now*."

Maybe claiming that Brian had ruined my life was what broke the seal on Brian's temper, but I suspect it was the fact that my father was yelling at me, taking his anger and frustration out on *me*, and, in not so many words, blaming me for what happened because I was dating Brian.

"*My* fault?" he roared. "I may be famous, and I may draw attention to Ella, but what happened to her today was not my fault. Have you seen that video? I'm not the person who suggested Ella give up her virginity for Christmas. I didn't drag her into a lingerie store and pressure her to push the boundaries of what she's comfortable with!"

"Brian," I whispered, trying to settle him a little.

He didn't stop. "Who dragged Ella into that store and picked out a bunch of lingerie for her? Who was joking around with her boyfriend about letting him pick out sexy underwear for her at seventeen years old? Those perverts were attacking your daughters because of *Ana's* bad choices! If she hadn't been at the mall with Ella last week, Erik Clarke might have got a cute video of Ella joking around in Barnes & Noble or Wizards of the Coast. I'd have been outed as a big nerd, and that's it. Nobody would be asking Ella to take her clothes off to make a statement for the world or throwing thongs in her face or *exposing* themselves to her. Today would have been nothing more than a few fans wanting to take pictures of us, and your family would still be blissfully obscure. If you want to blame someone for today's mess, blame *Ana*. This was her fault, and, in fact, she's been the cause of every horrible thing Ella's endured since moving to your home. If you're so concerned with your daughter's well-being, where the hell were you for the last few months while your other daughter tortured her and made her life miserable, huh? Or is it only the twins you're really concerned about?"

"Brian."

I tugged on his arm to get his attention and snap him out of his rant. He flinched and took several deep breaths when he met my gaze. "Sorry."

"It's okay. I know you're upset about all of this, but it wasn't Ana's fault. She didn't mean for this to happen. She was ambushed and tricked as much as I was."

I cast a glance toward Ana. She, Juliette, and Jennifer were all gaping at Brian. Ana's face was paler than I'd ever seen it. She noticed me looking her way, and instead of glaring at me like I expected, cast her gaze to the ground.

"I'm sorry," Brian said again. After another breath, he raised his voice a little louder and said, "Ana, I'm sorry. Ella's right. It wasn't your fault, either. I shouldn't have blamed you; I'm just frustrated. I never wanted this to happen to Ella or to any of you."

"Then you shouldn't have dragged her into your life," my dad snapped. "As long as you're dating her, you're going to keep hurting her. You're going to keep dragging her into the media, and you'll never be able to control it. And now your fame is hurting the rest of my family. I don't care whose fault today was. The truth is, if you weren't dating Ella, none of this would have happened. I can't stop her from seeing you, but I sure as hell can make you stay away from the rest of my family. I want you off my property, and

I want you to stay away from my family. If you don't, I'll have a restraining order slapped on you, and I'll have you thrown in jail any time you come near any of them."

"DAD!" I couldn't believe this was happening. Yeah, my dad is a prosecuting attorney, but I never dreamed he'd use that to hurt someone I loved. "You're being unfair."

"No, Ella," Brian said. His anger was gone. He was calm again. He shook his head as he stared at my father. "The man has a right to protect his family. I will respect that."

I wanted to punch my father right in his smug face. My jaw quivered as I fought the urge to cry. "Brian, this is *not* your fault." I took a breath and tried to get my voice to stop shaking. "Don't let him make you feel like you deserve this kind of treatment. You *don't*."

When Brian gave me a soft, sad smile, my heart stopped. I assumed my father had finally gotten to him and that he was going to break up with me for my own good. "Brian," I whispered, as all the blood drained from my face. "Don't listen to him, okay? I don't care about the fame. I swear. You've brought far more good to my life than anyone besides my mother ever has. I need you."

He surprised me by pulling me into his arms and kissing my forehead. "I need you, too, Ellamara. Don't worry; I am way too selfish to give you up."

Thank heavens the man was spoiled.

He squeezed me tightly and then pulled back to look into my eyes. "I will respect your father's wishes, because asking me to leave is his right. But..." He hesitated, a rare flash of insecurity crossing his face. He swallowed and reached up to tuck my hair behind my ear. "Will you come with me?"

"Of course." How could he think I wouldn't? Like I wanted to have Christmas dinner with my father after what he just did?

"No. I mean...will you come with me *permanently?* Will you agree to move in with me now?"

My dad gasped. *"What?"*

We both ignored his outburst. "You see what I mean about

Vivian's place not being safe for you, right?" Brian asked. "I love Vivian and her dads, and I wish you could go there because I know you would be happy and comfortable there, but you just *can't*. I'm so sorry."

"I know," I admitted with a shudder. "I won't go to Vivan's."

After what happened at the theater today, there was no way I was going to live somewhere where anyone could walk right up to my home and peek in the windows. Or break through them. And there was no way I'd even consider bringing that kind of drama to Vivian or her fathers. It was bad enough Juliette and Anastasia had been sucked in.

"So will you come?"

Before I could answer, my father took over the conversation. "No, she most certainly will *not* come," he growled. "She's staying here."

Brian closed his eyes and took a deep breath, trying once again to keep a lid on his temper. "Your father's place is better than Vivian's. I'll understand if you want to stay. But I would feel better if you came with me." He frowned. "Especially since I've just been banned from the property."

At the reminder, I glared at my father. He jutted his chin out and folded his arms, unwilling to relent in the slightest. He was as impossible as this situation. "Fine." I looked back at Brian and forced a small smile. "Okay." I blew out a breath as the enormity of what I was agreeing to settled in. "Okay, yes. I'll come with you."

Brian's eyes widened just the tiniest bit, as if he'd been sure I was going to stay home. "We're in this together," I said, squirming with sudden apprehension. I wasn't ready for this, but I didn't have another choice. "I need you, and if you aren't welcome here, well, then…" I took another deep breath, trying to settle my nerves. "My staying here isn't an option."

The expression on Brian's face right then was worth everything I'd been through this week. It was a face I'd only seen on him once before—when we had dinner together at FantasyCon. It was the wonder-filled look of a man who thought all of his dreams had just come true. His tiny, overwhelmed smile took my breath way. As did the light touch of his fingers when he took my face in his hands. "Thank you," he rasped, and brought my lips to his in a soft kiss. "I promise I will be a perfect gentleman." He paused, thought about it, and a ghost of a smile crossed his face as he tacked on, "Most of the time."

A quiet, semi-hysterical bark of laughter bubbled up from my chest. Brian registered my fear and leaned his forehead against mine. "Don't be nervous," he whispered. "This isn't about me, okay? It's about what *you* need. You have nothing to fear from me."

"Okay." Nodding, I gave myself a mental pep talk. I trusted him. I did. But I was still scared and completely overwhelmed by the idea of moving in with him. "Okay, just give me a few minutes to pack a bag. I can worry about everything else later."

He let go of me, and I took a small step back. I was really doing this. I was moving in with Brian Oliver. With *Cinder*.

I met my stepsister's eyes. "Hey, Jules?" I said quietly. "Will you help me pack a few things?"

Juliette looked as overwhelmed as I felt. She looked sad but understanding and gave me a small smile as she nodded. I got one step before my dad stopped me. Judging from the look on his face, he still didn't quite believe what was happening. "Ella-mara, no. Juliette, don't bother." He shot her a warning glance and then shook his head at me again. His mouth flopped open and closed several times, until his face finally flushed with anger and he found his scowl again. "You are not moving in with him. You've known him less than two weeks. It's…it's…preposterous. Out of the question."

Brian stepped up to my father and met his glare with a calm, confident stare. "This isn't your decision to make."

Brian spoke respectfully, but Dad was not about to take any kind of orders from him. "The hell it's not! She's my *daughter*."

"She's an *adult*," Brian said. "And she's better off with me."

Dad pulled in a breath so sharp it whistled in his nose. "You think you can take better care of my daughter than I can?"

Dad was grinding his teeth so hard I think he spit that whole question out with his jaw locked shut. Brian matched his rigid posture and leaned toward him, looking very much like a pit bull straining against a tight leash. "I have no doubt," he growled. "I've already been the main man in her life for over three years now. You may have brought her into this world, but you don't deserve to call yourself her father."

Dad's face went from red to purple. "How *dare* you suggest I don't deserve—"

"How dare you presume that you *do!*" Brian shouted. "You have no right to lecture her about her choices or try to tell her what to do. She is *ten times* the adult you ever were. You want to lecture Ella and me about our relationship? *HA!* At her age, you managed to knock a woman up who wasn't even your girlfriend, and then you blamed your *child* when the woman refused to get an abortion. Like it was *Ella's* fault you couldn't keep it in your pants."

Everyone gasped except me. I couldn't breathe enough to gasp. I was simply frozen in astonishment as I watched this train wreck. I didn't try and stop Brian. He'd had a problem with my dad's attitude since the first time they met. Dad had been awful, judgmental, and unfair to Brian from the get-go, and frankly, Brian deserved to rail on him for a change.

"You didn't even have the balls to divorce your wife before you started sleeping around on her. Nor did you bother to say good-bye to your daughter when you finally decided to abandon her. You left her for *ten years*, you bastard. You're nothing but an irresponsible, unfaithful coward who never wanted his daughter in the first place. You have no idea who Ella is or what she needs. So, *no.* You *don't* deserve her, and you're *damn straight* I can take better care of her than you. I already do!"

Brian's chest heaved as he worked to regain control of himself now that he'd spoken his peace. When he saw my stunned expression, he held his hand out to me again. He didn't apologize this time for the things he'd said in anger. I didn't think he'd ever apologize. He wasn't the least bit sorry.

"Fine," Dad spat when I took Brian's hand again. This time, he glared at us both. "If you want her so badly, then take her, you arrogant son of a bitch. And *good riddance*."

I sucked in a breath, and my knees nearly buckled from the pain that ripped through my chest. Candy Cane was the only thing that kept me on my feet until Brian wrapped his arm around me and held me upright against his chest.

"Ella may have signed up for your bullshit," my father continued to rant, "but my family didn't. I don't want them exposed to it anymore, so get the hell out of here, and don't ever come back."

I waited for tears to come, but they didn't. At the moment, I was too numb to cry. He'd hurt me too deeply this time. My dad checked himself when he saw whatever look of devastation was on my face, but it was too late for him. An apology would mean nothing to me after that.

"Your family?" I asked. I sounded as dead as I felt. "So once again, it comes down to you and your family, and me. Two separate things. And you're only claiming one of those things."

After he realized his error, his face fell and he choked out my name in a strangled apology. I pinched my eyes shut and shook my head, not wanting to hear his excuses. "No, I get it. Good riddance to me. I'm trouble, and your real family didn't ask for it. *You* didn't. Isn't that right?"

"Ella, I didn't *say* that."

"You didn't have to!" I screamed.

My voice cracked, and Brian hugged me to him even harder. He was holding me so tightly I could barely breathe, but I wished he could squeeze me even more. I was breaking apart, and he was the only thing holding me together. "Don't worry, Dad," I said, voice trembling with both anger and despair. "You just got what you've always wanted. You're free of me. Absolved. I'm not your problem anymore."

"Ella...I didn't—"

"No." I nodded toward Jennifer and the twins. Ana still looked pale, and both Jennifer and Juliette had tears streaming down their faces. "You go take care of them. They're the ones you really love. They're the ones you picked, after all. Now it's my turn to make a choice. I haven't needed you for years, and I don't need you now. Brian was there for me when you weren't. He wanted me when you didn't. He loves me unconditionally, whereas you can't."

I paused, a small part of me waiting for my dad to correct me. He didn't. It was another razor-sharp cut to my heart, but not a surprise. I nodded my acceptance of the truth and whispered, "If you can choose a new family, then so can I." I pulled my face away from Brian's chest and looked up at him. "If you'll have me?"

Brian's eyes fell shut as he pulled my head back to his chest. He trembled slightly as he held me. "Forever," he promised fervently. "You know that."

I nodded against his chest, and my eyes finally brimmed over with tears. I was so raw from being gutted by my father that Brian's complete and utter devotion to me felt equally as sharp as my heartbreak. I was so overwhelmed by his love that I couldn't breathe. The warring feelings of my father's rejection and Brian's acceptance were so intense I felt ready to collapse. Shaking so hard that my teeth clattered, I stuttered out my next request. "C-can w-we p-please g-get o-out of h-here?"

Brian ushered me to the back of the waiting limo without a word. As he opened the door for me, I refused to look back, even after my dad called out to me in a desperate plea. "Ella, wait."

It was Brian who responded. *"No."* His voice was as cold, hard, and as sharp as ice. "Ella is *done.* That was the last time you will ever break her heart."

The statement sounded like a threat. One that not even my father—a man who laughed at threats from some of the state's most vicious criminals—dared argue against.

"Let's go, Ella."

At his soft nudge, I climbed in the car. He scooted in beside me, gave his address to the driver, and silently held me all the way to his house.

After we walked through Brian's front door and it closed behind us, the reality of all that had just happened finally slammed down on me. "He did it again," I whispered. I took a step and stumbled as my body started to go into shock. "He gave me up. He told me to go. He chose his new family over me. *Again*."

Brian looked as tortured and heartbroken as me. "Ella, I'm so sorry."

He wrapped me in his arms, and this time when I buried my face in his chest, the dam holding back my emotions finally broke. I collapsed into violent sobs and barely felt it when Brian scooped me into his arms and carried me to his bed. He laid me down and then climbed onto the bed beside me. I curled into him and let myself shatter into a million pieces.

"I'm here," Brian whispered as he held me. "I've got you, Ella-mara, and I'm never going to let go. Not ever."

And he didn't. Not while I cried in his arms for hours, and not after I finally passed out. He stayed there in that bed, holding me tightly all night long. We missed dinner; we never bothered to change out of our clothes. Brian never even got up to pee. He literally held me without letting go, until long after the sun came up the next morning.

15

BRIAN

WHEN I WOKE UP EARLY THE NEXT MORNING TO THE FEEL OF ELLA snuggling up to me as if subconsciously seeking the warmth of my body, I realized that I was one incredibly lucky bastard. Her father's loss was my gain. Ella wouldn't have agreed to move in with me if she'd had another option. I knew she wasn't ready to live with me, even if I didn't understand why.

Maybe I was an ass for being grateful her hand had been forced, but I couldn't feel bad about getting my way. She was safer here, and I just plain wanted her with me. I wanted her in my bed every night. I wanted her to be the first thing I saw when I woke up every morning. I wanted her with me always—spending time together, laughing together, making decisions together, and making love. I'd marry her this instant if I thought it would help her, but I was confident laying that option on the table would only freak her out more.

Ella woke with a deep breath and a stretch that brought me back to the land of the living as well. I brushed a kiss to her forehead before giving her a cautious smile. I wasn't sure what state of mind she'd be in. "Good morning."

She looked at me in a groggy daze and then gasped when she realized we were snuggled up in bed together. Her eyes bulged, and she slowly ran her hand over my stomach, as if she needed to confirm to herself that she'd been sleeping on my bare chest and was too mortified to look. Her fingers brushed over my belly button, and she squeaked. She was too adorable.

"Don't worry. I'm still wearing my pants, and the only clothing I removed from you was your shoes."

Her eyes finally dropped to my chest, and she scrambled off of me, needing a few inches of space. I instantly felt cold and missed the feel of her pressed against me, but I let her go. She sat up, chest heaving. "Oh my gosh, I left home yesterday," she mumbled frantically. She turned to face me, eyes wide with panic. "I disowned my father and left home. I didn't even pack a bag. I don't have any clothes or even a toothbrush, or—"

"Hey." I sat up and pulled her into my arms. "It's okay. Everything's going to be okay. There's no need to panic." She started to tremble, so I gently lifted her chin and forced her to meet my eyes. "Everything's going to be okay, Ella. I'm here for you. We're in this together, and we'll figure everything out. One step at a time, okay?" She sucked in a breath. *"Okay?"*

Finally, she nodded.

"Okay." I gave her a smile. "First of all, I'm pretty sure I've got a spare toothbrush around here somewhere, and second, I'm completely okay with clothing being optional."

As I'd known it would, that snapped her from her panic. "Yeah, right," she said with an obnoxious snort. "Nice try."

I laughed. She was too easy. "Had to give it a shot."

She rolled her eyes but finally managed a smile. And when I propped the pillows up against the headboard, leaned back and opened my arms, she crawled into them without hesitation. She settled against my chest, resting her head against my shoulder, and we simply held each other for a few minutes.

I was so comfortable my eyes drifted closed again. I must have drifted off completely, because it took me a second to catch up when she finally spoke. "So what now?" she asked.

Groaning, I nuzzled in good and close until I had her right where I wanted her. I had no other plans than to stay right where I was for the entire day. Well, maybe eventually I'd add food to the mix. "Now…nothing," I muttered. "I'm good."

She laughed softly, so I gave her a lazy grin. "I'm serious. Now I really do have *everything* I want. I was only teasing when I said I wanted *you* for Christmas, but since you decided to take me literally, I fully accept, and there're no take backs. You're stuck with me now."

"Haha, Mr. Funny Man."

I could practically hear her eye roll, and it sparked that side of me that always took her sarcasm as a personal challenge. "I'm not joking."

If my tone of voice hadn't clued her into my sudden change in mood, the heat in my eyes as I pulled her mouth to mine certainly did. I was pleasantly surprised when she returned my kiss with enthusiasm. She leaned into me and locked her arms around my neck, making it way too easy for me to scoop her up onto my lap.

With her bad hip, I wasn't sure if she could straddle me like I was aching for her to do, so I settled her on top of me sideways, cradling her against me. Her arms unlocked, and she sunk one of her hands deep into my hair while the other fell to my chest.

Goose bumps exploded on my arms when Ella allowed herself, for only the second time, to explore my body. She was timid with her touch, barely grazing my skin with her fingertips, and though I wanted so much more, I buried my need deep inside because I didn't want to scare her into stopping. She needed to set the pace.

She ran her hand over my chest and down my abs, then followed my happy trail from my navel to the waistband of my jeans, brushing her fingers back and forth over it as if she enjoyed the feel of the thin, silky layer of hair. It felt so good that my eyes rolled back in my head.

Never in my life had a woman held so much power over me physically that a simple touch could make me come unglued. I let my head fall back against the headboard of the bed and sucked in a deep breath.

Her fingers immediately disappeared from my body.

"Please don't stop," I murmured. "You have no idea how much I love it when you touch me."

I opened my eyes just in time to see her blush deeply. When I met her gaze, she turned her head away and bit her lips. I lifted her chin with a finger and waited for her to look at me. Her cheeks remained deep crimson, but she eventually met my eyes. "Only what you're ready for," I promised, holding her beautiful blue eyes with mine. "Never anything more than that. Okay? You say stop, I stop."

We stared at each other for a heartbeat longer, and then she wet her lips and gave me a tiny nod. "Okay," she whispered.

She pulled her bottom lip into her teeth and sat frozen, as if she didn't know what to do next. I took her hand in mine, kissed her palm, and then placed it on my chest, guiding her fingers over my skin and brushing her thumb over one of my nipples because she'd been too shy to touch me there before. A shiver rocked her, and she swallowed audibly.

I fought to keep control of my excitement. I'd never had to do this before. Not once in my life had I ever had to be the aggressor with a woman or encourage one to touch me. I lost my virginity when I was barely fifteen and my seventeen-year-old costar at the time threw herself at me. I, being the stupid and eager teenage boy that I was, let her bring me into a world I wasn't nearly ready for.

I'd been way too young and not mature enough to realize it, but my mother was in Wisconsin by then, and I didn't have a father worth a damn to give me any kind of wise advice. After it happened, I felt overwhelmed. When I told my dad about it, my father had just patted me on the back and congratulated me for becoming a man and scoring my first with a hot, older girl who could properly show me the ropes.

That first time had pretty much set the bar for my sex life from then on. Women threw themselves at me, and I let them do what they wanted because it felt good, and I was lonely and looking for a deeper connection of some kind. I'd gained confidence over the years as I slept with more and more women, and I had no problem being in charge in the bedroom now, but I didn't want to become my seventeen-year-old costar taking advantage of someone younger and inexperienced.

Still gliding Ella's fingers across my skin, I quietly asked, "Do you want to stop?"

She looked at me again, and I waited. My body was screaming at me for more, but this was about her, not me. She bit her lip again and shook her head once.

"Will you say it for me?" I asked, needing verbal confirmation so that I could be sure I wasn't pushing her too far. "Out loud?"

She took a breath.

I waited some more.

"I don't want to stop," she whispered.

Sexier words had never been spoken.

Pressing her hand firmly against my chest in a prompt to leave it there, I let go of her and lifted my hand to her face. "Good," I said, kissing the corner of her mouth. "Because I really, really, really don't want to stop yet."

I grazed her jaw with my lips and then began trailing kisses down the side of her neck. She shivered again but quickly rediscovered some of the earlier courage she'd had before she clammed up.

After a few blissful minutes, I was ready to crack. Having her touch me like this, feeling both her vulnerability and her desire, was maddening. I needed to taste more of her, feel more of her. I scooped her off my lap and laid her back on the bed, never breaking the heated kiss we were locked in.

She gasped softly when I leaned over her, settling a good deal of my weight on her, sinking us down into the mattress. Her following shudder of pleasure told me it was the right kind of gasp, so I intensified the kiss and let my hands wander.

Ella was still dressed in the long-sleeve sweater and skinny jeans she'd worn the day before. They covered her from neck to toe. I knew the clothes had to stay on, but she gave me more freedom to roam over the top of them than I'd expected her to. She didn't put on the breaks until I rolled fully on top of her and settled myself against her in an attempt to ease some of the throbbing pressure in my pants.

"*Brian.*" She gasped in a way that made me sure she liked what she felt, even though it overwhelmed her. "Okay. I'm ready to stop."

I took a deep breath and lifted myself off her immediately. I gave her one more firm kiss and then propped myself up on my side next to her. She lay on her back, staring up at the ceiling, trying to catch her breath. She looked amazing with her hair mussed, lips swollen, and face flushed.

I took her hand and brought it to my lips before tangling our fingers together and holding them against my chest. I just couldn't seem to let her go. The kissing had stopped, but I still needed her in some way. She looked at our hands and then brought her free hand up to her flushed face. "I'm sorry," she whispered, looking away from me in shame.

I never wanted to see that look again. I didn't want her to feel bad about not being ready for sex. That's not something she should ever feel sorry for. If she did, then I was still putting too much pressure on her. I could say all of that to her, but I didn't want to sound like I was lecturing her, so I decided humor was the best route. "I'm not sorry. I got to second base."

I flashed her a naughty smile and wriggled my eyebrows. The tactic worked. For a split second, she was shocked, but then she rolled her eyes and cracked a smile.

I rubbed her blushing cheek and then ran my thumb over her swollen lips. "Ellamara, you are the most beautiful woman

I've ever seen," I murmured. I gave her a soft kiss and pulled back again. My eyes drifted to the top of her head, and I couldn't help adding, "With the most outrageous bed head ever."

"Oh, shut up."

I caught her hand again when she smacked me. "I'm serious. You are beautiful, and I can't believe I get to wake up to you every morning from now on."

Ella's face paled, reminding me that there was still a little more drama to sort out. She and I needed to clear some things up. I sighed. "I guess now's the time for that conversation you promised me the other day."

BRIAN

Ella knew exactly what I was talking about. She closed her eyes and groaned up at the ceiling. "I don't know what to say. I know you don't care about my scars, and you say you want to be patient with me about the sex, but—"

"Forget the sex and the scars. This isn't about that."

Ella frowned. I gave her a small smile and tangled our fingers together again. "I know you're shy about the scars and the sex. You aren't ready to share either of those things with me, and that is okay; I get it. I support it. I don't want you to worry about that. When you're ready to go there, we will. That's easy."

Ella blushed, because that's just what she did whenever the topic of sex came up. But her face stayed confused. "What else is there?"

I wasn't sure I could put it into words. The other morning, I'd flipped on the news as I made breakfast, and when the anchors mentioned Ella's first public interview since the premiere, I nearly spilled my coffee all over the counter. I hadn't a clue what they were talking about. She hadn't given any interview that I knew of. When they dropped Erik Clarke's name and website, I almost put my fist through the wall. I knew that bastard's game, knew he was good at it, and I could only imagine how much my feisty, fun, playful, trusting Ella would give a guy like him.

When I watched that video, I felt like I'd been smacked in the face with a two-by-four. It wasn't the things she'd said that upset me; it was the things she hadn't. "Not being ready to get so intimate right away is natural, Ella. But when you spoke on that video, you sounded scared and confused about *us*."

She shook her head. "I'm not."

I wanted to believe her, but there was something stopping me. She was still holding back. "But you are," I insisted. "In some ways, at least. I can feel it. You're scared of living with me. There's something about us—about our relationship—that you aren't sure about or comfortable with."

She bit her lip, and it made my gut clench. I was right. There was something really bothering her. My mind automatically turned to my insane life. She promised the fame didn't bother her, but after everything that happened yesterday, maybe she was worried that she'd made a mistake being with me.

"Ella...whatever it is...please tell me." I braced myself. I couldn't let her stay with me if she didn't want my lifestyle. I loved her too much to hold her prisoner. I never wanted to let her go, but if it was what she needed... "I don't want anything unsaid between us. I don't want you to hold back. Whatever you're feeling, I want to know it. And I promise you, whatever it is, we will find a way to fix it. If I have to give up my career and we have to move to Alaska and live under a rock, or undergo plastic surgery so that we're completely unrecognizable, we will."

She cracked a smile and squeezed my fingers. "Your insecurity is adorable," she said, shocking me. "And it's appreciated, too. Makes me feel more normal." She shook her head. "I told you, the fame doesn't bother me. What happened yesterday at the theater sucked, but it was nothing in comparison to having you by my side yesterday when my father rejected me. It could never erase the way you stepped up and claimed me as yours when he didn't want me. Or overpower the way you held me all night last night while I cried for hours. Fame is a very small price to pay for that, and I will gladly stand beside you in any spotlight if that's what it takes to be with you."

Holy shit, the woman was going to kill me. My chest tightened up so much I couldn't breathe, and my pounding pulse roared in my ears. I never could have imagined feeling this way. I thought I understood love. I'd cared about Ella for so long I was certain I knew what love was, but this...this was so much more than anything I could have imagined.

I cleared the emotion from my throat. "Then what is it? I can't stand the thought of you being scared or confused about anything, especially not when it comes to us. Please talk to me."

Ella must have detected my bubbling emotions, because she scooted forward and pressed her lips to mine. After a quick kiss, she nestled herself comfortably beside me. She rested her head on my shoulder and laid her hand on my chest. I was tempted to pull her thigh across me like it had been when I'd woken up this morning, but I might not stop there, and now was not the time for me to try and start something again.

"I'm not unsure about us," she insisted, once she was good and comfortable. "In fact, we might be the only thing I *am* sure about right now." She lifted her head up to look me in the eye. "And I'm not scared of you."

I raised a brow at that.

She shook her head. "I'm not. I promise. It's not that. It's just..." She sighed as she started absently brushing her fingers back and forth across my chest. The light scratch of her fingernails had my goose bumps coming back.

"Just what?" I whispered in a strangled voice.

"I think...you and I are just in different places right now."

Needing the physical connection as much as she did, I started running my hand up and down the length of her arm. "What do you mean?"

"I know you're ready for our Happily Ever After," she said. "You want to play house together and do the whole adulting thing."

I smiled at the mental picture she'd just put in my mind. She had no idea how badly I wanted that with her.

"I love that you want that life with me, and I want it with you, too, I do."

"But...?" I asked.

"But...I'm just not ready for it yet." She sighed again. "I've never been on my own. I haven't had any time to be an adult yet. I'm not ready to be a full blown grown-up."

I was starting to see what she meant, and she was right. There was a difference between becoming an adult and being a grown-up.

"There's supposed to be a transition between being a teenager living at home with your parents and the house with the white picket fence, two kids, and a dog."

"Cat," I said, chuckling.

"What?"

"I'm a cat guy," I admitted sheepishly. "Kittens are cuter, and then they grow up to be feisty, badass cats."

Ella lifted her head off my chest to look at me, pursing her lips together until finally a laugh burst through her defenses. "Okay, big, bad movie star. We'll get you a fluffy wittle kittie someday."

My grin doubled. I was so taking her to the humane society this week.

"Anyway," she said, rolling her eyes at me before dropping her head onto my shoulder once again.

"Sorry." I really wasn't that sorry. I didn't mean to make light of this whole moment, but I was just so happy. She was talking about this future together that I never thought I would get. Once I became a real superstar, I always figured I'd end up like my dad. I assumed that would be my only option. Ella's house with the kids and the white picket fence had my mind racing with all kinds of possibilities. Maybe it was possible to have my career *and* the typical American dream.

"I think what I really need is that transition. I haven't even been very well since the accident—physically, mentally, or emotionally."

Suddenly feeling like a jerk for teasing her, I dropped my playful attitude and kissed her temple so that she knew I was taking this seriously. She breathed in a deep breath and let it out slowly. "I need time to adjust. I need some stability for once, in an environment where I feel safe, comfortable, and in control."

"I can give you that," I promised.

Her cheek lifted against my chest, and I heard a smile in her answer. "I know you can. That's kind of the problem. I'm afraid you'll do your job a little *too* well. While I'm the baby bird finally flying away from the nest, you've already built your own and are looking for a mama bird to lay some eggs in it." I laughed at the metaphor and got a frown for it. "You've been on your own for years and are finally hitting that real grown-up stage."

I snorted. "My father should be happy to hear that. He's been calling me an immature ass and telling me to *grow up* for years."

"Maybe he should look in a mirror," Ella muttered under her breath.

I laughed again and hugged her to me. "Hey. I get what you're saying, and maybe there's some truth to it, but I can wait. What's a few more years of being an immature ass?"

Ella smacked my chest. "Shut up. I'm being serious."

"I know." I covered her hand with mine and held it against my chest. "And I mean it, too. I wasn't kidding about living more like roommates, if that's what you need to feel comfortable with this. I can do slow. Hell, it took me three years to work up the nerve to give you my number."

"Yeah." Ella scoffed. "And then it took you a week to ask me to move in."

The woman had a point. I'd held off for so long because I was afraid of telling her who I was. I had a good thing and thought revealing myself would ruin it. Once I learned it wouldn't, well, my instinct was to make up the lost time for those three years. "Okay, fine. That wasn't slow. But I can be patient now. I'm completely content with our current situation."

"Of course you are. You got your way, you big, spoiled celebrity."

I smiled to myself, unable to stomp out my pride. I *had* gotten my way. I got exactly what I wanted, and I was deliriously happy because of it. I hadn't done it on purpose, so I wasn't going to feel bad about it.

Ella looked up and caught my smug grin. Her face fell flat. "You are *impossible*."

"That's why you love me."

I don't think she wanted to smile at that, but she did. I ducked my head down and kissed her. "I understand what you're saying, and I promise I will follow your lead from now on. You have complete control of this relationship, woman. I know how you are." When she cocked a brow at me, I smirked. "You're not the only one who knows what they've signed up for. But don't worry. I happily relinquish my proverbial pants. You're welcome to wear them."

I got smacked again. Harder this time. It was totally worth it.

"You are such a dork, Cinder."

That did it. She called me *Cinder*, with her Boston accent slipping through extra heavily, like it does every now and then, and my mouth was on hers faster than you could say *cah*.

She indulged me for a minute but then let me go and sat up. I guessed the time for morning make outs had passed. That was okay. We had all day—forever, really—to find more opportunities. Mid morning, afternoon, evening, and bedtime make outs worked for me, too. If she wanted to take a break for some breakfast and a cup of coffee, I wouldn't complain.

"So…" She blew out a big breath and ran a hand through her messy hair as she looked around my room. She hadn't seen it before since it was upstairs. I'd given her a tour of the main level of the house the first time she came over, but we hadn't bothered to come upstairs because that was a difficult task for Ella. I wasn't sure what we were going to do about that, but one thing at a time.

The room wasn't anything special. It had the same modern decor as the rest of the house. Cool winter tones with a splash of bright color here and there. Bed—California King size—night tables on either side, TV mounted to the wall, sliding glass door to the master balcony, a chair in the corner…very basic.

"Home, sweet home, I guess," I muttered with a shrug. "Nothing fancy. I bought the place already furnished just over a year ago and never bothered to make any changes to it."

She nodded as if that explained a lot. "It's nice; just kind of… impersonal."

"Yeah, it's not really what I'd have picked, but I was in a hurry to get out of my old place, and this one had all the things I was really looking for. It's secluded, has a tall privacy fence all around the property—you can't see anything but the roof of the house from the road—and there are cameras and a state-of-the-art alarm system all along the property line."

"So, no stalkers peeking in your windows or paparazzi taking pictures with their super zoom-in cameras from nearby trees?"

"Exactly. I'm sorry there's not a bedroom on the first floor. I hadn't even thought of that before."

She shook her head. "We'll figure something out."

"Or I could just carry you to bed every evening," I said with another suggestive waggle of my eyebrows to make as light of the offer as possible. That might end up being our only option for now, but I knew she would loathe the idea. If she was really going to live with me now, perhaps it was time to call the real estate agent again.

There was something very appealing about the idea of Ella and I house hunting together, picking out something we both liked—arguing over color schemes and negotiating on the must-have features. No doubt she'd want a huge kitchen and a nice master bathroom, while I really only wanted a garage large enough for a future car collection and a great back patio for entertaining guests. But I knew better than to mention any of this to Ella, considering I'd just promised her not to be too grown-up. House hunting for our first house together, where we'd someday start a family, definitely fell in that category.

She broke through my daydreaming with a sigh. "Just one more thing to add to the to-do list, but that one can be dealt with later. For now..." She closed her eyes and shook her head. After a moment, she rubbed her temples and let out another heavy breath. "I don't even know where to start."

"How about we *don't* start?" I suggested, lying back on my pillow and propping my arm under my head. When she shot me an unimpressed look, I grinned and tugged her back down with me. "What if today we just lie in bed all day and pretend nothing outside this room exists? Life's going to start back up soon enough, but it doesn't need to start today. I think we earned a lazy day after yesterday."

Ella smiled as if she liked the idea as much as I did and snuggled right back up next to me, but then a frown spread over her face. "Life starts back up for *you*, maybe. I don't really have a life. The GED's out of the way now, so I've got no school, no job, no goals for my future..."

She made that sound like a bad thing. I thought it sounded like heaven. "You have time to figure all that out."

"I suppose I could start with college. There's a new semester starting soon. I could take a few classes at community college just to keep me busy while I figure out what I want to do."

I cringed. I was going to have to burst that bubble, and, yet again, it was because of my life. "Maybe that's not the best idea yet. After how bad things got yesterday, I think it's going to take a while for all of this hype to die down."

She stiffened beside me and spoke in a clipped tone laced with frustration. "So what am I supposed to do? Stay tucked away inside this house like a prisoner? Am I the princess locked away in her tower? Is that what life's going to be like for us now?"

"Not forever," I promised, pushing her hair out of her face. It seemed to calm us both down whenever I touched her. "Think of it more like we're Bonnie and Clyde lying low for a while. And we can still go out, but just randomly. You probably don't want to have anything so routine like a school schedule until we aren't the main story of every news broadcast. It will die down, like you said; it just might take a while. Besides, we have to get you all settled in, and you've got a surgery coming up in a few weeks, anyway. You've got plenty to worry about right now. School can wait a semester."

Ella shot up as if she'd just woken from a crazy nightmare. "Oh crap!" She looked at me with panic swirling in her eyes. "My surgery! I can't let my dad keep paying all of my medical bills. Not after I cut ties with him."

That was what she was so worried about? "Ella. Calm down. That's not a problem at all. We'll just have everything transferred into my name. I can take care of any debt that's still outstanding, and I'll have Scott look into adding you to my insurance policy. I bet if we're living together, I can add you, and if not, well, we'll just pay whatever as it comes."

Ella's face paled, and I could see her trying to come up with a way to refuse my offer. "Brian..." Her frown deepened as she struggled for words. Eventually, she settled for frantically shaking her head. "I can't let you do that. It's too much."

"Ella, I made fifteen *million* dollars for *The Druid Prince* alone, and my agents have already assured me they can get me thirty *apiece* for the next four films. And that doesn't even include any of my savings or investments or other sub rights and royalties. Trust me. It's *not* too much."

She glared at me. "You know what I mean."

I ignored the glare. Ella hand been raised by a single mom and had always had to live frugally. She was fiercely independent because of it. I admired her for that, and I knew it had to be incredibly hard for her to be so dependent after her accident—first on her father, and now on me. I wished I had another answer for her, but I didn't, and she really didn't have another choice. We both knew she had to let me do this; I just wished I knew how to make it an easier pill for her to swallow.

"Would it help if I say I *want* to do this for you? Or, that if you don't let me, I'll probably just spend all that money on another ostentatious car or two to keep Precious company, or other meaningless stupid stuff that will only make me more spoiled than I already am? Not to mention all the presents upon presents I would end up getting you because I'm a filthy rich celebrity who has nothing better to do with his millions of dollars."

Ella scrubbed her face with her hands, as if that might ease some of the tension building inside her or somehow miraculously solve her problem. When it didn't, she glared at me. "You fight dirty."

I grinned. Score another victory for me. "I'm sorry. I know you don't love the idea, but I really am glad I can help you with this."

"I know." She sighed, defeated. "I'll let you, because I have no other option right now, but I wish I didn't have to ask this of you."

"I can't think of anything I'd rather spend my money on than your health and well-being. In fact, this sounds so wrong, but I'm kind of thrilled that I get to pay all of your medical expenses."

She scoffed. "Not wrong. Perverse."

I sat up and scooped her into my arms, placing her between my legs and pulling her back against my chest. I rested my head on top of hers and just held her for a moment. "Thank you for letting me do this."

Slowly, she relaxed. "Thank you for doing it. It's not that I'm not grateful; I just don't want to be your responsibility. You're my boyfriend, not my caretaker. I want to be your *partner* in this relationship, not your dependent. Does that make sense?"

My heart warmed. "It does, and I respect that attitude more than you know. I've been used for my money many times. That you don't want me to spend so much on you only makes it that much easier to do. But I don't want you feeling like our relationship is out of balance. We're in this together. I want to be partners, too, not your sugar daddy." She snorted, and I laughed softly. "Okay, I actually wouldn't mind being your sugar daddy, but we'll figure out a way to get you on your feet. Right now, I might have to carry a little more of the responsibility, but we'll get a plan in place for you so that it doesn't always have to be that way. Or..." I squeezed her tight and kissed the side of her head. "We could always pretend we're back in the fifties. I can worry about the money and the bills, and you can do all the cooking and the cleaning and stuff." That got a laugh, so I added, "I mean, I have a cleaning lady who comes once a week, but I can always fire her and show you where the toilet brush is."

"Hmm..." Ella said. "Maybe we keep the cleaning lady, and you show me where the aprons are. I can handle cooking."

She grinned and offered her lips. I kissed those beauties and then moved mine to her ear. "If I get you an apron, would you consider cooking me breakfast wearing just that? Because that would be the sexiest—"

"OH MY GOSH, BRIAN! I am not going to give you any nude cooking shows! STOP!"

I burst into laughter. "You are so easy."

"Please. Like you were teasing."

"I was."

"Only because you knew I'd say no."

"So?"

"So nothing! You are such a perv."

I rolled my eyes. "I hate to break it to you, woman, but I am a completely *normal* man. You're just a prude." She scrunched up her face into a pout that made me laugh. "An adorable prude, but a prude all the same. There isn't a man in the world that wouldn't love to watch his girlfriend cook him breakfast wearing nothing but an apron."

"Fine. If you're so keen on the idea, why don't *you* cook *me* breakfast in just your apron and see how *you* like it."

Hell yes. That was all the green light I needed. "DEAL."

I was up and out of bed so fast she'd only managed a surprise squeak before I bolted out the bedroom's double doors.

17

BRIAN

Ella squealed as I left the room and headed downstairs. "Brian! Oh my gosh, *Brian!* I was joking! *Don't you dare!*"

One of the things I do like about my house is that it's very open. The whole front half has huge vaulted ceilings. The staircase leads up to a loft that overlooks both the living and dining rooms. It makes the place feel a lot bigger than it is.

At the moment, it also meant that Ella could hear me banging around in the kitchen from the master bedroom. By the time she got to the loft railing and leaned over it to yell down at me, I'd already shed my pants and purposely left them hanging over the back of the living room couch where she could see them from upstairs.

"Brian?" The same voice that had just spouted a string of Spanish that I was pretty sure would earn a film an R rating now sounded as if it were auditioning to play a mouse in an animated feature. Not a grown mouse, either, but a tiny little scaredy-mouse. "Brian, you aren't really naked right now, are you? Please tell me you have *something* on."

Have I mentioned how much I love that she's shy? I was grinning like an idiot when I called up to her from the kitchen. "You know, I don't think I actually have an apron. We'll have to pick one up next time we go shopping. But if you come downstairs and sit at the bar, you probably won't see much with me behind the counter. Why don't you come on down? I'm starting some coffee. It's excellent stuff. Some kind of fancy French roast."

"I'm not coming down until you put your pants back on!" she called out in a haughty voice.

I smirked. "I'm wearing boxers, babe. And I know for a fact that you've seen both of the teen comedies I did a couple years ago. Which means you've seen me in nothing but briefs before. The pants are staying off. Come downstairs! I'll make you some eggs and toast."

"That is different, and you know it!"

"Do you need some help? I can come get you if you want."

That earned me a frustrated groan. Damn, she was fun. "I'm going back to bed. You can bring me breakfast there when you're done being a brat."

My bedroom door clicked shut a few seconds later. I chuckled and rummaged around until I found a tray. Breakfast in bed sounded like a wonderful idea. I got right to work and managed coffee, juice, scrambled eggs, toast, and yogurt for two. I sighed a little as I slipped my pants back on. Another time, I'd be stubborn and leave them off, but she just got here, and I didn't want to push her too much. I wanted her to have fun and relax with me, yes, but I also wanted her to trust me and feel comfortable and safe in my home.

"I'm wearing my pants," I called as I entered my room. The dishes clanked quietly on the tray as I walked around to the bed. Ella wasn't in it.

"That's good," she called from out on the balcony, "because it's a little chilly out here, and I stole your robe."

Her voice was playful again as it drifted inside from the open sliding glass door. I carefully set the tray down on my bed and went to my closet. Lucky for her, I had more than one of almost everything. I found another robe, and then took Ella her breakfast outside.

The sun was shining, and there were only a couple of puffy white clouds in the otherwise blue sky above the canyon my house backed to. It was a little chilly, but just enough to nip at any exposed skin and make the robe feel warm and comforting.

Ella was sitting at the small patio table outside my bedroom door, with her eyes closed and her face turned to the sun. A small smile played on her lips, as if she loved the feeling of the sun rays hitting her face. She was swimming in my bathrobe, and her hair was a disaster, but she'd never looked better.

I could get used to this.

I set the tray on the table in front of her and kissed her cheek. "You are positively bewitching right now."

Her cheek lifted beneath my lips as she smiled. I waited for her to make a joke or call me cheesy, but she simply looked at the food in front of her and said, "Thanks for breakfast."

Not only did she accept my compliment; she rewarded me with a kiss. I laughed as I sat beside her and split up the food on the tray. "That was much better."

She slanted me a wry look. "I liked that one."

"Good to know."

I sipped my coffee while Ella salted and peppered her eggs and dug right in. We'd both skipped dinner last night. After a couple wonderful moments, I decided to get to the heart of it. "So today…do you want to worry about going to get some of your things, or do you want to just go shopping for some stuff and give it a week or so before you try to contact your family?"

Ella scowled at her plate. "I don't know. I'll call Juliette later and feel things out. Part of me never wants to go back there, but I have some things—like my mom's things—that I definitely want to keep."

"Okay. Well, why don't we—" I forgot what I was about to

say when the ringtone for the front gate started to sing. "Who in the world…?"

Ella set her fork down. "What's going on?"

I held up my phone before unlocking it. "I have it programmed to ring whenever someone buzzes the front gate."

"Someone's *here?* Who?"

I grinned. I'm not much of a techie, but I have fun with my security system. "Check this out. When I answer it, it'll show me the feed from the surveillance camera down there."

I answered the "call," and a little screen popped up on my phone, showing me the last person I ever expected to see. *"Mom?"*

"Hello? Brian, honey, is that you? Hello?"

I nearly dropped my cup of coffee. My mother was here? I couldn't believe it. My mother hates to travel almost as much as she hates my father. Traveling to the city where my father actually lived was the worst of both worlds, in her mind. She *never* came to L.A., if it was at all avoidable. She always made me come see her. She hadn't been to visit me in L.A. in three or four years.

"Mom, what are you *doing* here?"

When I spoke, she turned toward the sound of my voice coming from the small speaker on the gate box. She found the camera and gave me a petulant frown. "What do you think I'm doing here? I'm surprising my son for Christmas." She reached out her window and pressed the buzzer several more times before finally huffing in annoyance. "Brian, sweetheart, this thing is not working. The gate won't open."

I shook my head and swallowed a laugh. "That's the buzzer, Mom. It's like a doorbell. It doesn't open the gate."

"Oh. Well, how in the world am I supposed to open the gate, then?"

I glanced at Ella. She was watching my phone with fascination while biting her lips, as if trying not to laugh. I was glad to see her excitement. Though the timing wasn't ideal, I was sure Ella was going to love my mom, and I couldn't wait for them to meet. I shot her a wink and laughed at my mom. "You can't open the gate. I have to let you in."

Mom balked, as if personally offended. "Well, would you mind letting me in, son? We had to be at the airport at *4:00 a.m.* our time—it was the only flight they had for two days. We have been traveling for *hours*, and I would like to come in, put on a fresh change of clothes, and rest someplace comfortable."

"We?" I squinted at the tiny screen on my phone, trying to see past my mom to the passenger seat. "Is that Doug with you?"

"Well, of course it is. Who else would it be?"

"Hey, Doug!"

"Hello, Brian," my stepfather called out and then muttered, "You see? I told you we should have called him first."

"For heaven sakes, Douglas. How were we supposed to *surprise* him if we called him first?" She turned back to the camera. "Are you surprised, honey?"

"I—" Not surprised. I was stunned. Speechless. "Yeah. I'm surprised."

"Too surprised to open the gate for your dear old mother?"

Beside me, Ella slapped a hand over her mouth. Laughter spilled from her eyes.

I'm sorry, I mouthed.

"You'd better open the gate soon, or your mother's going to put you in time-out when she finally gets in the house," she whispered back, laughing.

I rolled my eyes, but Ella wasn't that far off, so I hit the code to open the gate and hung up the phone. I set it on the table and just stared at it for a moment. "Did that really just happen?"

"She seems fun."

"Fun." I blew out a breath and raked a hand through my hair. "If we survive, yes." I looked at Ella, wondering how to properly prepare her for what was about to hit us. My mother was...a handful. "I love the woman," I promised. "And you will, too, but she's..."

"Enthusiastic?"

I snorted. "Tenacious."

The doorbell rang four times in a row, eliciting a groan from me. "So much for a peaceful week." I shot Ella another look. "I apologize in advance. You have nothing to fear, but you will quickly see why the apology is necessary."

The doorbell rang again, as did my phone. "I'm coming, Mom," I grumbled when I answered it. "Let me just throw on a shirt, and I'll be right there."

"Throw on a shirt? Brian, it's ten thirty. Are you still in *bed?*"

"No. Sort of. Just hang on a sec. I'll be right there."

Ella followed me inside—our breakfast forgotten for now—and laughed as I put on yesterday's rumpled shirt. "Shut up," I warned. "It's not funny." At her evil grin, I added, "You mock me now, but her attention is only on me because she doesn't know you're here yet. She's not really here to see *me.*"

That wiped the smile off Ella's face. I should have felt bad when she bit her lip and tried to run her fingers through the tangled mess of hair on her head. But I didn't. She didn't have anything to worry about except being smothered to death by motherly affection, and I got the feeling Ella wouldn't mind that after the year she'd had. I kissed her forehead before heading out the door. "You look fine, and she's going to love you. Promise."

My mother was standing with one eyebrow arched, her arms folded tightly across her chest, a designer boot tapping impatiently by the time I got the front door unlocked. I wanted to be annoyed with her, but the second I saw the tiny brunette spitfire of a woman, I was a little kid again, giddy with excitement. "Hey, Mom!"

I threw my arms around her, and she melted, suffering from the same anticipation as me. "There's my baby boy!" she squealed, squeezing me in as tight a death grip as she could manage.

I let her go and gave Doug a quick, slightly awkward hug. I liked the guy, but we'd never spent enough time together for him to really feel like a father figure. "Good to see you, Doug. I hope the trip wasn't too strenuous."

Doug snorted, casting a glance at my mom, and I laughed. I

could only imagine Mom having to fly coach on a crowded flight at an ungodly hour in the morning. Doug was probably exhausted and very eager to pass Mom off to me.

I pulled back and just looked at them again after they shuffled into the entryway and I shut the door. "Wow." I was still trying to recover from the shock. "I can't believe you're here. Thank you for coming."

"Are you kidding?" Mom's giddiness was gone, and her you're-in-so-much-trouble face was back. "After you canceled your trip on us last minute? What else were we supposed to do? We had to wait until after Christmas, of course—Doug couldn't skip out on his kids—but Brian, I can't believe you ditched your mother for Christmas."

This time, I didn't hold back my groan. "Mom. I told you why I couldn't go. I couldn't leave Ella when I'd just thrown her into the spotlight."

Mom huffed. "I'd *hoped* you'd be able to convince her to come to Wisconsin. Did you even try?"

I rolled my eyes. "You know I didn't, and I told you why. It's not that she didn't want to come. She was just too overwhelmed with everything. We needed some time to ourselves."

My mom harrumphed her disapproval and led me by the arm to the living room couch, still in a lecturing mood. "Honestly, Brian, what kind of ungrateful son are you? My only child declares to the entire world that he's found the love of his life, and he couldn't take the time to call his own *mother* and let her know about it first? Then you don't even bring her to see me for Christmas?"

I laughed. Liz Crawford was a formidable woman—stubborn, opinionated, and determined. I think that's why she ended up married to my dad all those years ago. Also probably why they ended up divorced less than three years later. How she ever settled in a place like Green Bay, Wisconsin, with a quiet math professor I'd never know, but I was glad she was happy.

"Mom. Give me a break. We've only been dating for a week."

"*Love*, Brian. You used the word love. People don't fall in love in a week. You had three years to tell me about this mysterious young woman, and you never breathed a word of her. I am your *mother*."

She had a point, but I didn't feel bad that I'd never told her about Ella. I'd never told *anyone* about Ella. Ella had been too special from the very start. She'd been my secret. Mine alone. To completely geek out on you and borrow the words of Gollum— she'd been my precious. She'd been my One Ring that I needed to keep secret and safe.

I hadn't been embarrassed that I was talking to a stranger online. It was more that my life had never been normal, and Ella was so…regular. Not that she was ordinary. I always knew she was special. But she had a normal life. She was a link to a world I'd never qualify for but one I'd secretly longed to be a part of. She seemed too good to be true, and I was afraid if I told anyone about her, she'd disappear. Now that I knew she wasn't going anywhere, I was ready to show the entire world what a treasure I'd found.

"Okay, okay, I get it. I should have told you about her. And if you will quit lecturing me long enough to let me get a word in, I'll introduce you to her."

Mom's jaw dropped. "What are you—is she *here?*"

I relished the look of shock on my mom's face—it was her turn to be surprised, after all.

BRIAN

Smirking at my mom, I looked up to the loft railing above us where Ella was simply watching the scene unfold with amusement playing at the corners of her lips. Mom followed my gaze and squealed. "Oh, Ellamara, hello, dear!" She clasped her hands to her mouth and waited out a bout of emotions. "I'm sorry, I'm just so excited to meet you. Come on down here and give your future mother-in-law a big hug."

I slapped a hand over my face and groaned. *Future mother-in-law?* Not that I didn't think it was an accurate title, but I'd just been accused of being too grown-up and ready for things Ella wasn't. Things like marriage. Which my mother was mostly likely going to mention every five minutes for the next however long she planned to stay.

Luckily, Ella's attention was focused on something else. "It's good to meet you, too," she said. "And I would come down, but, um…" She grimaced and met my eyes. "Your stairs are kind of steep, and there's no handrail. I don't think I can manage them on my own."

The blood drained from my face and I hurried up the stairs, kicking myself the entire way. I was such an idiot. I never even considered that she hadn't come downstairs because she *couldn't*. She must have felt awful having to say that out loud in front of my mother. "Shit, Ella, I'm sorry," I whispered when I got upstairs.

She shook off my apology, but her smile was forced. I seriously could kick my own ass right now. "Do you need me to carry you?" I hated to ask, but I wasn't sure how much help she needed, and I didn't want to make her ask.

She sucked in a breath and shook her head. "I can make it; I just need to borrow this." She took my arm and linked hers through it.

I continued to mutter apologies as I walked with her to the top of the stairs. "I'm such an idiot, Ella. I didn't even—"

"It's okay, Brian. It's not your fault."

It felt like my fault. How the hell was she supposed to live here when she couldn't even get to and from her bedroom on her own?

Ella stopped at the top of the steps and frowned. She started chewing her bottom lip again.

"You okay?"

She gave me another grimace. "Um...well, it's just..." She eyed the steps again and sighed. "That's going to take me a while, and it's going to hurt, and I haven't showered or anything yet. If I'm just going to have to come right back up—"

I didn't let her finish. "Mom? Doug? Could you please come up here for a minute?"

The relief that washed over Ella's face made me want to kick myself again. "That's it. I'm calling the real estate agent this afternoon."

Ella's eyes bulged. "Don't be ridiculous. You can't *move* just because I have a hard time with stairs."

The hell I couldn't. "Watch me."

She didn't like my answer, but I was prepared to be stubborn about this. I never wanted to put her in this position again. And I definitely didn't want her to have to live somewhere where she'd have to either be carried—something she hates—or caused a lot of pain just to get to bed at night.

We were still glaring at each other when my mom and step-dad reached the loft. Mom's brow was creased with concern. "What's wrong, honey?"

"Nothing's wrong. Stairs just aren't an easy task for Ella. She wanted to meet you, but she's not quite ready to come down for the day."

Mom's eyebrows disappeared up under her bangs. "Well, why didn't you say so in the first place? Where are your manners?"

I half expected her to smack the back of my head, but she turned to Ella instead. "Sweetheart, it is so wonderful to finally meet you. I'd love to say I've heard all about you, but Brian has been extremely tight-lipped about the two of you." She shot me a scolding look and pulled Ella into a hug. "I suppose that doesn't matter anymore. You're here now, and we have all the time in the world to get to know one another. You must be quite the woman to make my baby boy give up his *horrid*, philandering ways. And just look at you!"

She pulled out of the hug and scanned Ella from head to toe. "You are positively…" She paused, cocked her head to the side as she looked closer at Ella's appearance, and her smile fell into a frown. "Well, you look like a bit of a train wreck, actually, and… have you been crying?"

"Mom."

Even Doug voiced a warning this time. *"Liz."*

Mom ignored us both and dragged Ella over to the small sofa along the wall of the loft. "What on earth happened to you? You look positively a mess. Please tell me my son normally takes better care of you than this."

The horror in my mom's voice made Ella crack a small smile. "Brian takes excellent care of me," she promised as the two of them sat down. Mom still clung to one of her hands and was now fussing with her hair as well. "He brought me here on the spur of the moment last night because I had an awful day yesterday. He let me be a complete girl and cry all over his shirt for hours until I passed out on him, and then he even made me breakfast in bed this morning, hoping to cheer me up."

That was my girl. Earning me brownie points with my mom, even though I'd only brought her breakfast after she'd demanded it in retaliation for me torturing her with my immodesty. Still, I *had* been trying to cheer her up, and I'd totally done all the other stuff, so I'd say the high praise counted.

My chest warmed with pride when my mom's face softened. She smiled at me as if I were still her little boy that she could tuck into bed at night and sing lullabies to. I couldn't help the grin that spread across my face in return. My mom's approval was hard earned. "It's good to hear he has *some* decorum," she teased.

I shrugged. "I had this insanely crazy mom who put the fear of God in me when it comes to treating women right."

Doug chuckled, and Mom rolled her eyes at both of us. "Well, somebody had to. Your *father* certainly wasn't going to do it." She turned her attention back to Ella with a sigh. "I'm so glad he's finally found himself a nice girl to look after him. I can tell how happy you make him." Her eyes misted over, and she sniffled. "I saw what happened on the news last night. It was *awful*. I'm sorry you had to go through that. I'm sorry his life has made yours harder, but thank you for sticking with my baby through all the craziness."

Ella gave my mom a watery smile and surprised her with a hug. She whispered something to her that I couldn't hear but that had my mom gripping Ella fiercely. "God bless you, sweetheart."

I shot Doug a look, and he just shrugged back with a look that said, *Women.* When they pulled back, Mom grinned at me. "This one's a keeper, Brian," Mom declared.

I smiled at Ella. "I know."

She let me pull her to her feet and kissed my cheek when I slid my arm around her waist. Mom stared at the two of us as if she was trying not to cry. "Well." She clapped her hands together, and in the blink of an eye transformed back into the formidable woman I knew her to be. "I suppose we should all get cleaned up and go to lunch to celebrate. Or did you two already have other plans with Ella's family? I'd like to meet them while I'm here."

Ella and I both cringed. When I gave her a questioning look, she sighed, knowing we were going to have to explain. Mom was bound to find out sooner or later. I hugged her to me closely and let her do the talking. "Actually...I cut ties with my family last night."

Mom gasped softly and clasped her fingers over her mouth. Doug stepped next to her, wrapping a supportive arm around his wife while looking at both Ella and me with concern. "What happened?" he asked.

"My dad was mad about my stepsisters being harassed. We fought. It got pretty ugly. He chose his new family over me, like he did when I was eight." Ella shrugged as if it were no big deal, but she was trembling again. "He told me if I was going to keep dating Brian, then I should leave, so I did. I didn't even pack a bag. Hence the train-wreck-slept-in-my-clothes-cried-my-eyes-out-all-night look I'm sporting this morning. Brian's pretty much all I have now."

At that last declaration, I took her fully into my arms and held her tight. I was suddenly as overcome with emotion as she was.

"It was because of what happened yesterday at the theater?" Mom asked quietly. When her worried gaze met mine, I knew what she was thinking—that my fame had cost Ella her family.

Ella could also sense my mom's fear and quickly shook her head. "It may have been the catalyst," she said quietly, "but my problems with my father were much deeper than that."

"Oh, you poor dear," Mom whispered. She snatched Ella away from me, pulling her into another firm hug. "Well, welcome to the family, then, honey. We're happy to have you. Aren't we, Douglas?"

"Of course."

I smiled at the way Doug's face softened when he nodded at Ella. He was a softy for the girls. It was probably a good thing he'd never had daughters, because they'd all have him wrapped around their little fingers. I had no doubt Ella would manage the feat before he and my mom went back to Wisconsin.

Doug's a good guy. He's a quiet man, and very kindhearted. But he's also sharp as a tack and appreciates a healthy dose of wit. And, obviously, since he married my mother, he likes strong, opinionated, feisty personalities. He'd probably love Ella every bit as much as my mom. In fact, the pair of them would probably make some great stand-in parents for Ella, if she needed.

"I've been waiting for a daughter my whole life," Mom said. "Even after I married Doug, I only inherited more boys— Doug has three from his first marriage, you know. They're all a little younger than Brian, so I haven't had the chance to gain any daughters yet."

My head was beginning to hurt. "Tone it down a little, Mom." Ella looked like a startled deer about to bolt. "We've been dating for barely two weeks. We aren't exactly picking out wedding rings or anything. You're going to scare her away."

Mom appraised Ella's overwhelmed expression and then frowned at me. "Oh, don't be ridiculous, Brian. No one here was thinking anything about *rings* or *marriage*." Her gaze narrowed on me. "Unless...*you* were."

Her eyes flashed with a hunger I recognized even if I'd never seen it in her before. "Mom, *no*. Don't even go there."

She pulled her shoulders back and lifted her chin in the air. "I didn't. *You* did." The smug grin she shot me was downright man-eater. "Honey, if you're considering—"

"Mom!" I snapped, sharp enough to startle her into silence. Her eyes rounded like baseballs, but she closed her mouth and waited for me to speak. That may have been a first. Ella was gaping at me, too. The feverish look in her eyes was a mixture of shock and panic. I groaned. How had this conversation derailed

so quickly?

Rubbing the tension out of my temples, I let out a long breath and looked at my mom with my sternest gaze. "No one is saying anything about *marriage*, okay? I just meant that you needed to back off a little because you're being extremely intense, and Ella's already had to deal with enough drama in the last twenty-four hours. Relax, or you're going to smother her, and she's too polite to say so."

Mom and I stared at each other for a moment, and when she opened her mouth to speak, I cocked a stubborn brow at her. "Resist the temptation, Mom."

"Well, you were the one—"

"Stop right there."

"But if you guys are—"

"No."

"Honey, I just think—"

"No thinking. The subject is dropped."

I folded my arms and waited out the frantic excitement in her eyes. She stood there a few more stubborn moments, bouncing her gaze back and forth between Ella and me. When she turned to Doug looking for help, he shook his head. "You heard the boy, Liz. You'd better just let it go."

"Well." She huffed hotly, then grumbled under her breath. "I was *not* being too intense. Of all the ridiculous…" She shook her head and smiled at my girlfriend. "Ella. Sweetheart. What do you say we let these men do what they really want to do today, which is crack open a six-pack and watch football, while you and I go shopping? If you didn't even get to pack a bag, you're going to need a few of the necessities until you can arrange for your things to be sent here."

"No," I said, before Ella could answer.

I cringed at the startled looks they both shot me. I was still too worked up. I hadn't meant for that to sound quite so forceful. "Sorry. Shopping is fine; I just don't want the two of you to go alone right now. Not after everything that happened yesterday. There's too much hype around Ella right now, and it's just not safe. We can all go shopping together, after we get some lunch or something, if you want to, but I'll call a security guard to trail us if we go anywhere too public."

Ella nodded. Last night had really shaken her. Mom reluctantly agreed after catching Ella's shudder. "Oh, all right. I suppose that's reasonable. Brian, honey, be a dear and go help your stepfather bring up our luggage from the car while I get Ella all taken care of."

Without waiting for me to answer, she started dragging Ella toward my bedroom, treating her as if she were four years old. "We'll draw you a nice hot bath, and I'm sure I've got something in my suitcase that you can wear for the day. You'll feel worlds better once you've been able to freshen up."

I watched them go, wondering if I needed to intervene, but Ella glanced back at me with a reassuring smile that allowed me to let her go. Mom was still babbling as they finally disappeared from my sight.

A hand came down on my shoulder with a playful pat, startling me from the daze my mother had left me in. "Look on the bright side," Doug said with a chuckle, "your mother's got someone new to fuss over this week, which means you're off the hook."

When I barked out a surprised laugh, he added, "Don't worry too much. Your mom knows what she's doing, and from the looks of it, your girl could use a little extra TLC for a few days."

He had a point. "Can't argue there. It is her first Christmas without her mom, and I know she's missing her pretty badly. Her relationship with her dad's been a real struggle this whole year, but I know how much she was hoping things would work out. She was pretty devastated last night. Mom might actually be the perfect distraction for her."

Doug smiled, proud of his wife. "Well, let 'em be, then. They can do their girl thing for a while."

"Yeah, I guess you're right."

Doug nodded his head toward the stairs. "Let's go get started on those bags."

I laughed as I led him downstairs. "She pack the whole house?"

"Only half of it." Doug smirked. "She ran out of suitcases."

19

Brian's mom was amazing. I could see why Brian had apologized for her in advance and had been worried about her barging into the picture after everything I'd been through the night before, but the truth was, she was exactly what I needed. She was so much like my mom—energetic and enthusiastic, with a true excitement for life. She was domineering, stubborn, opinionated, and outspoken, but she had a huge heart and was completely accepting. She'd been ready to love me long before she'd met me.

It was strange, though, because in ways, she was also a lot like my father. She was a go-getter. She was organized and efficient—something my free-spirited mama never could have managed. I don't think she'd ever had to support herself, but she still worked hard doing charity work and working for the alumni and boosters organizations at Doug's university. She'd been raised with money and had always run in important circles. I'd bet she'd get along really well with my elitist father. She just wasn't snobby or judgmental about it. Liz and Doug were both great, and frankly, I was relieved that between Brian and I we had at least one set of parental figures we could look up to.

Brian left with Doug to pick up his car from the movie

theater while I was in the shower. When I was done, Liz helped me downstairs, and by the time we reached ground level, I was rethinking letting Brian call his real estate agent. "It is always like that?" Liz asked when I had to go straight for a bottle of painkillers I kept in Brian's kitchen cabinet.

I nodded as I swallowed the medicine. "Stairs are the hardest physical activity I'm capable of. That I can manage them at all is a bit of a miracle. For a long time, the doctors didn't think I'd walk again, but I've got a wicked stubborn streak, and I wasn't going to be stuck in a wheelchair for the rest of my life."

I went to the refrigerator to see what I could scrounge up for lunch. Brian and I made breakfast late, but most of it went uneaten. Liz had brought our dishes back downstairs while I was in the shower, and was insistent that I get a proper meal in me. "Ooh. He's still got some shrimp. How does shrimp pasta salad sound?"

"Delicious." She blinked and glanced at me curiously. "Do you cook?"

I grinned as I pulled different ingredients from the fridge and set them on the counter. "It's one of my favorite hobbies. My mother loved it, too. It was something we always did together. Mama worked a lot of hours in order to pay the bills. She came home late a lot, and eventually I started waiting on dinner so that we could cook together after she got home. It helped her feel less guilty about being gone so much. After that, cooking sort of became our thing."

Liz smiled at the story, and I realized that I'd just openly talked about my mother without any sadness or fear of making things awkward. It was such a nice feeling. I never mentioned Mama at home because I knew it was a sore subject for Dad. I figured it was pretty awkward for Jennifer, too, and Ana seemed to have some kind of issues there as well. Juliette was the only one who ever asked me about her, and unless we were alone, I'd always give the shortest answers possible.

Here in Brian's home, Mama was not a taboo subject. It was

an unexpected but welcomed breath of fresh air. Another benefit of leaving my father's home. Maybe I could start to accept Mama's death a little better and really begin to overcome my grief. I made a mental note to remember this for my next therapy session with Dr. Parish, so she couldn't accuse me of running from my problems when I explained how I cut ties with my father. I was not looking forward to telling her that, but at least I had another week before our next appointment.

While I set a pot of water on the stove to boil and pulled out a frying pan, Liz began rummaging through cupboards and drawers. A wry smile crossed my face when I realized what she was looking for. "I don't think Brian owns an apron."

"Oh." She slid a drawer closed and reached for the chopping board. "I'll just be careful, then." She laughed in exasperation as she started cutting up one of the avocados I set out. "That boy. He's so much like his father. I worried he'd be an eternal bachelor. I'm amazed that there is anything in his fridge besides old take-out."

I laughed and threw some shrimp into a frying pan with a little olive oil, garlic, and lemon juice. "There wasn't the first time I came over. I made him take me grocery shopping. I couldn't stand to see a nice kitchen like this go to waste." At Liz's sigh, I added, "He's not hopeless, though. When I cook, he lets me put him to work without complaint."

"That comes from being raised by me." She shot me a wicked smile and winked. "He's used to taking orders."

"I should probably thank you for that, since I'm a lot better at giving them than taking them myself."

We both laughed and continued to enjoy ourselves as we cooked until the front door opened and an unfamiliar voice called out to us. "Hello?"

Liz and I were both startled by the intrusion. After the insanity at the movie theater yesterday, and all of Brian's platitudes about how he needed such heavy security, we were both freaked out. "Who's there?" I called back while Liz reached into a cupboard and grabbed a skillet.

I recognized the young, well-dressed blond who walked into the kitchen just in time to stop Brian's mom from beating the poor guy with a cast-iron frying pan. "Oh! Liz, wait. It's okay. That's Brian's assistant."

Scott jumped back, raising his hands in surrender. "Whoa! Sorry! I didn't mean to startle you. I didn't realize anyone would be here, or I would have knocked. Brian never has company, and he always says to just let myself in in case he's in the middle of a workout, or oversleeping, or hiding from a meeting he doesn't want to go to."

My adrenaline was pumping through me at an alarming rate, but I managed to laugh. It wasn't hard to imagine Brian oversleeping through something important or purposely not answering his door. "Does that happen often?"

My laughter made Scott relax. "Yeah," he admitted, with a shake of his head. "Often enough."

He held his hand out to me with a sheepish smile. "It's good to see you again, and meet, officially."

I cringed as I shook his hand. "Yeah, we didn't really get introduced last time, did we? It's Scotty, right?"

"I prefer Scott, if that's all right. My Nana is the only person who calls me Scotty. Well, and Brian, because annoying me seems to amuse him."

I laughed again. "That sounds like Brian."

Scott shrugged. "It's all right. There aren't that many people Brian genuinely likes, so I figure the teasing is a positive thing."

I smiled at that. "Very true. He really isn't much of a people person. And the torture is definitely a positive thing. He only messes with people he likes. He *adores* you. Can't get through a single conversation without mentioning your name."

Scott's smile turned wry. "How many of those times is he using it in the phrases *I'm sure Scotty won't mind* or *Scotty can do that for me?*"

"Only six out of ten," I promised, with a grin. "The rest of the time it's *We need to find Scotty a good woman* or *We should invite Scotty to that. He needs to get out more.*"

Scott shook his head as he set his messenger bag on the counter. "I can see why Brian likes you."

The compliment surprised me, but it was easy to return. "Ditto, *Scotty.*"

He chuckled at the taunt and flashed a nice smile at Liz when I gestured to her. "Have you met Brian's mom before?"

His eyebrows lifted in surprise as he shook her hand. "It's a pleasure to meet you."

I went back to finishing up the lunch prep while they got acquainted. "So what brings you by?" I asked once there was a lull in conversation. "I really hope Brian wasn't demanding your presence the day after Christmas."

"He did mention needing to sit down with you this week to go over a few things, but actually, I texted him this morning. He promised I could use him as an excuse anytime I needed to escape the house over the holiday, so I asked if this afternoon worked to have our meeting. He said it was probably best to do it as soon as possible. I decided to take that literally and came straight over."

I laughed. "You needed to escape that badly?"

Scott nodded gravely. "My sisters are all home for Christmas."

"*All* of them? How many do you have?"

"Six."

"Whoa."

"Yeah. And right now they're all at home helping my grandmother make online dating profiles for their poor single baby brother."

As soon as his words registered, I burst into laughter. "Right. In that case, make yourself at home. Just don't tell Brian what they're up to. He'd likely drive over there and help them."

Scott's answering sigh was adorable. *He* was adorable. I could see why people were always trying to set him up. "You hungry?" I asked. "I made plenty."

Scott's face lit up. "Are you sure? I don't want to intrude if this is a family thing. Brian didn't mention his parents were here."

"Brian didn't know we were coming," Liz said. "We decided to surprise him. And it's no trouble at all. With Ella's new predicament, squaring away a plan for her was already on the agenda for the day. Why don't you find some place settings for the table, and we can all discuss it over lunch? Brian and Doug should be back any minute."

Scott hopped up off the bar stool immediately. "Sure thing." As he started opening cupboards, he asked, "New predicament? You mean the Erik Clarke thing?"

Knowing there was no way to avoid the conversation, I started moving lunch to the table and told Scott all about the fight with my dad and how I would be staying with Brian until I could figure out a solid plan.

"You don't plan to stay with Brian?" Liz asked, startled.

Her face fell with both disappointment and concern when I shook my head. I hated dashing her hopes of the wedding she'd been mentally planning since Brian's slip of the tongue earlier. "I love Brian, Liz; don't worry about that. I'm just not quite ready to *live* with him yet."

Her frown grew even bigger, so I hurried on with an excuse she wasn't likely to question. "Besides, this house isn't going to work for me. As soon as I can figure out how to pay for it, I'm going to need to find an apartment or something that's a little more handicap accessible."

"That might not be as difficult as you imagine," Scott said, excitement lighting his eyes. "Brian mentioned needing to go over some things. Did he tell you what kind of things?"

"We didn't get into it, but I did hear something about film rights for my story and needing to get agent representation."

Scott nodded as he set five plates out on placemats. "Film rights are only one of a hundred offers you've received that could bring in some revenue for you."

My jaw dropped. That number had to be exaggerated. But Scott didn't seem like the type to embellish anything, and he had this focused way about him at the moment—like he'd gone into some kind of business mode. Fitting, considering he'd shown up wearing a nice pair of slacks, a white dress shirt, and a tie. It looked natural on him and made me wonder if he knew how to relax. His clean-cut appearance only added to how serious he seemed at the moment. "That many?" I asked.

He nodded, as if that number was insignificant. "Give or take a few, yeah. Don't worry; I've got a list for you, and I've prioritized it as best I could. Brian and I will go over all of it with you."

"Whoa." I had to sit.

I claimed one of the chairs at the table, and Liz brought me a glass of lemonade without being asked. "Don't worry, Ella. Brian knows what he's doing with all of this. He'll make sure it doesn't overwhelm you. And I'll help as much as I can until we have to go home."

Scott moved onto the silverware and gave me a confident smile as he placed a set of utensils around the plate in front of me. "It's not as bad as it sounds. And most of it will pay extremely well, so even if you only agree to a handful of the offers on your plate, you should have no problem getting yourself into an apartment, if that's what you want to do. Plus, I had this idea for turning your blog it into a viable business, if you're interested in that."

"Really?" I perked up at the idea of turning my blog into more than just a hobby.

"Yeah. If you did it right, you could be set for life."

With the table all set and lunch made, Liz excused herself to go *freshen up* for lunch. Once she wandered upstairs, Scott sat down at the table across from me. "Do you really think I could start making money from my blog?" I asked. "Like, turn it into a career?"

Scott barked an incredulous laugh. "Are you kidding? You've already done it, Ella. You just need to start cashing in on it."

"What do you mean?"

"With the following you've gathered since your online identity was leaked at FantasyCon, you're being contacted by advertisers left and right. People are desperate to throw their money at you."

"They *are?*" My jaw fell in my lap again, and my heart picked up its pace.

Scott smiled. "They're approaching Brian because you don't have any contact information listed, which means I'm getting the e-mails."

"No...yeah...sorry about that. I had to go completely dark after the whole Kaylee thing, and I just haven't had the time to start everything back up yet since I got out of the hospital. I planned to after the holidays."

"Well, when you do, your possibilities are endless. I was thinking you should convert your blog into a full-fledged entertainment e-zine. Keep it mostly entertainment review-based, but you could add subjects like music and video games to your review lineups. You could also create an entertainment news column and hire a reporter to keep current headlines running like *Variety* does. And you could do celebrity interviews. You've got the following already and every Hollywood connection you could possibly need. At the very least, you should consider creating a YouTube channel and doing some kind of weekly review show. If you did, and you set it all up correctly and monetized it, you could be pulling in more than enough to live off of with your first video upload."

I slumped back in my chair as my brain tried to keep up with Scott. I'd been blogging for so long, and I loved it. *Loved* it. If I could turn it professional and somehow support myself from it... He was basically telling me my dream was at my fingertips.

Even better than just loving the work, it was something I could easily do even with all of my physical limitations. I'd never have to worry about trying to go get a job and wondering if I could physically do it. This was something I could do right from the comfort of my own home, on my own schedule. And I could take it with me if, in the future, Brian ever had to leave for months at a time to film on location and wanted me to come with him. It could be perfect.

"That's it," I murmured, stunned. "It's *perfect.* The perfect thing for me to do. It's the solution to my problems and answers that big, gaping question mark that is my future."

I met Scott's eyes and was surprised to see so much encouragement shining back at me. He seemed as enthusiastic as I was about this. "You could definitely make it work," he said. "It wouldn't even be hard for you."

I shook my head as my brain continued to spin. I wish I had his confidence. "I guess...theoretically, but..." As excited as I was, the idea of making it happen was overwhelming. "I have no idea how to do any of that. I mean, writing reviews is one thing, but converting my blog over to a legitimate e-zine, that would mean major website reprogramming, hiring a few people to run some of the different columns, someone to handle marketing and advertising...essentially, it would be starting up my own business. My own *company*. I might have the following to get it successfully off the ground, but I'm not equipped to do any of that. I wouldn't have a clue where to even start."

"Well...actually..." Scott rubbed the back of his neck and a light layer of pink rose in his cheeks. "I...uh...sort of...already wrote up a business proposal for you...if you're interested."

It took me a minute to say anything. I was so surprised, and Scott looked so nervous it. It was adorable. "A business proposal?" I finally asked. "What do you mean? What kind of proposal?"

"Well..." Scott took a deep breath and forced his shoulders back. "I graduated from UCLA with a master's in business management last spring. My focus was entrepreneurial studies, so taking something like your blog and turning it into a real company that brings in revenue—that's exactly the kind of thing that I want to do. This specific project is perfect for me because I already know the entertainment industry so well. Working with Brian has given me a specific skill set that would be extremely helpful in this case."

"So you're talking about a partnership agreement. We go in together and split the profits?"

He gave me a shy nod. "Yeah. You'd be the creative head of the company—editor-in-chief of the content, and I'd be your business half—the behind-the-scenes guy. I don't have the experience yet, but I know I could do it, and I have every confidence that you could as well. You're entertaining and likable, and you're smart. You have a gift for creating content that people want. Honestly, I think, together, we could be really successful."

Something fluttered in my stomach. I could never do something like this on my own, but with Scott's help... Scott was like Superman. Brian always said so. If anyone could help me make this happen, he could. And he was right about being the perfect man for the job. He knew the entertainment industry a lot better than me, and with his education...

"I already spoke to Brian about it," Scott said. "I'm not trying to go behind his back or anything. I just noticed what was happening and figured it's a great opportunity for both of us."

I wish I could have been a fly on the wall for *that* conversation. What Scott was talking about would mean a full-time job for both of us. Maybe not right away, but once we hashed out a formal plan, there'd be a lot of work to do. Scott would eventually have to quit working for Brian. I smirked a little as I asked, "How'd that meeting go?"

Scott cringed, but his eyes sparkled with amusement. "Pretty much how you're imagining it."

"Lots of pouting? Whining about having to find a replacement?" Scott nodded. "He used the word *traitor*, didn't he?"

Scott's shoulders relaxed, and he shook his head, chuckling. "Several times. But, he also gave me his blessing, because he knows how much you'd love an opportunity like this—his words."

I had no doubt that was true. This was the opportunity of a lifetime for me. I was sure Brian knew that. I wouldn't have to be dependent on him, and I'd get to build a career doing something I loved and was passionate about.

A long silence stretched out between us as I thought over the idea again and again. Maybe I was just excited, but I couldn't find any downsides to this other than Brian losing his favorite assistant. Though, that might be good for him. Scott was right that Brian didn't care for many people, but he really did love Scott. If Scott wasn't his employee anymore, their relationship could morph into the real friendship that Brian kept trying to make it and Scott wouldn't allow because he was too professional.

When I met Scott's gaze, he squirmed in his chair. He seemed to be holding his breath as he waited for my reaction. "I accept," I said. "Where do I sign, partner?"

Scott laughed nervously, and the pink tint returned to his cheeks. "Well...um...you should really read the proposal first and talk it all over with Brian before you accept. And I know it's on the bottom of a very large stack of other offers and opportunities for you, so I know—"

"Stop trying to talk me out of it." I laughed. "I've always wanted to do what you're talking about—it's what I planned to go to college for—and I have no doubt you could handle it."

When Scott blushed, I smirked. "Brian calls you Super Scott behind your back. I had to talk him out of getting you your own personalized superhero costume for Christmas."

Scott's blush faded as the side of his mouth quirked up. "Seriously?"

I laughed. "Yes. He was thinking about making you wear it as your work uniform."

The fact that Scott's eyes went wide showed just how well he knew Brian. Anyone else would have thought I was joking. I wasn't. Brian had contacted his favorite comic book artist and was having the two of us drawn as superhero characters for a new webisode series for my blog. We were calling it *The Adventures of Cinder & Ella*. He had the guy make a drawing of Super Scott as well. It took a lot of effort to talk him out of having a real super suit made up for Scott.

"I appreciate the assist on that one," Scott said, grinning at the thought. "But maybe you should have let him do it."

I cocked a brow. "You have a thing for running around in skintight rubber suits, pretending to be an Avenger?"

"Not especially, but...do you know what he got me for

Christmas instead?"

That sounded ominous enough I was almost too afraid to ask. "No...what?"

He rolled his eyes. "I'll give you a hint. It's parked in the driveway and cost as much as he paid me this year."

A car? "He didn't."

Scott's flat look told me all I needed to know.

Brian and Doug came home before I could ask anything else. Doug entered first, and a smile burst out on his face as he inhaled deeply. "It smells *wonderful* in here."

"Yes, it does," Liz said, coming downstairs, having heard her husband arrive. "Ella is a closet gourmet chef, and she's made a spectacular lunch for us all."

Doug grinned as he headed for the dining table. He eyed the food and took another deep breath. "It looks delicious. You need to keep this one, Brian."

Brian had come in the door right behind him and proudly kissed my cheek at his stepfather's advice. "I plan to."

"Welcome back," I said. "I take it Precious is once again safe and sound in the garage, where she's supposed to be?"

"Yup. All is right in the world again. And I saw she's got some sexy company at the moment." Brian took a seat beside me and flashed a wide smile at Scott. "How'd she handle the turns in the canyon on the way here?"

Scott's face fell flat, and he cocked an eyebrow into a high arch. "A *car*, Brian?"

I wanted to be on Scott's side in this argument—the gift was completely inappropriate—but Brian's giddy excitement stopped me from voicing any objections. "Not just *any* car, Scotty. That's an Audi A8. That is a *pimp* ride."

Scott shook his head. "Thank you for the generous thought, but I can't accept it. It's too much."

"*Too much* is a relative term, my friend." He picked up his napkin and placed it in his lap with a flourish. There was a bounce in his every movement, as if surprising Scott with the car had made him ridiculously happy. "And besides, I *can't* take it back. I paid cash for it and put the title in your name, so technically, it's already yours."

Scott barked out an incredulous laugh and pinched the bridge of his nose as he shook his head. "You are insane, boss."

Brian took that as a compliment, grinning even more as he puffed up his chest. "Maybe, but you like me anyway. And the only way to get rid of that car now would be to sell it, but that would be a waste. I cherry-picked that one for you personally, and, dude, your Toyota is on its last leg."

"But—"

"Look. You work hard, you deserve it, and you need it. Just enjoy it. Take good care of her and don't name her something stupid, and I'll forgive you for leaving me for my girlfriend."

Brian winked at me before he gave his startled assistant a stern look. "I know you already told her about your traitorous plans. I can tell. She's *glowing*." He looked at me, and his stern gaze fell into a pout. "He's going to be a total crap partner, you know. Absolutely horrid."

Scott snorted, and I tried to keep from smiling at my boyfriend's tantrum. "Is that so?"

"Damn straight, it is. He's bossy, straight laced to the point of madness, and *completely* anal-retentive. He's going to drive you nuts."

"Gee thanks, boss."

"Brian!" Liz scolded. "Stop being so rude. Scott seems like such a nice young man."

Scott received another pointed look from Brian. "Except he's a traitor who's leaving me for my girlfriend. And speaking of traitors..." Now I was getting the pointed look. "The love of my life has just stolen my wonderful assistant."

My composure finally cracked. "I'm sorry I have to steal your wonderful, genius, irreplaceable assistant." I giggled. "But better me than somebody else, right?"

When I flashed him an innocent grin and batted my lashes,

he tried to hold his pout but caved. His answering smile was sardonic. "You're lucky I love you."

The quasi threat made me smile for real. "I know. And thank you. It's an incredible opportunity. I'm really excited about it."

Brian sighed in resignation. "I know. It's a good opportunity for Scott, too, and to be honest, I'm not sure I could trust anyone else with your future like that. You guys will be a great team."

20

THE NEXT WEEK WENT BY QUICKLY. A FEW TEXTS WITH JULIETTE resulted in me getting some of my things brought over to Brian's house. (Thank heavens for Vivian and her dads, who were willing to be the go-between.) Then, my new rehab team was informed of all the changes in my situation, and my appointments with all of them resumed.

My team informed Brian that because of my physical disabilities, I couldn't stay in his home permanently—which I already knew. He'd called his real estate agent the same day he'd met my physical therapist and asked her to come straightaway so that she could speak with Daniel about what kind of place would be best for me. She was more than happy to bend over backward for her star millionaire client.

I told them I wanted to find myself an apartment in a secure building with enough security to keep me both safe and give me privacy. Brian, of course, hated that idea and pouted like a big baby over it. He voted he would just find a new home that was suitable for me as soon as possible.

Liz had her own opinions on the issue, which mostly consisted of her taking Brian's side that I shouldn't waste the time and money on my own apartment, and that when we bought our first home together, we needed to think about our children's futures. Hints about the schools in Wisconsin were dropped several times.

I loved the woman dearly, but she was every bit as exhausting as Brian had warned me she was, and when she and Doug left on New Year's Eve, I felt like I was ready for a vacation. We waved good-bye to them from the driveway as they left, and once the gate closed behind them, we came back inside and fell to the couch together in an exhausted heap. "Finally, we have the place to ourselves," Brian murmured.

I laid my head down on his lap, and, with a moan and a stretch, curled up beside him, ready for a nice, long nap. "I could sleep for days."

Brian began running his fingers through my hair. "Sounds good, but it'll have to wait until tomorrow."

I groaned again. "Do we really have to?"

He laughed. "It'll be fun. I promise."

"If you say so."

Tonight was his talent agency's annual New Year's Eve party. It was a big deal. Mostly A-list and a very swanky, fancy affair. This was Brian's first invite to the bash. He'd only been with the agency since he switched after the FantasyCon debacle, and before that, he hadn't been considered important enough to merit an invitation.

He was proud and thrilled to have shed his teen heartthrob status and be considered a real star. I was proud of him, too, so I would go to the party and wear my best smile, but secretly I was terrified.

This would be my first public appearance with Brian in his world aside from the premiere of *The Druid Prince*. I'd been in enough shock that night that Brian had only introduced me to a handful of people and the conversation hadn't extended much beyond *Hello, it's nice to meet you.* Tonight would be different.

"We don't have to go if you really don't want to," Brian offered after I slipped into a fretful silence.

"Of course we do. You're looking forward to it, and it would be rude of us to skip out. I'm sure it'll be fun. I'm just nervous."

"You don't have to be," Brian said. "Most of them will be kissing your ass anyway, Miss Popular Entertainment Reviewer."

I snorted, but he raised a challenging brow at me. "Ella, you have power in my world now. Do you not remember what you did for my father on Christmas?"

I let out a half amused, half disgusted groan. "I can't believe I'm partially responsible for a Max Oliver *Drive Hard* monstrosity."

Brian laughed. "There will be plenty of people who enjoy it. *Drive Hard* is actually a really awesome video game. And, you have to admit, Dad *is* the perfect director for that type of movie."

I rolled my eyes. "Yes, he'll sexy it all up with the perfect amount of half-naked women and giant explosions, and teenage boys across the world will flock to it in droves—you included."

"There's nothing wrong with a good action film."

"Not when they have things like plot, story, and character development, no. Then they're great. But boobs and guns alone does not a good movie make."

"I dare you to impart those words of wisdom to Dad sometime, Yoda." Brian flicked the tip of my nose. "And fair warning. You'll be my date to the premieres of all of Dad's films from now on, so you'd better start mentally preparing yourself now."

I groaned again. "You think he'll disown me, too, once he reads the review I give him?"

Brian burst into loud, boisterous laughter. "You probably won't have to worry. He's egotistical enough that he'll just assume you love it and won't bother to actually read your reviews." He shook his head and laughed again. "But the media will eat it up. 'Cinder's Ella Trashes Father's Film.' It'll make a great headline."

The amusement in his voice made me grin. "Well," I said, "as long as you know it's coming ahead of time and aren't offended when it happens, then it doesn't really matter."

Brian chuckled. "I'd be shocked and worried if it was anything less than scathing. Now about this party tonight and that extremely sexy dress hanging in your closet…are you going to need any help getting into it?"

"HA! Most likely. But Vivian and Juliette are coming over to do my hair and makeup, so I think I'm covered."

"*Juliette's* coming?" Brian asked. "Your father's giving her permission to come to the evil movie star's house?"

My throat closed up at the surprise in Brian's voice. "Yeah. I guess maybe he thinks if he lets Juliette come over, I'll start answering his calls."

Brian was quiet for a moment and hesitantly asked, "Will you?"

"No." I scoffed.

Brian relaxed again. He would support me in whatever decision I made where my father was concerned, but I knew he was glad I'd cut ties entirely. He'd seen my father hurt me too many times and was afraid if I let him back into my life, it would only happen again. He wasn't the only one afraid of that, which was the main reason I'd been ignoring all of my father's calls for the past week.

"Well, I'm happy you and Juliette can still be friends," Brian admitted.

"Me too. I miss her."

"Don't tell her I said this, but I do, too. She's fun to tease. Even Ana's not so bad, in her own way."

My jaw fell open at that shocking statement, and Brian smirked. "She's sassy. I like that in a woman."

He gave me a very pointed look that I rolled my eyes at. "Whatever. Help me get upstairs before Jules and Vivian get here. It's going to take us a ton of time to make me A-list party worthy."

.   .   .   .   .

SOON ENOUGH, I WAS DRESSED AND BEING POKED AND PRODDED, painted and sprayed.

"Stop fidgeting, or I'm going to poke you in the eye with this mascara wand," Juliette warned.

It was the first time I'd seen her since my fight with my father, and her support couldn't have come at a better time.

"Sorry. I'm just nervous."

"You have nothing to be worried about," Vivian promised. "Not while you're wearing this dress."

She had a point about the dress. I'd panicked when Brian first informed me that this party would be a formal thing, so to ease my anxiety, he'd commissioned Vivian's dads to make me a dress. What they'd given me wasn't a dress but a work of art. It was a bright red, beaded, one-shouldered, floor-length gown that clung to me like a glove.

The one sleeve it did have went all the way to my wrist. Forgoing the other sleeve and leaving my good shoulder bare had given the dress a dangerously sexy vibe that made the gown look as classy and beautiful as anything anyone would be wearing that night, and yet it covered almost all of my scars. It was truly brilliant, and my eyes had misted over the first time I'd tried it on.

"Are you ladies *finished* yet?" Brian called, knocking on the door for the third time. "The suspense is killing me. I want to see my beautiful girlfriend."

We'd locked ourselves in Brian's guest room, and he'd been pacing outside the bedroom door since he'd finished getting ready himself.

"Oh my gosh, he is *so* romantic," Vivian crooned as she unleashed another cloud of spray on my hair.

She'd gone for a classic twisty up-do to leave my neck exposed and show off the bare shoulder even more. A hint of my scars peeked out around the neckline, but it wasn't much, and the sparkly body glitter Juliette had forced me to bathe myself in took the attention away from them quite nicely.

"If by *romantic* you mean *impatient* and *needy*, then totally,"

I teased, shaking the nerves out of my hands as I sat in a chair. I hadn't been allowed to look at myself since the girls showed up, either.

"Ella, a man as gorgeous as yours is allowed to need whatever or *whomever* he wants."

"Well, *he* would certainly agree with you." I cleared my throat and yelled, "Patience you must have, my young Padawan!"

His muffled grumble of *dork* came back sounding just irritated enough to make me snicker. "He's fun to annoy."

Juliette gave me an incredulous look as she coated my lips with a tube of sinfully red lipstick. "You two are so...I don't even know how to describe it. Blot." She shoved a tissue at me, and I pressed my lips to it. The print I left behind was as bright as my dress.

"Finished!" she declared, letting me stand so I could go look in the full-length mirror.

As I walked over to it and finally got a good glimpse of the fairy-talelike beauty my friends had transformed me into, all of the air left my lungs. I couldn't believe that after everything I'd been through since my accident, I was still capable of looking like this.

"Wait!" Vivian cried. "I forgot!"

She ran over to the garment bag in which she'd brought the dress over and retrieved a new cane from the bag. Like Candy, she'd given this one a makeover, too. She'd used the same red material as my dress and swirled it down the shaft opposite a white strip of fabric. It was even one of those canes that had a curved handle on the top so it literally looked like a candy cane. "I figured, since it's Christmas and all..."

The cane completed the ensemble in a dreamlike way that I never could have imagined. Vivian's creativity was in a league of its own. "Viv..." My voice was in danger of giving out. "It's *perfect*. You didn't have to do this."

"Oh, but I did," she said, accepting a big hug from me. "As much as I love Candy, she didn't match your dress at all, and I couldn't let you arrive with a standard plain ugly aluminum cane that reminds people of crutches. I figured if we had this second cane as a spare one, we could give it facelifts whenever the occasion calls for it, and we won't have to touch good old Candy Cane. Because changing Candy now would probably break my heart as much as you getting this fancy and having to use a cane that didn't match."

I barked out an incredulous laugh and hugged my crazy, stylish fashionista of a friend. "What would I do without you, Vivian?"

"Clash," she teased.

We all laughed again, and after giving Juliette a hug, too, we turned back to the mirror to simply stare at the winter wonder that I was. "You are seriously one sexy senorita," Vivian said. "You're going to put all of those starlets to shame."

Juliette waggled her brows evilly and added, "Especially that wench, Kaylee Summers."

I smirked at my stepsister in the mirror. "Unless she managed to talk someone into letting her be their plus one, I don't think she got invited." I shrugged. "Not cool enough."

It was petty, but I kind of felt proud that I'd snagged my own personal invite to this party tonight when Kaylee Summers hadn't. True, I was Brian's date, but his agency was trying to woo me into representation and had personally extended me my own invite. Brian had assured me Kaylee Summers wouldn't have made their guest list on her own when I'd asked if we were going to have to deal with her presence tonight.

Brian's irritated voice rang through the door again. "Guys, we're going to be late if you don't give me my date sometime this century!"

We all laughed. Juliette decided to take pity on Brian and unlocked the door. "Are you ready?" she asked, holding the door closed enough that he couldn't walk in.

"I've been ready for half an hour," he grumbled.

"I promise the wait was worth it," she said, swinging the door open all the way.

Brian stepped in the room just as I turned to face him, and his breath caught when he saw me. The heat that entered his eyes as he roved his gaze over me from head to toe made my whole body tingle. Face flushed, I slowly stepped toward him.

He didn't look so bad himself. All done up in his tailored tux, he was as handsome as any prince ever was. Tonight, he wasn't Prince Cinder, though; he was definitely working the Prince Charming look. His dark hair was sculpted with care, and his rich chocolate-brown eyes were extra warm as he continued to stare at me.

When I moved, it pulled him from his shock, and he joined me in the middle of the room, placing his hands on my arms with reverent gentleness. "Wow," he breathed.

"Back atcha, handsome." I twisted a little from side to side. "So what do you think? Will I embarrass you too horribly in front of all those A-listers?"

"What A-listers? There's no way we're going to make it to any party tonight." He stepped even closer and slid his arms around my waist. As his gaze dropped to my ruby red lips, he sucked in a sharp breath. When he could meet my eyes again, he locked his stare on me and called out to my friends. "Jules? Vivian? I'm eternally grateful for the work you've done this evening, but now I need you both to get out. Go home. Leave. And lock the door behind you. I need to unwrap this gift you've just given me and see if she tastes as good as she looks."

I would have shrieked at him and slapped his chest or something, except he was so not kidding, and his intensity left me frozen and unable to breathe. I was entirely at his mercy for the moment, and if he took my dress off, I didn't think I'd try to stop him. I was even wearing the sexiest bra and panties set I'd ever worn in my life at the moment.

Once I'd seen the dress, I couldn't bear to wear cotton grannies under it, and I'd secretly gone through the stash of Lindon's Lingerie that had arrived earlier this week, along with the suitcases

Juliette had packed for me. I'd been super annoyed with her for sending them over at the time, but now…with the lacy bright red bra and panties under the world's sexiest dress, making me feel like I deserved Lindon's offer to model for him, well, I was glad I'd had the option.

Brian and I were broken from our spell when he ducked his head forward and Juliette shrieked. "Noooooo! Don't you dare!"

Brian jerked his head back and blinked at me, as if resurfacing from a deep sleep. We both frowned at Juliette.

"You will mess up the makeup I just spent half an hour perfecting!" she shrieked. "No kissing on the mouth. Cheek, neck, shoulder—fine. But stay away from her lips. She's not going to go through the party tonight with smudges all over her face, like she had to at your movie premiere."

Brian smirked. "But that was hot."

"Down, boy," Vivian said, pulling us apart. "It was cute once, but it wouldn't fly twice. Now, be a gentleman and escort your gorgeous date to the party of the year and show her off to all of your friends."

Brian grinned at Vivian, finally returning to himself. "Yes ma'am."

21

THE STANDARD WAS A SWANKY, CUTTING-EDGE HOTEL IN DOWN-town Los Angeles. It was as trendy a place as they come and the nicest hotel I'd ever been to. I was a poor Latina girl raised in inner city Boston by a single mother. I was definitely out of my league here.

The party was being held on the hotel's rooftop pool and bar lounge area. My heart raced as Brian and I waited for the elevator, but surprisingly, I wasn't the only one with nerves. Brian was fidgeting like crazy. It was comforting to see that he was as anxious as me. Well, maybe not quite as much as me, but still, there was some discomfort, and it was nice to know I wasn't alone.

"Nervous?" I reached for his hand as the elevator doors slid open.

Brian startled at the touch and turned to me with a sheepish grin as we stepped inside. "A little bit." He jerked his head toward the ceiling as he hit the button for the roof. "That's the big leagues up there. It's my first time sitting at the grown-up table."

The analogy made me smile. "You're going to be great. They're going to welcome you to the cool kids club with open arms and wonder why they didn't do it years ago."

He laughed once and blew out a heavy breath. "If they do, it'll be because the woman on my arm has them all under her magical spell. What do you say, fair priestess Ellamara, are you ready to go win over our new kingdom with me?"

"I don't know," I teased. "Are you going to leave me for a dumb warrior princess, like movie Cinder did?"

Brian chuckled. "Of course not." After kissing my hand, he grinned at me over the tops of my fingers. "Besides, she won't be here. Not A-list enough, remember?"

If he was trying to make me feel better, it was working. I beamed a bright smile at him, letting him know I appreciated the Kaylee trash talk. He matched my grin. "You are the most beautiful woman I've ever seen. Thank you for doing this with me tonight."

He was every bit as breathtaking as he claimed I was. I was lucky to be his date. "You're welcome. Just…please don't ever leave me alone up there tonight."

"Promise." He held up our interlocked hands. "This, right here, not breaking for anything. You have my word."

"Thank you," I murmured as the elevator came to a stop.

We both took a breath as the doors slid open. "You ready?" he asked.

I didn't get the chance to reply, because two people noticed us walk off the elevator and called out to us straightaway. A man in a traditional tuxedo greeted us as if we were old friends, with hearty handshakes and an air kiss to my cheek. "Brian! Ella! So glad you could make it." He pulled back and looked me over, head to toe. "Miss Rodriguez, you look positively radiant this evening."

"Thank you." I looked to Brian for help, and he gestured toward my new friend with a small but genuine smile. "Ella, this is Samuel Weinhardt and Afton Marks." He gestured to the woman, and she echoed Samuel's hand-shake-slash-air-kiss thing. "Samuel and Afton are the leaders of my management team."

"So they're your agents?" I asked, trying to figure out how it worked.

"Say the word, and we'll be yours, too, Ella," Samuel said. "We've got a whole slew of offers that have come in for you—they've been coming to you care of Brian since no one knows how to contact you directly. We've already started putting together a plan for you. We'd love to schedule a meeting with you this week and get some of these contracts going."

The immediate talk of business surprised me since this was technically a holiday party, but I supposed it shouldn't have. Brian was always comparing his industry to a tank of hungry sharks. These two didn't just smell a new client; they already had a hundred ways to make money off me sitting in their e-mail inboxes. Of course they'd jump on that. I understood it, but they hadn't even managed a *Nice to meet you. How are you?* before assuming they could just snow me into submission. It irked me.

"That's very thoughtful of you," I said, plastering that same fake smile on my face that I'd used talking to those studio execs and Brian's dad. "I'm very interested in seeing what ideas you have in the form of a plan for me. I'll call your office Monday morning and schedule an interview appointment with you."

Afton laughed, a very polite yet condescending laugh. "Oh no, hon, that's not necessary. We're offering you representation. You don't need an interview."

Was this woman for real? I may have been new to this industry, but I wasn't naive. I'd spent the last year trying to keep up with medical professionals ten times more intelligent than me and refusing to let them treat me like a child. I wasn't going to let this woman, who couldn't have been more than ten years older than me and certainly didn't hold my life in her hands, do it.

I matched her patronizing laugh and said, "I meant an interview for *you*. I understand you've offered me representation, but so has every other agency in town. I'll be meeting with all of you before I make any decisions or sign any contracts."

My heart skipped a beat when Brian choked on a startled cough. Had I been too forward? Had I lost my temper too much? He'd been the one to tell me I can't let people push me around.

But I didn't want to piss off his agents or make him look bad.

When I glance at him, though, I realized he was trying not to laugh. He met my gaze, and though he didn't wink, his eyes sparkled with both pride and amusement. His approval gave me a boost of confidence, and my entire body relaxed.

Afton and Samuel, on the other hand, didn't seem nearly as at ease anymore. "Oh," Afton said in a very clipped tone, now full of forced friendliness. "I see. Well…"

"Well, they'll just have to be thoroughly prepared for your appointment next week, then, won't they?" a new voice cut in.

The newcomer was older, maybe in his sixties. He smiled brightly, but somehow he seemed even more authoritarian than his peers. It always surprised me that anyone could be more dominant than Brian, but this guy made Brian and his agents look like nervous little kids.

"Don't look so offended, Ms. Marks," he said to Afton. "It's wise to be cautious in this industry. Clearly, Miss Rodriguez is a very capable woman. Which is no surprise." The stranger took my hand and gave me a smile that made the corners of his eyes crinkle. "Your insightful critiques of the books and movies you review on your blog speak volumes about your intelligence, and any woman who could capture Mr. Oliver's heart has to have a sensible head on her shoulders. It's wonderful to meet you, my dear. I'm Harvey Buchman."

"Mr. Buchman's the head of the entire agency," Brian murmured.

Harvey turned his friendly grin on my very shocked boyfriend. "Please, Brian, call me Harvey."

Brian, stunned, shook the man's hand and said, "I will. Thank you, Harvey. It's an honor to finally meet you."

"Oh, the pleasure's mine, Brian. I've heard so much about you since you joined our agency." Harvey laughed with sincere amusement and grinned at me. "This young man gave our agency quite the shock the day we met with him the first time."

Brian laughed a little, but there was nervousness in it that made me wonder just how big of an uproar he'd caused the day he fired his old management team. Perhaps I should have let the mystery lie, but Harvey seemed in good spirits, so I couldn't resist asking, "Really? How so?"

Harvey laughed again. He studied the two of us together before deciding to be candid. "Frankly, with his previous résumé and reputation, and that stunt his old management team pulled after FantasyCon, we expected a young, spoiled hothead and were prepared to cater to a teenage heartthrob throwing a diva tantrum."

Brian chuckled softly. It made it easier for me to tease him. I shot Harvey a disbelieving look and said, "Are you trying to tell me you *didn't* get a young, spoiled hothead throwing a tantrum in your office that day?"

Mr. Harvey blinked at me and then laughed. "Perhaps there was some of that—not that we blamed him when we learned the truth of what his previous agency had done. No, it was his intelligence that surprised us. His scruples, his astute eye for the business, and his sheer determination to do right by you. He had my entire agency completely flustered within minutes."

Okay, *that* I could believe. Brian was formidable when he wanted to be. Just like his mother. "I'm sure he did," I agreed. "Brian is usually underestimated." When Brian slid me a look, I laughed. "Yes, I was guilty of it, too."

Harvey sighed. "That is the biggest problem with our young Mr. Oliver here, isn't it?"

Brian frowned. "What do you mean?"

Harvey placed a hand on Brian's shoulder and began leading us over toward the bar. "Well, being the paparazzi magnet you are—which, unfortunately, some stars just have that luck."

Brian scoffed.

"And," Harvey continued with a hint of chagrin, "with your father being who he is, most people in town had already made their minds up about you. It's hurt your career more than you know, but we're working to take care of that."

"I don't understand," I said. "I thought Max Oliver had a lot of pull in Hollywood."

"Pull, not respect," Brian said flatly.

"Ah." Enough said. "And, I guess movies like *Senior Trip* and *Screw the Prom Queen* haven't helped much, either."

"No. My former management team never did me any favors with the projects they lined up for me."

Harvey nodded. "Very true."

We reached the bar, and after making sure Brian and I both had something to drink—he didn't blink at my request for water, which was nice—Harvey smiled at Brian again. "Fortunately, we plan to change this town's opinion of you."

Brian took a small sip of a martini. "Do you really think you can do that?"

"Oh, absolutely. Starting tonight," Harvey gushed. "You've already done the hard part—you've forced everyone in town to question their judgment concerning you."

Brian and I shared a curious look and waited for an explanation. "Your performance in *The Druid Prince* really shook this town," Harvey said. "People were shocked at your depth and your ability to take a Max Oliver film, starring opposite Kaylee Summers, and turn it into such a moving performance. And *now*, surprising everyone again by dating a non-famous young woman with physical disabilities—forgive me for putting it so brashly, Miss Rodriguez; I mean no disrespect—it's really turned heads. No one in town knows quite what to think of the two of you."

Harvey led us to a vacant couch. The small sofa was one of four placed around a coffee table covered with plates of hors d'oeuvres. I was glad to be off my feet and looked forward to trying the stuffed bell peppers in front of me. Brian noticed me eyeing them and grinned. As he filled a small plate for the two of us to share, Harvey got down to business. "So, Miss Rodriguez," he said, having sat on the sofa nearest me. "Rumor has it you don't plan to take Lindon's up on their offered modeling contract."

I laughed harshly. "That would be correct. I have no desire to model for Lindon's Lingerie or anybody else. And I certainly don't plan to take my clothes off and bare my scarred and mutilated body to appease people's morbid curiosity."

Harvey's face fell into a frown. "I understand your reluctance, but I think it would be a mistake for you to pass on this opportunity."

"Excuse me?" I shook my head, bewildered that he could think such a thing. "Okay, first of all, the public may think Erik Clarke's suggestion that I model his winning lingerie is some kind of fun game, but it's actually my dignity, my feelings, and my reputation on the line. That's not a joke, that's my *life*. And second, did you happen to see the news Christmas Day? That kind of attention is not something I plan to sign up for willingly."

Brian squeezed my hand in an attempt to remind me to check my temper before I really lost it. Then he pulled me closely to his side, creating a very distinct *us* image. When he spoke, I was sure the move had been intentional. "With all due respect to you, Mr. Buchman, you *don't* understand Ella's reluctance on this issue. You couldn't possibly understand the things she's been through in the past year. You don't know what it's like to have a beautiful, perfectly healthy body taken from you and to be looked down upon and mocked and tormented because it's gone. Like she's lesser of a person now than she was before because of her injuries. This may be a power play to you, a trifle matter of smiling for a few pictures, but that's maybe one percent of the factors that would go into a decision like this."

My heart swelled to have Brian come to my defense in such a way. It wasn't that he was defending me no-holds-barred, it was that he got it. He understood that this wasn't about just the message I could send to the world.

Harvey wasn't deterred. "Which is why," he said, "Ella should sign with my agency." He turned his penetrating stare on me. "I may not be able to empathize with your situation, Miss Rodriguez, but I *do* understand it would be a very difficult and sensitive issue for you. What you're failing to consider is that the media has already thrust this mess on you, whether you want it or not. It won't go away. But if you embrace it, if you take control of it rather than letting it control you, it wouldn't have to be so painful for you."

I hated that he had a point. He was right that this problem wouldn't just disappear if I stuck my head in the sand long enough. Eventually, I'd have to face it.

"I did see the news Christmas Day," he said. "My heart went out to you and your family for having to endure that. Especially because of a video posted by *Erik Clarke*." He said Erik's name with as much loathing as I felt for the lying little jerk, which softened me and maybe even endeared me to Mr. Buchman a bit.

"I heard the things they shouted at you," he continued. "I know why they tackled that man to the ground, even if they didn't show it on camera. It wasn't hard to guess. Miss Rodriguez, I hate to say it, but that pervert who exposed himself to you will not be the last of his kind, if you don't take action. That is what my team would like to do for you. We could help you limit those kinds of experiences."

"How?" He sounded so confident, but it felt like an impossibility.

"By turning you into a hero instead of a martyr."

The force of his statement hit me hard, as did the meaning behind it. The air left my lungs, and it took all of my strength not to show this man how much he'd just affected me.

"A lot of doors have just been opened to you. Opportunities you don't even know exist. Endorsements. Modeling for basically anyone you'd care to work for. Numerous charities who would like your endorsement or help to support their causes. Your biography. A documentary. Everything from the major motion picture rights, to your own reality TV show, to a worldwide motivational speaking tour. There are so many ways we could spin your current situation."

My jaw fell a little further with each new suggestion he gave me. Brian and Scott had showed me the list of e-mails Scott had—it had mostly been guest appearance requests from people like Kenneth Long, Connie Parker, and *Celebrity Gossip*, and a long list of publishers and studios that were interested in advertising on my blog or having me review their projects.

What Mr. Buchman was suggesting was leagues above that. Worldwide motivational speaking tours? My own reality TV show? Not that I wanted any of those things, but who in the world would be that interested in me? I wasn't a hero. I was a complete disaster. An insecure emotional wreck.

Seeing that he'd overwhelmed me, Mr. Buchman toned down his intensity, softening his voice in an attempt to make his next words hit with less severity. "Do nothing, Miss Rodriguez, and everyone who has ever disparaged you *wins*. Stand up for yourself, and all of those pathetic, weak-minded bullies will see that you aren't a victim. So far, everything you've done, from that media footage of the two of you at FantasyCon, to stopping your blog posts and removing all comment features and contact information, to hiding from the media, and your terrified stroll to your car on Christmas Day, even the way Brian hovers around you so protectively tonight shows the world that you are every inch the meek, mild, terrified lamb ready for the slaughter. That crowd on Christmas Day was so out of hand because those people saw a victim. They sensed *prey*.

"You may be overwhelmed and in over your head at the moment, but watching you with my agents a few minutes ago, I know you can handle it. Show them you are strong, and they *will* back off. They will *fear* you. There is an inner strength in you. The same strength that had my agency falling over themselves at Brian's feet when he showed up demanding we cut all of our bullshit because he wasn't taking it anymore from *anyone*."

A startled snort of laughter escaped me that made Brian chuckle. "Yeah, that sounds like Brian."

"It's you, too, little miss *Ellamara's Words of Wisdom*," Brian teased.

I was as grateful as Harvey to have the tension broken. He

nodded with the smile back in place on his handsome face. "Allow my agency to help you get your head above the water. We can corral all of the chaos surrounding you right now and use it to your advantage. It wasn't Erik Clarke's suggestion on *Celebrity Gossip* that's fueling the public right now—he merely threw out an idea. Those people are reacting to *you* and your statements in that lingerie store. You've inspired the world, Ella, and now you have power at your disposal. A lot of it. Don't let it go to waste."

I blew out a breath, recognizing the end of his speech. It was a good one. I'd give him that. "You've definitely given me a lot to think about," I said honestly.

"Good." His answering smile was almost as much pride for me as it was for himself. "Hopefully, I've persuaded you."

The man was relentless…and very good at his job. "You've left an impression." I grinned, and he matched my dry smirk, knowing exactly what was coming. "I still plan to meet with all the others, too."

He laughed, accepting his defeat with grace, because he was sure in the end I'd come back to him. "You do that," he said. "But do me a favor." He pulled a business card from the inside breast pocket of his tux and handed it to me. Brian gasped softly when he saw that the card had Mr. Buchman's personal contact information on it. "If you should decide to go with ICM or good old Bill Morris, do me the courtesy of calling me before you sign so that I can have one last chance to counter any offers they may make that might sway you to them. I would take you on as my personal client, if that's what it takes to sign you."

Brian gasped again, louder this time. All I could do was stare at the business card that had the personal e-mail and phone number of the head of one of the largest, most powerful talent agencies in the world. It seemed so surreal. When I finally found my voice, I looked up again to see Mr. Buchman waiting for a response to his request. "I'll do that," I said, "if you'll answer one question for me. Honestly."

Harvey nodded, brows raised in curiosity.

"Why do you want me so badly? *You*, I mean. Personally. You could have let Brian's agents handle me tonight. I assume they're some of your best. If Brian really caused the stir you claim he did, I can't imagine you'd pair him with anyone but your top agents. But spending a good twenty minutes with me when everyone at this party probably hopes to gain your attention at some point? Why? It doesn't make sense. I may have a little hype right now, but I'm not star client material. I have no plans to be an A-list actor, the next chart-topping pop sensation, or even a supermodel. I'll never make you the kind of money someone like Brian will, so why give me your personal contact information? Why offer to represent me personally?"

When Harvey narrowed his eyes and suppressed a smile as if he were a cat caught with his whiskers in the cream, I shook my head at him. "Truthfully," I warned him, "or you'll lose my trust, and I'll cross you off the list of possibilities right here and now."

Brian didn't gasp again, but his whole body stiffened. Perhaps it was audacious of me to be so direct, but it didn't make sense, and I didn't like that.

Harvey chewed on my request for a long time, stretching out the silence between us until it was nearly suffocating, but I refused to let him off the hook. When he finally decided that whatever secret he held was worth sharing in order to keep me from walking away, he said the last thing I ever expected. "It's because I have a daughter."

He waited out a shocking bout of emotions, swallowing hard and taking a controlled breath before speaking again. "I have a smart, funny, caring daughter just a couple years younger than you. She is a *beautiful* young woman…with a strong Jewish nose, and my tight, frizzy curly hair, and my wife's freckles. The height gene skipped her, and she'll never be as thin as the girls in the magazines. Her beauty is unconventional, and she believes that equates to ugly. The kids at school act like her friends because of my status, and then they mock her behind her back. The only boys who ask her on dates are ones looking for an in."

He took another breath, as if needing to suppress a great deal of rage ignited by his protective instincts. I knew those instincts well. My father had them in spades. He'd banned Brian from his property, essentially cutting me from his life because he'd been angry that Juliette and Anastasia had been humiliated and put in danger on Christmas.

"The other agencies will want you because you will make them quick and easy money with your current attention and your A-list boyfriend. I don't want to make money, Miss Rodriguez. I want to make a *statement*."

His speech stole the air from my lungs. I was nearly moved to tears from it. I was also terrified, because he'd just made my decision infinitely more complicated and impossible to make. He'd made it real. He'd made it personal. From now on, every time I was faced with this topic, I would picture that adorably awkward teen girl struggling through high school, heartbroken and lacking self-confidence because she didn't feel beautiful enough.

Part of me wished I could unhear his story. But I'd asked him for the truth, and even though he hadn't wanted to give it, he did. "Thank you for your candidness," I whispered, still struggling to find my voice.

"Mr. Buchman," Brian said quietly, "my heart goes out to your family. More than you know. Because even with my support, Ella still struggles the same way your daughter does. It makes me want to set fire to the whole world sometimes when I have to hear the things people say about her."

Mr. Buchman's face fell slightly, and he gave me a sympathetic smile.

"Imagine," Brian said, "putting your daughter on TV, and on the front page of every magazine, in her underwear no less, so that she feels more vulnerable than she's ever felt in her life, and then circling all of those things she feels make her ugly with big red permanent markers so that the nation can gawk at her and debate whether or not she's beautiful, or whether she deserves to be with someone more beautiful and perfect than her."

"I can't," he said simply. His face had gone white at the picture Brian painted for him, and he swallowed hard. "I could never ask my daughter to go through that."

"And yet, that's what you're asking Ella to do."

I leaned against Brian, suddenly lacking the strength to sit up on my own. Mr. Buchman's eyes fell on me again, with a mixture of emotions. "I know that," he said. "I know what I'm asking of you. And I know that asking you to do it makes me a hypocrite. But I'm still asking. *Begging.* Please consider it. Because it's already happening to you, whether you like it or not, and you have the power to do something about it. Maybe you couldn't change the world, but you could change the lives of those who suffer from insecurity the way you do. You could be someone to look up to. Someone to make them believe *If she's beautiful, and worthy of a man like Brian Oliver, then maybe so am I.*"

His voice gave out, and he had to take a moment to compose himself. Brian and I both sat, stunned, that this man, probably one of the most powerful and influential people at this party— which was *really* saying something—was practically on his knees in front of me.

"Brian, you love Ella, don't you?" he asked.

"More than anything in the world," Brian replied, startled by the seemingly random question.

Mr. Buchman nodded. "Someday you'll have children, and the love that you have for Ella right now won't even compare to the joy those kids will bring into your life. And when they start to grow up, and you see them suffer, and you're unable to stop that pain, *then* you will understand how I could ask such an impossible task of Miss Rodriguez. Of the *both* of you."

He sucked in a deep breath and sat up straight, placing his hands on his knees. "And now..." He blew his breath out slowly. "If you'll excuse me, I do believe you were right that I have other guests I should probably attend to. Thank you both for your time, and please think about it." He rose to his feet, pointing at the card in my hand. "Hang on to that, and remember your promise. Call me first if you decide to sign with another agency."

"I will," I murmured.

"Thank you. Enjoy the party, you two, and Happy New Year."

With that, he slipped away, leaving a very stunned Brian and me sitting speechless on a sofa, staring at a business card.

BRIAN

WE STILL HAD AN HOUR TO GO UNTIL MIDNIGHT, BUT ELLA AND I were exhausted. We snagged an empty sofa in front of a fire pit and both sighed as we got off of our feet. It took Ella longer than normal to sit down, and I heard the wince she tried to hide. "How are you holding up?" I asked.

"I'm okay." She sounded breathy. I shot her a stern look, and she gave me a real answer with a sigh of defeat. "I should probably stay right here for the rest of the evening and maybe leave right after midnight."

I was afraid of this. I'd kept her off her feet as much as possible tonight, but there had been so many different people vying for our attention that it had still been a lot of up and down and standing around while mingling. Standing for long lengths of time was hard for Ella, especially when she wasn't in her special shoes, but she hadn't complained even once. She was doing that thing she does, where she was trying to act normal and refusing to be a "burden." The woman was so stubborn. Strong, brave, and amazing, but stubborn.

"Are you sure? We can leave now, if we need to. You don't want to overdo it again, like you did when you went shopping with the girls."

She sighed again, but this time it came out more of a frustrated huff. "We don't need to leave. I'll be okay. I just really have to sit and stay down this time."

She adjusted on the sofa, grunting softly as she fought her hips in order to settle her bad leg into a comfortable position. I knew that look. She needed to stretch her leg out and elevate her feet. I stood, put a small pillow against the arm of the sofa, and gave it a meaningful pat. Ella glared at me, but I knew that was only her frustration talking. We stared each other down until she finally broke. "Ugh, fine."

She moved to sit sideways but stopped and grimaced.

"Need some help?" I murmured. It was her least favorite question in the world, so I asked it as little as possible.

Her shoulders slumped, and she nodded. I gave her a small smile as I gently lifted her legs and helped her lay them out in front of her on the sofa. She didn't normally need that kind of help. Her hip must have really been hurting her. Her pinched expression and pale face as she settled into her new position told me I was right. "Ella, you should have said something sooner."

"I didn't want to." The defeat in her tone broke my heart.

"Ella—"

"You're the star tonight. This is a *big deal* for you. I just wanted to stand at your side and support you while you rocked the A-list for the first time."

I squatted down beside her, grinning as I took her hand. *Rocked the A-list.* She was adorable. This whole night had been crazy. After Mr. Buchman left us, it took a few minutes for the first curious person to approach us, but once the ice was broken, the introductions started and hadn't stopped for the last two hours.

She frowned at our clasped hands. "I know how excited you were for tonight. I wanted you to enjoy it, not spend it catering to me or worrying about me like you're doing now."

"This night has been amazing," I agreed, "but not worth risking you hurting yourself. Especially if you just needed to sit down. Haven't you ever heard of a throne? You and I seem to be king and queen of this party tonight. We could have found a comfy seat and let everyone come to us."

I took a quick glance around to make sure no one was close enough to hear the arrogant comment about to come out of my mouth. The coast was clear, but I still leaned close to Ella's ear and whispered my words. "They'd just have had to kiss our feet all night instead of our asses."

I got the response I knew I'd get, the one I'd been aiming for—a startled gasp and a smack to the chest. But she was laughing, and that was the important part. "Brian! Oh my gosh, shut up before someone hears you." She rolled her eyes. "Even if it *is* true."

I laughed at that. I couldn't believe the reception Ella and I had received tonight. People much more famous and influential than me had been congratulating me all night and welcoming me into their personal circles. Ella and I had received dinner invitations from just about the entire A-list. The whole thing was mind-boggling.

"Excuse me, Mr. Oliver?"

One of the party attendants had noticed me squatting beside Ella and brought me a chair. I stood with a stretch and shook the guy's hand. "Thanks."

"Of course, Mr. Oliver. If there's anything else I can do for either of you, please let me know."

His eyes flicked to Ella with concern, which endeared him to me and probably annoyed her. "Actually, we'd be grateful if you could track down some painkillers. Extra Strength Advil or Tylenol or something."

"Of course." The guy nodded to me and flashed Ella a smile. "I'll be back in just a few minutes."

Ella looked relieved as the guy scampered off to find her some pain reliever. She was really tired. I scooted my chair closer to her and took her hand again, bringing it to my lips. "Thank you for coming with me tonight. We can leave once you get those pain relievers and they start to kick in."

"We're staying." Ella shot me a defiant look. "I didn't get all glammed up just to duck out early and miss the chance to kiss my favorite A-list actor on a fancy rooftop at midnight."

My mind went gooey at the thought of finally getting to kiss her. She looked amazing tonight. Glen and Steffan had really outdone themselves with her dress. Ella had never looked more beautiful. It had taken all of my willpower to leave the house once I saw her, and I'd spent way too much time ever since thinking too many dirty thoughts. It's funny how I could love her dress so much and still want nothing more than to take it off of her.

Forcing my mind out of the gutter, I gave Ella my movie-star smile. "Well, you sure know how to convince a guy. I guess we're staying."

"Great. Could you go find Declan Simmons for me? I think he's around here somewhere, and it's getting kind of close to midnight."

I'd walked right into that one. I tried not to laugh, but Ella knew I was fighting a smile. When she burst into laughter, I finally lost my composure. "Declan Simmons? You're such a brat."

Ella laughed harder.

"Sounds like the real party's over here."

Our laughter faded into surprise as we looked up to see Astrid Graves smiling down at us. "Hope I'm not interrupting. I've been trying to snag a few minutes with you all night."

It took all of my acting skills to hide my shock. I'd been meeting the best of the best all night, but Astrid Graves was something else. She was only six years older than me and already had *three* Oscars—one of which she won at nineteen, making her the youngest woman to ever receive Best Actress at the Academy Awards. The beautiful brunette with eyes like ice had a regal air about her and was Hollywood royalty, if ever there was any—this generation's Audrey Hepburn. I'd never had the privilege of being in the same room with her, much less had her speak to me.

"Of course not," I said, rising to my feet to offer her my hand. "It's a pleasure to meet you."

"Likewise." She shook my hand and then smiled down at Ella.

Ella held her hand out but made no attempt to move. "Sorry. I need to stay off my feet if I'm going to last until midnight, but you're welcome to pull up a chair."

I offered her mine and quickly found another one to drag over. The two chairs next to the couch created this small, intimate circle in front of the fire pit that would be very difficult for anyone else to penetrate. Once I sat, I was just inches away from Astrid, and it was surprisingly hard to concentrate. Ella must have sensed I was flustered, because she reached for my hand and was trying very hard to suppress a smile. I narrowed my eyes at her, and she winked before turning her attention to the brilliant actress next to us.

The party attendant returned with some Advil and a bottle of water. Astrid waited politely for Ella to swallow a couple of pills and then said, "So…" Her gaze bounced back and forth between Ella and me, as if she were studying us. Eventually, she shook her head as if in disbelief. "The infamous Cinder and Ella in the flesh."

"Said *the* Astrid Graves," Ella quipped, shaking her head with her own fair amount of incredulity.

I was startled by Ella's playful taunt. Here I was, unable to string together a coherent thought, and Ella was *teasing* the woman. Was there anyone she wasn't intimidated by?

Astrid's eyes widened with surprise, but she quickly followed that with a laugh of delight. "Touché, Miss Rodriguez."

"Call me Ella."

"Only if you'll call me Astrid. It's nice to meet you."

"Is it lame if I say it's an honor? You're one of my favorites."

Mine too.

Astrid accepted the compliment with the grace of a true

princess and then studied Ella and me again. I still couldn't think of anything to say to her, so the silence stretched out. Just before it got awkward, Astrid clapped her hands together and said, "Okay, confession time. Zachary Goldberg is a dear friend of mine, and he's been hounding me for weeks to play Marguerite in *The Scarlet Pimpernel*."

Ella and I both gasped. Ella shot me a look that contained as much shock and excitement as I felt. Could I really get to work with both Zachary Goldberg *and* Astrid Graves? That was more than I would have ever hoped for. I held my breath as I waited for Astrid to continue.

"I've always wanted to do a period piece," she said, making my stomach flutter, "so I read the script the second Zachary sent it to me, and I loved it." She met my eyes. "But I hesitated when he told me that you were signed on to play Sir Percy. I've been sitting on an answer for weeks."

That fluttering in my stomach turned into a dull churning, but I forced my face to remain calm. I didn't think she'd explain all of this just to tell me I was the reason she passed on the project. I really hoped not, anyway. I wasn't sure I'd survive that kind of disappointment or rejection.

Ella knew me well enough to know I was freaking out internally, because she firmly squeezed my hand. When I glanced at her, she gave me a confident smile. "Breathe, Brian," she said softly. "I'm pretty sure you've got this one."

I about had a heart attack at Ella's boldness, but Astrid laughed and nodded her head. "She's right. I was curious about all the buzz, so I went to see *The Druid Prince* on opening day, and I called Zachary on my way home from the theater to let him know I wanted the Marguerite role. Contracts won't be signed until next week, but Zachary's promised me the part is mine, so it looks like you and I will be working together soon."

I sucked in my first breath in a full minute, and it immediately escaped my lungs in the form of a disbelieving laugh. I tried to speak but couldn't form any words. My head shook as I attempted to wrap my head around the news. I was going to star in a film directed by Zachary Goldberg opposite Astrid Graves.

"It seems you've rendered him speechless," Ella said. She nudged me playfully.

"Sorry. I'm just...wow. I'm honored. I've always wanted the opportunity to work on a serious production, but I never dreamed..." I let out an incredulous laugh, still reeling from my good fortune. "Thank you," I finally spit out. "For taking a chance on me."

Astrid shrugged, as if it were no big deal, even though I was sure she knew exactly how big of a deal this was for me. I appreciated her nonchalance. "I'm looking forward to it," she said, surprising me even further. "With Zachary leading the charge, it's going to be a first-rate production. I'm curious to see what you'll accomplish when you have some real talent to work with, for once." Her smile turned conspiratorial. "I suspect you'll shock the hell out of this town even more than you already have. I'm looking forward to being part of the next Brian Oliver scandal."

My jaw dropped again, and Ella smirked at me with enough amusement sparkling in her big blue eyes to make me blush. Barely restraining her laughter, she grinned at Astrid. "Being participant to one of Brian's scandals is an experience, for sure."

Astrid laughed, but I could tell her amusement was directed at Ella instead of me. I was certain the conversation was about to shift focus to my *infamous* girlfriend. Though that might normally make me nervous, I was relieved this time just to have the attention off of me. I needed a minute to recover from this conversation.

"Said the woman with quite the impressive scandal of her own," Astrid teased, throwing Ella's earlier jest back at her.

Ella laughed and repeated Astrid's earlier response. "Touché."

"And speaking of that particular juicy scandal..." Astrid took Ella's raised brow as permission to continue. "I have two good friends who have been watching us from the bar since the moment

I came over here, and they are salivating at the chance to talk to you. Would you mind if I introduce you?"

Ella seemed startled. "They want to talk to *me?*"

"Yup. Would you mind?"

"I guess not."

BRIAN

ELLA GLANCED AT THE COUCH SHE WAS TAKING UP AND THE LACK of room to include more people. When she started to move, I jumped up from my seat and stopped her. "Hang on. You stay put." I grabbed the end of the couch with Ella's feet and scooted it back away from the fire to make more space. Once I did, Grammy-winning country music star Carla Wilson and her famous photographer brother Nash joined us, snagging a few nearby chairs and widening our little circle.

After introductions were made, Carla looked Ella over from head to toe. With the way Ella was sitting, her feet were on display and her ankles were exposed. Her close-toed slipper-shoes hid most of the damage to her feet, but some of her scars were still showing. That's not what Carla was looking at, though; she was checking out Ella's dress.

"My brother and I have been discussing how beautiful you are all night long," she finally said to Ella.

"Positively breathtaking," Nash agreed.

Considering Carla was quite the vision herself and Nash could compete with me in the looks department, the compliment had some punch to it, and Ella blushed. "Thanks."

"Your dress," Carla said, scanning Ella head to toe again. "It's fabulous. It's like it was made to fit you, both physically and in personality. It's simplistic in its design and yet both classy and sexy. It shows off just enough while letting you still feel secure, I'd imagine."

It was a polite way of saying it covered Ella's scars while not looking like it was trying to. I agreed the dress was brilliant for that very reason. I didn't mind Ella's scars at all, but I knew she did, and when I saw her in this dress, and saw the way her entire face beamed, I knew I'd underpaid Glen and Steffan. And I knew I'd never let anyone else make a dress for her ever again.

"It does," Ella agreed. "I have some very good friends who can work magic with a sewing machine."

"Magic, indeed. I *knew* it was an original. It's too perfect for you." Carla leaned forward in her chair. "Who are your designers, and do they take other clients? Are they going to do your Oscar dress?"

I smirked. Carla was a cat ready to pounce. I understood her excitement, though; a great dress was powerful in the entertainment industry and hard to come by. And Ella's dress really was *that* good. If Glen and Steffan were looking for a career change, this dress was all they needed.

"*Oscars?*" Ella asked. She whipped her head toward me. "I hadn't thought of that."

Her panic was cute. "Relax. You've got time, and I'm sure Glen and Steffan will be thrilled to make you an Oscar gown."

"Glen and Steffan," Carla repeated. "Do they have last names? A business name? A phone number?"

Nash leaned forward, resting a hand on Carla's knee. "*Chill,* sis. You're coming across as desperate."

Carla huffed, and Nash rolled his eyes as he shot us an apologetic smile. "She ended up on a worst-dressed list after the

Grammys last year."

Astrid, Ella, and I all winced.

"See?" Carla muttered to Nash.

Ella relieved Carla of her misery. "Their last name is Euling. They're actually costume designers for the TV show *Celebrity Dance Off.* They make all the dresses for the dancers."

"Hmm," Carla said thoughtfully. "I haven't seen it. Guess I'll be binge-watching Netflix all day tomorrow." Her eyes flashed with hope. "Do you think they'd design me a dress for the Grammys?"

Ella shrugged her shoulders and shook her head. "I don't know. I know they love their gig, and I don't think they've ever designed anything for a private client before this. But I'd be happy to ask for you."

"Oh, thank you," Carla gushed. "Be sure to tell them how much I love your dress, and tell them I'm willing to make it very worth their while."

Ella laughed. "I'll do that."

Ella hadn't brought a purse, so I pulled my phone from my pocket and had Carla program her number in for me.

"Thank you, thank you, thank you. Oh, I hope they say yes. I am not being labeled worst-dressed *ever* again."

"That's great, sis; now shut up about the lovely dress," Nash said, waving her off with his hand. "On to more important things."

The smile he flashed Ella made me certain I knew where he was going to take this conversation. He was one of the most world-renowned photographers in the business and most known for working with people of interest in creative—often *nude*—ways. The poor bastard was about to get shut down hard.

"So, Ella, I heard Lindon's offered you a modeling contract…?"

His voice trailed off into a question. Knowledge of the contract was public; what he was asking was if Ella planned to accept it. Ella snorted right on cue. "Yeah. That's not going to happen."

Everyone laughed, but Nash's grin grew Cheshire. "I was really hoping you'd say that. Forget Lindon and his lingerie. Let *me* reveal you to the world."

Even suspecting the offer was coming, it was startling to hear. Nash Wilson didn't make offers; he accepted them. And at a very high price. Most of the people at this party—A-list status and all—would kill to do a photo shoot with him.

Nash must not have blabbed his intentions to his sister, because she and Astrid both gasped. "Oh, Nash!" Carla squealed, gripping his arm. "Will you *really?*"

"If she'll let me. I'll even do it for free. I just want to shoot her."

She squealed again and turned all of her giddy excitement on Ella. "Can you believe it? I was hoping he'd ask you, but I wasn't sure. I can't wait to see what he does with you! You're going to look so amazing!"

"Wait." Ella took in Astrid's amazement and Carla's excitement, then frowned at me before saying, "I don't understand." She pointed at Carla. "You, I recognize, and you said he's your brother…" She looked at Nash. "So…you're a photographer?"

Nash's eyebrows flew up, and both Carla and Astrid gasped again. I chuckled at their surprise. Nash seemed to take the lack of recognition in stride. "He's not just any photographer," I said, bringing her hand to my lips for another light kiss.

"No," Astrid agreed. "He's *the* photographer. And what he's offering you is *extremely* generous."

Ella looked to me for confirmation, so I nodded. Maybe she wanted more of an answer, but I didn't want to sway her one way or another. I wanted her to take him up on his offer, but I didn't want *my* desire influencing her decision. I didn't want her doing it if she was going to be uncomfortable.

"He's the best," Carla said. "But he's ridiculously expensive, and he's *beyond* snobby about who he'll photograph. He rejects 99 percent of his requests. This is the offer of a lifetime."

"No kidding," Carla said. "He's never even shot *me*, and I'm his sister. I'm so jealous right now."

Nash chuckled and patted Carla's shoulder. "Ah, sis, you

know you can't take it personally. I can't shoot just anyone—even if they're as beautiful as you."

Carla huffed, but I could tell she was mollified by the compliment.

"Why can't you accept everyone?" Ella asked. "What makes you decide who to photograph and who not to, if it's not just about money or beauty?"

"Everything and everyone has beauty in them somewhere. It's my job to recognize that beauty and enhance it," Nash said. His voice became earnest as he was overcome with passion. "You see, Ella, I don't simply take pictures. I'm not a photographer. I am an *artist*. I create works of art. My subjects are my canvas, and the camera is my paintbrush. I have to feel *inspired* to take on a project. The camera has to *speak* to me."

Ella considered his words and slowly nodded. "That makes sense. But are you really so inspired by *me* that you'd not only volunteer to take my pictures but do it free of charge?"

"*I'm* that inspired," I offered with a suggestive waggle of my brow. "Especially if we're talking about nude photos."

"BRIAN!" Ella shrieked. She started to yell some more, but then she balked and snapped her panicked gaze to Nash. "That's not what we're talking about, right? You can't possibly mean a *nude* photo shoot."

"I was hoping." Nash nodded cautiously. "Tastefully done, of course, and only showing as much as you're comfortable with. What I'd like to do is—"

Ella didn't let him finish. "*No way.* That's worse than asking me to parade around in lingerie."

Nash sat back, folding his arms over his chest, and frowned deeply at Ella. "What I'm suggesting is nothing even remotely as tacky as that."

"She didn't mean to insult you," I said quickly. "She's offended by the offer. She was raised very strictly and isn't used to such a liberal way of life. She probably can't picture what kind of photographs you're talking about."

Ella was perturbed that I'd spoken for her—and she'd yell at me for it later, I had no doubt. But whether she knew it or not, she didn't want to offend Nash. This opportunity really was special. Even if she didn't do a nude shoot—which I knew she wouldn't—after she really thought about it, she'd probably change her mind and take him up on the pictures. I'd try to help her understand later, when we had some time alone to talk about it privately. Once she quit yelling at me, of course.

Nash's eyes narrowed on me for a moment, but I managed to convince him she meant no harm. His shoulders relaxed, and he sighed. "I'm talking about *art*, Ella, not *pornography*."

"I *understand* what you mean," she growled, with a special glare for me. Oh yeah, I was in trouble. "But art or not, I'm not taking any naked pictures. At all. Ever. For anyone." Chalk up another dirty look for me. "Including *you*, mister."

That made everyone smile a little, so I hammed up a frown and pretended to be heartbroken. "Not even just a—"

"Don't even *think* about finishing that sentence, if you value your life."

She was getting more annoyed with me by the second, but the others were laughing at us now, which was a good thing. I kissed her hand again, tempted to just lift her up and set her in my lap so that I could kiss more than just her hand. But that wouldn't go over very well with her mad at me. "Sorry. I'll behave now. Promise."

She snorted as if she trusted that promise as much as she'd trust another chance meeting with Erik Clarke.

"Ella, it's not what you think," Carla said, coming to her brother's defense. "He'll make you the most beautiful woman alive. He has a way of making everything beautiful, so you don't have to worry about showing a little skin, scars or not. I promise you can trust him to make them look as natural as a dusting of freckles."

"Not completely nude, then," Nash negotiated. "I'm sure we could find something you're comfortable with, but the *point* is to show the world your scars and let them see how beautiful you still are. It would do no good to cover you up. Not that you don't look radiant this evening."

The anger bled from Ella's face, and insecurity washed over her. She took her hand out of mine and hugged her arms tightly around her while biting her bottom lip. If she weren't in a dress, she'd be hugging her knees to her chest right now. I hated seeing her that way and hated that the others were witnessing her fear. She probably hated that, too.

"Ella, it's only an offer," I murmured, moving from my chair to the edge of the couch. I forced her hands apart and purposely took the scarred one into my hands. "You don't have to do anything you aren't comfortable with. You *know* that. Forget Erik Clarke. The bastard lied to you, manipulated you, and then exploited you. No one who knows you will blame you if you can't share yourself with the world, and anyone else doesn't matter. You don't *owe* anybody anything."

Ella shut her eyes and took a deep breath, as if she were fighting back tears. I brushed my thumbs back and forth over her scarred hand. "I love you, Ellamara. No matter what you end up doing." My audiobook voice may or may not have been used intentionally. "*I* know what this means to you, and *I* know how brave you are just for being here tonight. I know how far you've come. Even if you never share yourself with the world, it won't mean you're weak, and I'll never stop being proud of you."

My softly-spoken words subdued the group around us. I wished this moment could have been private, for Ella's sake, but at least it made those watching us start to understand how hard this was for her.

When she opened her eyes, they were shiny, but she didn't cry. She met my gaze, and, with a timid nod, leaned forward to rest her forehead against mine. I smiled encouragingly and couldn't help sneaking an early kiss, even though it wasn't twelve yet.

"I'll promise you one thing, though," I said when she sat back. Some of the color had returned to her face, though she still looked visibly shaken. "Nash isn't Erik Clarke. He would never try and trick you into doing something you wouldn't do otherwise. He's not asking to take your pictures because he means to exploit you."

"Of course not," Nash whispered.

Ella finally glanced up and met the waiting looks of sympathy and encouragement. Carla even had tears in her eyes. She mutely shook her head. Ella eyed Nash and then pinned her gaze on her lap as she mumbled, "How can you be so sure? What other reason is there to make such an offer, if not for the fame and publicity or the money selling his pictures would give him?"

"For the art," Nash replied.

Ella met his eyes again, uncertainty clouded in her own.

"I don't need the money, Ella. And I'm already one of, if not the most famous, photographers in the world currently. I've already got more work than I need. But from the moment I saw you in that cute little yellow dress at *The Druid Prince* premiere, I've wanted nothing but the chance to work with you. You're a breathtaking woman, and the scars only enhance your beauty. Where others see imperfections, I see uniqueness. I don't see flaws; I see beautiful distinctions that set you apart from everyone else in the world. I see the miraculous creation that you are."

Ella swallowed, but she was calming down. I wasn't surprised. That was a hell of a speech. And because he meant every word of it, his sincerity shone through in spades.

"When I look at you," Nash whispered, his eyes slipping out of focus as he drifted into thought, "I see a mysterious and beautiful enchantress, much like the very woman you're named after. My hope is to do a shoot depicting that. I see you in a mist-filled magical forest beside a small brook, surrounded by tiny faerielike creatures. I picture you with flowers in your wild hair and delicate gossamer wings sprouting from your back."

He reached his hand out to Ella, to the one I still held—her scarred one. "May I?"

Ella sucked in a breath, and I froze, waiting for her to give me any kind of sign that I should intervene. A tense heartbeat of time passed, and then Ella reluctantly placed her shaking hand into his.

He held it for a moment, and then, very slowly, began brushing his fingers over her scarred skin. "Beautiful," he murmured to himself. "So much softer than I imagined." Without relinquishing her hand, he met her eyes. "If you'd let me, I'd put your skin on display in a beautiful and natural way. Elegant and tasteful. Nothing graphic would show. Maybe just enough of a curve here or there to pose as tempting—like a beautiful water sprite, playful and seductive at the same time, luring in your prey with your overwhelming beauty. I'd use soft mood lighting to even out your skin tones and then pull out the natural color of your striking eyes to give you the appearance of a mythical faerie goddess. I imagine you as the most breathtaking creature that ever existed, and your scars would only enhance your mystique."

My mouth went dry as I created a vivid image in my mind of the picture he painted. *Ellamara as my mysterious, exotic, magical, wild faerie goddess...* Holy shit, did I ever *want* those pictures. I wanted that entire day on that set. Hell, I wanted to play the role of the helpless lost woodsman under her spell. I wouldn't even have to act the part. Forget Cinder and Ella as superheroes. I had a new fantasy. And if anyone could bring it to life, Nash Wilson could.

"That *does* sound beautiful." Ella's quiet, shaky voice pulled me from my daydreams. "I...I'll think about it, okay?"

Nash, with a small, accepting smile, released her hand and sat back. "Come by my gallery sometime. I can show you plenty of examples of the kind of exposure I'm talking about, though I don't think any of them hold a candle to your potential. We could discuss every detail of the shoot beforehand—no surprises—and you could have final approval on every photograph released in any capacity."

Ella nodded again, lifting my spirits a little and giving me hope that she might find the courage to do the photo shoot. It would be so good for her, because Nash knew how to do his job well. Ella would, indeed, look so stunning that not even she would be able to hate the pictures. She would finally see herself as beautiful the way I see her. And the world could shut the hell up and leave her alone.

"I'll do that," she said. "I won't make any promises about doing the photo shoot, but I would like to see some of your work."

Nash grinned. "It's a date, beautiful. And…I suppose you could bring the boyfriend along, if you must."

His eyes briefly flicked to me, making my adrenaline spike. Was he going to invite me to join her? I knew better than to ask, but damn it, I wanted in. He must have seen the desire in my eyes, because his lips twitched before he looked back at Ella. "We might even be able to find some room for him in a picture or two, if you agree to the shoot." He glanced at me again, and his smile turned crooked. "You wouldn't look so bad bare-chested with pointy ears, wearing a pair of leggings."

Hell yeah! An elf is way better than a woodsman.

Ella snorted. And *not* softly. "If you think you're scaring him with the threat of tights, you're sorely mistaken."

Everyone laughed, and I shamelessly puffed up my chest, flashing them all a proud grin. "Oh, I'm all in. And unlike my modest girlfriend, I have *no* problems with nudity."

As I knew she would, Ella slapped her hand over her face and groaned.

24

THE WHOLE MONTH OF JANUARY WAS ONE BIG BLUR. THE FIRST thing I did was sign an agent. I met with several, but in the end, Harvey Buchman was the only one I trusted to consider my personal concerns and help me build the career I wanted versus building the one that would make me the most rich and famous.

Once it was official, we squeezed as much into the two weeks prior to my surgery as we could. We started contracts on a movie deal, and a documentary, and Brian and I did a few talk show appearances. Then, my surgery and all the extra physical therapy took up most of the second half of the month.

Any free time I had I spent plotting the layout of the new *Ellamara's Words of Wisdom* with Scott. We'd made a great start, and Scott had convinced me right away to start some kind of webisode series. I decided to start a sort of video diary. I called it *My Fairy Tale Life*. It was just little five to ten minute episodes where I chronicled all the craziness of my life now that I was suddenly a celebrity. People were eating it up.

It'd been a crazy, hectic month but a very good one. And the best part about it was that I found a fantastic apartment. Now, it was February first, and I finally had keys. Today was moving day, and things had been severely complicated when this crazy delivery of random packages was dropped off from my agency's office early this morning.

Vivian, my good friend Rob, and I were all sitting in the living room, sifting through a sea of letters and packages when Juliette arrived. "Come in," I shouted when Juliette knocked, because I was buried in *stuff* and unwilling to risk knocking over any of the piles I'd sorted or tripping and killing myself in the chaos. "Thanks for coming. You're just in time to help us sort through everything."

"Just in time?" Vivian laughed. "You'd be *just in time* six hours from now, too. We're going to be here all day."

"Whoa," Juliette said when she stepped inside. "What *is* all this?"

I looked around at the clutter and sighed. "It's a combination of get-well wishes, fan mail, and housewarming gifts."

Juliette blinked at the mess. My living room, which didn't even have furniture yet, was filled to the brim with cards, balloons, flowers, and all sorts of random household items. It looked like I was opening all the gifts from the world's largest wedding reception.

"Remember how in last week's webisode she gushed about how excited she was to be moving into her first apartment?" Vivian asked.

"And then," Rob added, "she naively joked that she was going to be sleeping on the floor and eating off paper plates forever because she couldn't physically go shopping for long periods of time, and she didn't have any of her own stuff yet?" He waved at the pile of gifts. "Meet the result of that joke."

I groaned. Having over five million subscribers on YouTube had repercussions I'd never expected. I'd been posting one *My Fairy Tale Life* video a week since the beginning of January, and in just one month, I was already ranked in the top 300 most popular YouTubers. It was *insane*.

After last week's webisode went live—the episode where I got to take the bandages off after my surgery and I introduced my rehab team to the world—the fan mail and gifts had started arriving by the next day. The only physical address anyone had for me was my new management team's offices, so that's where people sent stuff. Because my agent was the head of the entire company, they'd been kind and stored the stuff for me, since I wasn't in my apartment yet. But when they'd dropped off a truckload of mail this morning, they'd kindly asked me to invest in a P.O. box and warned me they would be forwarding all deliveries to my apartment from now on. I didn't blame them.

When Juliette finally got situated on the floor with us, Vivian handed her a giant stack of envelopes to open. "Here. You can start with these. A lot of them are from retailers and have gift cards as housewarming gifts in them. Keep those. We're going to collect them all and donate them to a battered women's shelter or a children's group home or something."

"And I'm going through all the actual *stuff*," I said, holding up a small crystal clock that would look great on a bookshelf… as soon as I had a bookshelf. "You're all welcome to go through it, too, and then we'll donate the rest of it with the gift cards."

"Wow," Juliette breathed as she tore through the seal of an envelope. "This is crazy."

"Oh, and skim the fan letters," Vivian added. "Ella can't possibly reply to everything, so we're just looking for anything that seems important. If it's like little ten-year-old Marcie who is a car accident survivor like Ella and sent a thank-you letter with a picture because she's in a wheelchair and is trying to learn to walk again and Ella's an inspiration, then keep it. Ella wants those. But if it's just normal gushy *You're so pretty and funny* fan mail or nasty, perverted stuff, toss it."

"Unless it's *so* creepy and stalkerish that we need to give it to the cops," I joked.

Juliette glanced at me, stunned. "Have there been a lot of those?"

"None yet." I laughed. "I've just been on a Janice Bishop kick since Christmas, so my mind keeps going to all these dark, twisted places."

Juliette shook her head, both scowling and laughing. "That's not funny. It's only a matter of time before some psycho really does try to go fatal attraction on you, you know."

"Sorry. I guess it's not that funny when you put it that way. But hey, I'm safe here. Promise. The security in this building is really tight. Brian wouldn't have let me move in otherwise."

"Yeah, I noticed the security."

Something in her voice made me look up from the box I was opening. "What is it?"

Juliette hesitated but quickly broke. "Dad came with me today."

My eyebrows jumped up my forehead so high my face hurt. "Dad was *here?*"

She nodded gravely. "He was going to come up and try to talk to you, but he wasn't on your approved list of visitors. The front desk guy said he could call you and ask if he could come up, but Dad said no and stormed out because he didn't think you'd say yes."

I didn't know what to say. I wasn't sure how I felt about that. I wasn't as angry with my father anymore as I had been at first, but I was resigned to a life without him. I was even mostly convinced that I was better off.

Juliette sighed. "He's going crazy. It's been over a month, and you still haven't answered a single phone call or e-mail."

I ground my teeth. "That's kind of the point of disowning someone."

Juliette nodded, but she looked sad. "I know, but he feels so bad. He didn't mean for you to sever all ties. He was just angry that day because of all those things those jerks said about us. He was *scared*, Ella. He didn't mean to hurt you."

I closed my eyes and let out a long breath as I shook my head. "He never *means* to hurt me, but he always does."

I didn't think Juliette would mention anything else about it, but she very quietly said, "I think he's learned his lesson this time.

I get it if you can't forgive him, but I really wish you would at least try."

When I finally looked at her, her eyes shone with a layer of moisture. "He's a wreck, and we all miss you. Even Ana does. She was finally starting to warm up to you."

I frowned. "But I still see you all the time, and how much can Ana really miss me? I've said to invite her every time you've come over since I left." I looked around the room. "I notice she's not here...again."

Juliette's eyes flashed with anger. "It's not the same, Ella. You were part of our family, and now you're not. And Ana is just embarrassed. She feels guilty. The lingerie thing was her fault. Even Brian said so. She thinks you both blame her and hate her."

"Oh, come on. Brian was just pissed at Dad that day. He even apologized right away."

"Yeah, but he still thought it enough to say it."

I sighed. "Well, technically she did start it, but in her own way she'd only been trying to help me, and if not for Erik Clarke— which she had no clue about—it would have been fine. We don't blame her. You know we don't."

"Yeah, *I* know you don't. But, have you ever tried to tell Ana that? Have you spoken to her at all since you left, or just invited her over through me?"

Juliette held my gaze with unrelenting directness while I mulled over her scolding. That was one of the things I loved about her. She spoke her mind. She loved me and supported me and was my friend, my sister, even. But when she was mad at me or disappointed in me, she let me know it. This time, she was right.

With a nod of acceptance, I pulled out my phone and dialed Ana's number—quite possibly for the first time ever. Juliette quirked a brow, but some of the light came back to her eyes and the side of her mouth twitched, threatening to turn up into a smile.

"Hello?" Ana's voice had an edge to it and held a fair amount of astonishment, but she'd answered, and it hadn't been with a

What the hell do you want?

Figuring Ana wouldn't appreciate some sappy apology, or even for me to bring the topic up at all, I simply said, "Get your bony butt over here. Dad brought Juliette over, so I know you have a car. Juliette will need a ride home eventually, and I need another minion to come help me sort through all this junk. And before you snark, minions get to claim any treasures they find that I don't want—of which, I assure you, there are plenty—so hurry up, before everyone else snags all the good stuff."

Amused grunts and snorts sounded all around me. One even came through the phone, and Ana said, "My butt is *not* bony." There was a short pause, and a less certain voice said, "I'll be there in twenty minutes."

I wasn't surprised when the call cut off. "There," I said, as I texted her the address and parking instructions. "She'll be here in twenty minutes."

I got a bunch of curious looks, but no one said anything. We all just got back to work. Juliette decided to break the silence as she ripped open a letter. "So I'm sure Rob didn't mention that he's seeing someone."

"*What?*" I gasped, whipping my head to my strong and silent friend. "You didn't tell me that!"

Rob rolled his eyes. "It's not serious."

"It's totally serious," Vivian said, earning a look of annoyance from Rob.

When I grinned, he shot that annoyance at me. "We're just kind of hanging out right now. It's nothing worth all their fussing."

He nodded toward Juliette and Vivian and went back to concentrating *really* hard on the envelope in his hands.

"Does she have a name?" I teased. "How did you guys meet? What does 'hanging out' mean? Kissing? Dating? Exclusive? Are you smitten? Come on, I want *details*. I hate that I'm so out of the loop now that I don't go to school anymore."

"Her name's *Marian* Fitzwalter," Juliette said, giggling hysterically. "Just transferred to Beverly Hills Prep after Christmas break.

She's a super cute brunette who seems kind of sweet but feisty."

"Kind of like someone else we know." Vivian laughed, giving me a pointed look. "Seems our coveted soccer captain has a specific type."

Rob shook his head at the jest and tossed the letter in his hands into a bulging trash bag before reaching for the next one on his pile.

I grinned when I noticed the slight blush on his cheeks. Rob had crushed on me for a while. People made it out to seem like it was this huge, epic crush, and I'd been afraid when I had to let him down, that I'd break his heart. But if he'd been left pining, he'd never shown it. We'd easily remained close friends. I was glad he'd found someone else.

"*Wait,*" I said, as something occurred to me. "*Robin Loxley* is dating a girl named *Marian?*"

Juliette and Vivian burst into laughter, as if they'd been waiting for me to make the connection this whole time.

Rob groaned. He *hated* Robin Hood references, and still hadn't forgiven his parents for naming him Robin when his last name was Loxley. They thought they were being clever, but instead, they'd simply cursed their son to a lifetime of torment. His only defense was that his last name was spelled differently than the old heroic outlaw from folklore. He always mentioned that, but it totally didn't help. The poor guy. He'd started punching anyone who called him Robin somewhere around the start of middle school, and the teasing mostly stopped after that. Rob has a mean right hook.

Deciding not to torture my friend any more than I'm sure he'd already been teased since the development of this new relationship, I settled for shaking my head. "What a crazy coincidence."

"Or maybe it's *fate,*" Juliette said, eliciting another groan from Rob.

He ripped into another envelope with a sigh, muttering something about *ridiculous parents* and then sprang to his feet when the apartment's phone rang. "I'll get it."

He moved so fast that we all burst into laughter. After a quick exchange, he handed me the phone. "It's your doorman."

"Hello?"

"Hello, Miss Ella?" I grinned at the greeting. My doorman was a sweet little Puerto Rican man named Yeriel. I'd gotten pretty familiar with him when the surprise delivery truck showed up. I'd told him that he could just call me Ella, but he couldn't seem to drop the *Miss*. "I have another delivery for you."

"Another one?" My stomach clenched. Would they just keep coming? I'd have to hire a whole team of people just to deal with my mail, if this kept up.

"Yes, Miss Ella. Not to worry, though. It looks like it's just your furniture. Shall I send them up?"

"My furniture?" I hadn't ordered any living room furniture yet. I hadn't had time. Furniture was supposed to be my main to-do this week starting this morning, but I'd been sidetracked by the mail. "Um...is there a note or a card or something?"

"Hold on. I can check." I started to explain what was going on to my friends when Yeriel's voice came back with an understanding "Ah."

"Ah, what?"

"It appears the furniture is another gift. Would you like me to refuse it?"

"Uh..." I honestly didn't know what to say. "Someone sent me a whole living room set? Seriously?"

"Is it ugly?" Juliette yelled.

"What?" she said, when I frowned at her. "You don't have any living room furniture yet."

Over the phone, Yeriel chuckled. "It looks very tasteful, Miss Ella," he said, having heard Juliette. "And expensive. It's nice. You might like it."

I sighed. "All right. Send it up, I guess."

Yeriel laughed again. "Straightaway, Miss Ella."

When I hung up the phone, Vivian was pointing my video camera at me. "Dude," she said. "You just got sent living room furniture as a housewarming gift from a random stranger. This totally belongs on *My Fairy Tale Life*."

"Well, watch where you point that thing. Juliette doesn't have a signed waiver from her parents to be on my webisodes, and I seriously doubt Dad is going to let me put her on the Internet."

Juliette frowned. "I have to get permission?"

I nodded. "Scotty's making me do everything by the rules. Something about not wanting to get sued. Everyone who appears on the show has to sign a release form. You aren't eighteen yet, so you can't sign it yourself."

"Lame." Juliette pouted. "I'll ask, but you're right. Dad definitely won't agree to it."

Vivian shrugged as she took shots of all the piles of mail. "Whatever. We'll just have your face blurred out or something."

"Double lame."

I laughed just as there was a knock on the door.

"Who just sends someone a whole living room set?" Rob asked as he helped me to my feet.

"I don't know. Some designer who hopes I film lots of webisodes while sitting on it?"

"Are you going to keep it?" Rob asked.

I shrugged. "May as well, I guess. I don't have any yet."

"What if it's totally ugly?" Juliette asked.

I shrugged again. "Yeriel said it looked nice."

When I opened the door, Juliette dashed past me into the hall and gasped. "Oh, Ella, it's *fabulous!* We're totally keeping this!"

"We?" I laughed. "If you want it to stay, then come in here and help clear a spot for it."

The delivery guys looked surprised when they saw the mess in the living room. I grinned sheepishly. "You aren't the first to drop off a surprise delivery today. I guess just set it along the wall in the hall for now? It's going to take us a few minutes to make room for it."

"Sure." The burly mover guy motioned to his crew to set the stuff down and handed me a clipboard to sign. "We've got to go get the rest anyway."

"*The rest?*"

The man seemed indifferent to my surprise. His mind was already back downstairs with the rest of his delivery. He looked at his clipboard and nodded. "This is just the living and dining room stuff. There's a bedroom set and some office furniture, too."

I supposed I should be used to the surprises by now, but I still gaped at the man. "They're furnishing the whole apartment? *Who?*"

"Dunno, ma'am. Some interior designer to the stars. There's a card somewhere. We'll be back in a minute with the rest of it." He eyed the mess in my apartment warily. "Try to at least clear a path so we can get furniture into the other rooms."

With that, the man gathered up his other three guys, and they headed back to the elevator. I left the door open for them and turned to face my friends, stunned. "It's the whole apartment."

"Crazy," Vivian murmured.

Everyone jumped to action, trying to clear as much space as possible. A minute later, the house phone rang again. Considering the only time it had done that all day was when Yeriel called me, I groaned as I answered it. "Please tell me it's not another delivery. I honestly don't have room for anything else."

Yeriel laughed. "No, Miss Ella. Mr. Oliver and Mr. Thompson are here, but they have a couple of guests with them who are not on your list." He cleared his throat and spoke a little lower. "He, uh, said he recruited a little extra manpower to help with the move. May I send them up?"

I laughed once. "Yeah, sure. Brian and Scott are welcome to bring up whoever they want. Tell them they're right on time."

When I hung up the phone, I grinned at my friends who were still scurrying about the living room. "Excellent news. Brian's here, and he's brought help."

"*Brian Oliver* recruited help?" Vivian set another box out of the way and picked up the video camera again. "This ought to be good."

Not two minutes later, Brian called out using some kind of deep cheesy porno voice as he knocked on my door. "Special delivery for Ellamara Rodriguez."

I shrugged at the inquisitive looks my friends all shot me. "What can I say? He's a dork."

"Perfect." Vivian hit record on the video camera and gave me a cheeky grin as she pointed it toward the door. "We need shots of him when he's in a silly mood, because he's usually so grumpy or serious toward the public."

I let her have her fun. After all, the girl had a point. Even Brian's agents had mentioned I was good for his image because I made him seem more personable. "Come on in," I called. "Just be careful and watch your step. We've cleared a little room, but it's still pretty chaotic in here."

Brian walking through the door carrying a small coffee table wasn't wholly unexpected. The fact that he was *shirtless*, however, was a bit surprising. When I cocked a questioning brow at him, he gave me a big, cheesy grin to match the ridiculous porn star voice he'd adopted. "I've got a nice big package for you, Miss Rodriguez. Is there anywhere special you'd like me to stick it?"

My eyes bulged, and I slapped a hand over my reddening face. "Oh my gosh, *Brian!*" I shrieked while Juliette, Vivian, and even the extremely reserved Rob burst into laughter. "You did *not* just say that."

Brian finally lost his composure, and, after setting the coffee table down, scooped me into his arms to give me a kiss and a very insincere apology. "Sorry. I couldn't resist. And I didn't realize you'd have company."

He noticed Vivian holding the video camera and looked startled. "Did you just get all of that on film?"

"Oh yeah," Vivian said proudly, still aiming the camera at him.

Brian shot me a pleading look. "You'll edit that out of your webisode, right?"

I laughed louder than he had a minute ago. "Are you kidding?

What's more fitting for *My Fairy Tale Life* than Porn Star Brian delivering me *packages?*"

Brian narrowed his eyes at me, trying to figure out if I was serious. I held my smirk like a pro. Of course I wouldn't post it if he really didn't want me to, but he didn't have to know that yet. "Would you cut it if I gave you something better?" he asked.

"Better than Porno Brian?" Juliette asked. She sounded skeptical that something better existed. I have to admit, I shared her skepticism.

Brian whistled loudly. "Okay, boys! Bring it on in!"

I turned my eyes to my open front door just in time to watch two of Hollywood's biggest action stars—also minus their shirts—carry my new couch into my apartment.

My jaw dropped.

Jesse Ramos was a popular action movie star. If you needed a display of muscles, lots of guns, and explosions, Jesse topped your list. He'd been in a couple of Brian's dad's films, and I assumed that's how the two met.

Rhett Kessler was more of an action-thriller star. He was the sexy, smart, espionage type. His movies had lots of fancy parkour stunts and ninja fights for the action lovers and the quippy sarcasm and dreamy smiles that got the women to the theater along with the men. Brian had mentioned him before, and I'd gotten the impression Rhett was one of Brian's closer friends.

They were both *very* easy on the eyes. And they were standing, *shirtless*, in my living room waiting for me to tell them where to set down my new couch.

"Is it just me," Rob muttered, "or did the cast of *Hostile Take-over* just show up to help Ella move?"

"Holy crap!" Juliette said.

Vivian nodded. "Okay, yeah, we can erase Porno Brian for this. Talk about a fairy tale."

Both startlingly familiar faces grinned at my friends before turning their smiles on me. "Hope you don't mind us showing up unexpectedly," Rhett said, flashing me a boyish grin as he and

Jesse found a spot in the living room clear enough to set the couch down.

Jesse stretched after dropping the sofa and nodded in agreement. "Yeah, we ran into Brian at the studio, and when he mentioned you might need a little extra muscle today, well…" He flexed his arms and flashed me a cocky smile.

I finally managed to stop gaping and shot the man a wry smirk. "I'd say the two of you definitely qualify as muscle."

They both laughed, and Jesse stepped toward me, hand outstretched. "It's a pleasure to finally meet you."

"Finally?"

I shook his hand and held mine out to Rhett next. He ignored it and pulled me into a gentle hug, surprising me with both his sense of familiarity and his awareness of my condition. Never mind that he was *shirtless* and I was so much shorter than him that my face was plastered against his bulging pectorals. "Yeah, finally." He laughed. "This fool has talked about nothing but you since he met you at FantasyCon. I've been asking him for weeks when he was going to let me have a proper chance to steal you from him."

Brian laughed but pulled me away from his friend and tucked me tightly to his side. I was relieved to have the breathing room, but I gave a mental eye roll at the silent display of possession. I didn't think Brian even realized he was doing it. *Men.*

A knock and a tentative "Excuse me, miss?" had us all turning toward the door. The delivery guy was back with the rest of the furniture and was eyeing all the shirtless men in the apartment warily. When he realized who they all were, his mouth fell open. He glanced back at me with wide eyes, and I couldn't think of anything except to shrug helplessly and say, "Need some extra muscle to bring everything in?"

WHEN BRIAN STARTED TO FOLLOW ALL THE MEN OUT THE DOOR to start moving furniture in, I grabbed him and pulled him back to me. "Let them do it," I said, sliding my arms around his waist and leaning in. He didn't put up a fight. After a quick kiss hello got his complete attention, I said, "How was your day? How'd the table read go?"

The Scarlet Pimpernel was fully cast now, and today had been the first time they'd all gotten together to do a full read-through of the script. Brian had been a bundle of nerves and excitement this morning when he left.

"Incredible." His whole face lit up, and he shook his head in awe. "I still can't believe I get to work with all of those people. This film is going to be *amazing*. I'm the only one in the main cast without an acting award nomination."

"Well, next year you'll have one. You'll be a shoo-in thanks to this film."

Brian took a deep breath and nodded as if he was trying to convince himself that was true. He hadn't made the final list of nominees for Best Actor this year, but rumor had it he'd been close. He was a little disappointed, but not too much considering he'd never dreamed he'd get award buzz at all. It also helped that this year he was going to be the lead actor in a film that was sure to sweep next year's awards ceremony.

"I'm glad the read-through went well today. I was worried you'd be too starstruck having to work with your big fat celebrity crush on Astrid Graves."

"What?" Brian flinched at the accusation, and his face turned pink. "Where did that come from? I do not have a crush on Astrid."

"You're totally blushing right now."

Brian put his hand to his cheek and cursed when he realized it was warm. He got as flustered as he'd been New Year's Eve and then glared at the grin on my face. "Shut up, woman. It's not a *crush*."

This was so fun. "It's completely a crush."

"It's *admiration*," he grumbled. "Don't tease."

I couldn't help bursting into a fit of giggles. "I wouldn't dream of it."

His eyes narrowed on me, and he squeezed me tighter. "I'm sure you have a celebrity crush, too."

I totally did, but I couldn't let Brian know who it was. He'd kill me. "Pshhh. Who me? No way."

"No, you do." Brian shook his head, refusing my answer. "*Everybody* goes fangirl over someone eventually. When I find out who your celebrity crush is, you're going to be sorry."

I grinned evilly, not ready to stop tormenting the man yet. "Maybe there is *one* person who could make me swoon if I met him in person, but I'm not telling *you*. That's a secret I'll take to my grave."

I made that sound like a playful taunt, but I really hoped Brian never discovered my crush on rock star Kyle Hamilton that was a borderline fangirl obsession. Kyle is the lead singer of my favorite band. He was the first person whose poster I ever put up on my bedroom wall. He was also one of Brian's least favorite people on the planet. I'd mentioned liking Tralse once to him in an e-mail years ago, and I'd gotten quite the earful about what a douche bag Kyle was in real life, and that I should hate the whole band on principle. I hadn't mentioned it again.

"It's got to be someone really embarrassing, or you'd just tell me," Brian said, staring at me as if he were trying to extract the truth with his eyes.

Maybe someday I'd admit I went weak in the knees every time his arch nemesis stepped up to a microphone, but today wasn't going to be that day. I went for the shameless subject change. "How goes the search for the new assistant? Any acceptable candidates?"

Brian's grin turned into a pout, and I almost laughed. I knew that would distract him. "Hopefully horrible," he grumbled. "Then Scotty won't be able to leave me."

"There were a couple of potentials," Scott offered from across the room, happy to contradict his boss. He'd been the one holding interviews this morning while Brian was at his table read. Anyone who applied for the position had to get past Scott before getting an interview with Brian. Knowing Scott, I doubted there were very many who measured up.

I flashed Scott a smile. "Great. Would you mind forwarding me all the best applicants after Brian picks one?"

Scott raised his eyebrows with a laugh. "In the market already, are you?"

"Take a look around. I'm pretty sure I'm going to need help, if for nothing more than the fan mail situation."

"I'll say," Scott muttered, eyeing the boxes of letters and gifts he was currently helping stack on one side of my living room. "I pity your future assistant."

I laughed. "Me too."

Right about then is when Ana waltzed into the apartment with a puzzled look on her face. "Did I just see...*Rhett Kessler* and *Jesse Ramos* carry a desk down that hallway?"

"*Shirtless,*" Juliette chirped, bobbing her head enthusiastically. She patted the empty space on the couch beside her with a huge grin on her face. "Come have a seat, and enjoy the show with us."

"Just watch out for Jesse," Brian said, with a chuckle. "He's the biggest flirt in L.A., and he won't care that you're underage."

Ana shook off her shock and smirked at Brian. "If that's supposed to be a warning to stay away from him, your technique could use some work."

"He's got crabs," Brian offered.

Ana snorted. "Better."

"Is that true?" I whispered as Ana took a seat beside Juliette.

Brian grinned. "Doubtful. But now that's all she'll think about whenever he hits on her."

I was still laughing when a couple of the delivery guys stopped in front of me, carrying a giant headboard for what looked like a queen-size bed. "Miss, could you show us how you'd like the bedroom to be arranged so we can set up the bed?"

That question ended my moment with Brian, but he did come with me to offer his thoughts on how my bedroom should be set up—which he was surprisingly opinionated on. He didn't want the bed in the corner because he didn't want to have to crawl to the foot of the bed to get out of it whenever he had to pee at night.

When I reminded him that it was *my* room and that he had his own up the canyon, he muttered the word *technically* and told the men putting the bed frame together that he planned on staying over often enough that he deserved an opinion.

The delivery guys sided with me, of course, but I ended up caving and not placing the bed in a corner, even though it made the room feel a lot smaller. I had a feeling that moving out of Brian's apartment wasn't going to give me as much space as I'd planned on. It looked like I was going to have an unofficial roommate most of the time. I didn't know why that wasn't quite as scary as an official roommate, but it wasn't.

Once my presence was no longer needed, I was put in charge of ordering the pizza, since I couldn't do any lifting or moving. I had no idea how many pizzas it took to feed men as big as Rhett and Jesse, so I ordered a lot to be on the safe side and got a ton of chicken wings, too.

The food arrived just after the deliverymen left, and my guests attacked it with gusto. With everyone settled in, I got back to sorting my mail. Having a couch to sit on and shelves to put the knickknacks on helped.

Ana was the first to join me, while the others all laughed and joked in the kitchen. She sat down on the couch with caution and hesitated before speaking. "So...um..." For a moment, I almost thought she was going to try and apologize or something; guilt and remorse were all over her face. But she seemed to talk herself out of it at the last second and said, "What can I do to help?"

The offer was almost as surprising as an apology. I guess because, in a way, that was her saying she was sorry. I wanted to tell her not to worry about it. I really didn't blame her for the Erik Clarke thing. But I figured Ana was the type who didn't want to hear it. I was sure she just wanted to move past it and pretend it never happened. I could give her that much.

After handing her a box of unopened cards and explaining what I needed her to do, she got straight to work. The silence was awkward, so I tried to think of a way to break it. "Hey...um, have you ever heard of Nash Wilson?"

"The photographer?"

When I nodded, Ana shrugged and went back to skimming the current card in her hand. "Sure. My mom is a huge fan of his work. I think she'd faint if she ever met him in person. We went to some fancy event held in his gallery once, and she could hardly stand still. Have you seen his stuff? It's incredible."

It was the most normal conversation Ana and I had ever had. It was strange but nice, and I wanted to tread carefully so that I wouldn't take ten steps backward after this giant leap forward. "Yeah," I agreed. "Brian and I visited his gallery a couple weeks ago. His work was much more beautiful than I'd expected."

"What made you bring him up?"

"Well..." The question was again very cautious, and when I

looked up, Ana was watching me through wary eyes. I wondered if talking to her about this was a mistake. There was a good possibility she'd think I was trying to brag or shove Nash's offer in her face as a way to make her see that she was wrong about me. Hopefully that wouldn't be the case, though. "He's approached me. He wants to do a photo shoot to help me reveal my scars to the world."

Ana's eyes widened and then narrowed. "Why are you telling *me* this?"

I took a breath and met her eyes. "Do you think I should do it?"

Her eyes bulged to their limits this time, and her jaw went slack. "You're asking *me*? Why would you care what *I* think?"

I shrugged. "Because you won't hold back. You won't tell me what you think I want to hear. You won't lie and say everything will be easy, and wonderful, and perfect. You won't sit there and say that I'm so beautiful and it's the opportunity of a lifetime." I smirked and added, "You won't just say I should do whatever I want, either. I know you'll have an opinion, and I know you'll have your reasons for it. I want to know what they are. Please?"

Ana watched me for a moment, considering my words and whether or not I really meant them. She had an opinion, all right—a strong one—and she was trying to decide if I really wanted to hear it. Determination flashed in her eyes, and she sat up straight, pulling her shoulders back. She'd just decided to tell me whether I wanted the truth or not.

"Fine. I think you should do it."

I wasn't as surprised by that answer as I thought I'd be. She'd sided with her mom the night we first heard Erik Clarke's interview. I matched her resolve, lifting my chin a little and taking a breath. "Okay. Why?"

"Because you *need* to."

Okay, *now* I was surprised. Ana read the confusion in my expression and shook her head. "You are the most stubborn, confident, bravest person I've ever met."

I'd tried for a poker face but just couldn't manage one. Ana ignored my shock. I think she'd expected it. "You have it together in every aspect of your life, except where it comes to your scars. You're terrified of them. You're scared of what people think of them."

She had a point. Even just hearing her say it out loud like that had my heart racing. "With good reason," I mumbled.

Ana shrugged, unwilling to accept the excuse. "You say whatever you want on your blog. You rip books and movies apart, knowing there will be people who think you're an idiot for your opinions. You don't care. You don't care what anyone says or thinks about you. It's not what other people think of your scars that makes them so crippling to you. It's what *you* think about them. It's what you think about yourself."

When I realized my mouth was hanging open, I snapped it shut. I'd never thought about it quite like that before, but Ana was right. In every aspect of my life, I didn't care one iota about what people thought of me. Except my scars. And my limp. When it came to my physical disabilities, I was different. I was weak.

"You're confident to the point of arrogance," Ana continued, "with your thoughts and opinions on just about anything. That's why you can hold your own in a relationship with a guy like Brian. The two of you are equally matched. In every aspect except physical appearance. You have no self-esteem there at all."

Again, she was right. I probably was my own worst critic when it came to my physical appearance and capabilities. Every horrible thing I'd ever heard anyone say about me was nothing worse than the things I'd already thought of myself. Maybe that's why they hurt so badly. Because I believed they were true.

"It's holding you back," Ana said.

I frowned, confused, and Ana shrugged. "You have *Brian freaking Oliver* worshiping the ground you walk on and sleeping in your bed at night. I bet you've never taken your clothes off for him. I bet he's never seen all of your scars. I bet you've never let him touch them."

I blushed and glanced toward the dining room. To my

horror, the conversation around the dining table had fallen silent. They were giving Ana and me our space, but the whole room was listening intently to this conversation.

My stomach rolled, and I considered running to my room and testing out my brand-new bed, but I'd asked Ana for her opinion, and I'd said I wanted it because she'd tell me things even if I didn't want to hear them. I definitely didn't want to hear this, but I'd made my bed and now I was stuck in it. The best I could do was take a few deep breaths and force the bile to stay in my stomach.

"No," I whispered, because Ana seemed to be waiting for an answer, even though she already knew the truth. "I haven't done any of that." I tried to defend myself. "I'm just not ready. It's not because—"

"Oh, please." Ana rolled her eyes. "Yeah, you're a scared little virgin, for sure. But it's not your shyness that's holding you back. That's just the excuse you're using to lie to yourself about what the real problem is."

I stiffened. That was the first harsh statement that made me remember I was talking to Ana. It was blunt, abrasive, and cold. But was it the truth? She wasn't being malicious right now; she was just being honest.

"Prudes get over themselves pretty quickly when they find the right person. Brian is your one. You love him, and you have no doubt that he loves you, too. You've been living together for over a month. If you haven't gotten that far with him yet, it's not modesty holding you back; it's fear."

She was right. As much as I hated to admit it, she was absolutely right. I wanted to be with Brian. I really, truly did. And sometimes when we kissed, I physically ached with the need for more. But I always held back.

"You need to take those pictures because you need to face your fear," Ana said, bringing us back to the original topic. I'd completely forgotten all about Nash Wilson's offer. "*You're* the one judging yourself based on your looks," she said. "And until you get over it, you're never going to be ready for an intimate relationship. You're going to hold yourself back, you're going to keep yourself from Brian until he just can't stand it anymore, and you're going to drive a wedge between the two of you. You guys are a forever couple. If you don't make it, it'll be for this reason, and it'll be your fault."

It wasn't until Ana finished her speech that insecurity washed over her. I was surprised to see it. Surprised that she cared whether or not she'd pushed me too far. Before, she wouldn't have. Before, she probably would have reveled in the fact that I was frozen with emotion right now. That I was so overwhelmed by her words that I was too close to tears to even breathe.

Seeing the vulnerability on her face and the quick, nervous glance she shot toward Juliette and Brian in the kitchen, I realized she was doing the same thing I was. She was making an effort. Trying to find some kind of middle ground between us. Maybe we'd never be close the way Juliette and I are, but we didn't have to be enemies anymore. I got the feeling that our entire relationship in the future depended on how I responded to this very moment. I'd given her a chance, asked her to be herself, and she'd stepped up to the challenge.

Inside, I was a wreck. Her lecture had gutted me. But I'd asked her for it, and I was grateful she'd had the guts to give it. "Thank you," I mumbled. "I appreciate the honesty."

I forced myself back into motion, reaching for a new card. I pulled the gift card out of it and set it on a stack with the others.

"You're not going to do it, are you?" Ana asked. She was still watching me closely. "You're not going to take his offer."

I sucked in a deep breath and let it out slowly. "I'm not sure I can," I admitted.

Ana seemed to accept this and turned her attention back to her own stack of mail. "For what it's worth," she said with a softness in her voice I didn't know she was capable of, "I'm sure he'd make you look beautiful."

The compliment hit me as hard as her lecture had, because

it was equally as raw. I looked up, meeting her eyes, and had to swallow a giant lump in my throat before I could form any words. "Thanks."

She continued to look at me, and though she didn't smile, she nodded with 100 percent sincerity.

We both fell into silence after that and went back to our tasks. But the silence was comfortable now. Something had changed between us. We'd reached our middle ground. It was more than a truce. It was acceptance of one another. It was a long time coming, and it was a nice feeling.

I risked a glance toward the dining room and found Juliette beaming at me with watery eyes. When our gazes met, her tears spilled onto her cheeks and she grinned as if she were so happy it was painful. It made me chuckle. But then I saw everyone else trying not to look at me and realized that things may have been good between Ana and me now, but everyone else was drowning in awkwardness.

I cleared my throat and forced some cheer into my voice as I said, "So, Rhett, I was wondering something the other day…"

Rhett, surprised to be singled out, glanced around the group before giving me a curious look. "About me?"

I smiled. "Yeah. See, I read *Murder in Motown* last week, and Brian mentioned you were playing the lead in the movie."

The question broke the tension, and people slowly started to move again, throwing out their paper plates and napkins. Rhett wandered into the living room and found a seat on the floor near me. "Yeah, we wrapped on filming in December. It was great. I'm looking forward to the release."

"Glad to hear it. How was it doing a romantic suspense instead of the normal action thrillers on your résumé? I'm sure you were great in the role; I'm just surprised. I was wondering what made you take the job?"

Rhett's face lit up at the question, as if he were genuinely flattered by my interest. "Oh, well, actually, it happened because the author of the book had posted somewhere once that she'd always pictured me as her lead detective in this book. I guess her fans rallied behind her choice enough that the producers approached me first." He shrugged with surprising modesty. "It was pretty flattering, so I read the script out of curiosity, and then I read the book out of curiosity, because I liked the script so much." He grinned. "I've become a bit of a Janice Bishop fan since then."

I laughed. "You and me both. I just found out on Christmas that my dad was a super fan of hers, so I read her new one out of curiosity as well. I've been making my way through all of her books since then. She's good."

Rhett beamed a proud smile at me. "The premiere is in a few weeks. I've got a few extra tickets to give away still. You and Brian should totally come. Bring your dad, too. Janice Bishop will be there. I'd be happy to introduce you."

"Oh…" The mention of my father completely startled me. "Thanks, that's really sweet of you, but…"

"We'll totally take you up on that," Brian said, joining the conversation. He didn't mention my father at all, so I ignored it, too. It hurt too much to think about it.

"Cool. I'll get your names on the list."

Brian sat on the floor beside my legs, resting his back against the couch. He draped an arm over my lap and grinned at his friend. "Remember that thing I was telling you about for Ella's blog? When I showed you the artwork I had drawn up?"

Rhett was holding a big box in his lap, eyeing it as if it were a Christmas present he was trying to guess the contents of. He lifted his eyes from the package to nod at Brian. "The Cinder and Ella adventures web series thing?"

"Yeah."

"Hey, why don't you do me a favor and open that," I interrupted, pointing at the box in Rhett's hands. The curiosity was clearly driving him nuts. "See what's inside."

He winked at me and ripped off the brown packaging paper.

Brian picked up a box and opened it as well, while keeping up the discussion. "Your premiere would make a great first feature for *The Adventures of Cinder & Ella*. If you wouldn't mind letting Ella and me interview you for a minute that night."

Rhett laughed, but Jesse's snort was even louder. "So that Ella could post it on her super blog to all of her five *million* subscribers? Pretty sure he's not gonna mind. In fact," Jesse shot me a devastating grin, "if you're ever up for a *real* adventure, come visit me on my set sometime. I'm filming *Maximum Force 3* right now. If you come on the right day, we'll get you in some harnesses and let you feel an explosion."

His enthusiasm for pyrotechnics was cute. And so predictable that I laughed. "As awesome as that sounds, I think my nurse and my physical therapist would both have aneurysms if I tried that." When his face fell in disappointment, I said, "But we could totally blow up Brian. That could be fun."

"Yeah, sounds like a real *blast*," Brian said drily.

That got a good groan from everyone.

Jesse's grin was back with full force. "It's a date, *mamacita*. Don't back out on me, either, because when I tell the studio I landed us a feature on *Ellamara's Words of Wisdom*, they're going to be kissing my ass the rest of production."

I laughed again, but he wasn't joking. The influence I now had on Hollywood was completely surreal. I glanced at Brian, and he shrugged his approval, so I nodded. "Okay, it's a date," I agreed.

"Ooh!" Brian realized what Rhett was holding in his hands and yanked it away from him. "An espresso machine. A nice one." He grinned at me. "We're totally keeping this."

26

My father agreed to sign Juliette's and Ana's waivers to be on my web series under one condition—that I agreed to have dinner with him, just the two of us, so that we could talk. I didn't want to do it, but one look at Juliette's face and there was no way I could say no. I knew she was excited to be part of my video diary—and really she was such a big part of my life that it would be hard to work around her if she couldn't get permission—but more than that, I knew she was hoping I'd make amends with my father.

Jules had always been pro family healing. She hated the rifts that had been caused since I'd arrived in her family's life. After seeing how happy my smoothing things over with Ana had made her, I knew I needed to at least hear my dad out. Just once. But there was no way in hell I'd meet him alone. I told him I was bringing Brian with me and that he could take it or leave it. He'd agreed surprisingly easily, and, for some reason, that put me on guard even more.

Brian made reservations for a restaurant in Santa Monica that you weren't supposed to be able to get reservations for less than a month in advance. But I suppose that's what happens when the nation's current most famous couple calls and asks if it's possible to get a table for the evening. Magically, one always opens up.

Brian didn't make the reservation to impress my father. He did it because the restaurant had a reputation for privacy and discretion. The situation had the potential to be tense, and neither of us wanted the drama with my father to get leaked to the media. I would have suggested he come talk to us at Brian's house or my new apartment, but Brian said he and my father would both probably behave better if we were someplace public. Less chance of fighting then. It was sound logic.

"No wonder you picked this place," I muttered after we were given an amazingly secluded table that was almost fully enclosed in its own little cove.

"We'll have privacy," Brian promised. He noticed my knee bouncing beneath the table and placed his hand on top of it. "Relax, Ella; it'll be okay. He called you. Not the other way around. He's not coming here to start another fight."

"That doesn't mean he won't," I muttered.

"Hey." Brian pulled me into his side and held me close. "If he does, we'll just leave. And then we'll know for the future not to meet with him again."

I blew out a breath, trying to calm my pounding heart and twisting stomach. He was right. I no longer had to put up with my father. If I didn't like what he had to say, I didn't have to listen.

I stiffened when he arrived, and Brian removed his arm from around me to sit up straight. He took my hand beneath the table, though, and I laced our fingers together in a death grip. Assuming we made it to the actual act of eating dinner, he was going to have to eat one-handed because I wasn't letting him go until my father was out of sight.

Dad murmured hello as he sat down across the table from us and nodded when the server who'd shown him to the table offered to pour him a glass of wine. We all ordered dinner and then fell into a deafening silence. I was not going to speak first. This meeting had been at his request. If he wanted to talk, then he could talk. I'd only promised to listen.

When it was clear I wasn't going to give him so much as a greeting, he sighed and said, "Thank you for coming."

He looked pale and had dark circles beneath his eyes, as if he hadn't slept at all in the last six weeks. His wrinkles and few streaks of gray hair were more noticeable than normal, too. He'd had a rough month and a half since I'd left. *Good.*

"Ella…honey…"

My jaw clenched. Brian must have been watching me carefully, because he squeezed my hand once to lend support. It prompted me to release a breath I hadn't realized I was holding.

"I'm sorry," Dad murmured. He sighed and started twisting his napkin in his hands. "That doesn't sound like enough."

I shook my head, closing my eyes over a layer of moisture. "It isn't enough," I said. "Not this time."

His face crumpled, and his entire body sagged with the weight of my words. "I don't know what else to say."

"I'm not sure there is anything else you *can* say. You've said it all already." I steadied my voice and looked at him. "How many apologies have I received from you since moving into your home, Dad? They don't mean anything to me anymore, because I know that even if they're sincere, I'm just going to need another one in a few days, or weeks, or months."

"Sweetheart, I'm doing the best I can."

I shook my head in short, quick shakes that bordered on panic. "It's not good enough. I can't let you keep breaking my heart. One of these times it's going to be so broken that even Brian won't be able to glue it back together. You *crushed* me on Christmas. Permanently. I can't just get over that. I can't just accept your apology and pretend it never happened. Having you in my life, hurting me over and over and over again, *kills* me."

A shudder tore through me, causing Brian to pull me into his arms. He took his napkin and wiped at the few tears that had rolled down my cheeks.

I stiffened as the server brought our dinner to us, but Brian continued to hold me tight and did all the speaking necessary. Once the waiter was gone, Dad and Brian both reluctantly picked up their utensils, but I just stared at my plate.

Brian noticed I wasn't eating. He gave me another hug and put his own fork to his mouth but didn't bother telling me I should eat. He knew how upset I was right now. He knew there was no way I'd be able to choke down even a single bite.

Dad sighed when he realized I wasn't going to eat. When I looked up, he put his fork down as well and bored his misty blue eyes into mine. "Ella…" His voice gave out, and he had to wait out a bout of emotion. "I didn't mean to hurt you, baby. I love you."

I didn't want to have this conversation, but hashing it out was the whole reason for being here, so I steeled myself and forced the words out. "I know, Dad, but you can't help hurting me, either. You may love me, but I'm still your biggest regret in life."

"That's not—"

"No, I am." I wouldn't let him finish his sentence. I didn't want to hear the lies. He wouldn't lie on purpose, but he was lying to himself. "Jennifer, Juliette, and Anastasia…they're your pride and joy. I can tell in the way you talk about them, the way you smile at them, the way love them. It's different with me. We both know that."

"It's not that I don't love you, too; it's just complicated, baby. Your mother—"

"You're trying." I cut him off, not wanting to bring Mama into this. I didn't think I'd survive that. "I know you are. And I'm grateful for the effort. But even though you may like me, I'm your *consequence* more than your daughter. I'm a reminder of your mistakes and your regrets. You can't seem to get past that, so I'm not going to make you try anymore."

"Ella…baby…you're not *making* me try. I *want* to. I've wanted to make this work from the second the police called me to tell me about your accident. Not having you in my life this past month was a nightmare. You had surgery, and I couldn't be there.

You have a new apartment…a new life…I hate not being a part of it. Maybe things aren't perfect between us yet, maybe there will always be a slight difference between my relationship with you and the one I have with Jennifer and the twins. But what we have is better than nothing at all. Trying is better than losing you."

"For you, maybe. For me, it just hurts."

I sucked in a deep breath and held it a few seconds before letting it go in a slow rush of air. More tears spilled down my cheeks, and as I looked at my father and then felt Brian's warm, solid arm around me, I suddenly knew why I hurt so badly. "I don't want to be anyone's *consequence*. I want to be someone's pride and joy."

A silent sob wracked me, and I crumpled against Brian's chest. He scooped me up tight and leaned his head against mine. "You're more than my pride and joy," he said, softly stroking my hair with one hand. "You are my *life*, Ellamara. My heart. My soul. My everything."

Minutes passed. Neither man said a word while I soaked Brian's shirt with my tears. Once I got hold of myself, I sat back up, wiped my eyes and nose on my napkin, and took a sip of water. I was still shaking a little and I couldn't stop the straggling tears, but the ugly, uncontrollable sobbing was over.

I set my water glass back down and snuggled back into Brian's embrace before braving a look at my father. His eyes were red rimmed and his face was a mask of devastation. He met my gaze and then seemed to take in the whole picture before him, of Brian and me together—the way Brian held me, the way I clung to him for dear life, with complete trust. As he studied us, he shook his head in an absentminded gesture that was barely noticeable. "You aren't what I regret, Ella," he said quietly. "My mistake was walking away from you."

I wished I could believe that.

My dad sat back in his chair, eyes still roving over Brian and me together. "Your mother and I needed to divorce, but I shouldn't have left you both." His gaze came into focus, and he looked directly at me, beseeching. "You were an unexpected gift."

His eyes slid to Brian. "*He* is my consequence."

I frowned, unsure what he meant.

Dad sighed, eyes still locked on the man holding me. "I owe you an apology, too."

Brian didn't react, but I gasped softly. I hadn't excepted my dad to acknowledge his sins against Brian.

"I love my daughter," he said, his tone becoming firm but not angry. "I worry about your fame and how it will affect her. I worry about your reputation and your past history with other women. It's hard to believe you so suddenly changed, and that you won't hurt my baby girl."

"Understandable," Brian said, surprising me. "I would expect as much from a father who cares about his daughter. Now, understand this: the fame can't be helped, but I will do everything within my power to keep Ella safe and protected as we deal with it together. She will *never* be alone in this." Dad's jaw clenched, but he kept silent. "And as for the women…they were nothing but my misguided way of coping with Ella's loss in the first place."

Brow furrowed, Dad opened his mouth to ask a question, but Brian supplied him with an explanation before he could get the words out. "All of those years that Ella and I wrote to each other, I dated here and there, but never anything serious, and nothing to warrant my reputation. Even then, before I'd met her in person, Ella was the only one I wanted. I'd been waiting for her to turn eighteen. I planned to fly out to Boston after her birthday to meet her and her mother in person. I was ready to explain to them who I was and how I felt.

"After Ella's accident, when I thought I'd lost her forever, a part of me died. The women that followed were nothing but my way of trying to fill the void Ella's disappearance created. It was a stupid way to grieve, but that's what I was doing. Not one of those women ever came close to giving me even a fraction of the happiness I get from a single text from Ella."

Okay, as far as romantic declarations go, that one was pretty good. My face flushed, and I squeezed Brian in a tight hug, letting him know that I loved him just as much. His past didn't bother me a single bit. I understood, and I knew with all my heart that he was telling the truth. Those women meant nothing to him, and he'd never need them again.

He hugged me back and kissed the side of my head before continuing. "Since the second I received that first e-mail after Ella's accident, there hasn't been even a *thought* about another woman. Ella is the only one that matters. This sudden 'change' you're concerned about isn't a change at all. This is the real me, finally finding my way back from a dark place. I'm not going to hurt your daughter. I'm not going to leave her and go back to being a player. In fact, when we're old and gray and it's time to move on, even God himself will have a hell of a time prying her away from me. He's going to have to take us together."

I cracked a smile, picturing myself caught in a tug-of-war between Brian and the Almighty. It wasn't that hard to imagine.

"I understand your concerns where it comes to my relationship with Ella." Brian's voice lowered, turning hard as he said, "But the animosity you have toward me stops *now*. It's unnecessary, and it hurts her. If you can't accept me, you will lose her for good—if you haven't already."

Man, I loved my boyfriend whenever he went all alpha male on my father like that. It was always a little startling, and exciting, and just so, so, so *hot*. There was a reason he made the perfect Cinder on-screen. He had the confidence and the dominance to pull it off. My man could totally be a kickass warrior prince in real life.

I hid my grin for my dad's sake, because he didn't appreciate Brian's brashness the way I did. In fact, he loathed it. But this time, to my surprise, he took it. He swallowed his pride, and though every muscle in his entire body was stiff and his teeth ground together, he gave Brian a curt nod. "Fair enough. The two of you have my blessing," he said, shocking me so much I reared back as if the words had smacked me in the face. When he noticed my disbelief, he sighed again. "As I said before, I owe Brian an apology."

Dad rubbed his head and sipped his wine. Brian sat in silence, giving my dad time to figure out the words he needed to say. I held my breath, waiting for the explanation. Could my father have meant what he said? Could he really stop hating Brian and actually give us his blessing? It seemed too much to hope for.

"I know you love her," he finally said, his words directed at Brian. "That's been obvious since your appearance on *The Kenneth Long Show*. Any fool can see it."

And here I thought he couldn't shock me any more than he already had. I hand to pick my mouth up off the table to say, "I don't understand. If you know how much we love each other, then why hate him the way you do?"

Dad stared at me as if he knew the answer to my question and just didn't want to admit it out loud. After a quick glance at Brian, he grimaced and said, "Jealousy."

I blinked. He was *jealous? Of Brian?*

I glanced at Brian, but he was just as confused.

Dad sighed. "I'm bitter and resentful, and it was easier to take my anger out on him rather than own up to the fact that it's *my* fault you'll never be my baby girl."

"What?" I gasped.

Dad shrugged. "Everything he said to me on Christmas was the truth." His gaze lifted to Brian. "You *are* the man in her life, and you were long before I came back into the picture. She used to call out for you—for Cinder—when she was in the hospital. When she was half conscious and the pain was too much, or she was grieving for her mom, she'd cry your name, over and over. I never understood what she meant at the time."

My eyes widened at this unknown truth, and Brian hugged me just a little bit tighter.

"You're the one she turns to for everything," Dad said, defeat thick in his voice. "You're the one who makes her feel better, who puts smiles on her face, the one she trusts... You *do* know her better than me, and you *can* take better care of her."

Brian's body tensed ever-so-slightly. It was the only clue he gave that he was affected by my father's words. I knew him well enough to know what it meant. He was trying not to get his hopes up.

Brian's own father was a difficult man, and as much as Brian disliked the guy, deep down, he still sought his approval. Earning it didn't happen often. He'd been so excited to meet my dad the first time. I believed he saw himself as a perfect catch for a woman. He was smart, responsible, independent, he could provide for any woman he dated, and he was sincere in his feelings for me. He'd expected my father to be happy about our relationship and to be proud to have him dating me.

Reality was a severe blow to my confident boyfriend's ego. He'd never said so, but my father's disapproval hurt him. It showed in the way he was so quick to lose his temper with my dad and become defensive. Brian never bothered to get defensive with anyone unless he truly cared what they thought about him. My dad got under his skin so easily because, just like with his own father, Brian wanted to earn my dad's approval. He wanted my dad to like him and be proud of him. He wanted his trust and wanted him to see how well he could take care of me.

"Dad…"

My father's eyes snapped back to me at the sound of my quiet voice, and I almost chickened out of speaking. Brian started stroking my hair again, giving me the strength I needed. "All of those things you just said about Brian…those are *good* things. Fame issues aside, he is exactly the kind of man any father would be proud to have dating his daughter."

Dad glanced at Brian again, and then his face softened when he looked back at me. "I know, baby. And I'm glad that you've found someone who can take care of you and loves you as much as he does. I've been unfair to you both, and I'm sorry for that." His eyes bounced between the two of us again. "You really do have my blessing. It's just a hard pill to swallow."

"But *why?*"

Dad gulped and answered my question in a voice rough with

emotion. "Abandoning you was the biggest mistake of my life. Not having you, and not being with your mother, but *leaving* you. I knew that the second I heard about your accident. I sat in that hospital, and I thought either I'd watch you die and that would be my punishment…or you'd live and I'd be given a chance at redemption. When it became apparent that you were going to survive, I knew God had given me an opportunity to fix my mistakes. And I wanted it, baby. I wanted you. You were my little girl, and I was overjoyed to have a second chance. I was so excited to bring you home and make you part of my family. But that turned out to be a lot harder than I thought it would. I'd hurt you too badly. I saw how deep your wounds were, and I didn't think you'd ever forgive me."

He looked away and cleared his throat as he took another sip of his wine. When he composed himself again, his eyes found Brian instead of me. "When Ella reached out to you, and the two of you started talking again, the change in her was instantaneous. With you back in her life, she was a completely different young woman. I knew, then, that I was too late. She'd never be my little girl. I'd already lost her to you. I'd been the fool to leave her, and in my absence, she found you. Not only that, but you did such a good job picking up my slack that she didn't have any need for me at all."

"Dad…" He wasn't trying to make me feel bad, but I was starting to feel a little sorry for him.

He shook his head, his eyes never leaving Brian's. "You are a better man than I am, Brian Oliver, and you deserve her more than I do. I finally realized that when I hurt her so badly she handed her fate over to you and walked out of my life without so much as a glance back. The worst part was, I couldn't blame her. I'd been the one to drive her away. I'd been the one to break her heart.

"I couldn't even worry about her because she was with you; I knew you would take care of her. I knew if anyone could fix some of the damage I'd caused, you'd be the man to do it. I *hate* you for that. And I love you for it, too."

"Dad…" My tears had returned. I hadn't noticed.

"I'm sorry, Ella." He shut his eyes and shook his head. "So incredibly sorry."

After a deep breath, he opened his eyes again and met my gaze. "I've failed you every step of the way. I've hurt you so badly I feel like an ass for even wanting this, but please don't cut me out of your life entirely. Don't walk out on me the way I did to you. *Please*, baby. I don't want to lose you again."

My head was shaking before I knew how to answer him. "Dad…I just don't know. I can't keep doing this with you. We go in circles, and every time it hurts that much worse, cuts that much deeper."

I sniffled, and Brian handed me his napkin. I shamelessly blew my nose in it. The restaurant was probably charging two hundred dollars a plate for our dinner. They could afford to replace one cloth napkin.

Pain flashed across my dad's face and he shut his eyes again. "It'll be different this time," he whispered. The promise sounded sincere, but I couldn't trust it. "I've been humbled, Ella. You finally got through to me. I understand that you can't be my little girl— you *aren't* a little girl. You don't need someone to raise you anymore. I missed out on that opportunity. *That* is my regret—my consequence that falls entirely on *my* shoulders. I can't even really claim the role of your father—I lost that privilege when I gave you up. I will accept that, if you give me one last chance. I'll stop trying to be someone to you that I don't have a right to be. I'll accept Brian in your life and simply be grateful that you found someone to fill the spot I left vacant. I'll welcome him into the family like the son I never had, if that's what it takes to prove myself to you."

He looked to Brian again, and I saw the sincerity in his eyes when he said, "You're a good man. I was wrong to judge you so harshly, and I'm sorry. If you can find it in you to forgive me, I mean it that you can be as much a part of my family as Ella is. The two of you are a package deal. I'm ready to accept that."

"Thank you," Brian murmured, sounding more reserved than I'd ever heard him. "I appreciate that."

Dad met his eyes again and shrugged. "Kind of have no choice. All four of my girls love you too much."

One side of Dad's mouth quirked up into a half smile to let Brian know he was teasing him. Brian returned the gesture with a ghost of a smile and a small nod, but he said, "It'll always be Ella's call. She's my priority. I'll support whatever she decides 100 percent."

"Of course." Dad's head bobbed up and down, and then he looked at me with hope bleeding from his eyes.

My stomach churned with indecision. I couldn't say yes, but I couldn't say no, either. "I need some time," I whispered.

Dad's face drooped. Some of the light left his eyes, but he tried to hide his disappointment. "I understand. Take as much time as you need. I'll wait." He swallowed again. "I really am so sorry. I hope you can forgive me someday, and even if you can't, thank you for not giving up on my girls because of me. Believe it or not, Ana needs you in her life, and Juliette would be devastated to lose your friendship."

I shook my head and finally managed a small smile of my own. "She won't."

I looked down at my untouched plate, and my stomach rolled again. I felt my dad's eyes on me, knew he was wishing and hoping that I'd suddenly become okay. That somehow, through the course of this dinner, I'd accept his apology and tell him he was forgiven and that we could have a relationship. I wasn't ready to make that decision, and I couldn't sit here under the weight of his hope.

"I'm sorry," I whispered, and looked up at Brian desperately. "I need to go now."

Brian didn't ask questions. He flagged down our watchful server, signaling for the check, and two minutes later we were on our feet. My father just sat in his seat, staring at his own untouched plate. "I do appreciate the apology," I said. "And I *will* think about it."

He nodded, unable to lift his eyes to mine. I suspected they were full of tears he didn't want me to see.

27

Rhett Kessler's red carpet interview for *The Adventures of Cinder & Ella* was golden. Who knew Rhett was such a comedian? He'd come to the premiere tonight armed with a slew of cheesy pickup lines that he'd memorized in Spanish and kept using them on me randomly throughout the interview. I couldn't stop laughing, and Brian was annoyed because he didn't know what Rhett was saying. To be honest, I don't think Rhett knew half of what he was saying, either. Especially not when he outed himself as a homosexual. I started laughing so hard I couldn't stop.

"Oh come on, that one was romantic," he said, pouting when I hunched over my cane, unable to breathe from laughing so hard.

"You're right. It was." I gasped, clutching my aching side. "Very romantic. Do you realize you just told me that I'm so beautiful I make you wish you weren't gay?"

"*What?*"

Rhett's face paled, and I doubled over again. This time, Brian burst into laughter with me.

"And the one before that, you compared loving me to having *diarrhea*."

"That *bastard*." Rhett grumbled something under his breath

that I was fairly certain I'd have to bleep out before posting the video. Then he shot me a sheepish smile. "I guess that's what I get for trusting a friend to translate some pickup lines for me." He scowled into the camera. "Thanks a lot, Jesse. I hope you enjoyed that one, you jackass."

Brian's laughter spiraled nearly as out of control as mine. "You trusted *Jesse Ramos* to translate for you? Were you *crazy?*"

Rhett frowned. "He's the only person I know who speaks it. I didn't want to just google translate a bunch of stupid crap. I wanted to sound authentic."

"It was very authentic," I promised. I tried to stop laughing for the poor guy, but I just couldn't calm my giggles. "You used perfect grammar, and your pronunciation was great, too. You were loud and clear for all my Spanish-speaking viewers."

I lost it again and had to grab onto Brian's arm so I wouldn't fall over. "We should probably call it quits now," Brian said, patting Rhett on the shoulder sympathetically. "Before you kill my girlfriend with laughter or admit to the world you have impotence issues or something."

They were *both* going to kill me. "Oh my gosh, stop! I'm dying! My stomach hurts, and I'm not wearing waterproof mascara!"

"Right," Brian said, laughing into the camera. "I think things have deteriorated to a point of no return so, we'll just call it for the night. We're off to see the show!"

"Thanks for tuning in," I added. "It's definitely been an *adventure*. We'll see you next time!"

I'm pretty sure the last thing the camera caught before it was shut off was Rhett cursing Jesse Ramos and promising retribution when we filmed Jesse's feature.

While Brian laughed with Rhett, I caught my breath and then took my camera back from my dad with an awkward thank-you. I'd finally broken down yesterday and invited him and Jennifer to come tonight. It had been last minute, and I didn't think he'd show because he doesn't like the whole celebrity scene, but he'd surprised me and shown up right on time, dressed in one of his best suits.

Jennifer was draped on his arm in a beautiful floor-length cocktail dress, like the perfect arm candy. She'd been smiling the entire time, looking a little starry-eyed to be on the red carpet, but Dad had been very reserved so far. "That was, um…interesting." He spoke gruffly, but the side of his mouth was twitching like he really wanted to smile. It helped ease some of the tension.

I smirked. "I met Jesse a couple weeks ago. He's quite the character. Rhett probably should have known better."

"I think it turned out cute," Jennifer said. "People are going to love it. You'll have to subtitle everything he said on the video."

"Oh, I will," I promised. "It's too good not to."

"You'll help me get him back, right?" Rhett asked, clasping a hand lightly on my shoulder. "I've got to do *something* to restore my dignity."

I patted his hand and kissed his cheek. "We'll think of something. Promise."

His grin returned. "We'll do lunch sometime and come up with a plan. For now, come with me. There's someone I want you all to meet."

We were already inside the lobby of the theater. Rhett had needed to do the press thing with the *actual* press on the red carpet, so we'd waited for him to make his way inside. The movie was supposed to start soon, and most people were making their way into the theater to sit down, so the crowd in the lobby was starting to thin out. I noticed right away who Rhett was heading for and smiled to myself when I heard my father's quiet intake of breath.

Janice Bishop isn't how I'd picture a typical writer. She seems more like someone who would work in my father's office. She's beautiful and looks younger than she is. She's stylish and sharp and just radiates intelligence. It makes sense now that I've read some of her books. Her attention to detail is phenomenal, and the subject matter is so intense and complicated. It would have to take a very smart, very patient woman to write the way she does.

When she saw us nearing her, she beamed a bright smile and held out her hands to me. "Ella! Darling! I'm so glad you could make it!"

Not at all surprised by the informal greeting from a total stranger, I gave her my one good hand to squeeze and leaned in for the kiss to the cheek, addressing her by her first name as if we were old friends. "Janice. It's a pleasure."

I was so getting this Hollywood thing down.

"I can't tell you how surprised I was when my publisher told me you'd requested the new book and would be reviewing it. I was honored that you'd take a chance on me and a new genre."

I might have been getting used to the Hollywood *people*, but the idea that I had real power and influence among them was still so hard to believe. Every time someone flattered me, I just didn't know how to respond. It was so strange. "Really, you have my father to thank. He's such a big fan of yours that it made me curious. He's a hard man to please." I let go of her hand and pulled my dad in front of her. "Janice Bishop, this is my father, Richard Coleman. He's a district attorney for L.A. County."

"Oh, *wow*." Janice's eyes lit up with pleasure. I thought she might like that. "No pressure, huh? I hope I got everything right."

My dad chuckled and extended his hand to her. "Always," he said as they shook. "Your knowledge of the way things work astonishes me. You truly have a gift, Ms. Bishop."

"Oh please, call me Janice. And may I call you Richard? You know…my next manuscript is going to be set here in Los Angeles, dealing with some of our local gang activity. I've got a lot of research to do still. A district attorney for our great county would be the perfect man to have on my speed dial."

My dad puffed up his chest with obvious pride. I'd never seen him look so pleased in my life. "Call me anytime, Janice," he said. "I'd be honored to answer any questions you have."

I stepped back, letting him introduce Jennifer and enjoy his moment with *his* celebrity crush. I wondered if meeting her might soften him to Brian's world a little. I hoped so. I know he said he'd welcome Brian into the family, but I wasn't sure that welcome would include Brian's career or lifestyle. I worried he'd still keep Brian at arm's length or try to keep the twins from doing things with us because of the fame. Hopefully, tonight would show him that it's not always like it had been on Christmas. So far, so good.

Brian sneaked up behind me and lowered his mouth to my ear. "Let's head in." When I glanced at my dad, Brian chuckled. "He looks like he's doing just fine."

Sitting down sounded like the best plan ever. I'd been on my feet a long time now. "Dad, we're going to go find our seats. We'll see you in there."

Dad was chatting away with Janice and didn't hear me, but Jennifer nodded. Her face softened when she looked at me and she mouthed, *Thank you*. I gave her a nod and a smile of my own and then watched them a moment before heading into the theater with Brian. He squeezed my hand, as if sensing my sudden insecurity. "You okay?"

"Did I do the right thing? Inviting my dad tonight?"

Brian looked back at my father and sighed. "I think it's the right thing, because you want it to be."

He was right. I did want things to work out with my dad. We had our issues, and they were huge, but he was my *dad*. Dr. Parish had encouraged me to try one more time with him. She seemed to think it would be easier now that I wasn't dependent on him and he wasn't responsible for me. I hoped she was right.

"I do want it," I whispered. "But I still can't help worrying that I'm just setting myself up for more disappointment."

"He came tonight, Ella. He's here."

I sighed. "You're right. He is. And I know he hates this kind of thing."

Brian chuckled. "He doesn't seem to be hating it right now."

No. He didn't. He, Jennifer, and Janice were all laughing about something, and Dad was using his hands as he spoke, waving them around animatedly. "I'm glad he's having a good time."

"Me too."

With nothing else to say on the subject—only time would tell if letting my father back into my life was a mistake—we headed into the theater. Someone had been kind and reserved the handicap-accessible seats for Brian and me so that I wouldn't have to walk up any stairs or try to climb past any people down the cramped aisles.

The theater was full and slightly on the warm side. I wanted to take off my jacket before I sat down, but it took me a second to work myself up to it. The shirt I was wearing beneath it was a halter-top that revealed both of my shoulders and most of my back. I'd worn my mother's dress to Brian's premiere, so people had seen some of my scars before, but that didn't make it any easier to show them off this time.

I'd asked Vivian for help with my first outfit for *The Adventures of Cinder & Ella*. I'd told her I needed a different look for the show so that it felt different from my webisode that I did at home. She'd been *thrilled* with the opportunity to dress me, but she'd gone pretty daring.

I'd promised her and Juliette at Christmas that I'd start wearing more things that showed off some of my scars, and she was cashing in on that promise tonight. She'd told me that this was a good first step in getting me more comfortable with Brian. She said it was like taking baby steps. I kept repeating those words in my head, trying to convince myself she was right.

Baby steps. This outfit was a step in the right direction…if I could only take my jacket off…

I had on a long, stylish bright red halter-top blouse that was backless, sleeveless, plunged a little low in the front, and clasped behind my neck. Vivian had coupled it with these shiny black leather jeggings, a cute black leather jacket, sparkly ballet flats, and a bowler hat. Candy had stayed home this evening, and I'd gone with a classic black cane. I looked like some kind of rock star mobster. My outfit was funky, fancy, and informal all at once. I *loved* it.

Brian loved it, too. It was probably the sassiest I'd ever looked, and Brian's mouth had fallen open when he first saw me. He was definitely enjoying the bold, sexy style, though. I'd caught him staring a number of times tonight. And he hadn't even seen me without the jacket yet.

Baby steps. Baby steps. Baby steps. Take off the jacket, Ella.

"You okay?"

Startled, I shook off my nerves and focused on Brian. He was watching me with a worried look, waiting for me to sit down. "Sorry. Yeah, I'm fine." I slowly blew out a breath and pulled in a new one, holding it in my lungs as I peeled my jacket off one shoulder at a time.

Brian's eyes widened when he saw my top, but not all of his shock was due to my choice to wear something that revealed my scars. Heat filled his gaze. I blushed under his scrutiny and turned to lay my jacket across the back of my seat before sitting down.

When I turned around and Brian saw the back of my shirt, or rather, the lack thereof, he sucked in a sharp breath. He grabbed my hips and pulled me against him, my back to his chest. His hands slid around me and clasped together against my stomach, locking me in his arms. Burying his face in my hair and taking a deep breath, he moved his mouth to my ear and unleashed the full force of his audiobook voice on me. "Ellamara…" His lips pressed against the soft, sensitive skin just behind my ear. "Do you have any idea what you are doing to me this evening?"

Goose bumps exploded up my arms, and I shivered. "Maybe a little." Amusement seeped through my breathy confession. "Maybe that was the point."

Brian's grip on me tightened, and he growled quietly before saying, "I'm staying at your place tonight."

Not a question. A demand. One I was more than happy to succumb to, but I still teased him. "You have to be up early tomorrow, and your place is a lot closer to the studio than mine."

"I. Don't. Care."

I turned around in his grip to smile at him and snap him out of his mood before he acted way too inappropriately for being in a crowded movie theater. "Good. I was just making sure."

Right before he lowered his mouth to mine, a cute couple maybe a year or two older than me passed us, and the girl stumbled to a stop. *"Wicked scars,"* she said, startling Brian and me from our private moment.

We turned to her, a bit shocked. "Excuse me?"

The girl was tall and slender with long, bright red hair pulled back in a ponytail. She was wearing jeans and an old-school Dead Kennedys T-shirt made to look vintage. Her eyes were locked shamelessly on my shoulder and arm. I'd have been offended if I weren't so stunned by the look of awe on her face. "Those are so hard core," she said. Her eyes flicked to mine, and she smiled. "How'd you get 'em?"

I startled again, and Brian stiffened next to me, offended on my behalf by her brazenness. I was so shocked that my response was automatic. "Fire. Car accident."

"Whoa. They're freaking sweet. You look like a total badass."

"Ellie," her boyfriend hissed. He gave Brian and me both an apologetic grimace.

The guy was maybe Brian's age and very good-looking. Tall with dark hair and blue eyes that popped as much as mine did. The sympathy in them was easy to see. "I'm sorry. She has no filter. Or tact."

"What?" the girl scoffed. "I'm *admiring* her scars. That's not rude." She glanced at me again, her smile a little less sure. "Seriously. You're awesome. I've got one, too. Not quite as cool as yours, but check this out…"

Brian and I glanced at each other as the woman lifted her shirt to show us a series of long slashes across her stomach. I gasped, horrified, because what on earth could have caused a scar like that? It looked like she'd been sliced open.

The guy sighed as if this was a common occurrence for the audacious woman. Oddly, I found myself endeared to her. If only I could be as confident about my scars as she was with hers. Any offense I'd felt disappeared, and I smiled at her. "That is impressive. How…" I started to ask the same question she'd asked of me but couldn't quite get the insensitive words out.

This girl didn't care at all. "I got knifed," she said proudly as my jaw fell wide open. Brian looked just as appalled. The girl noticed our shock and shrugged, as if it were no big deal. "I'm from Detroit."

This, she said as if it were supposed to explain everything. I cracked a smile, and a small laugh escaped Brian.

Ellie's boyfriend, looking relieved to have the tension broken, held out his hand. "Hi. I'm Seth Bishop."

"Bishop, as in Janice Bishop?" I asked as we shook.

He grinned. "Her nephew." He shook Brian's hand next and nodded toward the redhead. "And this crazy woman is my girl-friend, Ellie."

"Hey, me too," I said as I shook her hand. "Well, close. I'm Ella."

She arched a brow. "Short for Eleanor?"

"Ellamara."

She huffed. "Lucky you. I'm Eleanor. Ellamara is way better. It's, like, exotic. Eleanor is such an old, crotchety grandma name. I'm going to feel compelled to yell at children in my old age."

Brian and I both laughed. She was too funny.

"So," I said as their names registered in my brain. "Seth and Eleanor. I'm sensing a distinct correlation between you and the two lead characters in this film."

Seth laughed, and Ellie rolled her eyes. "Unfortunately," she said. "Get involved in a serial murder case when you live across the street from Janice Bishop, and that's what happens."

Serial murder case? I looked to Brian, but he seemed just as confused. Seth took pity on us. "Do you remember the Saturday Night Murders in Detroit about five years ago?"

"Of course. That's the case *Murders in Motown* is based on, right?"

Everyone had heard of that serial killer. He was the only thing on the news all summer. The guy killed a girl a week until he was caught. Always on Saturday nights—hence the nickname. He had a particular taste for redheads and used knives as his weapon of choice... My gaze went to Ellie's fiery hair again and then to her stomach. When I put the pieces together, I clasped a hand over my mouth to stifle a gasp.

"You're Eleanor *Westley?*" Brian asked quietly. Guess he remembered all the news from five years ago, too.

Ellie's smile turned wry. "In the mangled flesh." She proudly patted her stomach.

A surprised laugh bubbled out of me before I could stop it. "I can't believe you can joke about that."

Ellie blinked at me, unable to fathom why not. "Are you kidding? I joke about it all the time. I tangoed with a serial killer and lived to tell the tale. You bet your skinny butt I'm gonna own that story. Can you believe after my wound healed the doctors offered to do plastic surgery to *remove* the scar?"

"You didn't want them to?" I asked, shocked by the horror in her voice. Her scar went across her entire stomach in an ugly zig zag of angry lines. She looked like she had quite an athletic body, but bikinis were definitely out. Then again, she was happy enough to pull her shirt up for me a moment ago. She probably wouldn't care about a bikini.

"Heck no," she said, and up went the shirt again. She rubbed her hand over the raised jagged lines. "This is my battle scar. I *earned* this. No way was I going to let some dumb yahoos take it away from me. Think about it." She pointed to my damaged arm. "You've obviously been through something horrible. *Fire?*" She shuddered at the thought of being burned. I shuddered with her, at the memory, and Brian pulled me into his arms again, as if he hated thinking about it.

"Look at you now," Ellie said, waving a hand at Brian and me. "Strutting around here, looking freaking gorgeous, and dating Brian freaking Oliver. No stupid car accident's gonna get you down. After everything you went through and how much you must have had to fight to survive something like that, wouldn't it suck to just one day wake up and look *normal* again? Like none of it ever happened?" She rubbed her scar again. "I know I'd be sad."

"I'd be sad, too," Seth murmured. He pulled Ellie back against his chest and held her tightly just as Brian had held me earlier. "I love your scar," he murmured against her ear, rubbing his hand over Ellie's stomach. "It's proof of just how kickass you are, my sexy little firecracker."

Ellie snorted. "You didn't find my missing teeth sexy, and that proved how kickass I am, too." Ellie flashed Brian and me a wide smile. "Front two teeth are fake. I play women's ice hockey for the University of Minnesota. Took a high stick right in the mouth during last year's championships. They had to call time to wipe all my blood off the ice and find my missing teeth."

I blinked. This girl really was slightly crazy. But in a very cool way. Brian and I laughed again while Seth shook his head at her. "That was different. I couldn't kiss you while your face was broken. Your scar, though…that is very, very kissable."

Seth's hand disappeared beneath the hem of Ellie's shirt. Though Ellie had just pulled her shirt up to expose her stomach and had rubbed her scar, Seth's actions were completely different, and I blushed.

Ellie elbowed Seth so hard he was forced to let her go. "Later," she grunted, glaring at him. "Sorry," she said to me, with a roll of her eyes. She took in my burned arm again and then smirked. "But I guess you know how it goes. Guys and scars, right? Can't seem to keep their hands off them." Her grin turned wicked. "Another reason I'd be really sad to lose it."

My eyes widened, and she laughed, pointing up the stairs to where their seats were. "Anyway, the show's going to start any minute, so we're going to go sit. It was nice meeting you both."

"You too," I muttered.

I watched them climb the steps to the seats near the back of the theater, shaking my head in awe of the woman. She was so different. And her attitude toward her scars was…well, I didn't even have words for it. She seemed so happy and confident and proud of her damaged stomach. And there was no question she liked it when her boyfriend touched it. And there was *definitely* no question he liked to do that. Her stomach was a mess, and yet, Seth had been turned on by it. He really, truly found it sexy.

I swallowed at the thought that Brian might be that way, too. He never tried to touch my scars like that, but then, I'd never offered him the chance. I kept them covered as often as possible. He probably thought I didn't want him touching them. And maybe I didn't. But… I thought of the strange couple again and how comfortable they both were with Ellie's body. Maybe I was wrong to not let Brian touch me. Maybe I—maybe *we*—were missing out on something special.

BRIAN

I'd never met a woman quite like Eleanor Westley before, and it was clear as she and Seth walked away from us that Ella hadn't, either. Ella stared after them, lost in deep thought, until they found the row where their seats were and slipped into the crowd.

"Interesting woman," I said, tugging Ella's hand, prompting her to take her seat. She'd been standing for a long time now, and I was sure she was sore.

"Very," Ella agreed absently.

She sat down very slowly, as if feeling stiff, but she still seemed so lost in her thoughts that I didn't bother to ask if she was all right. I hoped she wouldn't hurt too badly after resting through the movie. After the New Year's Eve party, she'd started bringing her bottle of prescription painkillers with her to events and parties in case they turned out to be as taxing on her as that had been.

I didn't want her to have to take them tonight, though, because they made her tired and out of it. I didn't want a tired and spaced out girlfriend tonight. Not when she looked as hot as she did and had braved the shirt she was wearing. I wasn't sure what had prompted her actions, but they'd had major effects on me. Effects that I would be feeling all night long.

Ella wouldn't just miraculously be ready to go all the way with me tonight. Hell, the sleeveless blouse was probably the limit on what she could handle. She'd probably run home and change into a pair of sweats before she let me come anywhere near her, but I didn't care. Whatever the change in her tonight was, it was a step in the right direction, and I would take it without complaint.

"You okay?" I asked. She seemed so heavily weighed down all of a sudden.

"Huh?" Her eyes snapped into focus, and she seemed to realize she'd zoned out. "Oh yeah. Sorry. I'm good. I was just thinking…"

I waited for her to share her thoughts, but she simply fell into them again. I decided to be patient. She'd talk to me when she was ready. Now wasn't the time, anyway, sitting in a crowded theater where the lights had just gone dim. When the movie started to play, she smiled softly at me, surprised me with a kiss to the cheek, and said, "I love you."

Again, I didn't know where this was coming from, but it was oddly touching. I lifted the armrest between our seats and tried to contain the burning feeling in my chest when she snuggled against me. "I love you, too, Ella."

Ella stayed in her strange, quiet, withdrawn mood through the whole film and passed when Janice Bishop, Seth, and Ellie invited Ella, me, and Ella's dad and Jennifer to join them for a late dinner after. I didn't question her, but I was really starting to worry.

We said our good-byes, and I resisted the temptation to speak all the way back to Ella's apartment. She would tell me. Once we were inside and settled, and it was just the two of us, she would tell me what happened.

I wanted to be patient. I wanted to let her be the one. But

when we got up to her apartment and I closed the door behind us, the words were out of my mouth before I realized I was speaking them. "Ella, what's wrong? What happened? What can I do? You're really starting to worry me."

She gave me another loving smile as she'd done just before the movie and kissed me. "Sorry. I'm fine, I promise."

She started to take off her jacket. I helped her out of it and hung it on the rack near the front door, then joined her on the couch.

"Did you see them together tonight?" she asked.

"Who?" I was caught off guard by the random question.

"Ellie and Seth."

Ah. So that was the direction of her thoughts. I tried to relax a little, but I still didn't know exactly what about them had made Ella so contemplative. "They were interesting."

She cracked a crooked smile as she stared off into nothing. "They were so comfortable with each other. Physically, I mean."

I automatically thought of Seth lusting over Ellie's scars and wondered if that's what we were talking about here. "True. But it sounded like they've been a couple for a long time."

Ella's gaze snapped into focus suddenly, and she looked me straight in the eye. "I want that with you."

I froze. The direct statement on a topic that had always been near impossible to broach with her made my pulse spike. "I want that, too," I said carefully.

She looked away from me. I didn't want to lose this connection we had. I didn't want her to withdraw. She'd braved sharing her thoughts with me. I didn't want her to stop now. Swallowing my nerves, I reached for her undamaged hand and held it clasped in both of mine. "We'll get there, Ella." When she met my eyes again, I said, "We *will* have that someday."

"I'm trying," she whispered, suddenly becoming overwhelmed with emotion.

My heart cracked at the sadness and frustration in her voice. "I know."

I pulled her face into my hands, cupping her cheeks gently as I pressed my lips to hers. When I sat back, I looked at her bare shoulders and decided to take a risk. I reached to gently grip her shoulders—both of them. I moved slowly, giving her time to stop me if she needed to. She swallowed loudly and trembled slightly when my hand rested on her burned shoulder, but she bravely allowed my touch.

"I was so proud of you tonight," I said.

I ran my hands down the lengths of her arms, both the healthy and the scarred one, until I reached her fingers and tangled them in mine. Her eyes fell shut, and her lashes trapped a couple of teardrops.

"*So* proud," I whispered again.

I leaned forward, skimming my nose along her jaw, and kissed the side of her neck once. Then, pushing her further than I ever had before, I dragged my lips down her neck and over her bare shoulder. She gasped as I pressed my mouth to her scars. The oddly textured skin tasted as heavenly as the rest of her did. I wanted to feel and taste it all. I wanted to explore every inch of her. One day, I would. Today, I would just be grateful for this small preview, for this new branch of trust I was being offered.

I threaded one of my hands in her hair, pulling her close to me, and ran the other up and down her damaged arm while dropping another kiss to her shoulder. "You are strong, brave, and beautiful, and I will take as much or as little as you are willing to give."

I sat back and met her eyes again. "If this is what you're capable of tonight, then this is what you're capable of, and it's enough. The rest doesn't matter yet."

She pursed her lips through a bout of emotion and then whispered, "Thank you."

I shook my head. "Thank *you* for trusting me this much."

I claimed her mouth, throwing some of the heat rising inside me into the kiss. Ella responded, but when I started to lay her back on the couch, she stopped me. "Would you give me a minute?"

"Of course," I said, though I wondered what was wrong again.

Reading my worry, she offered me a smile and rose to her feet. "I just want to take some Tylenol and change out of these clothes. I'll just be a minute. Want to make us something warm to drink?"

I smiled at the much more normal response. "Coffee for me, and hot chocolate for you?"

"Perfect." She kissed me again and then disappeared down the hall.

I took a deep breath as I headed for the kitchen. I needed to calm down. Ella often described me as intense. I didn't think she minded that, but I didn't want to overwhelm her, and after allowing me to kiss her scarred shoulder, I knew she must be feeling a lot. That's why she'd stopped the real kissing before it even began. She was in her room right now, probably layering herself in two or three layers of clothes just to feel like she was in control again.

That's not a step back.

I had to tell myself that over and over as I turned on the coffeemaker and heated some water in a mug for Ella's hot chocolate. I had to prepare for her being covered from head to toe and no longer in the mood to kiss when she returned. I had to be ready for that, because, no matter what, I couldn't let her see any disappointment.

I was stirring the chocolate in her mug when the tiny sound of a throat clearing alerted me to Ella's return. "Brian?" she said softly.

Thank heavens I hadn't been holding the mug of hot liquid in my hands, because I would have dropped it when I turned around and took in the sight of her. She'd changed from her clothes into a very sexy black satin kimono that barely went to her mid thigh. She looked...she looked...wow.

I blew out a big breath.

What the hell was she wearing beneath the robe, and why was she standing in front of me in it?

I leaned back against the kitchen counter, gripping it tightly so that I wouldn't step forward and use my eager hands on her. I wasn't sure what was going on here, but I knew it couldn't be what my body wanted it to be.

I drank in the sight of her and had to slow both my breathing and my thoughts before I could speak. "That's a nice robe." I cleared my throat and tried to sound nonchalant as I added, "Is it new?"

I wasn't fooling anyone. Ella's cheeks flushed, but she giggled and shrugged. "I found it in one of those boxes Lindon's sent me."

"It's very pretty." I had to clear the frog from my throat again. Twice. "So…um…what's the occasion?"

She glanced toward the living room as she rubbed her arms as if she had a sudden chill. I wanted to go to her. Heaven knows I had plenty of heat in me at the moment to warm her up with.

"No occasion," she whispered, still unable to meet my gaze. "I just…"

I waited for her to collect her thoughts. I could see them running away from her.

When she shivered again and shifted her weight, I finally stepped away from the counter and offered her my hand. "Let's go sit down. You've been on your feet a lot tonight. And you're shivering. I'll get you a blanket."

She took my hand, but instead of following me toward the living room couch, she led me back to her bedroom. My breathing quickened again. *Get a grip, Brian. This is not happening.*

Once inside, I waited for instruction, having no clue what she intended and not willing to presume anything. She sat on the edge of the bed and patted the spot next to her. I sat and laced my hands together in my lap, once again, forcing them into restraint.

Ella broke my grip and claimed one of my hands. I fisted the other one at my side, tempted to sit on it because Ella's robe was not tied very tightly, and it would be all too easy to figure out what was beneath it.

"You said you wanted to sleep over tonight," she said quietly.

I gulped. "Yes. I would like that. If that's what you want, too."

She nodded, causing another surge of adrenaline to rush through me.

"Would you still want to stay if I planned to sleep in…what I have on under this robe…but all we did was sleep?" Her voice shook, and she kept her eyes focused on the carpet.

Desire bubbled up inside me so thick I choked on it. My body and my head warred with one another, but there was no question of my answer. It wouldn't be easy, but I would stay all night and not lay a single finger on her, if that was what she asked. But I *would* stay. After putting such a promise in my head, she couldn't pry me away from this bed before sunup for anything.

"Yes." My voice was so thick I could barely form words. "I would still want that very, very much. As long as you wanted me to stay."

She sucked in a sharp breath and let it out slowly. "I do want you to stay. I want you to see me. What there is to see, anyway. But I can't do anything else." She finally met my eyes. "*That* is what I'm capable of tonight."

"Okay." I stayed calm. I don't know how I managed it, but I steadied my heartbeat, calmed my thoughts, and relaxed. Ella was anxious enough. She needed me to be the sure one right now. She needed calm and reassuring. I would be that for her.

What was happening right now may have been something I wanted very badly, but it wasn't about *me*. Ella was not doing this for me. This was for her, and so I would put aside all of my myriad emotions, needs, and desires. *I* would have to wait.

I suppressed a smirk. If Ella could hear my thoughts now, she'd fall over in a dead faint. The woman was not wrong that I am spoiled and self-centered. This might have been the first time I'd ever truly been willing to forget about myself and what I wanted.

"Are you sure?" I asked, though the question tasted like dirt on my tongue. "Because you don't have to. If you aren't ready for that, Ella, we can wait."

"No." She shook her head. "I want to."

Thank the Lord for his small and tender mercies.

"Tonight, watching Seth and Ellie, it just clicked," she said. "He didn't care. He even *liked* her scar. He was *turned on* by it."

I knew how he felt. It wasn't the scars themselves I found appealing. It was just Ella, and she, as she was, was beautiful to me. The scars were part of her. I couldn't imagine her without them. But I knew she struggled with them, so the thought of her letting me touch them, letting me see all of her, of her trusting me with her biggest fears and insecurities, *that* was enticing as all hell.

"He's not the only one who feels that way about his girlfriend, Ella."

I let my desire leak through in that statement; let her see the lust in my eyes. Hers widened slightly in response, but she quickly tampered her fear. "I believe you." She bit her lip and frowned at the floor again.

Ella sat for a moment, collecting her thoughts, and then shifted on the bed slightly so that she could face me. "I was thinking about it tonight, and I think... I'll never feel completely secure with you if I don't learn to like myself. It's not you I'm uncomfortable with. I'm afraid of my body."

"Ella, there's nothing wrong—"

"Let me finish."

I closed my mouth and took her hand in mine. She gave me a small, timid smile. "The truth is, you're probably a lot more comfortable with my flaws than I am, and if I can't figure out how to accept my body on my own, then maybe I should let you help me."

I brought her scarred hand to my lips but said nothing. As much as I wanted to shout that *of course* I was fine with Ella's body and that helping her realize how beautiful she was was all I'd wanted to do for her for months, instead I sat there silently and let her work it out on her own. I could tell her these things until I was blue in the face—I'd tried a hundred times—but the truth would never matter until she accepted it. I couldn't make her do that.

Ella stared down at our joined hands and threaded our fingers together. "If I can't show you all of me, then I'm not really trusting you all the way, even if I thought I was. But maybe…" She paused a moment, hesitating as if she once again couldn't figure out how best to put her feelings into words.

I waited some more. It was all I could do. Finally, I was rewarded with those big blue eyes, shiny from a layer of moisture, staring at me as if permitting me entrance to Ella's soul. "If I could just give you my *complete* trust and let you love my flaws *for* me, I might be able to finally see that they aren't so bad."

The breath left my lungs. She was finally getting it. I'd been trying to tell her this for months. I owed Ellie and Seth big time, because I would have never been able to get through to Ella the way they did with one quick conversation. But whatever she realized tonight, it was finally sinking in like it should have back when we first met.

"Watching Seth tonight with Ellie, and seeing her respond to him. And just seeing her so…proud of herself—I *want* that." Ella's expression changed, filling with determination and turning fierce. "I *did* survive hell. I've worked so hard to get to where I am now, and Ellie was right; if I woke up tomorrow completely healed with no physical reminders of everything I've been through, part of me would be sad about that."

I reached up and tucked a lock of her hair that was shielding her beautiful eyes from me behind her ear, offering her the smallest, sincerest smile. "I would be *devastated* by that."

She looked surprised, but it was the honest truth. She wouldn't be *my* Ella any other way than she is now.

She sucked in another deep breath and then nodded, as if accepting the truth of my feelings. Then she pulled herself to her feet and turned to face me. "I trust you, Brian," she murmured, reaching for the belt holding her robe closed. "I trust you to love the things about me that I don't."

She took one last deep breath and held it as she pulled the tie loose and let her robe fall to the floor.

29

I trembled as I pulled myself to my feet. I needed to do this. I didn't feel ready, but I was beginning to think I'd never feel ready, and I was tired of being afraid. I was sick of not being with the man I loved because I was too scared to let it happen. I wanted Brian. I wanted to be with him in every way. I wanted the physical relationship that went along with two people being as in love with each other as we were. Sure, I was a bit of a prude, but Brian was Brian, and if I hadn't had the physical issues I did, I wouldn't have lasted three days against the temptations he presented.

Brian sat patiently, unmoving and quiet, making sure I had 100 percent control of this situation. It was the perfect reaction. I couldn't do this any other way.

Looking at him now, his eyes were on mine and filled with nothing but love and encouragement. That surprised me. I'd expected shock, anticipation, excitement, lust, or even some of the nervousness I felt, but none of that was there. It was as if he wasn't thinking about the fact that he'd see me almost naked in a moment or that he was going to see the full extent of my damage. His thoughts were on *me*, not my body—how hard this was for me and what a huge step I was taking.

He was supporting me, not thinking about anything else. The look of pride and unconditional love in his eyes was the *only* reason I was able to pull on the tie that was holding my robe shut. "I trust you, Brian." The words were whispered because I was terrified, but they were fervent. I did trust him. "I trust you to love the things about me that I don't."

I wanted to close my eyes or look away as I tugged off my robe. Fear made me not want to see his face as he took in the sight of me. But I needed to watch his reaction. Brian openly wore his emotions on his face. His feelings would be there for me to see, and that was the whole point of this—for me to see that he wasn't sickened by my appearance. He wasn't going to flinch, or shy away, or curl his lips in disgust. *He wasn't.*

As I maneuvered the soft material off my shoulders and let it fall to the floor, I forced myself to hold Brian's gaze, but I stopped breathing and shook like a leaf. I hadn't been this terrified since my accident. "This is me. What's left, anyway," I whispered, holding out my free hand as the other leaned on my cane for dear life. I was so scared I felt like I was going to pass out at any moment. Candy Cane was the only thing keeping me on my feet.

Brian's gaze held mine for a second before he let it drop, and then he simply looked. He wasn't overcome with lust. He didn't make some romantic comment about how beautiful I was. He just...took in the sight of me. It was almost a clinical assessment of my injuries. I didn't take it personally. It was a lot to process.

I didn't have a normal body with some pale, discolored splotches hinting at a past injury. It was so much worse than most people could imagine. I was covered in angry, bumpy scars and skin grafts that tugged together unevenly, making my skin look as if it had been unnaturally stretched over my body. (Which it had been.) It wasn't pretty; it was shocking and horrific. I looked like a Barbie doll that had been held over an open flame and melted. I was literally deformed in places.

I didn't realize that Brian wasn't breathing until he gasped for air and let it out in a quick puff as if he still needed to take another breath. When he met my gaze again, his eyes were shiny with unshed tears.

He completely startled me when he suddenly pushed to his feet and grabbed me in a passionate kiss. He cupped my face in his hands and claimed my mouth as if his life depended on it.

The kiss was all emotion. It was the same reaction he'd had when we were sitting in that restaurant at FantasyCon and I'd first told him about my injuries. He was overwhelmed and reacting to the violent assault of feelings that had blindsided him.

"Ellamara," he whispered gruffly as he tried to calm himself. He brushed his lips against mine and corded his hands into my hair. "Ella..."

He wasn't the first to be overwhelmed by my scars. Jennifer had been so startled she'd dropped a glass of lemonade on the floor and burst into tears. She'd literally run from the room because she couldn't deal with it. Juliette had bawled, and Ana had turned white as a ghost and avoided being in the same room as me for over two weeks.

Seeing me all at once was not a casual thing. The first time people saw the full extent of my injuries was the first time they really understood the nightmare I'd lived through. And it was when people decided that my insecurities, as deep as they were, were justified. That realization must have hit Brian harder than it would anyone else. He loved me so much that my pain and suffering became his as well.

He kissed me again, this time a little more tenderly, but still completely in an unconscious reaction to his emotions. He urged my lips to part, needing a deeper connection. When I let him in, he kissed me so deeply and intensely that I could taste his sorrow, his fear, and his desperate need to prove to me how much he cared for me. It was as if he were trying to heal me with his kiss, or, at the very least, erase all of the anguish I'd endured since my accident. He was feeling that anguish now, firsthand.

I let him kiss me as much as he wanted. Not that I minded, of course—Brian could kiss me whenever he felt like it, and I would welcome and cherish it—but this particular kiss was different. Brian *needed* this kiss, so I held still and let him take it. I kissed him back, letting him know his advance was welcome, but I let him stay in complete control. It was his turn. He'd waited patiently for me to get through my speech and work up the courage to share myself with him. Now I needed to be the calm and collected one, while he tried to make sense of the devastation coursing through him.

"I'm sorry, Ella," he whispered in a shaky voice once he was finally able to break our kiss. His hands still held my face, and he leaned his forehead against mine, eyes closed as he tried to calm down and regain his composure. "I almost lost you," he muttered. "I always knew that, but…"

With a slow shake of his head, he took a deep breath, and his entire body shuddered. He pressed another small kiss to my lips. "Thank you for surviving," he murmured. "Thank you for fighting so hard and for not giving up, and for finding your way to me."

My eyes fell shut, a few tears leaking from the corners. "Thank you for giving me something to fight for."

When I sniffled, Brian finally released me. He wiped the tears from my face, either ignoring or not realizing that he had trails of wetness down his own cheeks. "I'm sorry," he said again. "I told myself I wasn't going to overreact, but I just…all of a sudden I pictured you in that hospital and realized I came so close to never having you in my life. Thought of having never met you…" He shut his eyes against the words, as if they brought him physical pain. "Having to live my whole life never knowing what happened to you. Never having the chance to see your smile in person, or hold you in my arms, or kiss you. I can't imagine a life without you."

Swallowing back another lump of emotion, I shook my head. "I can't imagine life without you, either." I wrapped my arms around his neck and stole a small kiss of my own, smiling for the first time since we'd entered my bedroom. "Thank you for loving me so much."

"You're welcome." The atmosphere in the room shifted suddenly as a playful grin crept across Brian's face. "And thank *you* for not going with the blue *or* the pink. This is much better."

My eyes nearly bugged out of my head, which of course made Brian laugh. His gaze dropped to my chest. With a wicked smile that spiked my pulse, he removed my hands from around his neck and stepped back so that he could take another look at me.

My face flamed as the fact that I was standing in my underwear suddenly became about my nakedness and not my scars. This time when Brian's gaze raked over my body, I saw the heat and the hunger that he'd been suppressing this whole time.

I swallowed hard and tried to stand proud in the simple lacy matching underwear I'd put on. It'd caught my eye because it was the same canary yellow as my mama's dress, but I liked it because it was understated compared to most of the stuff I'd received from Lindon's. It was sexy without being overly sexed up. It was actually more on the playful side, if anything, and it seemed to be having that exact effect on Brian now that he'd recovered from the initial shock of seeing my scars. "Yellow is *definitely* my favorite color," he said, unable to take his eyes away from my body.

I choked out a surprised laugh. "Shut up. It is not. It's midnight blue, like the custom paint job you had done on Precious."

Brain shook his head, eyes still trained well below my face. "Nope. It's yellow. Has been since the night of *The Druid Prince* premiere." He wet his lips and swallowed audibly. "This confirms it. I'm a yellow guy."

Finally, he pulled his heated gaze back to mine. It made my heart race so fast I wasn't sure I wouldn't rather him stay enthralled with my boobs. He stepped close again and lifted my arms back around his neck. "You are beautiful, Ellamara. The most beautiful woman I have ever seen."

I laughed without thinking. "Are you sure? That's quite a bold declaration, considering you've seen a *billion* women."

Brian's eyes flashed at the quip, and he scooped me into his arms with a playful growl. "That's it," he said as I yelped in surprise. "You are going to learn to take a compliment, woman."

He walked me around the side of the bed and laid me down on it. I have no doubt he'd have *dumped* me on it, if I weren't breakable.

My breath hitched when he ripped his shirt over his head, dropped his pants to the floor, and then climbed on top of me, straddling my thighs and hovering above me on his hands and knees. He stared down at me with heat blazing from his eyes. His chest heaved with desire. "I am going to kiss *every inch* of your body until you no longer laugh when I tell you that you are the most beautiful woman on Earth," he said.

Holy crap!

I'd unleashed a beast. A feral, hungry, determined animal. He'd skipped his audiobook book voice and wandered into alpha werewolf territory. It was low, rough, and promised both danger and pleasure. The threat—and it *was* a threat—sent a shiver through me, spiking my pulse and heating me from the inside out.

"I'll remember what you said," he told me. "We won't go any further than this. I promise. What's covered now will stay off-limits." He grabbed both of my hands and held them against the pillow above my head, weaving his fingers in mine. "But I want to taste every inch of you that isn't."

My lungs seized up. I was overcome with the feeling that I was captured prey, but my nerves took a backseat to the intense desire that swept through me. Fear turned to excitement and then quickly to need. He was terrifying and mesmerizing like this, and so help me I wanted him to *devour* me.

Whatever he read in my expression pleased him. He smirked both knowingly and hungrily, then slowly lowered his mouth to mine. After a torturously delicate kiss, he moved his lips to my ear. "Give me permission, Ella."

I sucked in another breath and shivered again. When I nodded, he growled. "Not good enough. I need you to tell me, Ella. I want to hear it."

302

So direct. So demanding. And yet I didn't feel pressured at all. He was being his dominant self, but he was making sure that this was what I wanted. Heaven save me if he ever figured out exactly how much I wanted it. "Okay," I rasped.

"Okay what?"

"You have my permission."

Brian pulled back and looked into my eyes again. "I have your permission for what? What would you like me to do, Ella?"

He wanted me to say it. He liked the talk. Did he know how hard that was for a shy woman? How scary and embarrassing? But I couldn't deny his forwardness was a turn on, and I couldn't blame him for wanting to know exactly what he was and wasn't allowed to do with me. He didn't want to cross any lines accidentally. I was grateful to him for that, so if he needed vocal confirmation, as uncomfortable as it was, I would give it. I met his waiting gaze, took a deep breath, and with as much confidence as I could muster, said, "I want you to explore me, Brian."

His eyes flashed again, and he sucked in a sharp breath through his nose. I thrilled at the thought that I'd made him respond that way, and it made me bold. "I want you to kiss me and touch me everywhere. I want you to get to know my body as well as you know me, so that I'll never fear you again." My voice cracked, and I quietly added, "Help me accept this, Brian. Make me feel beautiful and desired. Please."

The sizzling lust that had been driving Brian faded at my request. He smiled tenderly as he brushed my hair away from my forehead. "You have nothing to fear from me," he said softly, claiming my lips with his. "And you are going to accept the truth because you *are* beautiful and *so* damn desirable. Ellamara, you are *perfect*."

His mouth quickly found my jaw, and he began trailing light kisses down my neck. "You're perfect here," he murmured when his mouth met the base of my throat.

Instead of moving his lips lower to the cleavage my tiny yellow bra put proudly on display, he swept his mouth along my collarbone until he found my shoulder—the same damaged one he'd kissed earlier. "You're perfect here," he murmured as he pressed his lips to the scarred skin.

My eyes fluttered shut as I soaked in the tenderness of his kisses. Each one made my heart ache in the sweetest way, as if Brian was repairing all the invisible cracks and tears in it one at a time.

He shuffled above me, and then I gasped when his lips swept over my stomach, searching for their next spot to kiss. He placed his hands on my hips, dropped his lips to my stomach just above my navel, and pressed down firmly. "You are *definitely* perfect here."

My eyes burned as I enjoyed the sensation. My stomach had taken severe burn damage and was a complete mess. To have Brian's mouth there, caressing me as if I were precious, stole my breath from me.

Tears leaked from the corners of my eyes as I lay there, completely at his mercy, and allowed him to become intimate with the worst parts of my body. They were tears of love, gratitude, joy, and relief.

Since my accident, I'd given up on the possibility of ever having a moment like this. I didn't think anyone would ever be able to accept me for what I am and love me despite my flaws. Yet, here Brian was, and he wasn't just doing this to humor me or make me feel better. He *wanted* this. Wanted *me*. In fact, from the way he'd become so tense, I knew he was struggling not to take this even further, to places I wasn't ready to go. To him, I really was beautiful and desirable. To him, I was as perfect as he was to me. It seemed like a miracle.

He continued his heavenly torture, kissing scar after scar, until a sob burst my chest and I began to cry in earnest. It was all just so overwhelming. It was so beautiful, and so much more than I ever thought I'd be able to have. It was the best moment of my life.

Brian understood my tears, and instead of asking if I was all right, he climbed off of me and pulled the covers back on my bed. We crawled in together, and he held me against him, constantly running his fingertips over my bare back while I had a good cry in his arms. Once I started to settle down, he kissed the side of my head and said, "That's enough for tonight. Sleep now, my beautiful Ellamara."

The line was so something out of a melodramatic movie, but I didn't laugh this time. I smiled to myself, secretly grateful that he constantly spouted cheesy romantic nonsense. He was an actor. Movie dialogue was what he knew. And I loved that about him.

Resisting the urge to tease him, I sniffed away the last of my tears and settled against his chest with a sigh of contentment. He continued to graze my skin with his fingertips, lulling me into a state of blissful relaxation. I never wanted to move from this spot ever again. Never wanted to leave the security of his arms. Never wanted to spend another night alone in this bed. Already drifting into a sleepy daze, I realized something and muttered a drowsy curse. "Darn, you were right. I should have just let you buy us a new house."

I fell asleep to the sound of his soft chuckle.

30

When I woke up the next morning, I wondered if I would feel awkward lying in bed with Brian, both of us in only underwear. But when he shut his alarm off with a groan and pulled me against his warm, bare chest snuggling in like he had every intention of going back to sleep, I was too sublimely happy to be anything but relaxed. If only we could enjoy this moment longer. "Sorry, mister. You've got a seven o'clock call time in Glendale. You've got to get up."

"Five minutes," Brian grumbled, hugging me tighter to him, as if I were his prisoner.

"Fine. Five minutes, but then we're getting up."

Brian groaned. "Why, of all mornings, did I have to be scheduled early today?" He took a deep breath, stretched, and pulled his face back to look at me. "You okay this morning?"

His concern was touching. I smiled warmly. "More than okay. No regrets. I needed that."

Brian dropped a kiss to my forehead. "Me too."

"Sorry it ended with me being an emotional, blubbering mess. I promise I wasn't upset over anything you did. It was the opposite. Last night was so incredible it *hurt*. That sounds crazy, but I don't know how else to describe it." I paused a moment, suddenly worked up emotionally again. "You've given me something that, since the day I came out of my coma, I didn't think I'd ever get to experience."

Brian raked his fingers through my horrible mess of bed hair, grinning a little at how crazy it was, and then sighed when his eyes met mine. "Ella, you have more emotional trauma to work through than anyone I've ever heard of. I completely understood the tears last night. I can only imagine that the good moments are probably just as overwhelming for you as the bad."

"More overwhelming," I admitted. "I'm used to the bad ones. The good ones still take me by surprise."

How a face could portray so much emotion I would never understand, but with just one look, Brian expressed a lifetime of love and devotion. "Sounds like I've got some work to do, then." He found one of my hands and kissed it before holding it against his chest. "From now on, we'll make so many good moments that the bad ones will be all but forgotten."

"Moments like this one," I said, offering him a smile before lying my head down on his chest and letting go a contented sigh. I loved this man so much my chest constantly threatened to burst from it. "I wish you had a normal job that didn't cost people thousands upon thousands of dollars if you called in sick."

It was Saturday, but film shoots didn't exactly follow the normal Monday through Friday nine-to-five schedule. They were intense, packing as much work as possible into the shortest amount of time possible because they were so expensive and had to coordinate with a hundred people's different scheduled projects. They were insane, and Brian missing a day would set back production, throwing everyone off. It was out of the question.

Brian chuckled and hugged me tight. "I'm tempted to do it anyway."

"Not happening. I'd feel terrible."

Brian sighed. "Well, we don't want that. How about you come with me today? My workdays are 70 percent sitting around waiting for everyone else to be ready anyway, and I have my own trailer. We could hide out there, same as here."

That was a true statement, if I'd ever heard one. I was surprised the first time I visited him at work at the amount of hurry-up-and-wait that goes on on a movie set. But when it takes a hundred people doing a hundred different things just to get one shot, well, that's just how it goes. But it works out nicely for me when I want to go keep Brian company at work. No one ever cares that I'm there, and mostly we just get to hang out while he waits.

"Tempting. But actually..." I pushed my lazy body into a stretch, hoping it would motivate me to get out of bed. "I was thinking I'd call Nash Wilson and see if he'll meet me for lunch today."

Brian raised his brows in surprise, and I let out a breath I'd started to hold. "I'm going to tell him yes."

"Ella..." Brian sat up, taking on a sudden intensity I didn't know he was capable of so early in the morning. My man was definitely not a fan of the a.m. "Are you sure?"

The way he searched my face for clues and seemed on the verge of either panic or excitement was startling. I couldn't tell what was going on inside his head, but he was holding his breath at the moment as he waited for my answer.

"Yeah," I said, surprised at how confident that answer sounded. I thought about it again and then nodded. "I'm sure."

Something sparked in Brian's eyes, and then he surprised me with a hard kiss. "What was that for?" I asked when he let my face go.

"I'm so proud of you." He wasn't even smiling. He was too full of whatever emotion was overwhelming him. "I've been hoping you'd decide to do this."

"Really?"

I blinked. Where was this intensity coming from? Everyone had had an opinion on this subject since it first came up, but Brian was the only one who never said anything one way or another.

"I didn't want you to feel pressured," he said, "but Ella, I want you to take those photos more than anything."

I knew he was serious, so when I joked it was only half-hearted. "You just want to see me all decked out as a mostly naked faerie goddess."

Heat filled his eyes, and I knew I was at least partially right.

"You bet your cute little ass I do," he said.

The growly wolf-man voice was starting to make a comeback. He had to shake himself from his lustful thoughts in order to stay focused. "Ella, you are beautiful. I know you think I'm biased—and maybe I am—but it's still the truth. And Nash is going to make *you* believe it. He's that good. He won't be transforming you into something you aren't; he'll be shining a spotlight on you in a way that makes everyone see what I see. Even you will see it. That's what I want."

I grinned a little. "You want me to do the photo shoot just so that I can have some pretty pictures of myself?"

He still wasn't playing when he nodded. "Yes. I do. You need them. And so does the rest of the world. You need to believe in yourself. It's just like last night. Forcing yourself to let me see you even though you were scared—what was the end result?"

"Um…" I looked at myself and then at him and wondered what, exactly, he was asking. "Spending the night with you in our underwear…?"

"*Confidence*, Ella." He smirked. "Though, spending the night with you in our underwear was definitely a nice perk, too."

His eyes dropped down my body, making me blush again. I'd hoped I might get over the shyness after last night, but when he looked at me that way…I was probably going to blush for the rest of my life.

He took my hand in his. "You got past the fear, and you have more confidence this morning. I can already see it. It'll be the same with the photos. It'll be scary, but once you conquer the initial fear, you'll find your courage."

That's exactly what I was hoping, too. I was sitting here with all my scars exposed to Brian, and none of the crippling anxiety and insecurity I've felt since the day we met was there. I was comfortable with him. I was in my underwear, for heaven's sake, and I was just sitting here having a conversation with him as if it were completely natural.

"You said you want to love yourself," Brian said with a soft smile. "You said you want to feel as confident about yourself as Ellie did. Do this photo shoot and release the pictures. Give the haters the metaphorical middle finger. I think it will free you. I think it's exactly what you need to get past your accident once and for all and really find the strength to live your life. To *love* it, Ella. To truly be happy."

His speech was exactly what I needed. His faith and support solidified my resolve, and now I'd be able to meet with Nash confidently. Brian was right. I needed to get past this hurdle of insecurity, and if it took giving the world the *metaphorical middle finger*, then so be it. Any scorn and ridicule that came my way wouldn't matter because Brian would be there to hold me at night and kiss any doubt away.

Brian seemed to be waiting for me to say something, so I grinned at him and slid my arms over his shoulders. He wasted no time pulling me tightly against him so that our chests were flush against one another. I shivered, even though all I felt was heat. "I already love my life," I promised. "You've made me as happy as any person can get." I kissed him with just enough passion that it was going to be difficult for him to get out of bed, and then I grinned. "But I'll do the shoot anyway, so that you can have a picture to keep in your wallet for bragging purposes."

"Hmm. A woman who understands what's *really* important to a man. I have the best girlfriend in the world."

Brian laughed and pressed his mouth to mine again, forcing my lips apart because he wanted a deeper connection.

It took us another five minutes—or maybe it was ten—before Brian finally got out of bed and got ready for work. A few hours later, when the rest of the city might finally be awake, I called Nash and asked him to meet me for lunch. Then I called my father, because a plan had formed in my mind over the course of the morning that I couldn't let go.

"Ella?" he sounded worried.

"Hey, Dad."

"Hi, honey. It's good to hear from you. What's up? Is everything okay? You looked like you weren't feeling well last night. Jennifer and I were worried."

A smile crept over my face as I listened to his concern. He wasn't perfect, but he did love me. That could be enough for now. "Nothing's wrong," I said. "It's great, actually. I was just wondering if you'd be able to meet me for lunch today. All of you, Jennifer and the girls, too?"

"I—" Dad sputtered, surprised by the request. "Well, yes, I suppose we could make that happen. I'm at the office going over some depositions for court on Monday, but I can sneak away for an hour. A man's got to eat, right?"

I smiled again. "Great. Can you meet me at the Ivy at one?"

"The *Ivy?*"

I chuckled. It had been Nash's suggestion, so I told him I'd make the reservations.

I'd never been to the restaurant, but it was infamous for business lunches in the entertainment industry. Many a deal had been made at the quaint little café on Robertson Blvd. Apparently, Nash was hoping this would be a productive lunch date.

"Yeah. A friend made the suggestion, and it seems to be the place to go among most of Brian's friends, so I figured I'd give it a try. I've got some news I'd like to share with you all. A proposal, really."

Dad made a choking noise. "Have mercy, Ella! Are you telling me you're getting *married?*"

He sounded scared, but there was no hostility in his voice. I don't think he was scared of me marrying Brian; I think he was scared of weddings. Brides and cakes and centerpieces and having to give his little girl away." I laughed. "Relax, Dad. It's not that. I'm not engaged. I'm also not pregnant."

The gush of air he breathed into the phone made me laugh again. "Dad." My voice softened as sympathy seeped into my chest. "I may not be your eight-year-old little girl anymore, but I'm not in a rush to grow all the way up, either. I need the adjustment time as much as you do. And, I promise, when marriage and babies and all of that does come, I'll give you as much warning as I can."

"Thanks, honey."

I chuckled again at his relief. Was that a thanks for not being ready for marriage and babies yet? Or thanks for the promise of warning?

"You're welcome. So can you meet me at one, or should I change the reservations?"

"One is fine. We'll be there."

"Would you mind picking me up? Jennifer and the girls can meet us there. If you're at the office, it'd be on the way, and a little one-on-one time might be nice."

Dad cleared his throat, and when he spoke, his voice was a little gruff. "I'd love to."

"Thanks. Twelve thirty?"

"I'll be there."

"Great. Oh, and Dad? Can you tell everyone to dress nice?"

Dad laughed. "You think Jennifer or the girls would be seen at the Ivy in anything less than their absolute best?"

I laughed. "You have a point. I'll see you soon. And..." I hesitated a moment before I managed a quiet "Thanks."

There was a slight pause before Dad's reply as well. "Anytime, honey. I mean that."

31

DAD AND I DIDN'T TALK ABOUT MY NEWS ON THE WAY TO THE restaurant. Instead, I asked him how he liked the premiere last night and what he thought of Janice Bishop. He admitted the premiere wasn't as bad as he'd expected it to be and relented that red carpet events weren't the same as what we'd gone through on Christmas Day. And then he'd *gushed* about Janice Bishop for the rest of the ride. Someone had a serious author crush. It was cute, and I was proud I'd been able to do something so special for him.

Things were comfortable between us when we reached the restaurant, which seemed a miracle in itself. Then we were shown to our table, where Jennifer and the twins were already waiting for us. Ana was just as anxious and excited to figure out what my big secret was, too. "Let me see the ring!" she demanded, nearly pushing Juliette out of the way to get to my hand first.

I laughed. "Sit down, you bridezillas. I'm not engaged."

"Then what is it?" Juliette asked. "I'm dying. You're killing us."

"Just sit down already. I'll explain in a minute. We're still waiting for one more person."

"I thought Brian was filming today," Juliette said.

"He is. We're waiting for a friend of mine."

Jennifer and the girls sat, and Dad pulled out my chair for me, but before I could sit, Nash's voice called out across the room. "Ella, my beautiful doll! Please tell me that this lunch is your way of accepting my offer."

I laughed as I greeted him with a hand squeeze and a cheek kiss. "It is."

His eyes lit with delight as I presented him to my family. "Nash, I'd like you to meet my family. Everyone, this is Nash Wilson."

Dad shook his hand, nodding cordially, having no idea who he was. Juliette and Ana looked surprised, but they'd both known I knew him and that he'd asked to take my pictures, so their surprise was nothing compared to Jennifer's shock.

After a few minutes of Jennifer's gushing—which Nash proudly accepted with enthusiasm—everyone got seated and gave the server our orders.

Ana was the first to bring up the subject the second we were alone again. "You're really going to take his offer?"

"Yeah." I grinned at Nash. "If you're still feeling inspired, anyway."

Nash brought his fisted hands to his pursed mouth, as if trying to keep from cheering out loud or possibly trying to hold tears at bay. Then he suddenly took my face in his hands and kissed both my cheeks with so much flourish that my whole family laughed. "You lovely, courageous woman! You are going to be my *pièce de résistance!*"

"I hope so, if we're really going to release the pictures to the entire world," I joked.

Nash sobered instantly and took my hand in his. "You have my word, Ellamara. You are going to be the most beautiful, ethereal, heavenly being ever to be captured on camera."

I swallowed a lump of emotion. "Thanks."

Our lunch arrived, and I gave everyone a chance to dive into their meals before I brought up the reason I'd requested they all come. Once we were all settled in, I finally broached the subject. "So Nash…are you still thinking faeries in an enchanted forest?"

Nash cocked an eyebrow at me. "Is it not a perfect idea for the mystic druid priestess and her beloved druid prince?"

I grinned. "More perfect than you know. I just wanted to make sure you were still thinking that direction, because I wanted to run an idea by you."

Nash put his soup spoon down to give me his full attention.

"Okay, I know this is your shoot. I understand you have to be inspired and all, and I'll trust your judgment, but I had a thought this morning after I decided I wanted to really do this."

I took a breath and cast a quick glance around the table. "What if we make it a family session instead of just me?"

Jennifer gasped, so startled she dropped her salad fork, while both Juliette and Ana looked at me with wide eyes. Dad frowned, as if he was trying to figure out what the big deal was.

I held Nash's gaze while he narrowed his eyes on me. "Look at them," I said. "And tell me what you see."

Nash humored me and looked—really looked—at my family. He took his time, and I could see him really thinking about my question. "I see a beautiful, picture-perfect family," he said, shaking his head as if they were nothing more than ordinary.

"Exactly," I said. "You see perfection. You see beauty, elegance, and grace. You see Hollywood's mold wrapped up in a perfect package. And then there's me…"

Nash's eyes flashed to me.

"One of these things is not like the others, Nash."

His eyes widened, and he sat straight up in his chair, looking at my family again but seeing them with a new perspective. I could tell he understood what I was getting at. "You're absolutely right," he whispered reverently. "They're perfect. They're exactly what the world demands. They're so beautiful and perfect that they'll blend together."

His head snapped back to me, and then he rose from his chair to take a step away from the table and see us all together as a whole. "It's *brilliant*," he muttered. He held his hands up, as if putting us all in a frame together. "The most beautiful and perfect creatures all together, and among them, you will shine. Your differences—your imperfections—will stand out among them and set you apart. And imperfect truly will be more beautiful."

His eyes met mine, and I knew he was onboard.

"Brian will be disappointed not to do it, but—"

"No, we still need Brian," Nash said. "Having you two as a couple in the photos with the others will only make everything that much more powerful. The powerful fey prince claiming his princess, only she's not the one the world would choose upon first sight."

A huge smile bloomed on my face. "I hoped you would say that. My cosplay-loving boyfriend really would have been devastated to be left out of this photo shoot."

Juliette and Ana burst into laughter. They loved that Brian, of all people, was, at heart, a huge geek.

Nash and I grinned at each other, and he kissed my face again before sitting back down. He was speechless for an entire minute before he looked around the table. "Will you do it?" he asked my family.

There was excitement and even desperation in his plea. He would beg, if he had to. Which was a good thing, considering he was going to have to convince my father to dress up like a faerie, bare-chested and in tights, and allow his daughters to be photographed in what I assumed would be some pretty skimpy faerie outfits showing a hefty amount of skin. Begging was definitely going to be necessary.

Jennifer shook as she asked, "You really want *us* to join Ella's photo shoot?"

"Mrs. Coleman." He shook his head, shooting her a smile that made her blush. "I would love nothing more. You have a beautiful family, and together with Ella, you complete a picture so breathtaking it will mesmerize the entire world."

Tears formed in Jennifer's eyes. Even if she wasn't the main focus of the pictures, being photographed by Nash Wilson was a dream come true for her, and having those pictures in her portfolio would open a world of new opportunities. The twins, if they wanted to follow in the footsteps of her modeling career, which I was pretty sure Ana did—would be set.

Jennifer shook her head in disbelief and then laughed a startled laugh that was mixed with a tiny sob. "We would be honored. Wouldn't we?"

She looked to the others. Juliette and Anastasia nodded immediately, heads bobbing like bobbleheads and eyes as wide as anime characters. "I can't believe this," Ana whispered. "We're going to get to do a *Nash Wilson* photo shoot."

All eyes turned to my dad, seeking final approval. He frowned at me with eyes so wary it was hard not to laugh. "Hold on now; you said something about faeries in an enchanted forest. Just what kind of family pictures are you thinking of taking?"

I let Nash explain, and as he spoke, Juliette's, Ana's, and Jennifer's expressions got dreamier and dreamier, while Dad's slowly became so horrified I worried he was going to have a stroke.

He wanted to say no. I could see it in his eyes. A little of his hesitancy was because of his daughters, but mostly it was for his own dignity. Brian may have had no problem dressing up in skintight leggings and pretending to be a faerie for the world, but Richard Coleman, power-lawyer who ate criminals for breakfast? Not likely.

"Dad," I whispered when he opened his mouth to say no, "I can do this on my own. I can take these pictures myself, and with Brian—I'll do that no matter what you decide—but it would mean a lot to me if you all did this with me."

Dad's mouth shut, and he turned a very conflicted set of eyes on me.

"I know I'm asking a lot," I whispered. "But the thing is…I'm doing this as a way to heal. Deciding to show myself to the world is something I need to do to accept myself. But I need to accept my *family* as well."

"Ella…" My dad shook his head as his voice trailed off. He didn't know what to say. That was all right, because I'd sort of prepared this speech ahead of time.

"I called my agent this morning after I agreed to meet with Nash. We had a long conversation about what this photo shoot would mean for me and what I would want to get out of it. Ultimately, I'm looking for closure. I think I'm going to try and write my autobiography. I want to share my story. I think if I just face my fears and lay it all out there, I'll find the acceptance over everything awful that's happened to me. I need that acceptance with you and your family just as much as I need to accept my body."

I lifted my gaze away from Dad and met the eyes of my stepmother and sisters. "I have never truly felt like I belonged with you. From the moment I arrived in California, I was one giant, imperfect mess trying to mold myself into your beautiful picture-perfect world. I wasn't surprised that my father had left me for you. Why would he want me, when he had such a better offer?"

"Ella—" My dad choked on the name and reached out to me.

I surprised him when I took his hand. "I'm sorry. I know that sounds awful, but it's the truth. I've been so intimidated and scared of your perfect life that I haven't been able to let myself be a part of it. I *need* this. I need to feel like I can be every bit as worthy to be a Coleman as the rest of you. I need to face the insecurities I have where you, Jennifer, and the twins are concerned if I'm ever going to conquer them. So even though it's going to make you uncomfortable, I'm still asking. Please do this for me, Dad."

My dad looked at me for a moment before his face crumpled, and he let out a heavy sigh. "Honey, from the moment I brought you home, all I've wanted was for you to feel welcomed into my family."

"Then do this with me, Dad. Let's be a family, for once. All of us. Together. I'm about to do the most terrifying thing I could possibly ever do. I may have decided to do it, but it is going to be *hard* for me." I took a breath to stave off tears that were suddenly stinging my eyes. "I could really use the extra support."

Dad's shoulders slumped, and resignation washed over him. "Okay." He met my eyes with the same big bright blue ones he'd passed on to me. "If you really need this—if you really think it will help you feel like you belong in this family, then we'll do it. *I'll* do it."

Jennifer, Juliette, Ana, and Nash all broke out into cheers, while my father and I just looked at one another. I couldn't believe he'd agreed. Yeah, I'd totally played an underhanded card there, but I still hadn't thought it would work. It had been the truth, though, every single bit of it. I needed this with them. And now that he'd agreed, my chest burned with as much excitement and anticipation as it did with nerves.

I'd tried so hard to stay dry-eyed, but I finally lost that battle, and my eyes welled up with tears. I threw my arms around my father and sniffled as I hugged him. "Thank you, Dad."

"I love you, sweetheart."

My throat closed up even tighter, and I couldn't let him go. He didn't seem to be in any hurry to end the hug, either. "I love you, too," I whispered.

When I pulled back, I wiped my eyes with my napkin and blushed as I looked around the table. When my eyes met Ana's, she smirked her classic dry smirk. "You've always been a Coleman, stupid."

Stupid was a term of endearment this time, because her lips twitched. Juliette laughed and added, "Glad you're finally ready to own it."

I rolled my eyes at the twins as they both giggled, and then met Jennifer's watery gaze. She smiled brightly and chuckled a little as she said, "Welcome to the family, sweetheart."

For the first time since coming to California, the invitation felt sincere, and I was finally ready to accept it. "Thanks. It's nice to have one again."

Epilogue

FOUR MONTHS LATER

I BOUNCED WITH NERVOUS ENERGY AS BRIAN AND I DROVE UP to the beautiful two-story brick home with white colonial pillars. This was my first time visiting Brian's mom and stepdad, but it wasn't hard to pick out which house on the street was theirs, considering it was the only one decked out in full Christmas attire.

Garland was twined around the front porch railing and the pillars, a gorgeous wreath hung on the front door, and glowing white reindeer stood proudly in the front yard. Liz and Doug had even gone so far as to cover the sprawling green lawn with a layer of puffy white fluff to masquerade as snow. The lights on the house were just becoming visible as twilight hit the lovely city of Green Bay, Wisconsin. I'd timed my travel plans just right. It was perfect.

As we pulled into the driveway of Brian's mother's home, he gaped up at the decorations as if he thought his mother had lost her mind. I couldn't blame him. It was almost August, after all. "What in the world…?

"That's so strange," I agreed.

Brian glanced at me, suspicion shining through his narrowed eyes. I wasn't the actor in this relationship, that was for sure. I was hard-pressed to keep the grin off my face as I opened the door and got out of the rental car. "Let's go find out what's going on."

Brian didn't believe my innocence for a second, but he got out of the car without demanding answers and walked arm in arm with me up the driveway. Brian's mom and stepfather were waiting on the front porch before I got all the way up the front steps. "You're here!" Liz squealed.

She quickly hugged Brian and then pushed him aside to squeeze the life out of me. Not that she loved me more than Brian, of course; she was just excited because she knew what I'd planned.

After a quick, warm hug from Doug, they ushered us into the house. The inside was as beautifully decorated as the outside was. The Christmas tree was massive, reaching easily twelve feet high in the vaulted living room, and sure enough, there were a small pile of presents lying beneath it, waiting to be unwrapped. There were even soft carols playing and a fire roaring in the fireplace. It may as well have been Christmas Eve instead of July 25.

"You're right on time," Liz gushed. "I just put dinner on the table. Roast beef and mashed potatoes, green bean casserole, homemade rolls, and pumpkin pie. I've been cooking all day, so I hope you're both hungry."

"Starving," I admitted. "It smells fantastic."

"It smells great," Brian agreed. "But Mom...what is going on? It's *July*."

He got no reply, because Liz had already disappeared into the formal dining room. A beautiful feast sat laid out around a lovely Christmas centerpiece, and she'd pulled out the china and the silver for the occasion. I'd never sat at a table so fancy before. "This looks wonderful, Liz." My throat tightened at all the effort she'd put into this evening. All I'd asked her to do was set up a small Christmas tree. This was above and beyond. "Thank you for going to so much trouble."

Liz waved us off. "No trouble at all. Come in and sit down.

Let's eat before it gets cold."

"Mom…?" Brian tried again.

He got a stern look in response that made me giggle and had him shaking his head as he pulled out a chair for me. Yup. He definitely thought his mother had lost all of her marbles.

Once we were all seated, Doug gave a blessing, and then the plates began to fill. When I complimented Liz on her excellent Christmas dinner, Brian finally couldn't stand it anymore. "Okay, seriously. It's July. Mom, have you gone mental?"

Liz frowned, fork halfway to her mouth and huffed, affronted. "No, I have not *gone mental*, son. What I have done is gone to a lot of trouble to help your extremely thoughtful girlfriend recreate the good Lord's birthday."

Brian turned his *you're insane* stare on me. I answered it with a patronizing smile. "Haven't you ever heard of Christmas in July? When I realized we'd scheduled this trip on July 25, I thought it might be fun to try a do-over since our first Christmas together was, in a word, awful."

Brian's face immediately went from skeptical to adoring. "Last Christmas was pretty bad, wasn't it?"

After Brian's father had ambushed us at the movie theater and mine had cast us out of his life, yeah, I'd say it was pretty horrible. "It was," I said. "And the one before it I was coming in and out of a coma and had just lost my mother. I want a good Christmas, and I want it before the next one, just in case I'm actually cursed or something and have to break the cycle."

Laughing, Brian leaned over and kissed my cheek. "The only thing you are cursed with is a high-maintenance boyfriend, *Cinderella*."

"Very true," I agreed.

I laughed to myself when Brian rolled his eyes at my easy agreement and finally dug into the food on his plate. People always joked that I had Brian whipped, but in reality, I was just slightly more stubborn. We argued now as much as we ever had as Internet buddies, except now we did it vocally instead of via e-mail. Brian was a man very used to being adored by everyone and always getting his way. He would forever make demands and expect people to cater to him.

The last seven months that we'd been a couple had been a learning process for me. The trick was figuring out when I needed to stroke that fragile ego of his and when I needed to knock it down a peg. The fact that I was as stubborn as a mule and, okay, maybe a little self righteous, was, oddly enough, one of the reasons we worked so well as a couple. He needed someone who would push back instead of just rolling over to his demands like everyone else. I never had a problem pushing back. I was always pretty quick to apologize or forgive, too, which may have been my saving grace.

"So, how was Boston?" Doug asked.

I couldn't help the grin that escaped me. Things got so crazy so fast for me that I never did end up getting Brian a gift for Christmas. It had been Valentine's Day when he finally pulled out his gifts to me and demanded I take them. One of them had been a trip back East. He said he wanted to be properly introduced to Mama, *Abuela*, and Papa. We'd had to wait until filming was wrapped on *The Scarlet Pimpernel*, but in June we finally managed to go back home. "It was amazing," I admitted. "I didn't realize how much I missed the East Coast. It was nice to go back home. We even got in touch with a few of my old friends from high school. It felt a little like visiting a dream, but I got to say good-bye. The closure was good for me."

"Plus, the Red Sox won the game we went to, so Ellamara was a happy camper the whole trip, and when she was back there, her accent came back really heavy. It was adorable."

I stuck my tongue out at him. His infatuation with my Boston accent was laughable. He'd spent most of the trip giggling and making me say different words.

"And how's the autobiography coming along?" Liz asked.

I nodded my head as I cleared my mouth of food. "Really good. I've been working with a non-fiction writer who's done several celebrity biographies. I've learned a lot from him, and Dr. Parish has helped me, too. Putting all my experiences down on paper has made a lot of headway in my therapy sessions. I bring Dr. Parish each new chapter as I write it, she overanalyzes every single sentence, I use up a whole box of tissue, and somehow I feel just a little bit better after each session. By the time the book is done, I might just be a fully-functioning, well-adjusted, mentally stable woman."

Liz and Doug both stopped eating to blink at me, but Brian snorted, not surprised in the least that I was joking about my therapy and my mental health. The thing is, I'd found that humor is the best medicine, and while I had a lot of things to work through, it was easier to deal with them if I could joke about it. Besides, I really had made a lot of progress with Dr. Parish. Things weren't so touchy for me anymore. Even my relationship with my father was getting pretty solid.

"No one with your temper could ever be called well-adjusted," Brian said.

It was my turn to roll my eyes at him, even if he did have a point. A *small* one.

After dinner, we all decided we were way too full and needed to take a break before eating pie, so we headed into the living room to relax. Brian and I sat down on the loveseat, while Doug sat on the sofa, and Liz headed to the Christmas tree to grab the gifts and hand them out. She flashed Brian the biggest smile when she handed him the small square box with his name on it. He read the *To: Cinder From: Ella* on the tag and chuckled. "You really did go all out for this, didn't you?" he asked me.

I shrugged, and he pulled me to him for a kiss.

"I'm surprised you managed to find something for me," he teased. "Have you been looking this entire time? Because you know there's only five months until next Christmas, and my birthday is only three weeks away."

That earned him a groan. "Don't remind me. We'll just say

this one counts for your birthday and Christmas for the next fifty years."

He laughed again and started to open it, but I stopped him. "Wait. Let your mom and Doug open theirs first."

They each had large poster-size frames that I'd gift wrapped and sent ahead of time. Liz said Doug had been going crazy with curiosity for weeks, but I had their word that neither of them had peeked. Doug wasted no time tearing the paper off his gift. His lifted eyebrows and slack jaw when he saw the framed Green Bay Packers jersey signed by the entire team made me grin. "Is this the whole team?"

I nodded proudly. "From last season, yeah."

Doug blinked at me in shock, and Brian shot to his feet to go get a better look at Doug's gift. "What? You thought of something this awesome for Doug and couldn't even think of a single thing for me? Dude. I want one of *these*."

Liz and I shared a look as we both laughed. Men and their sports. I loved my Red Sox on principle and enjoyed a game here or there, but the obsession that guys seemed to have with sports had always escaped me. Liz didn't really understand it, either, but she found the men's giddy excitement over the prized jersey as endearing as I did.

"This is incredible, Ella," Doug said. "Thank you so much. How did you *get* this?"

"And why didn't you get me one, too?" Brian said, pouting at the small box in his hand that clearly didn't hold a signed football jersey.

Rolling my eyes at Brian, I shrugged. "Well, I tried to get season tickets first, but apparently there's been a waitlist for those since like 1960 or something, and no amount money or celebrity status could get them to put you on the top of the list. Believe me. I called and asked about it."

Doug blinked again, and Brian laughed. "And you call *me* a diva."

"I was *not* a diva about it. I simply asked if there was anything they could do to help me out, and when they said no, I said thanks and asked about getting something signed instead. They were happy to send this after I asked if *The Adventures of Cinder & Ella* could come visit them during pre-season camp and highlight them on our web series."

Brian's head snapped to me, eyes shining with childlike excitement. "What? You did? Did they say yes?"

I laughed again. "They were very flattered to learn that Brian Oliver was a huge fan and honored to be Cinder and Ella's first adventure into professional sports. I may have to shake some pom-poms in a Green Bay cheerleading outfit and you might get creamed by their offensive line once or twice, but yes, this week, Cinder and Ella are going to a day at training camp with the Green Bay Packers. They've invited Doug and Liz as well."

After a shared look of shocked excitement with Doug, Brian was back across the room in two giant steps and scooped me into his arms, carefully holding me against his chest as he lifted me off the ground and twirled me around once. "You beautiful woman! You are the best girlfriend ever."

"I know. Now put me down so Liz can open her gift, too."

After Brian and I were seated again, which didn't happen until after he'd kissed me enthusiastically enough to make me blush, he pulled me tightly to his side and turned his attention to his mother.

The look on her face before she tore the paper away from her gift suggested she was a little worried there might be a second signed football jersey waiting for her. Her gasp when she saw what it was was worth it. "Oh, Ella!" She covered her mouth with her hand, and tears pooled in her eyes. "It's so beautiful."

She held the large framed collage from our fairy-tale photo session with Nash Wilson up to show Doug and Brian. The photos had turned out more magical than I could have imagined. We'd gone to the Redwood forest in northern California for the shoot. I'd never been there before, but the place had to be one of the most mystical and wild places on Earth. It was simply breath-taking and my new favorite place in the whole world.

Doug whistled, and Brian sucked in a breath. "I want one of those, too," he muttered.

I snickered. "Is there anything you *don't* want?"

"Lots of stuff," he said absently, his eyes locked on the picture collage. It was a combination of some of the best group shots, couples shots, and solo shots of both Brian and me. He was on his feet again and back to his mother's side. He knelt down to get a closer look at the collage. Pointing to the frame, he shook his head. "This is not a want. I *need* one of these."

My favorite picture from the entire shoot was actually one of just me. I sat atop a huge downed tree trunk in the thick of the wild forest. A single beam of sunlight penetrated the trees and shone down on me like a spotlight. Nash had given me large, pointy ears and huge, glittery gossamer wings tinted an ice blue. He'd dressed me in the tiniest little blue skirt and top that was really nothing more than a binding to cover my breasts and a skirt that would make Tinker Bell blush. He'd given my hair a wild windswept look and weaved tiny blue flowers through it. I'd never seen *anyone* look more beautiful. It was hard to believe the creature in the picture was me.

I was sitting in a fetal position and the picture was taken in profile, but my head was turned toward the camera, and I was looking up through my eyelashes. Nash had been right; my eyes popped, making me look magical. The greatest thing about the photo was that the rough texture of my scars was actually complemented by the bark of the old tree, making me look as if I were a part of nature itself, like some kind of forest faerie goddess. That photo was going to be the cover of my book.

Nash had unveiled the photos in his gallery in April. Mr. Buchman had helped Nash and me put together a huge event for it where I gave my first speech about my experiences and what the photos meant to me. Nash's photos and my speech had earned us a cover and an in-depth interview in *Time Magazine*.

"Seriously, Ella. I have to have one of these," Brian said again.

"Good. Now I know what to get you for your birthday." I actually already had a different set of three framed collages for us to hang above the living room couch in the apartment.

Brian frowned. "That's three weeks away."

I laughed. "You'll survive, you big, spoiled man. Why don't you worry about the present you have now instead?"

I held up the small box that he'd set down next to me when he'd gone to look at the photos, and gave it a small shake. Brian flashed me a bright smile as he returned to my side and took the box. He started to open it again but paused and frowned at me. "I don't have anything for you."

I laughed. "You already gave me my gifts. Plural. Remember? A whole trip to Boston, among other things. I don't need anything else."

Brian's frown deepened. "That's not the same. I didn't actually give you a gift last Christmas, either, if you recall. You should have told me about this do-over. I would have come up with something awesome."

"It's fine, Brian. I don't need a gift." A wry smile crossed my face, and I smugly sang the line from my new least-favorite Christmas song. "All I want for Christmas is you."

Brian narrowed his eyes at me and squished his face up into a grimace. "Was I really that annoying?"

I burst out laughing. "Yes! For *weeks*. You totally deserve this. Now open your present already."

He tore the paper off and raised his eyebrows at me when he found the signature baby-blue box from Tiffany's. I only grinned in response to his unasked question. He opened the box and got even more curious when he found the ring box inside. I had to bite the inside of my cheek to keep from giggling when he opened it and frowned at the ring inside. "You got me an engagement ring?"

"Oh no," I chirped, trying as hard as I could to keep my composure. "That's for you to put on my finger."

When his eyes flashed back to mine, I waggled my eyebrows. "Guess you got me something after all."

His hand fell to his lap, ring all but forgotten as he stared at me with wide eyes. "Are you asking me to *marry* you?"

I brushed off the question as if it was the silliest one he'd ever asked. "Heavens, no. That's your job. I'm just dropping a subtle hint that I might be ready for you to do that. Whenever you're ready, of course."

Once Brian got over his shock—which took a good fifteen seconds—his lips quirked up into a crooked smile, and he held up the ring. "This is your idea of subtle?"

"*Subtle* is relative. It all depends on the density of the person needing the clue."

"I am *not* dense. You're the one who refused to move in with me and gave me all those lectures about how you weren't ready for serious grown-up things like marriage and babies."

"Oh, I'm still not ready for the babies," I promised quickly, ignoring the small huff of disappointment that came from Liz's direction. "But the marriage thing I could do, and the new house, too, as soon as my lease is up and we find a place we like."

Brian's eyes glossed over, and his mind wandered into some fantasy of his. He's always had this fascination with the idea of our twisted Hollywood version of the American dream. Movie premieres and awards ceremonies mixed with the kids and the white picket fence. And a cat. Not a dog. Which I happen to think is adorable. My big old strong, dominant man loves cuddly little kitties.

"We'll call the real estate lady as soon as we get home," Brian said. "She'll be happy that I'm finally ready to look for a place seriously."

He'd been on the hunt for a place that was friendlier to my needs when I'd first moved out of my father's home, but he'd given up the search once I moved into my apartment. "We should probably wait until we get back from New Zealand," I reminded him.

Brian was scheduled to film the rest of the Cinder Chronicles movies starting in August, right after his birthday. The first film had done so well—broken box office records—that they'd automatically green lighted the rest of the series. They were filming them all at the same time to save on production costs, which meant Brian would be on location in New Zealand, where they'd filmed the first one, for roughly the next eight months. I was going with him, of course, and I was crazy excited to get to travel out of the country for the first time in my life. We were leaving right after his birthday. I could do most of my work with my website online, and Scott would still be in L.A. to take care of anything that had to be done from home.

"Fine. But it's the first thing on the agenda when we get back. You promise?"

"Promise." I grinned and picked up his hand—the one still holding my engagement ring. "So, about this ring…"

Brian's crooked smile returned, and he raised one eyebrow into an arch. "I thought you weren't asking me to marry you."

"I'm not." For once, I managed a completely innocent look. "I'm simply explaining my gift to you. Read the engraving on the band."

Brian focused on the ring, noticing for the first time that it had tiny words scrawled into the band. When he read them, his smirk grew. "And they lived happily ever after."

I finally let myself grin the way I'd been dying to. "*That* is my gift to you."

"Happily ever after?" he clarified.

I nodded, smirking again. "Assuming you quit diddling and ask me to marry you, already."

I wiggled my hand at him as if he should stop wasting time and slip the ring on my finger. The move earned me Brian's stern *I'm-Brian-Oliver-and-I-bow-to-no-man* look. "I don't *ask* for things; I make demands," he said, puffing out his chest and folding his arms tightly across his chest. "*And,* I'm not going to propose just because you told me to. You are so unromantic. I'm going to plan out the most creative, beautiful, epic, romantic proposal ever."

I met his gaze and lifted an eyebrow, shaking my hand again, stubbornly waiting him out. He narrowed his eyes and folded his arms defiantly across his chest. Giggles drifted to us from across the room, but we ignored our audience, refusing to look away from each other's stare. He broke first. "Fine," he said with exasperation. "But I'm eating your pie for this."

I laughed, but adrenaline shot through me as he got down on one knee in front of me and took my hand in his. I grinned at his mother over the top of his head, happier than I could ever remember being, and she beamed a brilliant smile back at me.

"Ellamara Valentina Rodriguez," Brian purred in that deep voice that I loved so much.

When I met his gaze, he gave me the most loving smile. Maybe I'd planned this, but it was still the most perfect moment ever. I waited with bated breath to hear whatever over-the-top romantic silver-screen-worthy proposal he would come up with. He paused for a good five seconds, no doubt for dramatic effect, and then his lips twitched at the corners. His eyes twinkled with mischief as he said, "Marry me, woman." And yes, it was definitely a demand.

So much for cheesy movie romance. I actually snorted and burst into laughter, saluting him. "Yes, sir!"

When I finally settled down, Brian was still kneeling in front of me. I flashed him a grin so giddy he rolled his eyes at me as he slid the ring on my finger. I admit, I got really girly then and squealed a little bit.

Brian finally lost his composure and laughed, shaking his head as I examined the ring on my hand for a moment. "Look at that; it's a perfect fit," I teased.

"Shocker," Brian deadpanned.

I laughed as he stood and pulled me to my feet. He stopped my giggles with a kiss, and that seemed to be the signal that it was okay for Liz to finally interrupt us. She tackled us before we even broke our kiss. "Oh, I'm so happy! Congratulations! I can't believe my baby is getting married!"

The hugs and kisses and tears started and didn't stop until Doug intervened on our behalf. "Liz, calm down. Give the poor kids a moment to themselves."

"But Doug—"

"*Liz.*"

I giggled when the command actually made Brian's mother stop her fussing. I hadn't realized the old softy had it in him. He winked at me and then took his wife's hand. "Why don't we go cut the pie now?"

She huffed, but when Doug didn't relent, she threw her hands up in defeat. "Oh, all *right.*"

Brian had me back in his arms before his mother was out of the room. "I love you," he whispered.

I slid my arms around his neck. "I love you, too."

He gave me a quick kiss and then surprised me with a frown. "Not that I didn't love my surprise, but you really should have given me the chance to get you something, too."

"You give me gifts all the time."

"So?"

Brian had told me when we first got together that I should be prepared to receive gifts on a regular basis. He'd delivered on that warning. No one loved giving gifts like Brian did. I loved that he was so generous even if he did go overboard way too often. I was sure it was killing him that I'd finally had the chance to get him something when he didn't have anything to give in return. But that had all been part of my plan, too.

"I'll tell you what," I said, stepping out of his arms and taking his hand in mine. "There is one thing I want that you can give me tonight. If you're really so desperate to give me a gift."

"What?" he said eagerly. "Anything."

A smile crept over my face as I leaned in and whispered exactly what I wanted from him. And since I knew how much he appreciated a little talk, I was very specific.

Brian sucked in a sharp breath, while I giggled again. When

I pulled back, he stared at me with eyes as big as baseballs. After a moment, he swallowed hard, licking his lips as if his whole mouth were suddenly as dry as the desert. "Are you sure?"

My whole body was full of nervous flutters, but I was ready. Very, very ready. I wrapped my arms around his neck and gave him a small kiss. "I already told you," I said. "All I want for Christmas is *you*. I meant it."

He blinked twice and then threw his mouth on mine as if he was ready to make it happen right here in the living room.

"Brian! Ella! Dessert is ready!"

Brian broke the kiss, chest heaving and eyes burning. He glanced toward the dining room and then looked back at me. The conflict in his eyes made me snicker. "It's just pie," I whispered.

I'd meant that eating pie wouldn't take long, but Brian took my statement as more of an *It's okay if we skip it.*

"Sorry, Mom. Ella and I have to leave," he hollered as he scooped me into his arms. "We'll be back tomorrow."

Liz dashed into the living room. *"What? Where are you going?"*

"Somewhere where I can make wild, passionate love to my fiancée without my parents down the hall."

I really should be used to the man by now, but I still gasped in horror, and my face turned redder than it ever had. *"BRIAN!"*

Liz echoed my screech. *"BRIAN!* Don't be so crass!"

"Sorry, Mom." He was so not sorry. And he was walking toward the front door. "We'll be back in the morning, promise. Er—make that the afternoon."

"Brian Oliver, you stop right this instant. You just got here. Your…physical needs can wait until after you at least eat your pie."

Brian opened the front door. "They really can't, Mom. Just put it in the fridge for me."

"Brian!"

"Liz, I think the boy is determined," Doug said, trying and failing not to grin.

He was definitely determined. And as much as I was horrified that his parents knew where he was taking me and why, I didn't have the willpower to put my foot down and make him stop. I peeked over his shoulder and shot Liz an apologetic smile. "I'm sorry, Liz. I promise we'll be back for lunch tomorrow, and we can talk about wedding plans."

That seemed to appease her a little, and out of the corner of my eye, I saw Brian cringe. *Served him right.*

He walked outside, placed me in the passenger seat of our rental car, ran back to get my purse and my cane, waved to Doug, kissed his mother's cheek, grinning at her frown of disapproval, and then jumped in the car. "Was that really necessary?" I asked when he practically peeled out of the driveway.

"Yes." He took my hand, twining our fingers together, and brought it to his lips. "So, about the wedding…" When I looked at him with amusement, he grimaced again. "I don't suppose you'll be nice and let us do the Vegas thing before we leave the country? If I get a choice, I'd much rather have that for my birthday than the picture."

I almost felt bad for him. Almost.

After a lighthearted laugh that bordered on obnoxious, I gave him my most pitying look. "Oh, sweetie, I am so sorry, but there is *no way* this Cinderella princess is starting her happily ever after without her fairy-tale wedding."